THE GRAPHIC NOVEL
William Shakespeare

ORIGINAL TEXT VERSION

Script Adaptation: John McDonald
Character Designs & Original Artwork: Will Volley
Coloring: Jim Devlin
Lettering: Jim Campbell
Design & Layout: Jo Wheeler & Jenny Placentino

Associate Editor: Joe Sutliff Sanders
Editor in Chief: Clive Bryant

Romeo & Juliet: The Graphic Novel
Original Text Version

William Shakespeare

First published: December 2009
Reprinted: October 2010, October 2011

Published by: Classical Comics Ltd.

Acknowledgments: Every effort has been made to trace copyright holders of
material reproduced in this book. Any rights not acknowledged here will be
acknowledged in subsequent editions if notice is given to Classical Comics Ltd.

Images on page 161 reproduced with the kind permission of The Shakespeare Birthplace Trust.

All enquiries should be addressed to:
Classical Comics Ltd.
PO Box 7280
Litchborough
Towcester
NN12 9AR
United Kingdom

info@classicalcomics.com
www.classicalcomics.com

ISBN: 978-1-906332-61-7

Printed in the USA

This book is printed by CG Book Printers using environmentally safe inks, on paper from
responsible sources. This material can be disposed of by recycling, incineration for energy
recovery, composting and biodegradation.

The rights of John McDonald, Joe Sutliff Sanders, Will Volley, Jim Devlin and Jim Campbell
to be identified as the artists of this work have been asserted in accordance with
the Copyright, Designs and Patents Act 1988 sections 77 and 78.

Contents

Romeo & Juliet

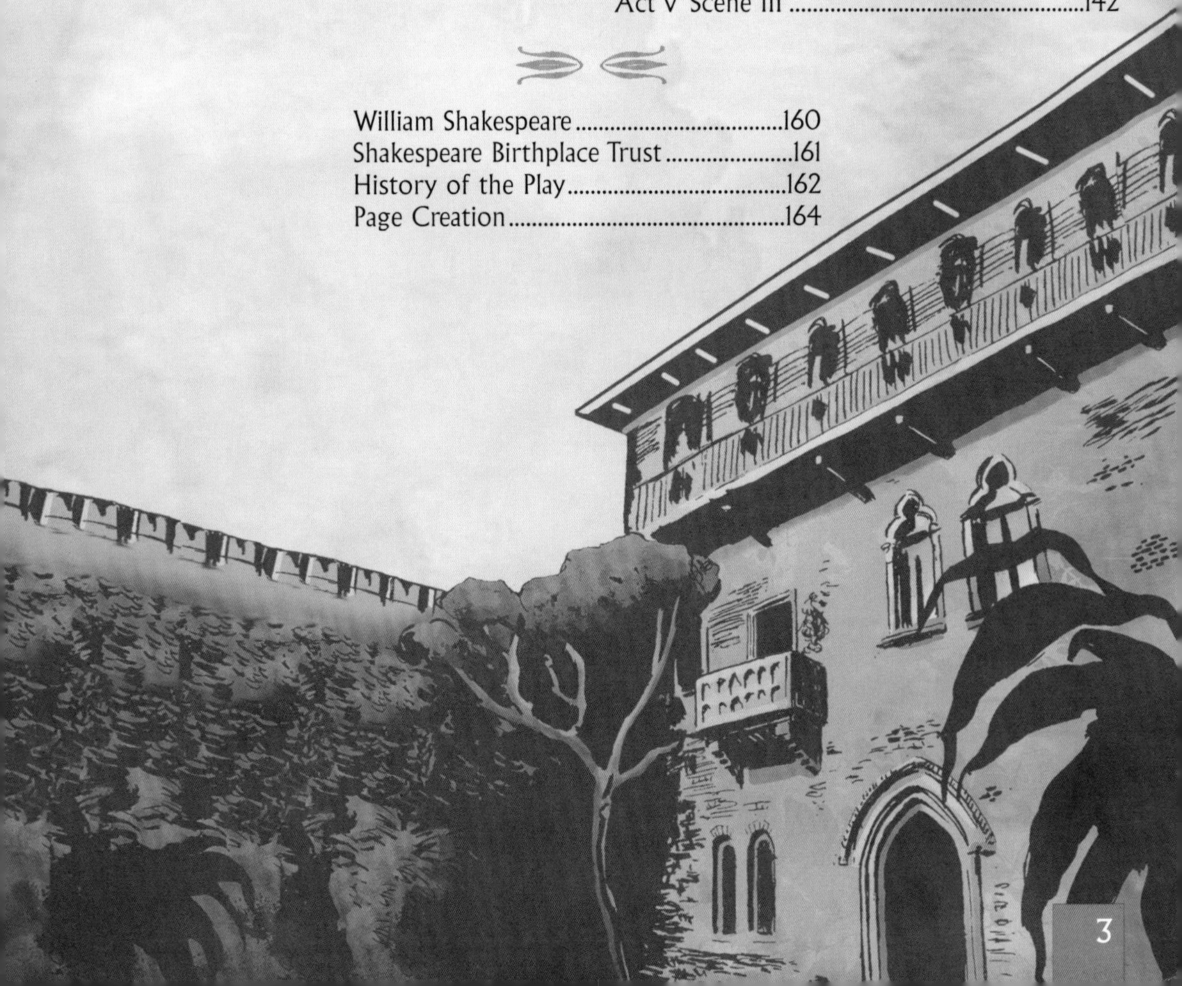

Dramatis Personæ

Romeo
Son to Montague

Chorus
*Introduces the first two acts
of the play*

Lord Montague
*Head of the Montague house
(a Veronese family), at feud
with the Capulet family*

Lady Montague
Wife to Montague

Benvolio
*Nephew to Montague and friend
to Romeo and Mercutio*

Balthasar
Servant to Romeo

Abraham
Servant to Montague

Escalus
Prince of Verona

Mercutio
*Kinsman to Escalus, Prince of
Verona, and friend to Romeo
and Benvolio*

Paris
*A young nobleman, kinsman to
Escalus, Prince of Verona*

Juliet
Daughter to Capulet

Lord Capulet
*Head of the Capulet house
(a Veronese family), at feud
with the Montague family*

Lady Capulet
Wife to Capulet

Tybalt
Nephew to Lady Capulet

Nurse
*A Capulet servant and Juliet's
foster-mother*

Peter
A Capulet servant to Juliet's nurse

Sampson
Servant to Capulet

Gregory
Servant to Capulet

Friar Laurence
A monk of the Franciscan Order

Friar John
A monk of the Franciscan Order

Romeo & Juliet

A Note on Pronunciation

As you go through this Original Text version, you will notice how some words that usually end in "-ed" are written "-'d", whereas others are written out in full.

Shakespeare wrote much of his plays in verse, where the rhythm of the speech formed strings of "iambic pentameters", each line being five pairs of syllables, with the second syllable in each pair being the most dominant in the rhythm.

To help with enunciation and voice projection in early theaters, words that ended with "-ed" had that last syllable accented — unless to do so would have spoiled the iambic rhythm, in which case it was spoken just as we say the word today.

This speech by Prince Escalus at the end of the play:

Some shall be pardon'd, and some punished:
would have been said as:
Some shall be pardon'd, and some punish–ed:
so that the syllable pairs (five of them in the line) are correct in number and in emphasis (if you say it as "punish'd" you'll see how the rhythm of the line is destroyed).

Whereas, the "pardon'd" cannot be pronounced "pardon-ed" because to do so would give eleven syllables in the line, and would not allow the right emphasis to be placed on each syllable.

In short, whenever you see a word ending "-ed" it should have its 'e' pronounced to preserve the rhythm of the speech.

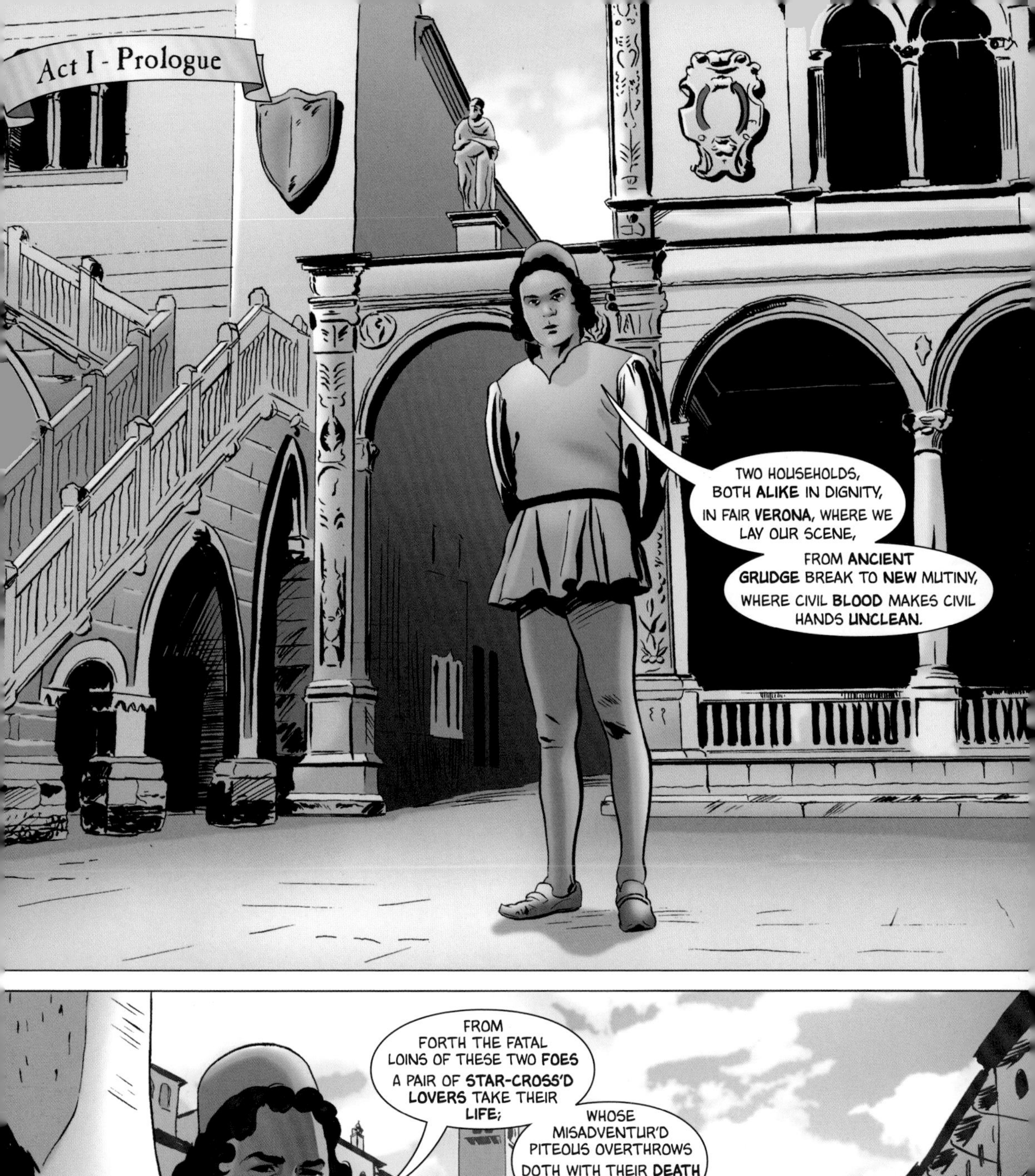
Act I - Prologue
TWO HOUSEHOLDS, BOTH ALIKE IN DIGNITY, IN FAIR VERONA, WHERE WE LAY OUR SCENE,
FROM ANCIENT GRUDGE BREAK TO NEW MUTINY, WHERE CIVIL BLOOD MAKES CIVIL HANDS UNCLEAN.

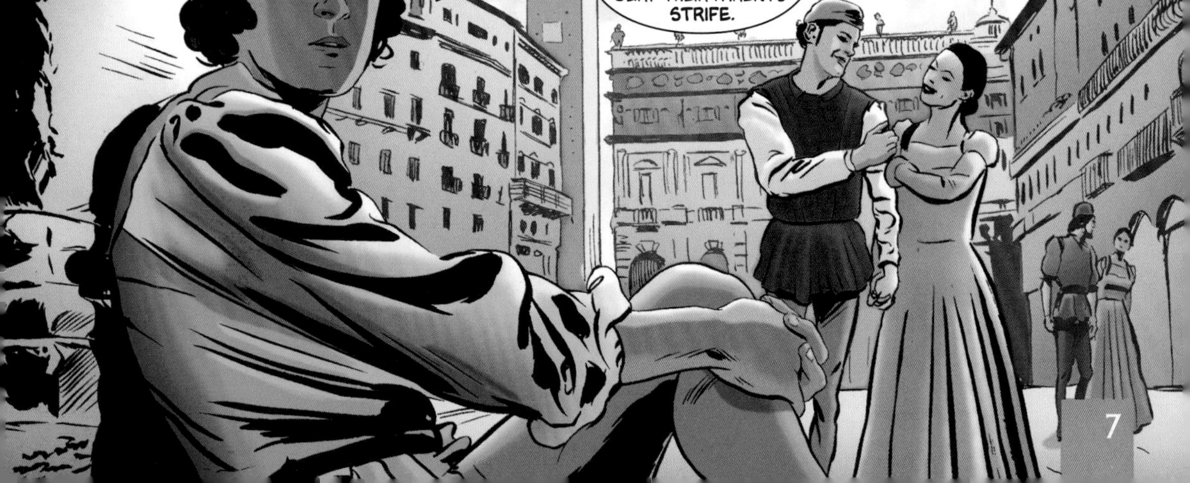
FROM FORTH THE FATAL LOINS OF THESE TWO FOES
A PAIR OF STAR-CROSS'D LOVERS TAKE THEIR LIFE;
WHOSE MISADVENTUR'D PITEOUS OVERTHROWS
DOTH WITH THEIR DEATH BURY THEIR PARENTS' STRIFE.

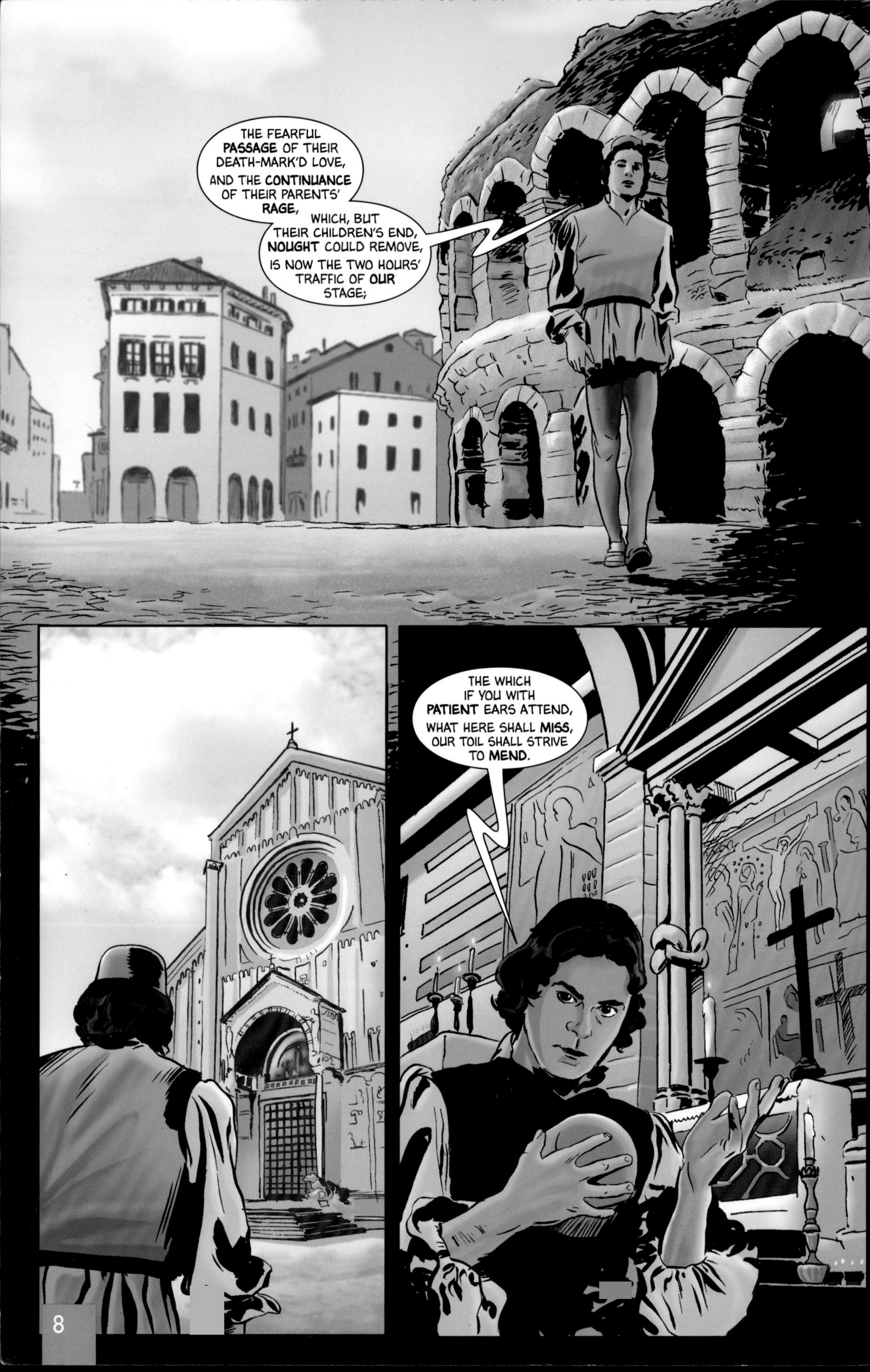
THE FEARFUL PASSAGE OF THEIR DEATH-MARK'D LOVE,
AND THE CONTINUANCE OF THEIR PARENTS' RAGE,
WHICH, BUT THEIR CHILDREN'S END, NOUGHT COULD REMOVE,
IS NOW THE TWO HOURS' TRAFFIC OF OUR STAGE;
THE WHICH IF YOU WITH PATIENT EARS ATTEND,
WHAT HERE SHALL MISS, OUR TOIL SHALL STRIVE TO MEND.

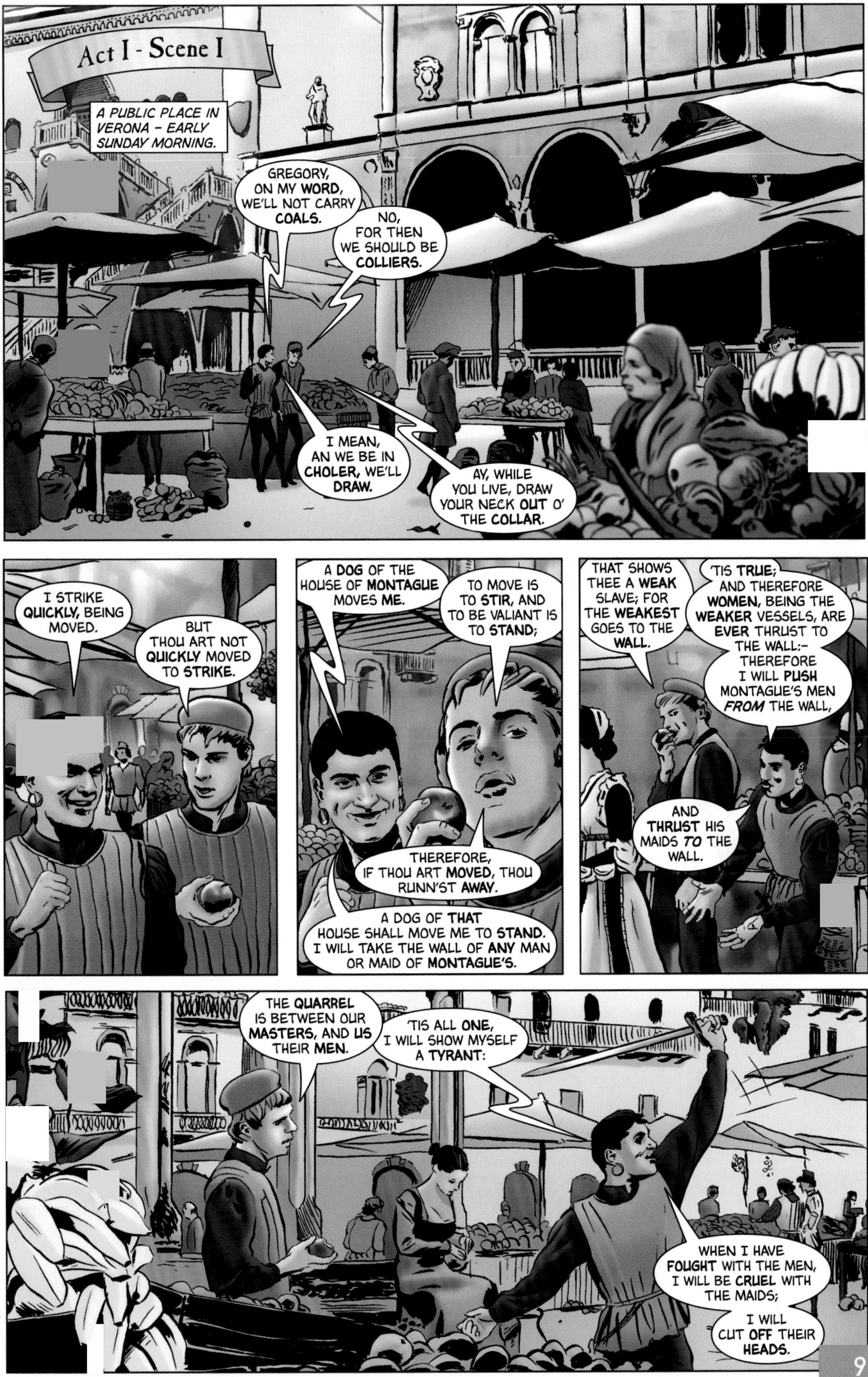

Act I - Scene I
A PUBLIC PLACE IN VERONA – EARLY SUNDAY MORNING.
GREGORY, ON MY WORD, WE'LL NOT CARRY COALS.
NO, FOR THEN WE SHOULD BE COLLIERS.
I MEAN, AN WE BE IN CHOLER, WE'LL DRAW.
AY, WHILE YOU LIVE, DRAW YOUR NECK OUT O' THE COLLAR.
I STRIKE QUICKLY, BEING MOVED.
BUT THOU ART NOT QUICKLY MOVED TO STRIKE.
A DOG OF THE HOUSE OF MONTAGUE MOVES ME.
TO MOVE IS TO STIR, AND TO BE VALIANT IS TO STAND;
THEREFORE, IF THOU ART MOVED, THOU RUNN'ST AWAY.
A DOG OF THAT HOUSE SHALL MOVE ME TO STAND. I WILL TAKE THE WALL OF ANY MAN OR MAID OF MONTAGUE'S.
THAT SHOWS THEE A WEAK SLAVE; FOR THE WEAKEST GOES TO THE WALL.
'TIS TRUE; AND THEREFORE WOMEN, BEING THE WEAKER VESSELS, ARE EVER THRUST TO THE WALL:– THEREFORE I WILL PUSH MONTAGUE'S MEN FROM THE WALL,
AND THRUST HIS MAIDS TO THE WALL.
THE QUARREL IS BETWEEN OUR MASTERS, AND US THEIR MEN.
'TIS ALL ONE, I WILL SHOW MYSELF A TYRANT:
WHEN I HAVE FOUGHT WITH THE MEN, I WILL BE CRUEL WITH THE MAIDS;
I WILL CUT OFF THEIR HEADS.

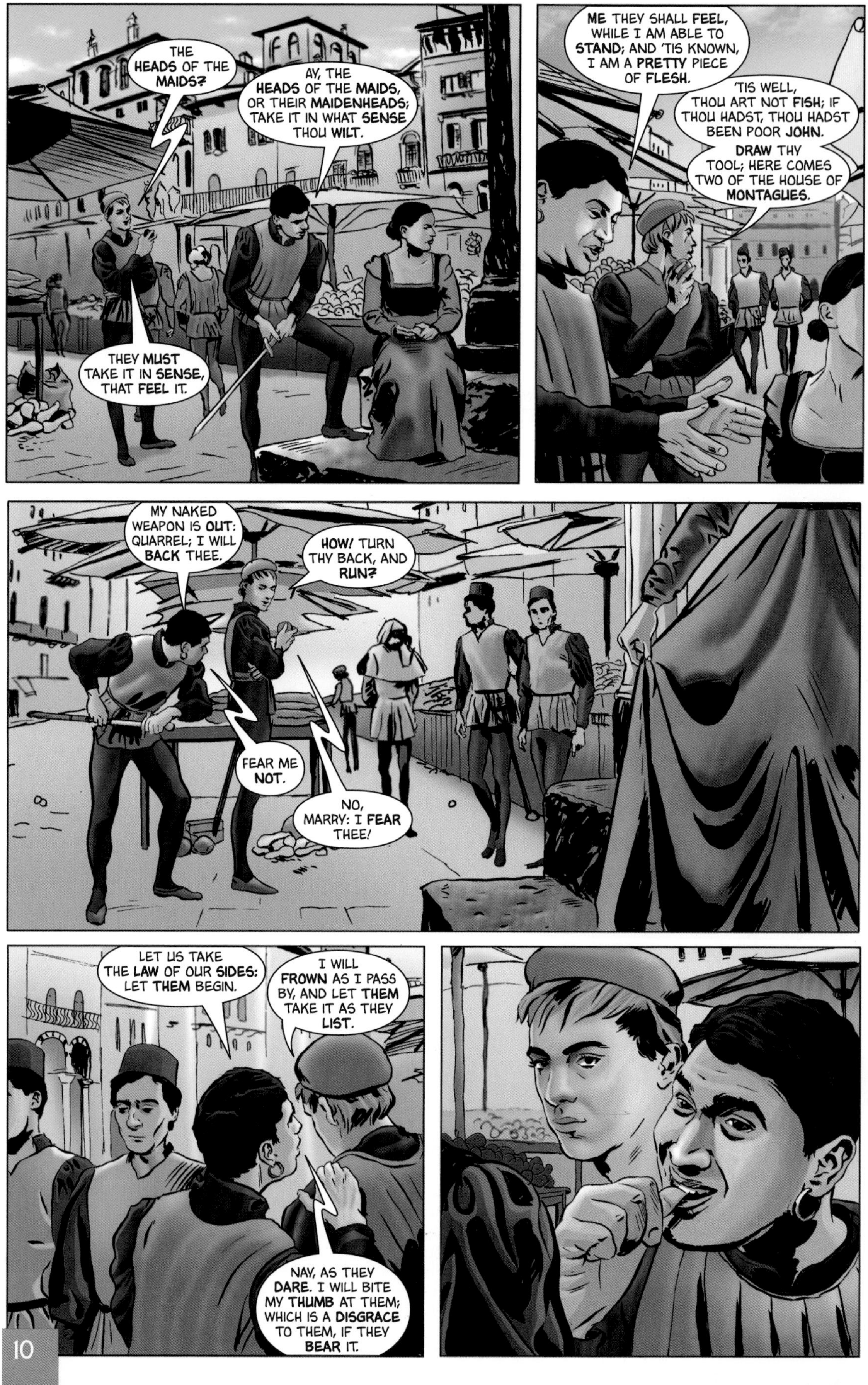
THE HEADS OF THE MAIDS?
AY, THE HEADS OF THE MAIDS, OR THEIR MAIDENHEADS; TAKE IT IN WHAT SENSE THOU WILT.
THEY MUST TAKE IT IN SENSE, THAT FEEL IT.
ME THEY SHALL FEEL, WHILE I AM ABLE TO STAND; AND 'TIS KNOWN, I AM A PRETTY PIECE OF FLESH.
'TIS WELL, THOU ART NOT FISH; IF THOU HADST, THOU HADST BEEN POOR JOHN.
DRAW THY TOOL; HERE COMES TWO OF THE HOUSE OF MONTAGUES.
MY NAKED WEAPON IS OUT: QUARREL; I WILL BACK THEE.
HOW! TURN THY BACK, AND RUN?
FEAR ME NOT.
NO, MARRY: I FEAR THEE!
LET US TAKE THE LAW OF OUR SIDES: LET THEM BEGIN.
I WILL FROWN AS I PASS BY, AND LET THEM TAKE IT AS THEY LIST.
NAY, AS THEY DARE. I WILL BITE MY THUMB AT THEM; WHICH IS A DISGRACE TO THEM, IF THEY BEAR IT.

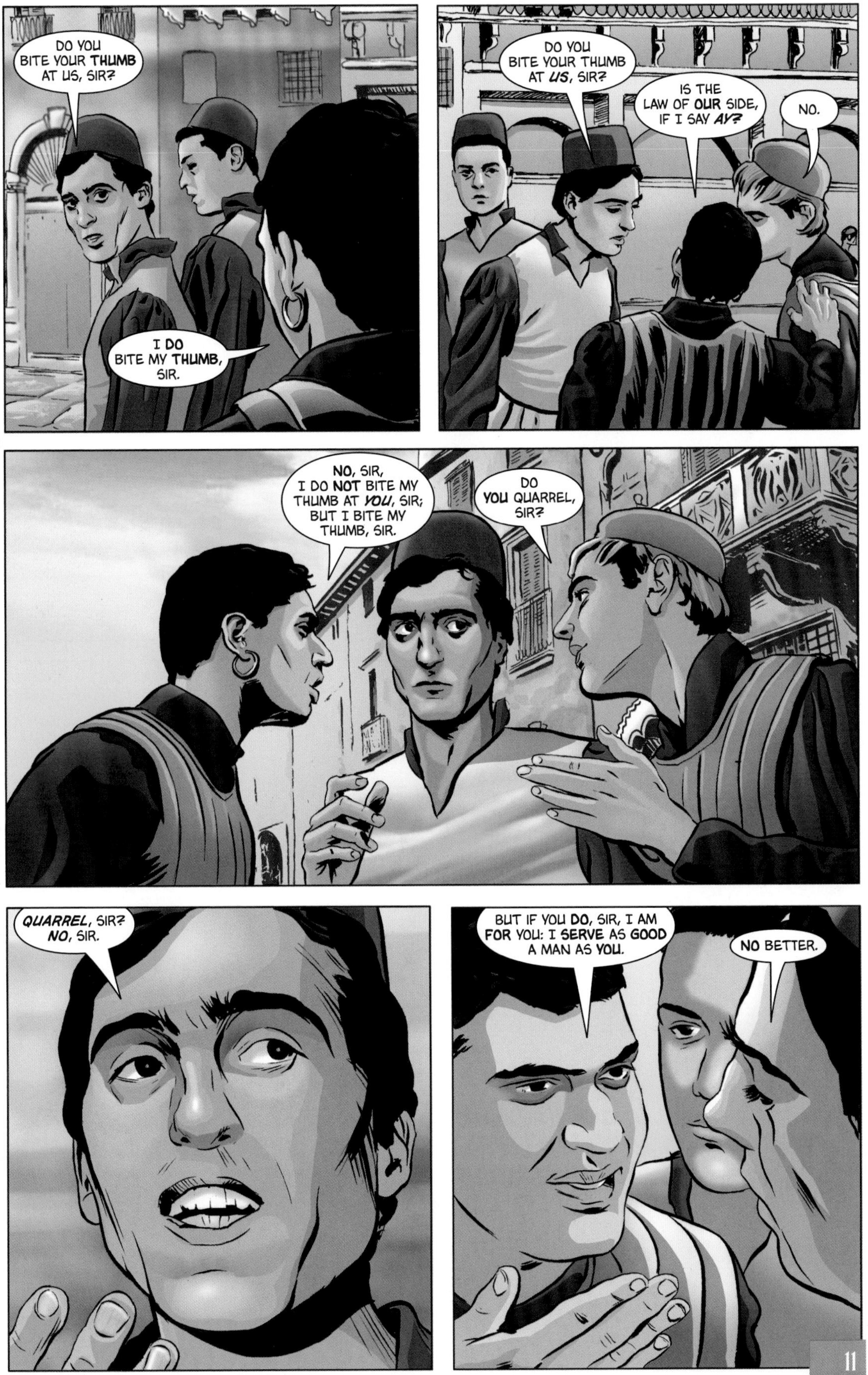
DO YOU BITE YOUR THUMB AT US, SIR?
I DO BITE MY THUMB, SIR.
DO YOU BITE YOUR THUMB AT US, SIR?
IS THE LAW OF OUR SIDE, IF I SAY AY?
NO.
NO, SIR, I DO NOT BITE MY THUMB AT YOU, SIR; BUT I BITE MY THUMB, SIR.
DO YOU QUARREL, SIR?
QUARREL, SIR? NO, SIR.
BUT IF YOU DO, SIR, I AM FOR YOU: I SERVE AS GOOD A MAN AS YOU.
NO BETTER.

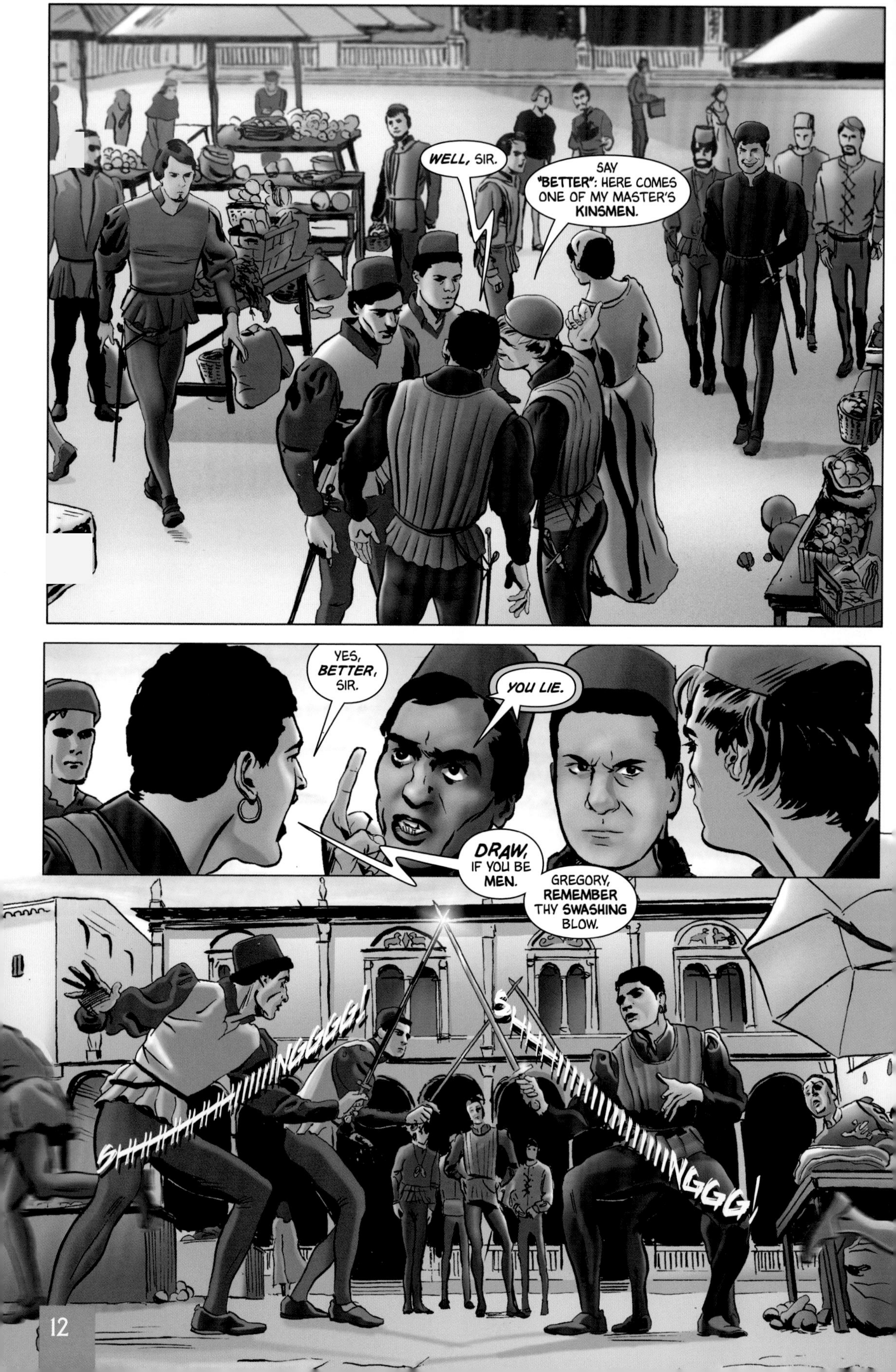
WELL, SIR.
SAY "BETTER": HERE COMES ONE OF MY MASTER'S KINSMEN.
YES, BETTER, SIR.
YOU LIE.
DRAW, IF YOU BE MEN.
GREGORY, REMEMBER THY SWASHING BLOW.
SHHHHHHHHIIIIIINGGGG!
SHHHHIIIIIIIIIIIIINGGG!

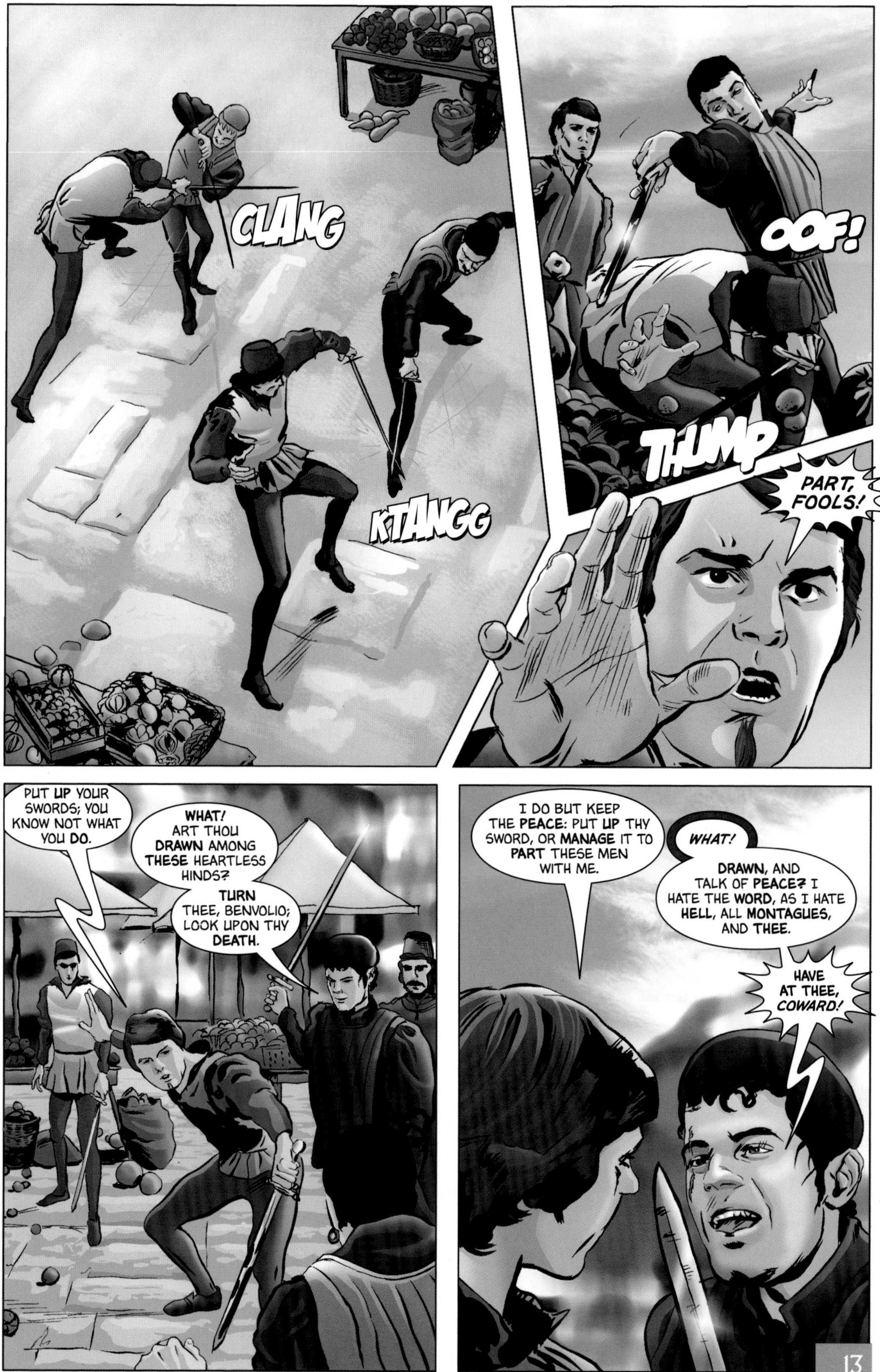
CLANG
KTANGG
OOF!
THUMP
PART, FOOLS!
PUT UP YOUR SWORDS; YOU KNOW NOT WHAT YOU DO.
WHAT! ART THOU DRAWN AMONG THESE HEARTLESS HINDS?
TURN THEE, BENVOLIO; LOOK UPON THY DEATH.
I DO BUT KEEP THE PEACE: PUT UP THY SWORD, OR MANAGE IT TO PART THESE MEN WITH ME.
WHAT!
DRAWN, AND TALK OF PEACE? I HATE THE WORD, AS I HATE HELL, ALL MONTAGUES, AND THEE.
HAVE AT THEE, COWARD!

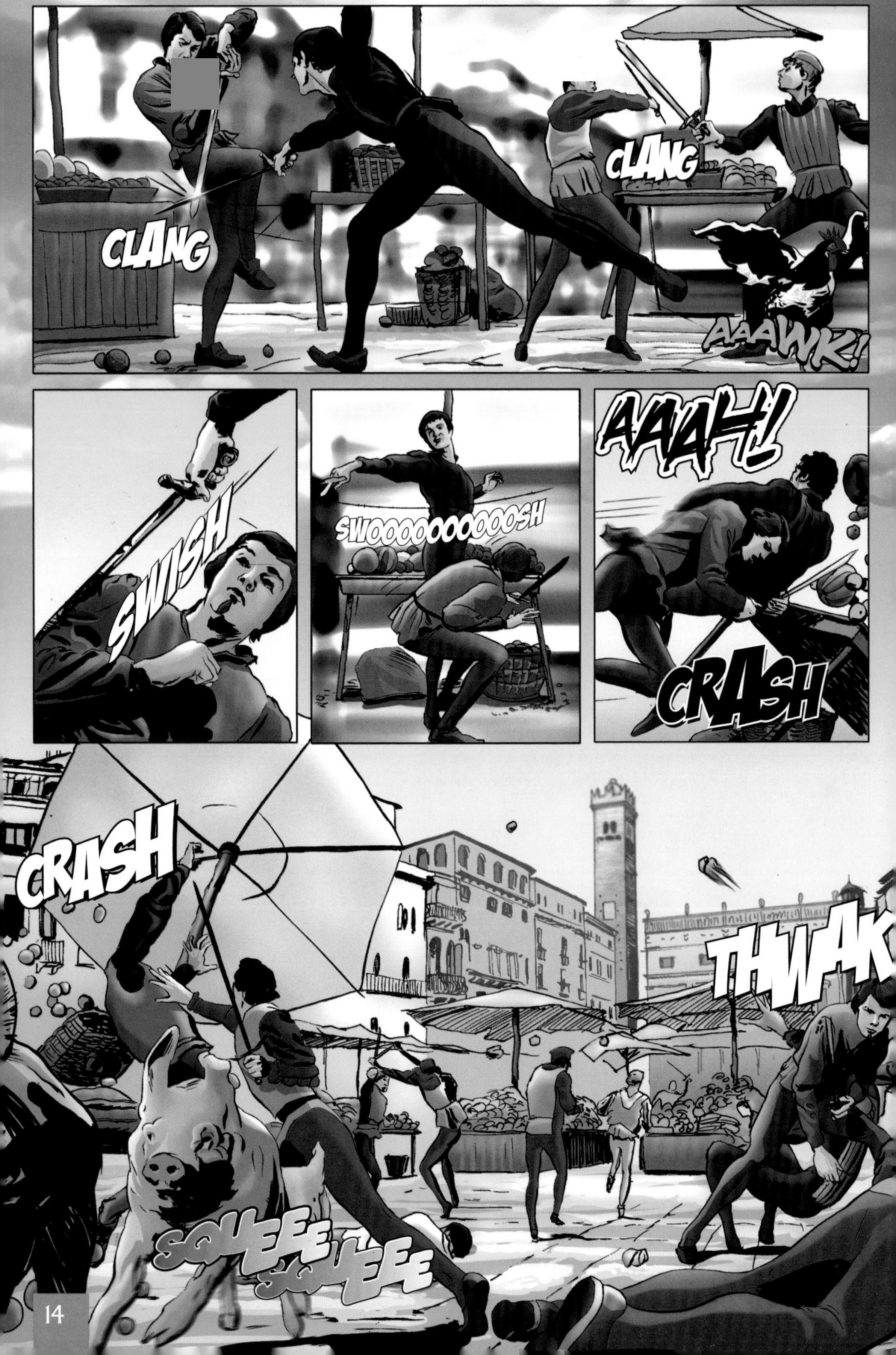
CLANG
CLANG
AAAWK!
SWISH
SWOOOOOOOOOOSH
AAAH!
CRASH
CRASH
THWAK
SQUEEE
SQUEEE

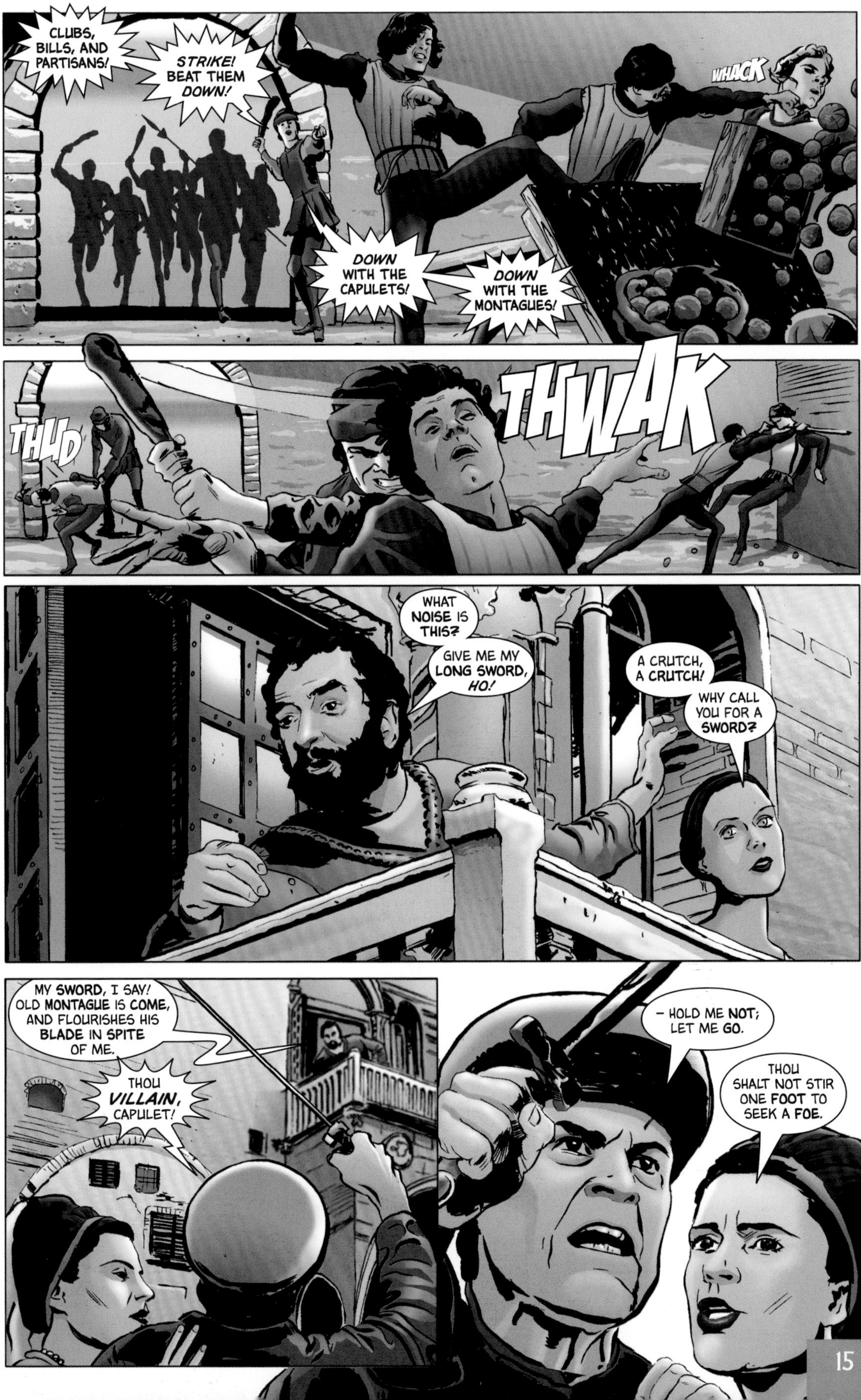
CLUBS, BILLS, AND PARTISANS!
STRIKE! BEAT THEM DOWN!
WHACK
DOWN WITH THE CAPULETS!
DOWN WITH THE MONTAGUES!
THUD
THWAK
WHAT NOISE IS THIS?
GIVE ME MY LONG SWORD, HO!
A CRUTCH, A CRUTCH!
WHY CALL YOU FOR A SWORD?
MY SWORD, I SAY! OLD MONTAGUE IS COME, AND FLOURISHES HIS BLADE IN SPITE OF ME.
THOU VILLAIN, CAPULET!
– HOLD ME NOT; LET ME GO.
THOU SHALT NOT STIR ONE FOOT TO SEEK A FOE.

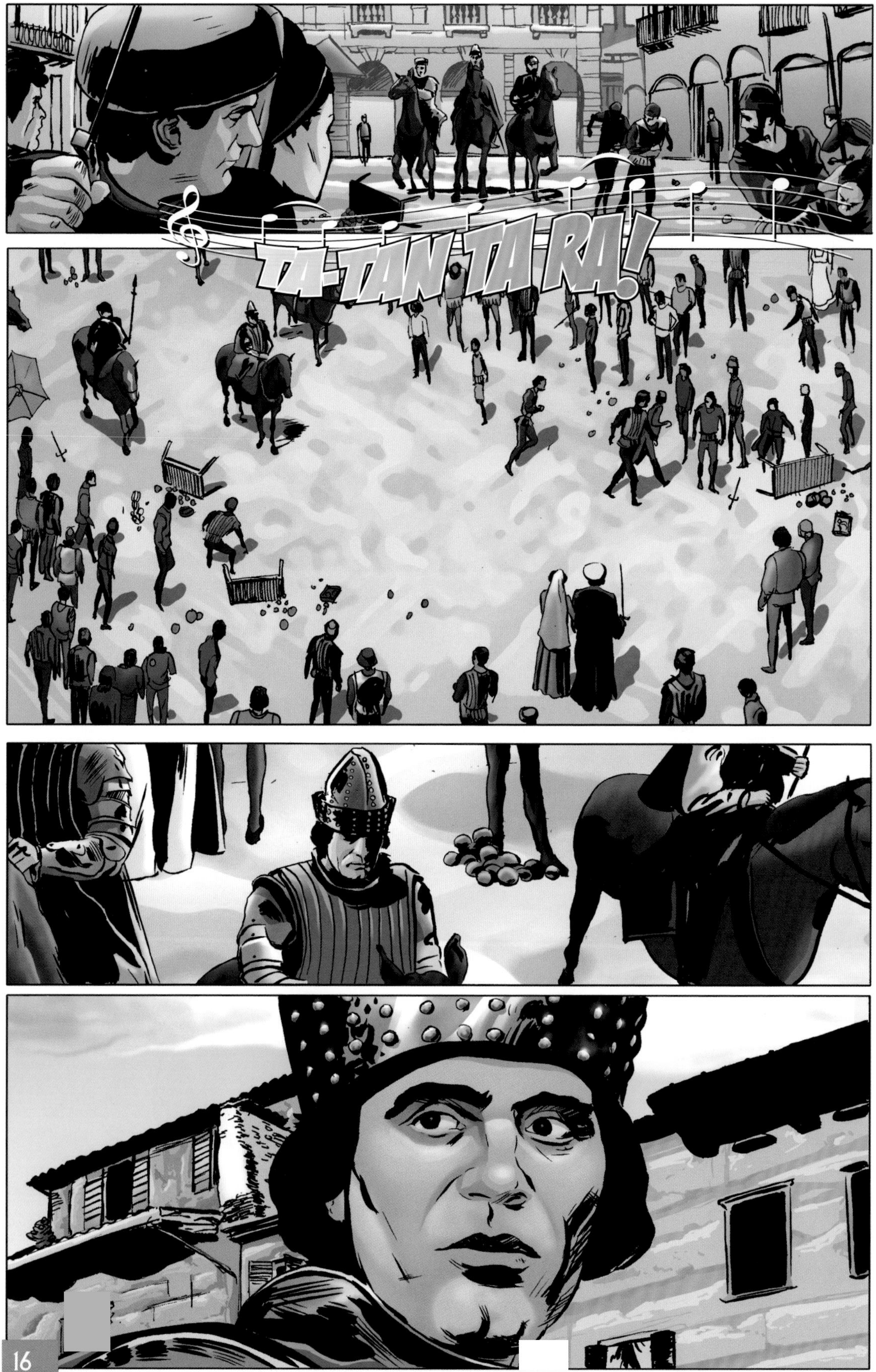
TA-TAN TA RA!

REBELLIOUS SUBJECTS, ENEMIES TO PEACE, PROFANERS OF THIS NEIGHBOUR-STAINED STEEL,

– Will they not *hear*?

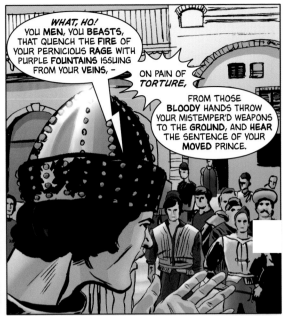

WHAT, HO! YOU MEN, YOU BEASTS, THAT QUENCH THE FIRE OF YOUR PERNICIOUS RAGE WITH PURPLE FOUNTAINS ISSUING FROM YOUR VEINS, –

ON PAIN OF *TORTURE,*

FROM THOSE BLOODY HANDS THROW YOUR MISTEMPER'D WEAPONS TO THE GROUND, AND HEAR THE SENTENCE OF YOUR MOVED PRINCE.

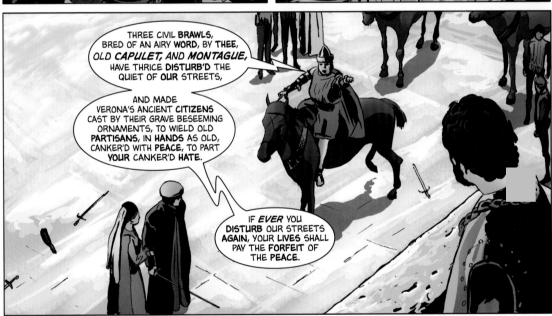

THREE CIVIL BRAWLS, BRED OF AN AIRY WORD, BY THEE, OLD *CAPULET,* AND *MONTAGUE,* HAVE THRICE DISTURB'D THE QUIET OF OUR STREETS,

AND MADE VERONA'S ANCIENT CITIZENS CAST BY THEIR GRAVE BESEEMING ORNAMENTS, TO WIELD OLD PARTISANS, IN HANDS AS OLD, CANKER'D WITH PEACE, TO PART YOUR CANKER'D HATE.

IF *EVER* YOU DISTURB OUR STREETS AGAIN, YOUR LIVES SHALL PAY THE FORFEIT OF THE PEACE.

FOR THIS TIME, ALL THE REST DEPART AWAY:

YOU, CAPULET, SHALL GO ALONG WITH ME;

AND, **MONTAGUE**, COME **YOU** THIS AFTERNOON, TO KNOW OUR **FURTHER** PLEASURE IN THIS CASE, TO OLD **FREE-TOWN**, OUR COMMON JUDGEMENT-PLACE.

ONCE **MORE**, ON PAIN OF **DEATH**, ALL MEN **DEPART**.

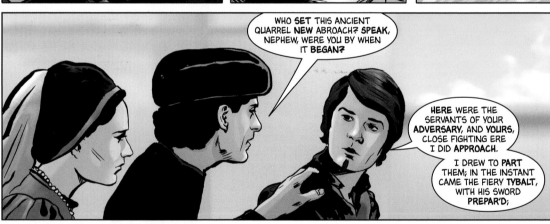

WHO **SET** THIS ANCIENT QUARREL **NEW ABROACH**? SPEAK, NEPHEW, WERE YOU BY WHEN IT **BEGAN**?

HERE WERE THE SERVANTS OF YOUR **ADVERSARY**, AND YOURS, CLOSE FIGHTING ERE I DID **APPROACH**.

I DREW TO **PART** THEM; IN THE INSTANT CAME THE FIERY **TYBALT**, WITH HIS SWORD **PREPAR'D**;

WHICH, AS HE BREATH'D **DEFIANCE** TO MY EARS,

HE SWUNG ABOUT HIS **HEAD**, AND CUT THE WINDS, WHO, NOTHING HURT WITHAL, HISS'D HIM IN **SCORN**.

WHILE WE WERE INTERCHANGING **THRUSTS** AND **BLOWS**, COME MORE AND MORE, AND **FOUGHT** ON PART AND PART,

TILL THE **PRINCE** CAME, WHO **PARTED** EITHER PART.

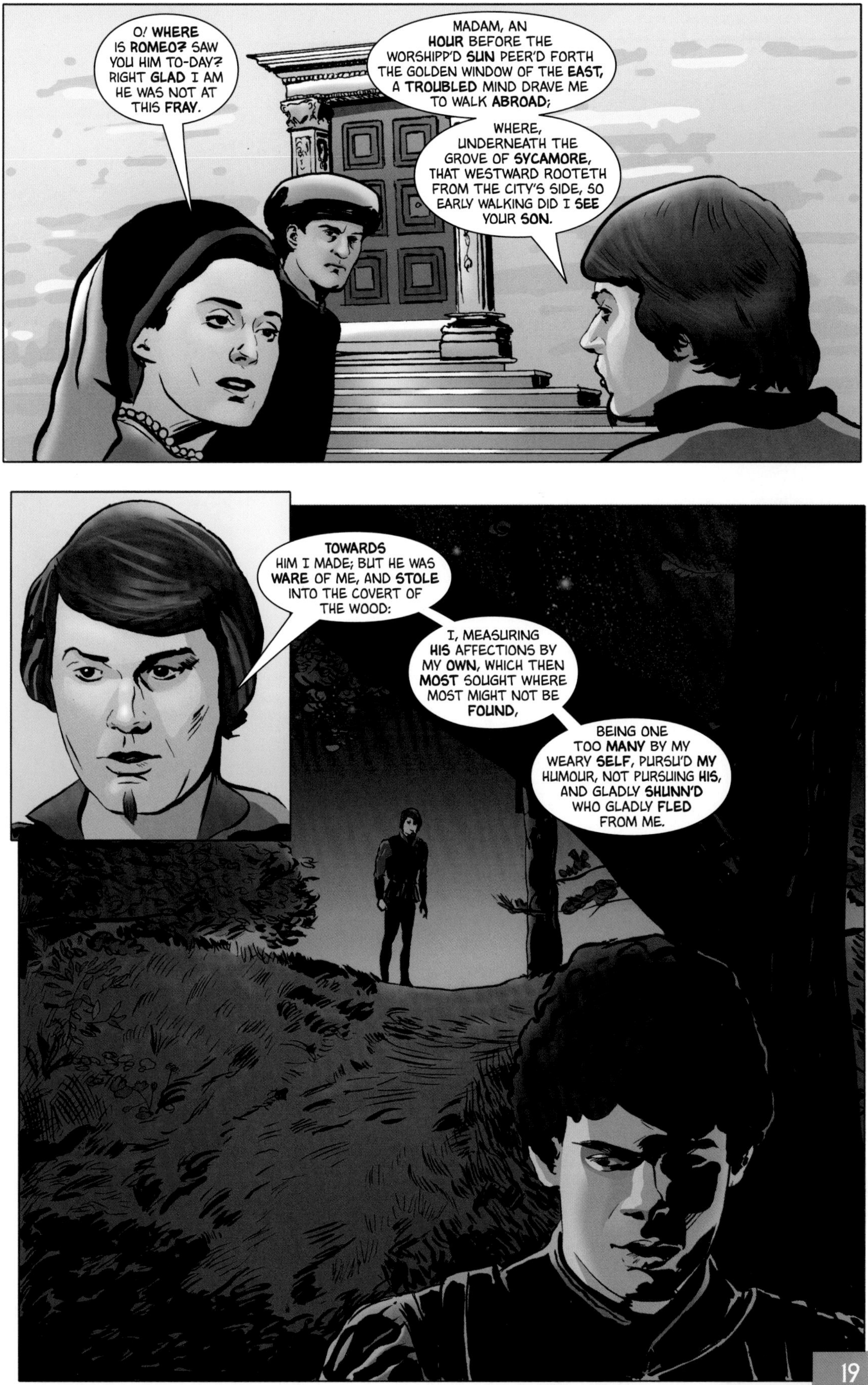
O! WHERE IS ROMEO? SAW YOU HIM TO-DAY? RIGHT GLAD I AM HE WAS NOT AT THIS FRAY.
MADAM, AN HOUR BEFORE THE WORSHIPP'D SUN PEER'D FORTH THE GOLDEN WINDOW OF THE EAST, A TROUBLED MIND DRAVE ME TO WALK ABROAD;
WHERE, UNDERNEATH THE GROVE OF SYCAMORE, THAT WESTWARD ROOTETH FROM THE CITY'S SIDE, SO EARLY WALKING DID I SEE YOUR SON.
TOWARDS HIM I MADE; BUT HE WAS WARE OF ME, AND STOLE INTO THE COVERT OF THE WOOD:
I, MEASURING HIS AFFECTIONS BY MY OWN, WHICH THEN MOST SOUGHT WHERE MOST MIGHT NOT BE FOUND,
BEING ONE TOO MANY BY MY WEARY SELF, PURSU'D MY HUMOUR, NOT PURSUING HIS, AND GLADLY SHUNN'D WHO GLADLY FLED FROM ME.

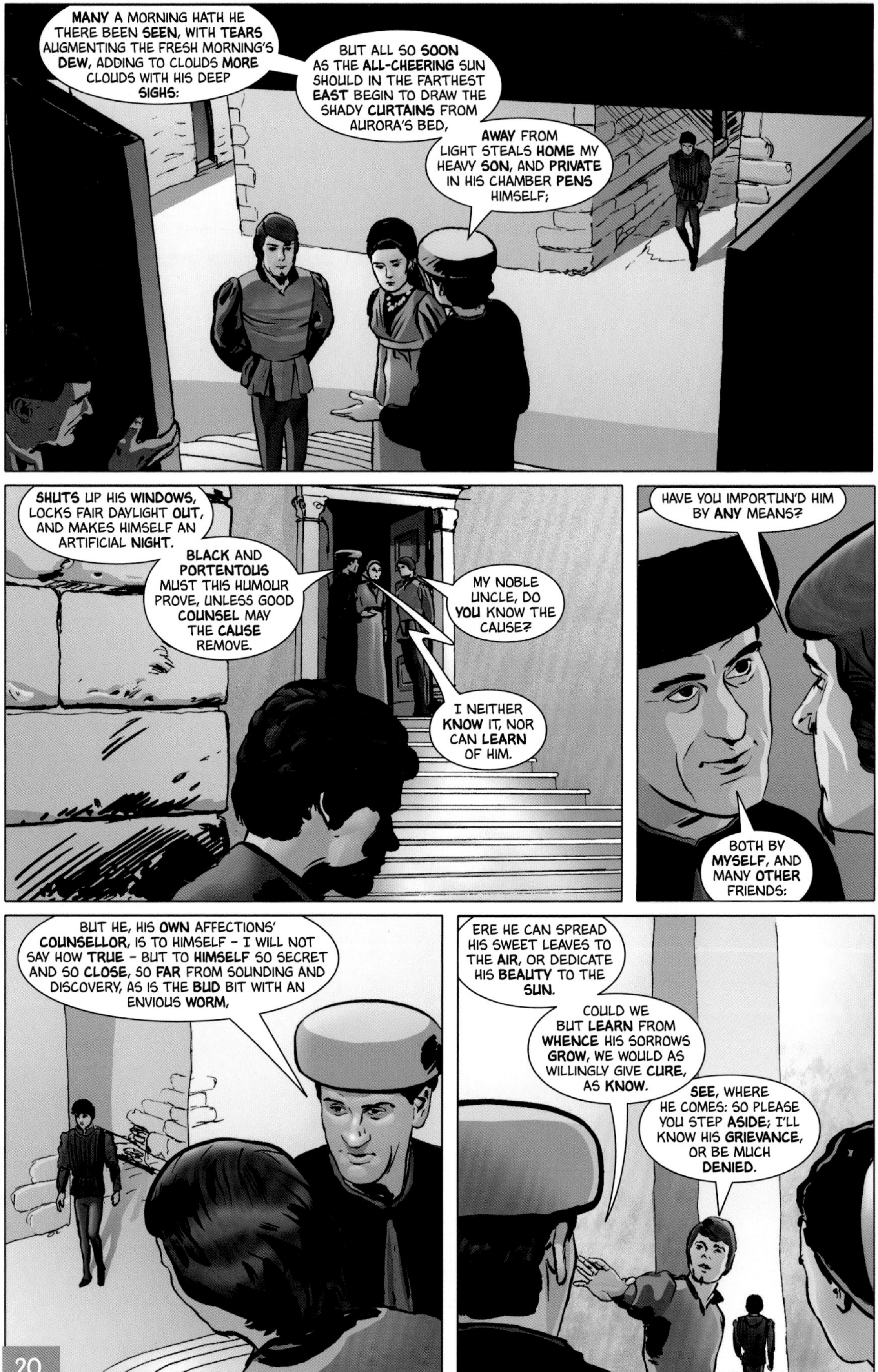
MANY A MORNING HATH HE THERE BEEN SEEN, WITH TEARS AUGMENTING THE FRESH MORNING'S DEW, ADDING TO CLOUDS MORE CLOUDS WITH HIS DEEP SIGHS:
BUT ALL SO SOON AS THE ALL-CHEERING SUN SHOULD IN THE FARTHEST EAST BEGIN TO DRAW THE SHADY CURTAINS FROM AURORA'S BED,
AWAY FROM LIGHT STEALS HOME MY HEAVY SON, AND PRIVATE IN HIS CHAMBER PENS HIMSELF;
SHUTS UP HIS WINDOWS, LOCKS FAIR DAYLIGHT OUT, AND MAKES HIMSELF AN ARTIFICIAL NIGHT.
BLACK AND PORTENTOUS MUST THIS HUMOUR PROVE, UNLESS GOOD COUNSEL MAY THE CAUSE REMOVE.
MY NOBLE UNCLE, DO YOU KNOW THE CAUSE?
I NEITHER KNOW IT, NOR CAN LEARN OF HIM.
HAVE YOU IMPORTUN'D HIM BY ANY MEANS?
BOTH BY MYSELF, AND MANY OTHER FRIENDS:
BUT HE, HIS OWN AFFECTIONS' COUNSELLOR, IS TO HIMSELF - I WILL NOT SAY HOW TRUE - BUT TO HIMSELF SO SECRET AND SO CLOSE, SO FAR FROM SOUNDING AND DISCOVERY, AS IS THE BUD BIT WITH AN ENVIOUS WORM,
ERE HE CAN SPREAD HIS SWEET LEAVES TO THE AIR, OR DEDICATE HIS BEAUTY TO THE SUN.
COULD WE BUT LEARN FROM WHENCE HIS SORROWS GROW, WE WOULD AS WILLINGLY GIVE CURE, AS KNOW.
SEE, WHERE HE COMES: SO PLEASE YOU STEP ASIDE; I'LL KNOW HIS GRIEVANCE, OR BE MUCH DENIED.

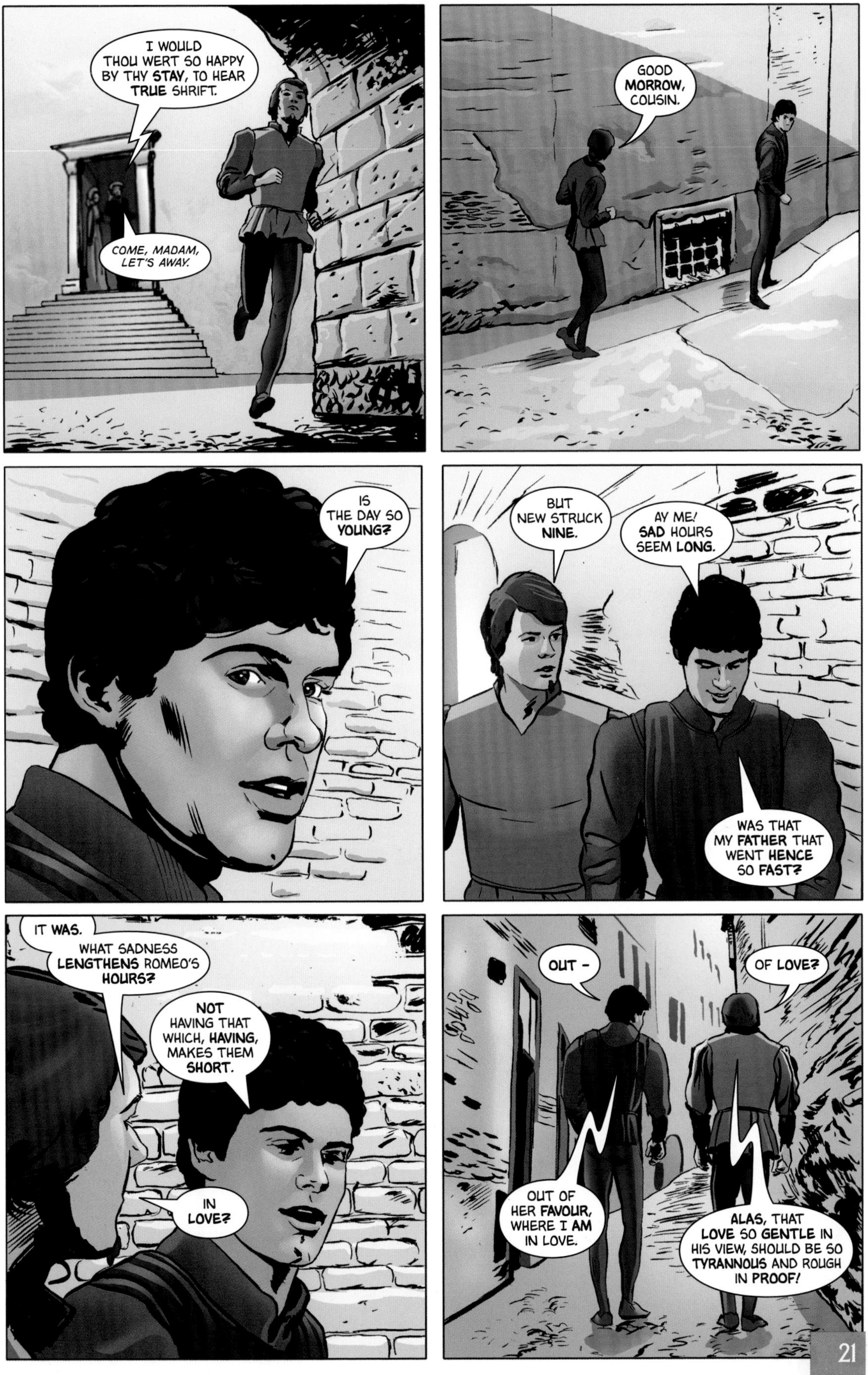

I WOULD THOU WERT SO HAPPY BY THY STAY, TO HEAR TRUE SHRIFT.
COME, MADAM, LET'S AWAY.
GOOD MORROW, COUSIN.
IS THE DAY SO YOUNG?
BUT NEW STRUCK NINE.
AY ME! SAD HOURS SEEM LONG.
WAS THAT MY FATHER THAT WENT HENCE SO FAST?
IT WAS.
WHAT SADNESS LENGTHENS ROMEO'S HOURS?
NOT HAVING THAT WHICH, HAVING, MAKES THEM SHORT.
IN LOVE?
OUT -
OF LOVE?
OUT OF HER FAVOUR, WHERE I AM IN LOVE.
ALAS, THAT LOVE SO GENTLE IN HIS VIEW, SHOULD BE SO TYRANNOUS AND ROUGH IN PROOF!

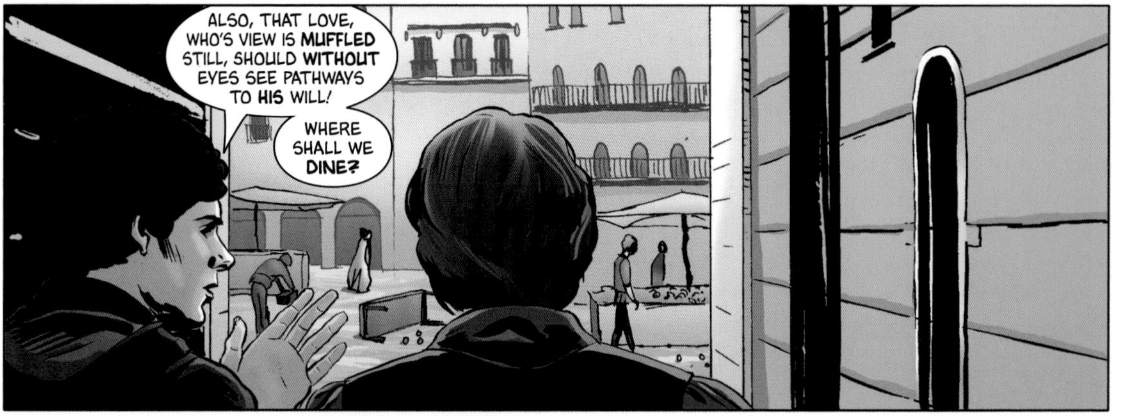
ALSO, THAT LOVE, WHO'S VIEW IS MUFFLED STILL, SHOULD WITHOUT EYES SEE PATHWAYS TO HIS WILL!
WHERE SHALL WE DINE?

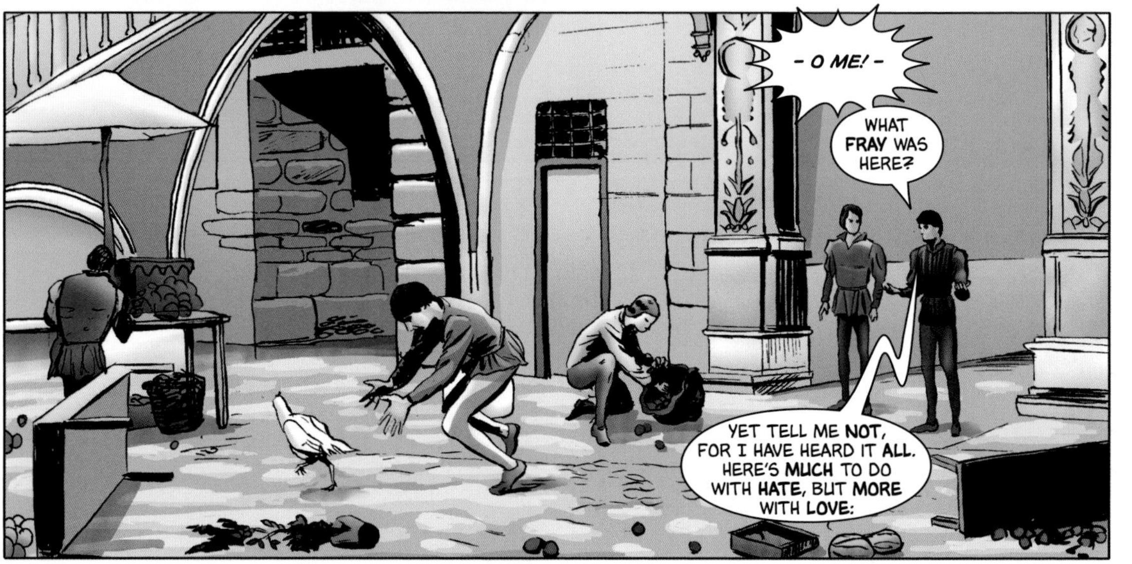
- O ME! -
WHAT FRAY WAS HERE?
YET TELL ME NOT, FOR I HAVE HEARD IT ALL. HERE'S MUCH TO DO WITH HATE, BUT MORE WITH LOVE:

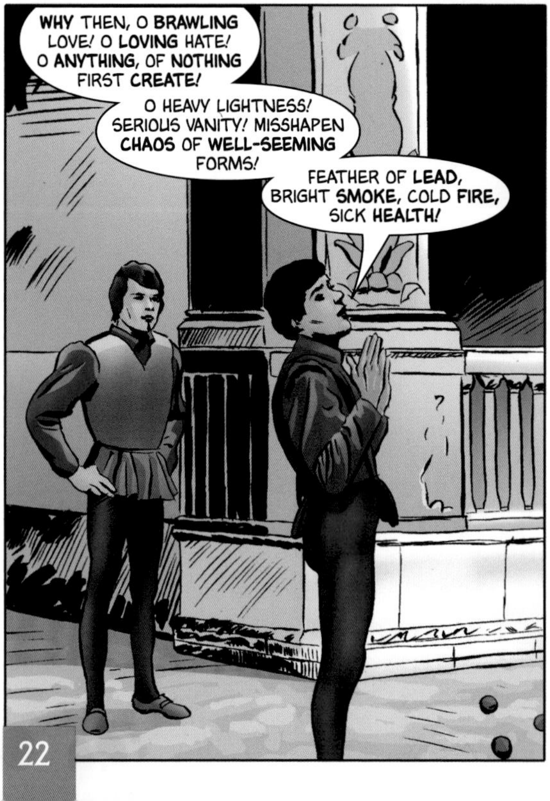
WHY THEN, O BRAWLING LOVE! O LOVING HATE! O ANYTHING, OF NOTHING FIRST CREATE!
O HEAVY LIGHTNESS! SERIOUS VANITY! MISSHAPEN CHAOS OF WELL-SEEMING FORMS!
FEATHER OF LEAD, BRIGHT SMOKE, COLD FIRE, SICK HEALTH!

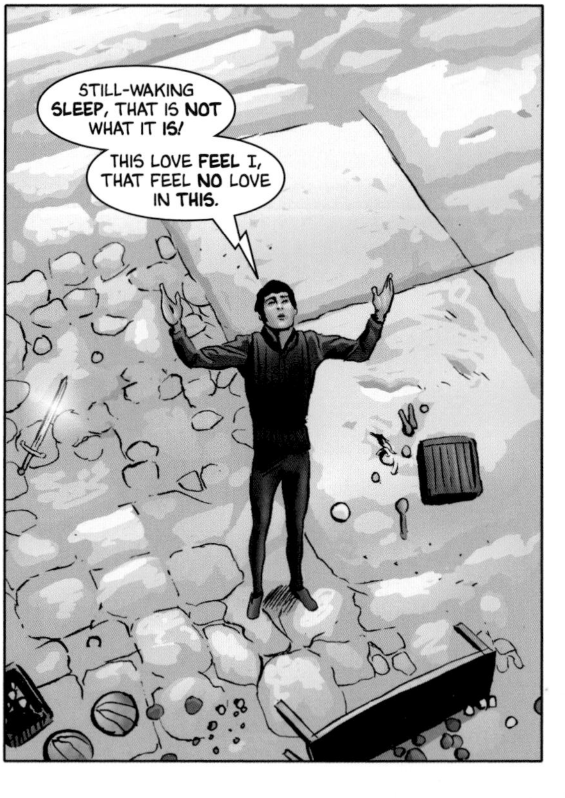
STILL-WAKING SLEEP, THAT IS NOT WHAT IT IS!
THIS LOVE FEEL I, THAT FEEL NO LOVE IN THIS.

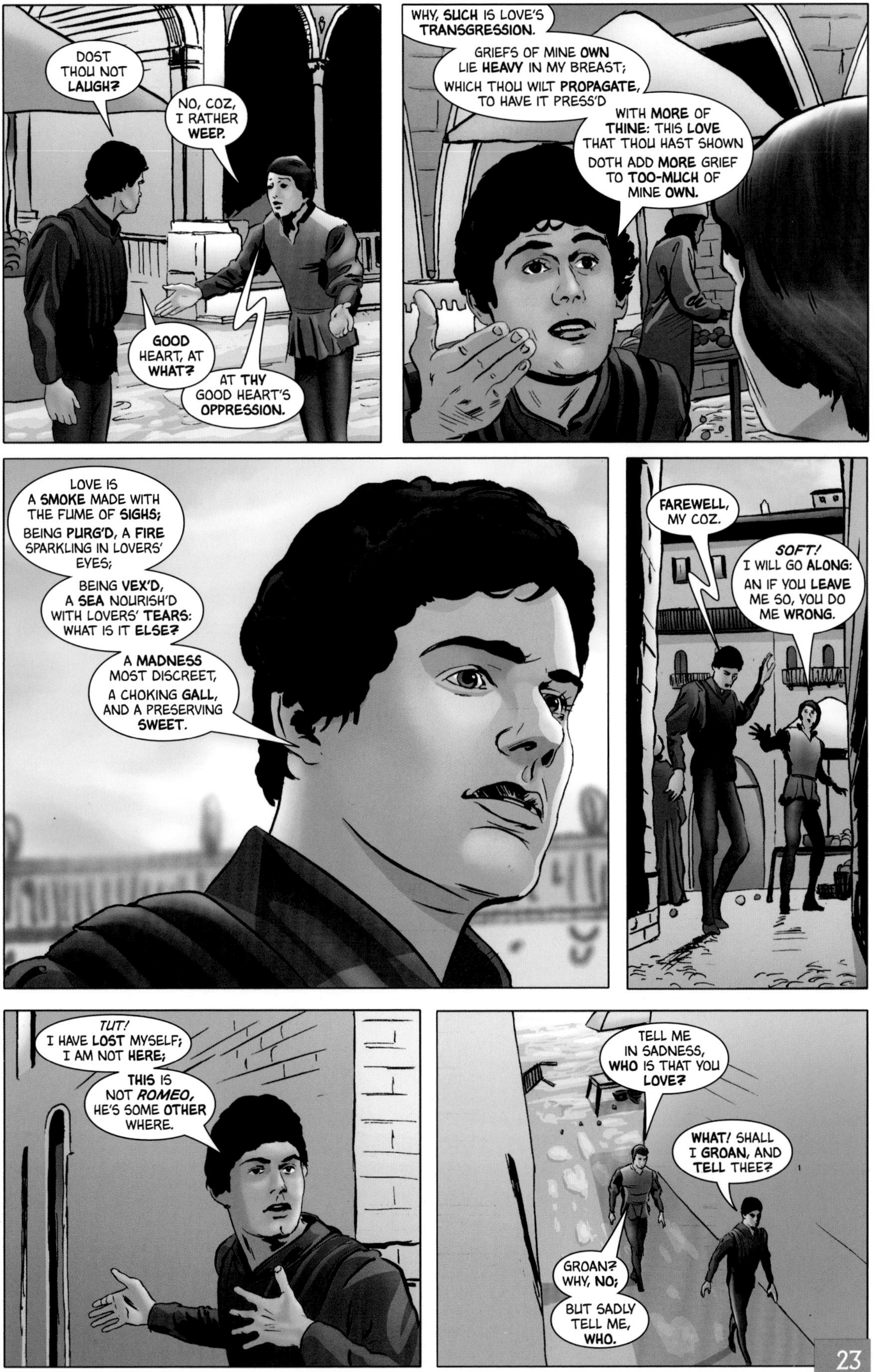
DOST THOU NOT LAUGH?
NO, COZ, I RATHER WEEP.
GOOD HEART, AT WHAT?
AT THY GOOD HEART'S OPPRESSION.
WHY, SUCH IS LOVE'S TRANSGRESSION.
GRIEFS OF MINE OWN LIE HEAVY IN MY BREAST;
WHICH THOU WILT PROPAGATE, TO HAVE IT PRESS'D
WITH MORE OF THINE: THIS LOVE THAT THOU HAST SHOWN
DOTH ADD MORE GRIEF TO TOO-MUCH OF MINE OWN.
LOVE IS A SMOKE MADE WITH THE FUME OF SIGHS;
BEING PURG'D, A FIRE SPARKLING IN LOVERS' EYES;
BEING VEX'D, A SEA NOURISH'D WITH LOVERS' TEARS: WHAT IS IT ELSE?
A MADNESS MOST DISCREET, A CHOKING GALL, AND A PRESERVING SWEET.
FAREWELL, MY COZ.
SOFT! I WILL GO ALONG: AN IF YOU LEAVE ME SO, YOU DO ME WRONG.
TUT! I HAVE LOST MYSELF; I AM NOT HERE;
THIS IS NOT ROMEO, HE'S SOME OTHER WHERE.
TELL ME IN SADNESS, WHO IS THAT YOU LOVE?
WHAT! SHALL I GROAN, AND TELL THEE?
GROAN? WHY, NO;
BUT SADLY TELL ME, WHO.

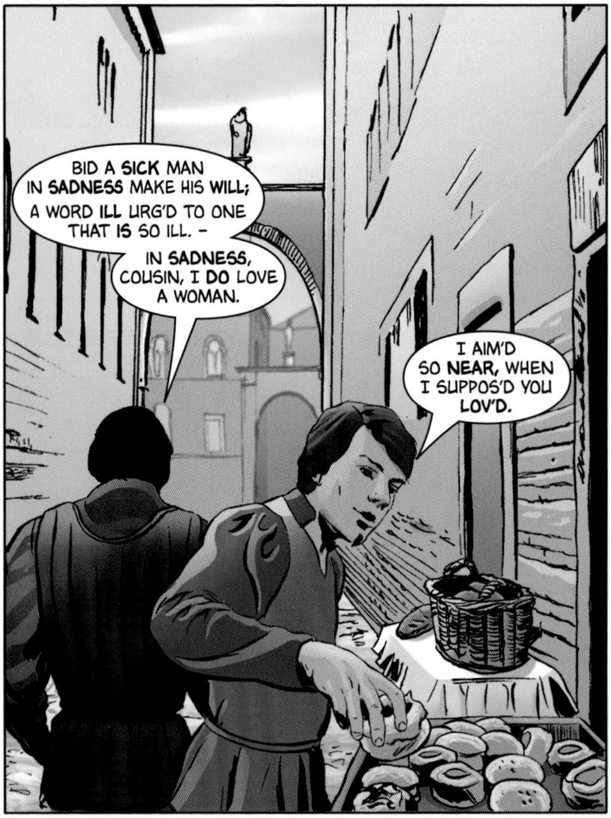
BID A **SICK** MAN IN **SADNESS** MAKE HIS **WILL**; A WORD **ILL** URG'D TO ONE THAT **IS** SO ILL. –
IN **SADNESS**, COUSIN, I **DO** LOVE A WOMAN.
I AIM'D SO **NEAR**, WHEN I SUPPOS'D YOU **LOV'D**.

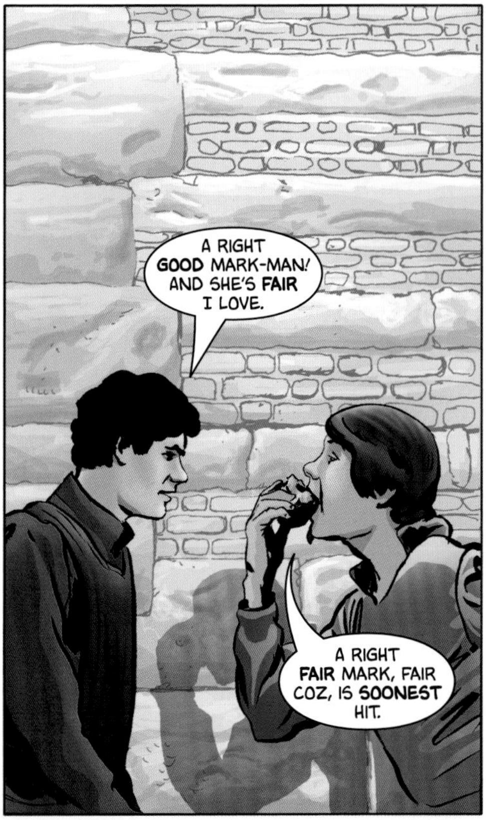
A RIGHT **GOOD** MARK-MAN! AND SHE'S **FAIR** I LOVE.
A RIGHT **FAIR** MARK, FAIR COZ, IS **SOONEST** HIT.

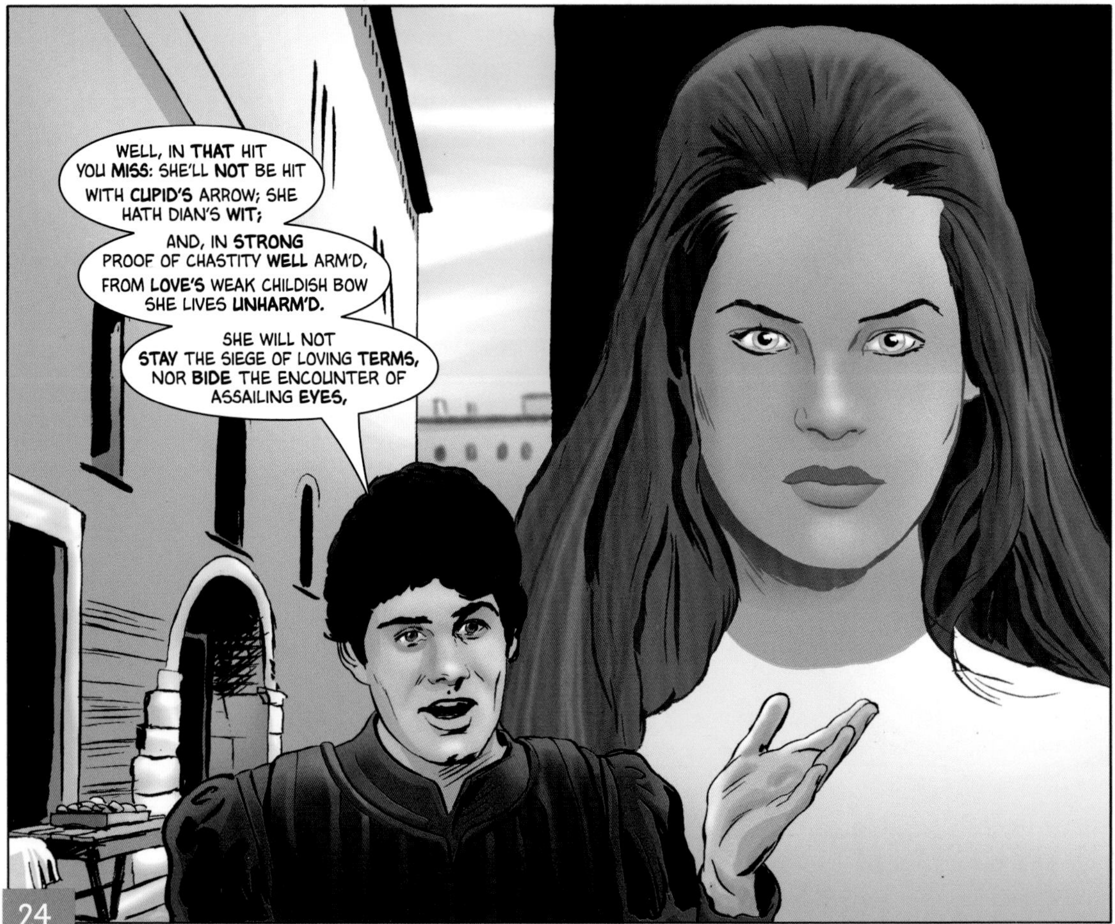
WELL, IN **THAT** HIT YOU **MISS**: SHE'LL **NOT** BE HIT WITH **CUPID'S** ARROW; SHE HATH DIAN'S **WIT**;
AND, IN **STRONG** PROOF OF CHASTITY **WELL** ARM'D, FROM **LOVE'S** WEAK CHILDISH BOW SHE LIVES **UNHARM'D**.
SHE WILL NOT **STAY** THE SIEGE OF LOVING **TERMS**, NOR **BIDE** THE ENCOUNTER OF ASSAILING **EYES**,

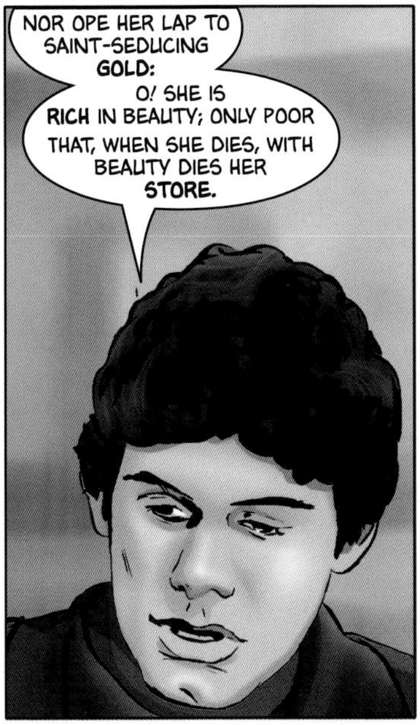
NOR OPE HER LAP TO SAINT-SEDUCING GOLD:
O! SHE IS RICH IN BEAUTY; ONLY POOR THAT, WHEN SHE DIES, WITH BEAUTY DIES HER STORE.

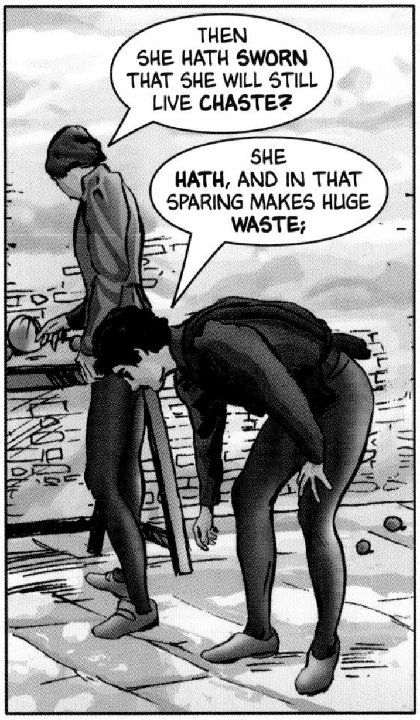
THEN SHE HATH SWORN THAT SHE WILL STILL LIVE CHASTE?
SHE HATH, AND IN THAT SPARING MAKES HUGE WASTE;

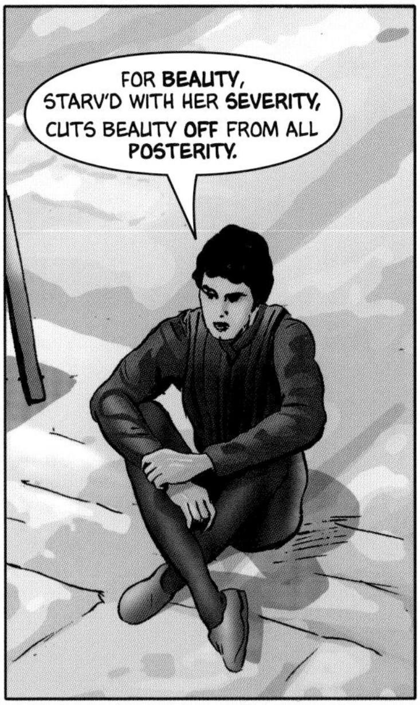
FOR BEAUTY, STARV'D WITH HER SEVERITY, CUTS BEAUTY OFF FROM ALL POSTERITY.

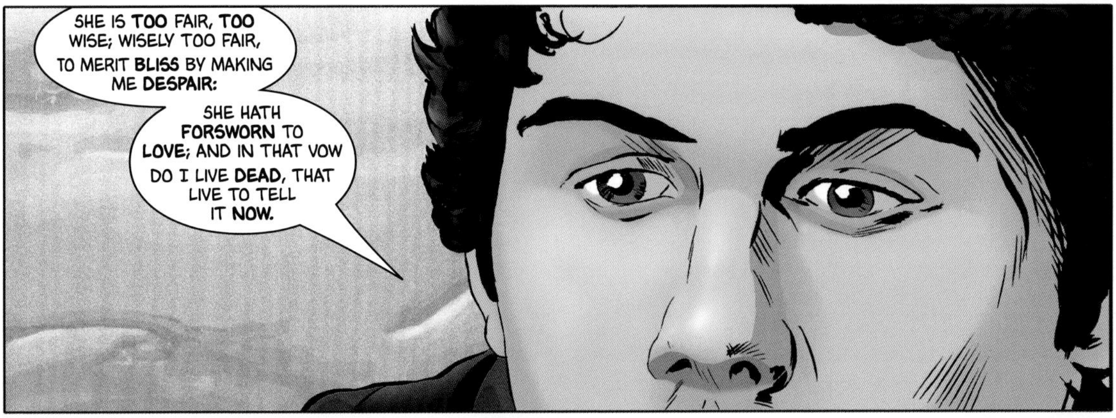
SHE IS TOO FAIR, TOO WISE; WISELY TOO FAIR, TO MERIT BLISS BY MAKING ME DESPAIR:
SHE HATH FORSWORN TO LOVE; AND IN THAT VOW DO I LIVE DEAD, THAT LIVE TO TELL IT NOW.

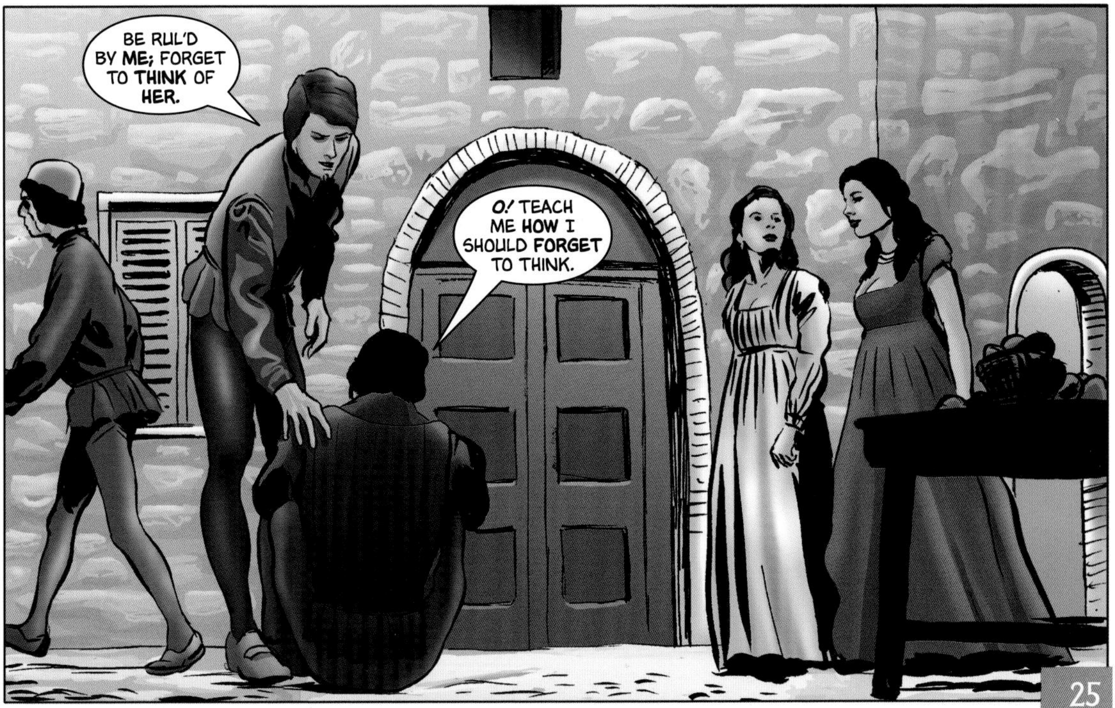
BE RUL'D BY ME; FORGET TO THINK OF HER.
O! TEACH ME HOW I SHOULD FORGET TO THINK.

BY GIVING LIBERTY UNTO THINE EYES: EXAMINE OTHER BEAUTIES.

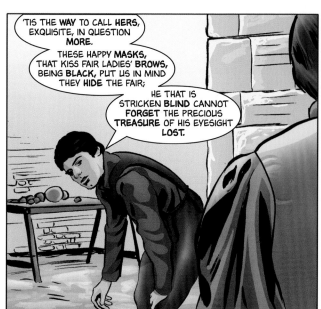

'TIS THE WAY TO CALL HERS, EXQUISITE, IN QUESTION MORE.

THESE HAPPY MASKS, THAT KISS FAIR LADIES' BROWS, BEING BLACK, PUT US IN MIND THEY HIDE THE FAIR;

HE THAT IS STRICKEN BLIND CANNOT FORGET THE PRECIOUS TREASURE OF HIS EYESIGHT LOST.

SHOW ME A MISTRESS THAT IS PASSING FAIR, WHAT DOTH HER BEAUTY SERVE BUT AS A NOTE WHERE I MAY READ WHO PASS'D THAT PASSING FAIR?

FAREWELL: THOU CANST NOT TEACH ME TO FORGET.

I'LL PAY THAT DOCTRINE, OR ELSE DIE IN DEBT.

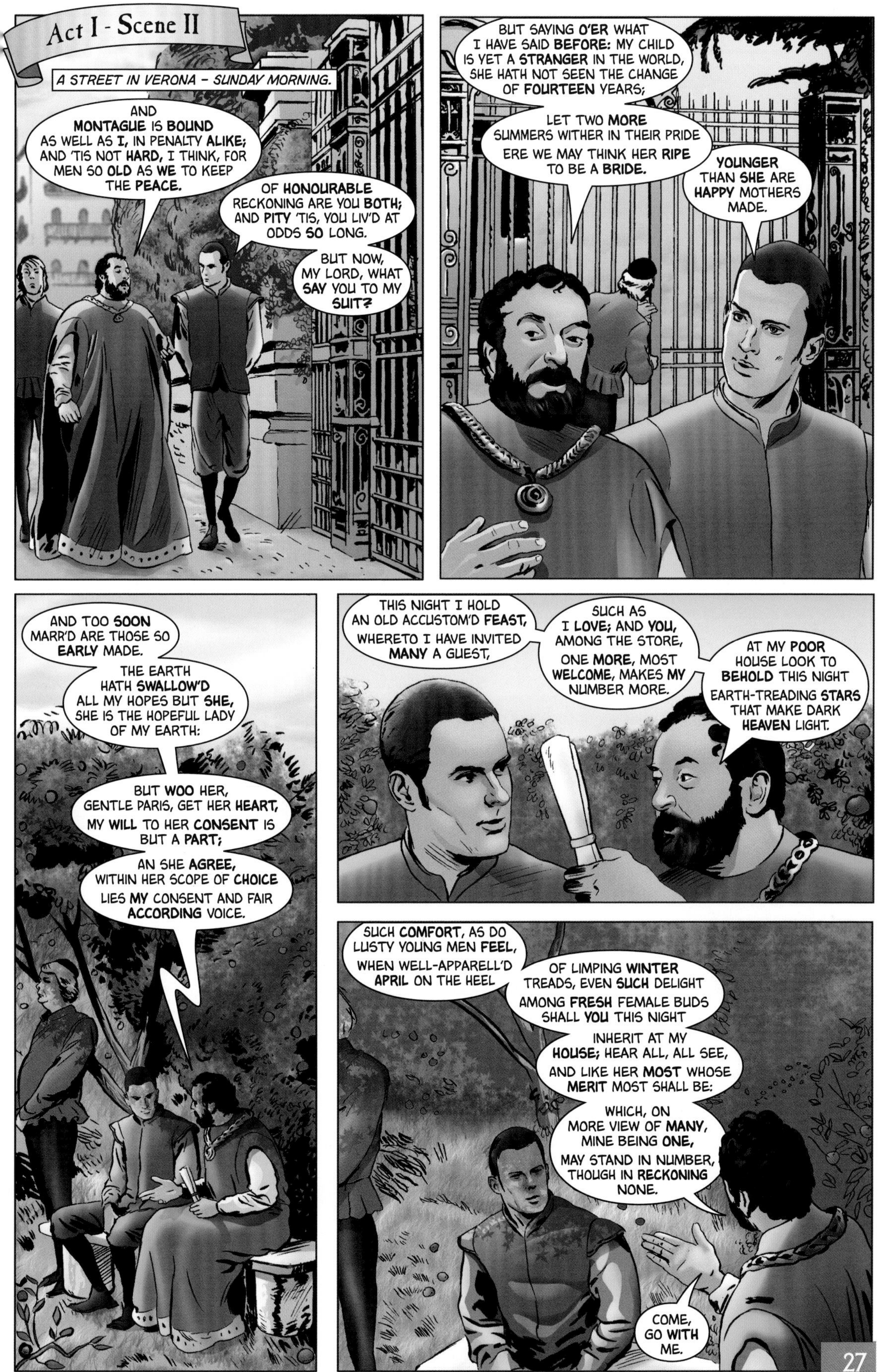
Act I - Scene II
A STREET IN VERONA – SUNDAY MORNING.
AND MONTAGUE IS BOUND AS WELL AS I, IN PENALTY ALIKE; AND 'TIS NOT HARD, I THINK, FOR MEN SO OLD AS WE TO KEEP THE PEACE.
OF HONOURABLE RECKONING ARE YOU BOTH; AND PITY 'TIS, YOU LIV'D AT ODDS SO LONG.
BUT NOW, MY LORD, WHAT SAY YOU TO MY SUIT?
BUT SAYING O'ER WHAT I HAVE SAID BEFORE: MY CHILD IS YET A STRANGER IN THE WORLD, SHE HATH NOT SEEN THE CHANGE OF FOURTEEN YEARS;
LET TWO MORE SUMMERS WITHER IN THEIR PRIDE
ERE WE MAY THINK HER RIPE TO BE A BRIDE.
YOUNGER THAN SHE ARE HAPPY MOTHERS MADE.
AND TOO SOON MARR'D ARE THOSE SO EARLY MADE.
THE EARTH HATH SWALLOW'D ALL MY HOPES BUT SHE, SHE IS THE HOPEFUL LADY OF MY EARTH:
BUT WOO HER, GENTLE PARIS, GET HER HEART,
MY WILL TO HER CONSENT IS BUT A PART;
AN SHE AGREE, WITHIN HER SCOPE OF CHOICE
LIES MY CONSENT AND FAIR ACCORDING VOICE.
THIS NIGHT I HOLD AN OLD ACCUSTOM'D FEAST,
WHERETO I HAVE INVITED MANY A GUEST,
SUCH AS I LOVE; AND YOU, AMONG THE STORE,
ONE MORE, MOST WELCOME, MAKES MY NUMBER MORE.
AT MY POOR HOUSE LOOK TO BEHOLD THIS NIGHT
EARTH-TREADING STARS THAT MAKE DARK HEAVEN LIGHT.
SUCH COMFORT, AS DO LUSTY YOUNG MEN FEEL,
WHEN WELL-APPARELL'D APRIL ON THE HEEL
OF LIMPING WINTER TREADS, EVEN SUCH DELIGHT
AMONG FRESH FEMALE BUDS SHALL YOU THIS NIGHT
INHERIT AT MY HOUSE; HEAR ALL, ALL SEE,
AND LIKE HER MOST WHOSE MERIT MOST SHALL BE:
WHICH, ON MORE VIEW OF MANY, MINE BEING ONE,
MAY STAND IN NUMBER, THOUGH IN RECKONING NONE.
COME, GO WITH ME.

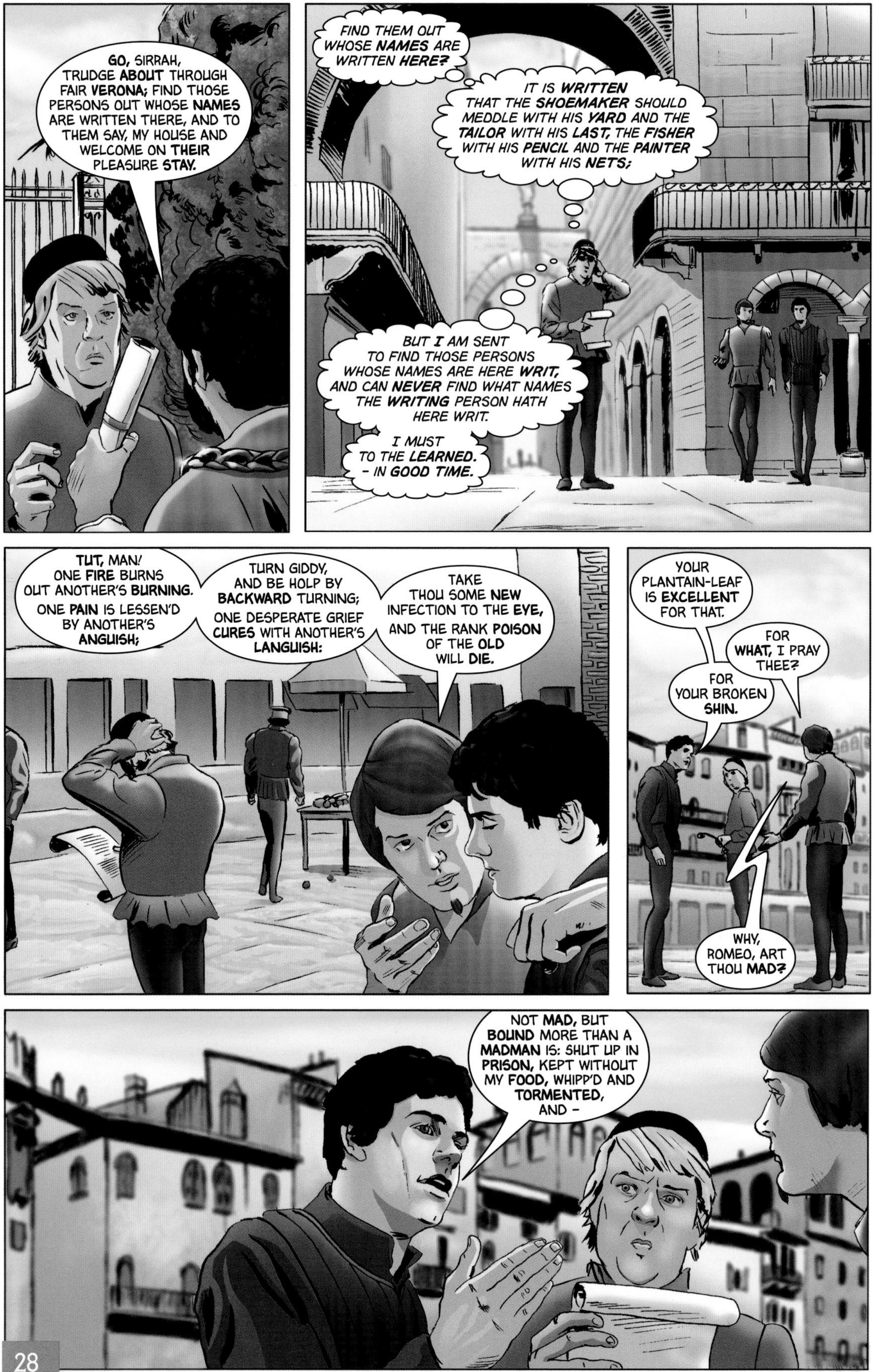
GO, SIRRAH, TRUDGE ABOUT THROUGH FAIR VERONA; FIND THOSE PERSONS OUT WHOSE NAMES ARE WRITTEN THERE, AND TO THEM SAY, MY HOUSE AND WELCOME ON THEIR PLEASURE STAY.
FIND THEM OUT WHOSE NAMES ARE WRITTEN HERE?
IT IS WRITTEN THAT THE SHOEMAKER SHOULD MEDDLE WITH HIS YARD AND THE TAILOR WITH HIS LAST, THE FISHER WITH HIS PENCIL AND THE PAINTER WITH HIS NETS;
BUT I AM SENT TO FIND THOSE PERSONS WHOSE NAMES ARE HERE WRIT, AND CAN NEVER FIND WHAT NAMES THE WRITING PERSON HATH HERE WRIT.
I MUST TO THE LEARNED. - IN GOOD TIME.
TUT, MAN! ONE FIRE BURNS OUT ANOTHER'S BURNING.
ONE PAIN IS LESSEN'D BY ANOTHER'S ANGUISH;
TURN GIDDY, AND BE HOLP BY BACKWARD TURNING;
ONE DESPERATE GRIEF CURES WITH ANOTHER'S LANGUISH:
TAKE THOU SOME NEW INFECTION TO THE EYE, AND THE RANK POISON OF THE OLD WILL DIE.
YOUR PLANTAIN-LEAF IS EXCELLENT FOR THAT.
FOR WHAT, I PRAY THEE?
FOR YOUR BROKEN SHIN.
WHY, ROMEO, ART THOU MAD?
NOT MAD, BUT BOUND MORE THAN A MADMAN IS: SHUT UP IN PRISON, KEPT WITHOUT MY FOOD, WHIPP'D AND TORMENTED, AND -

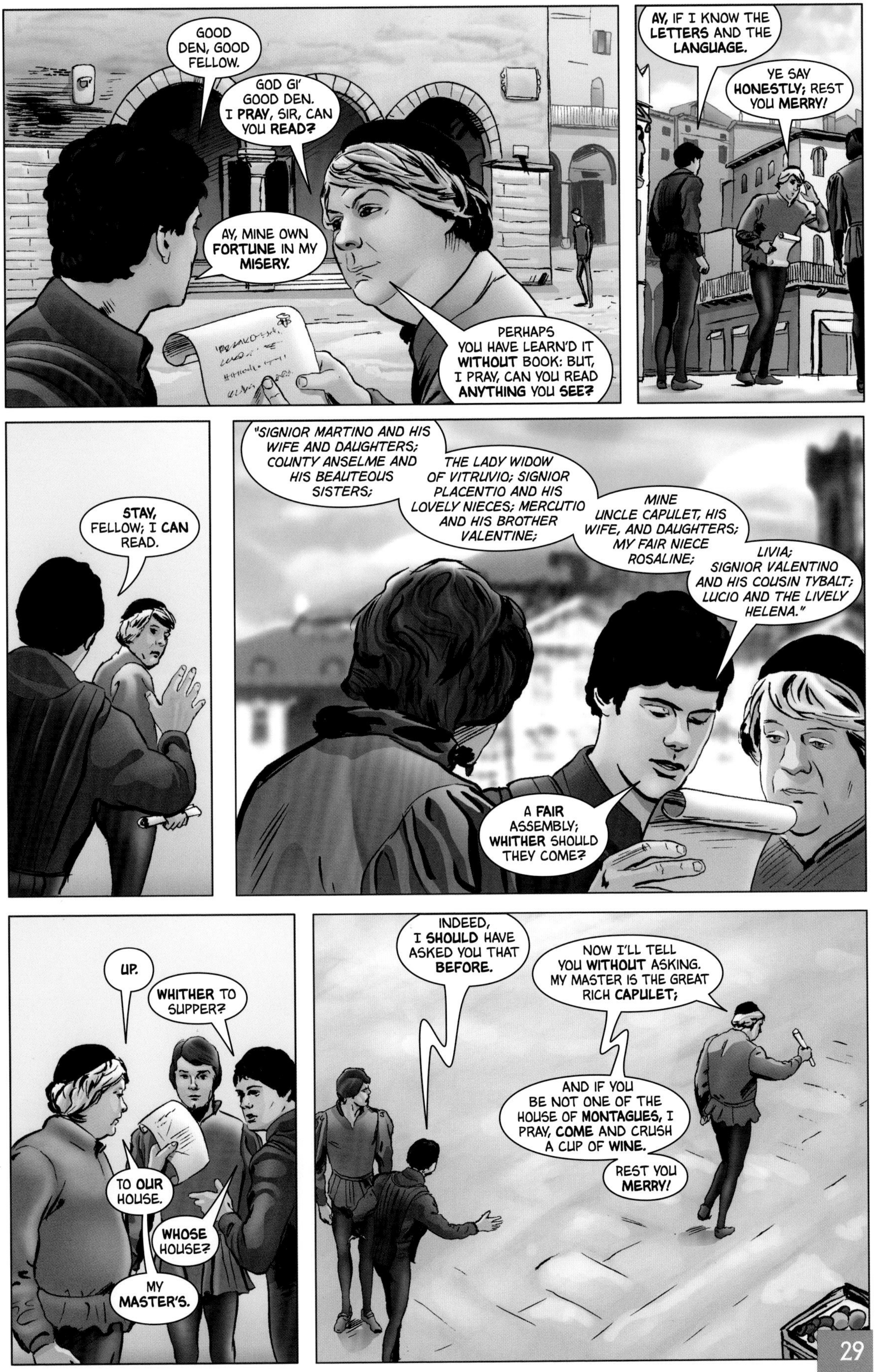
GOOD DEN, GOOD FELLOW.
GOD GI' GOOD DEN. I PRAY, SIR, CAN YOU READ?
AY, MINE OWN FORTUNE IN MY MISERY.
PERHAPS YOU HAVE LEARN'D IT WITHOUT BOOK: BUT, I PRAY, CAN YOU READ ANYTHING YOU SEE?
AY, IF I KNOW THE LETTERS AND THE LANGUAGE.
YE SAY HONESTLY; REST YOU MERRY!
STAY, FELLOW; I CAN READ.
"SIGNIOR MARTINO AND HIS WIFE AND DAUGHTERS; COUNTY ANSELME AND HIS BEAUTEOUS SISTERS;
THE LADY WIDOW OF VITRUVIO; SIGNIOR PLACENTIO AND HIS LOVELY NIECES; MERCUTIO AND HIS BROTHER VALENTINE;
MINE UNCLE CAPULET, HIS WIFE, AND DAUGHTERS; MY FAIR NIECE ROSALINE;
LIVIA; SIGNIOR VALENTINO AND HIS COUSIN TYBALT; LUCIO AND THE LIVELY HELENA."
A FAIR ASSEMBLY; WHITHER SHOULD THEY COME?
UP.
WHITHER TO SUPPER?
TO OUR HOUSE.
WHOSE HOUSE?
MY MASTER'S.
INDEED, I SHOULD HAVE ASKED YOU THAT BEFORE.
NOW I'LL TELL YOU WITHOUT ASKING. MY MASTER IS THE GREAT RICH CAPULET;
AND IF YOU BE NOT ONE OF THE HOUSE OF MONTAGUES, I PRAY, COME AND CRUSH A CUP OF WINE.
REST YOU MERRY!

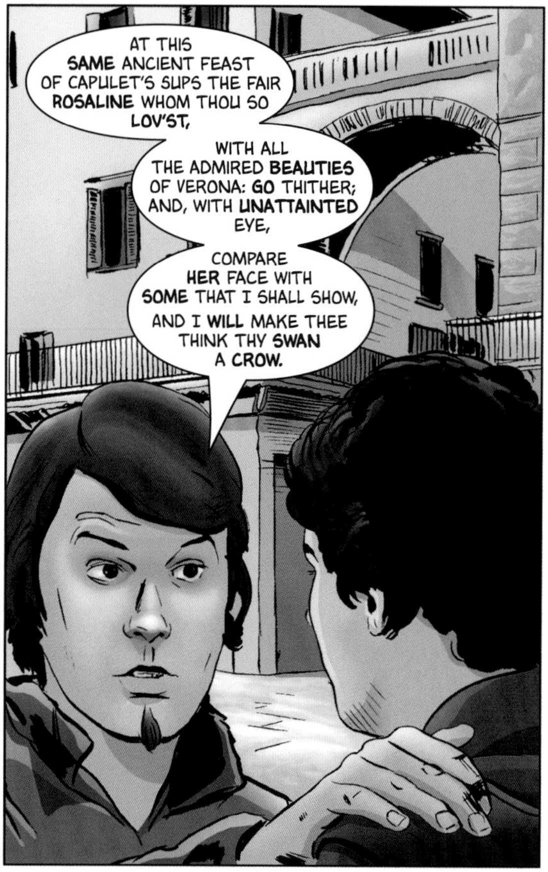
AT THIS SAME ANCIENT FEAST OF CAPULET'S SUPS THE FAIR ROSALINE WHOM THOU SO LOV'ST,
WITH ALL THE ADMIRED BEAUTIES OF VERONA: GO THITHER; AND, WITH UNATTAINTED EYE,
COMPARE HER FACE WITH SOME THAT I SHALL SHOW, AND I WILL MAKE THEE THINK THY SWAN A CROW.

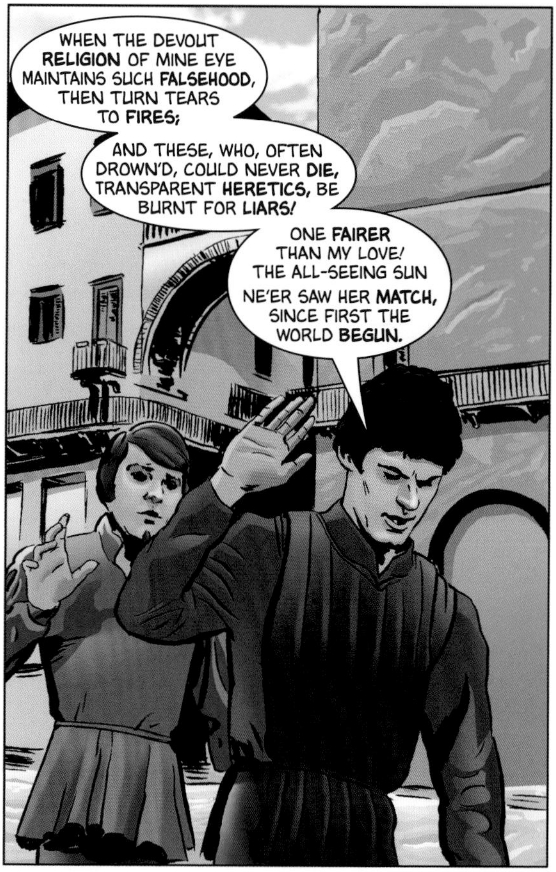
WHEN THE DEVOUT RELIGION OF MINE EYE MAINTAINS SUCH FALSEHOOD, THEN TURN TEARS TO FIRES;
AND THESE, WHO, OFTEN DROWN'D, COULD NEVER DIE, TRANSPARENT HERETICS, BE BURNT FOR LIARS!
ONE FAIRER THAN MY LOVE! THE ALL-SEEING SUN NE'ER SAW HER MATCH, SINCE FIRST THE WORLD BEGUN.

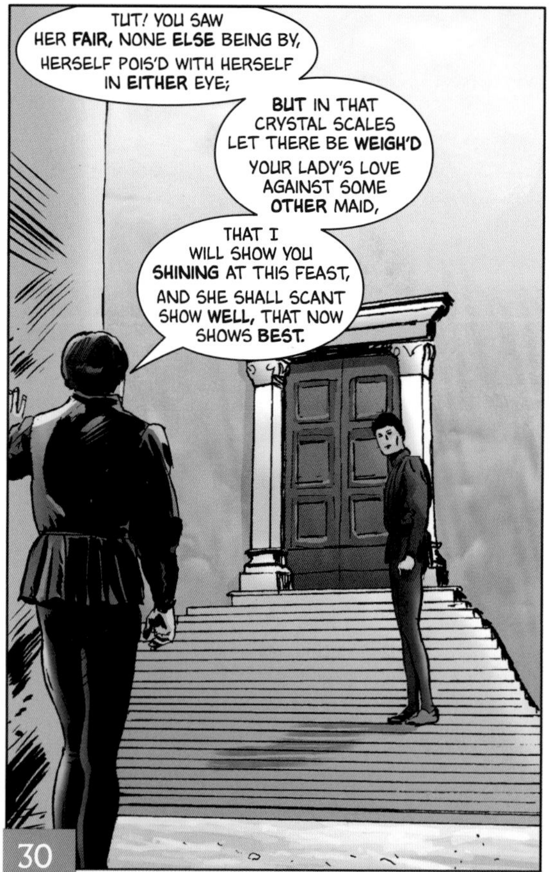
TUT! YOU SAW HER FAIR, NONE ELSE BEING BY, HERSELF POIS'D WITH HERSELF IN EITHER EYE;
BUT IN THAT CRYSTAL SCALES LET THERE BE WEIGH'D YOUR LADY'S LOVE AGAINST SOME OTHER MAID,
THAT I WILL SHOW YOU SHINING AT THIS FEAST, AND SHE SHALL SCANT SHOW WELL, THAT NOW SHOWS BEST.

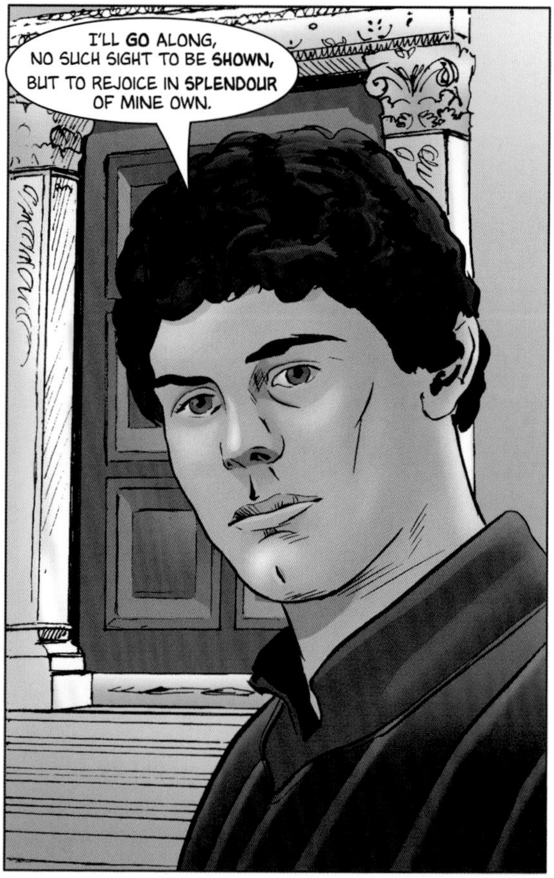
I'LL GO ALONG, NO SUCH SIGHT TO BE SHOWN, BUT TO REJOICE IN SPLENDOUR OF MINE OWN.

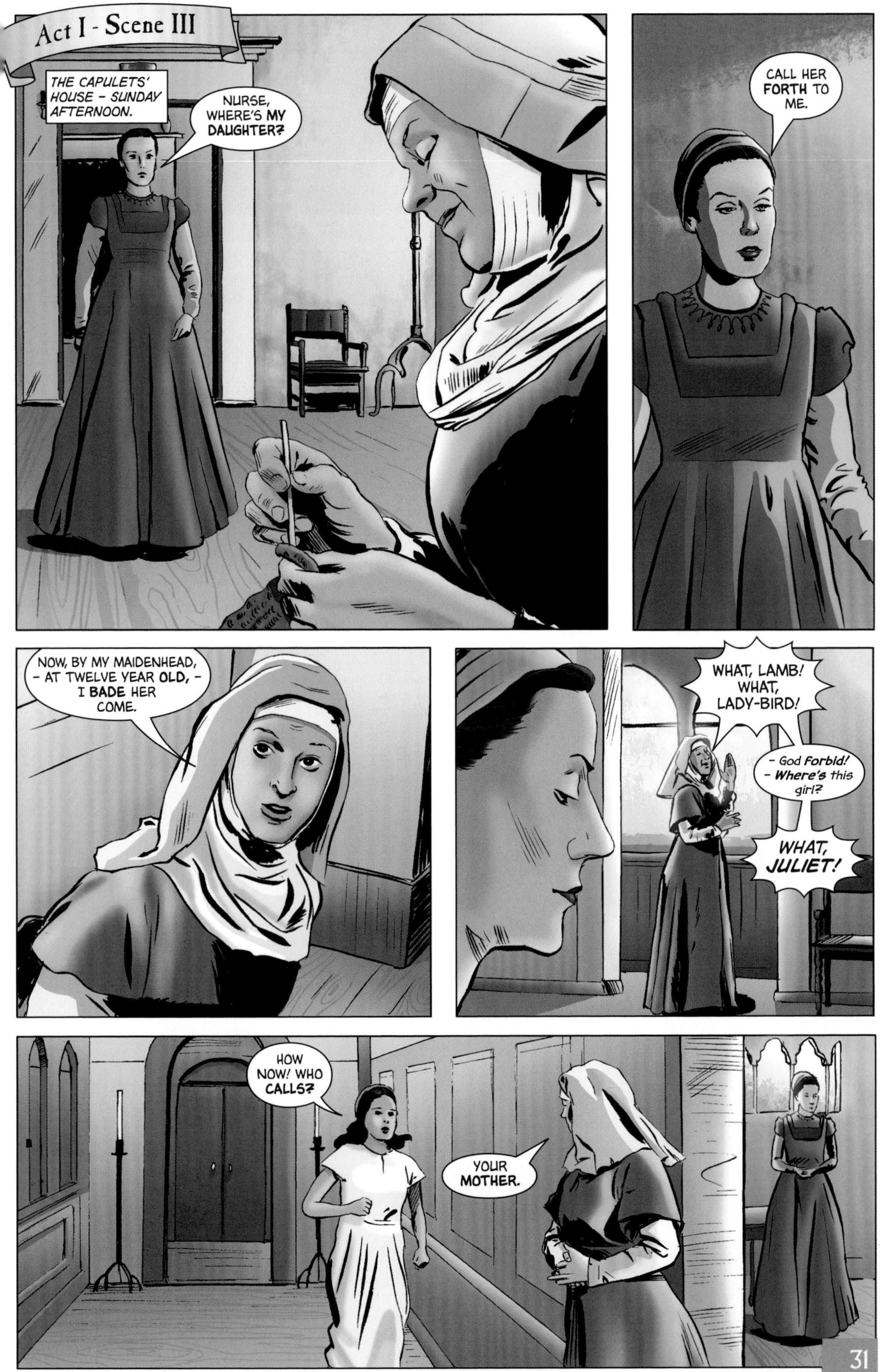

Act I - Scene III
THE CAPULETS' HOUSE – SUNDAY AFTERNOON.
NURSE, WHERE'S MY DAUGHTER?
CALL HER FORTH TO ME.
NOW, BY MY MAIDENHEAD, – AT TWELVE YEAR OLD, – I BADE HER COME.
WHAT, LAMB! WHAT, LADY-BIRD!
– God Forbid! – Where's this girl?
WHAT, JULIET!
HOW NOW! WHO CALLS?
YOUR MOTHER.

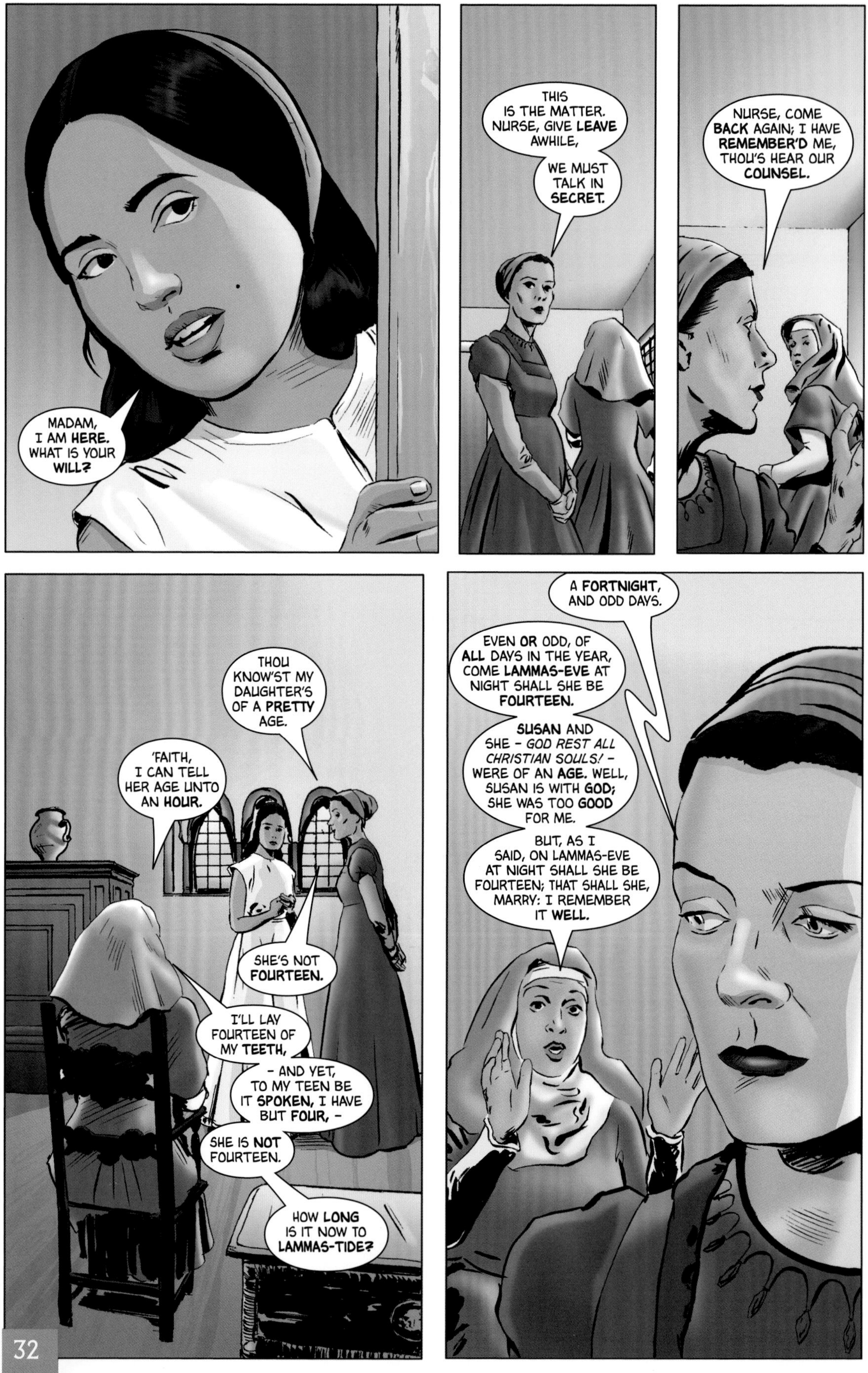
MADAM, I AM HERE. WHAT IS YOUR WILL?
THIS IS THE MATTER. NURSE, GIVE LEAVE AWHILE,
WE MUST TALK IN SECRET.
NURSE, COME BACK AGAIN; I HAVE REMEMBER'D ME, THOU'S HEAR OUR COUNSEL.
THOU KNOW'ST MY DAUGHTER'S OF A PRETTY AGE.
'FAITH, I CAN TELL HER AGE UNTO AN HOUR.
SHE'S NOT FOURTEEN.
I'LL LAY FOURTEEN OF MY TEETH,
- AND YET, TO MY TEEN BE IT SPOKEN, I HAVE BUT FOUR, -
SHE IS NOT FOURTEEN.
HOW LONG IS IT NOW TO LAMMAS-TIDE?
A FORTNIGHT, AND ODD DAYS.
EVEN OR ODD, OF ALL DAYS IN THE YEAR, COME LAMMAS-EVE AT NIGHT SHALL SHE BE FOURTEEN.
SUSAN AND SHE - GOD REST ALL CHRISTIAN SOULS! - WERE OF AN AGE. WELL, SUSAN IS WITH GOD; SHE WAS TOO GOOD FOR ME.
BUT, AS I SAID, ON LAMMAS-EVE AT NIGHT SHALL SHE BE FOURTEEN; THAT SHALL SHE, MARRY: I REMEMBER IT WELL.

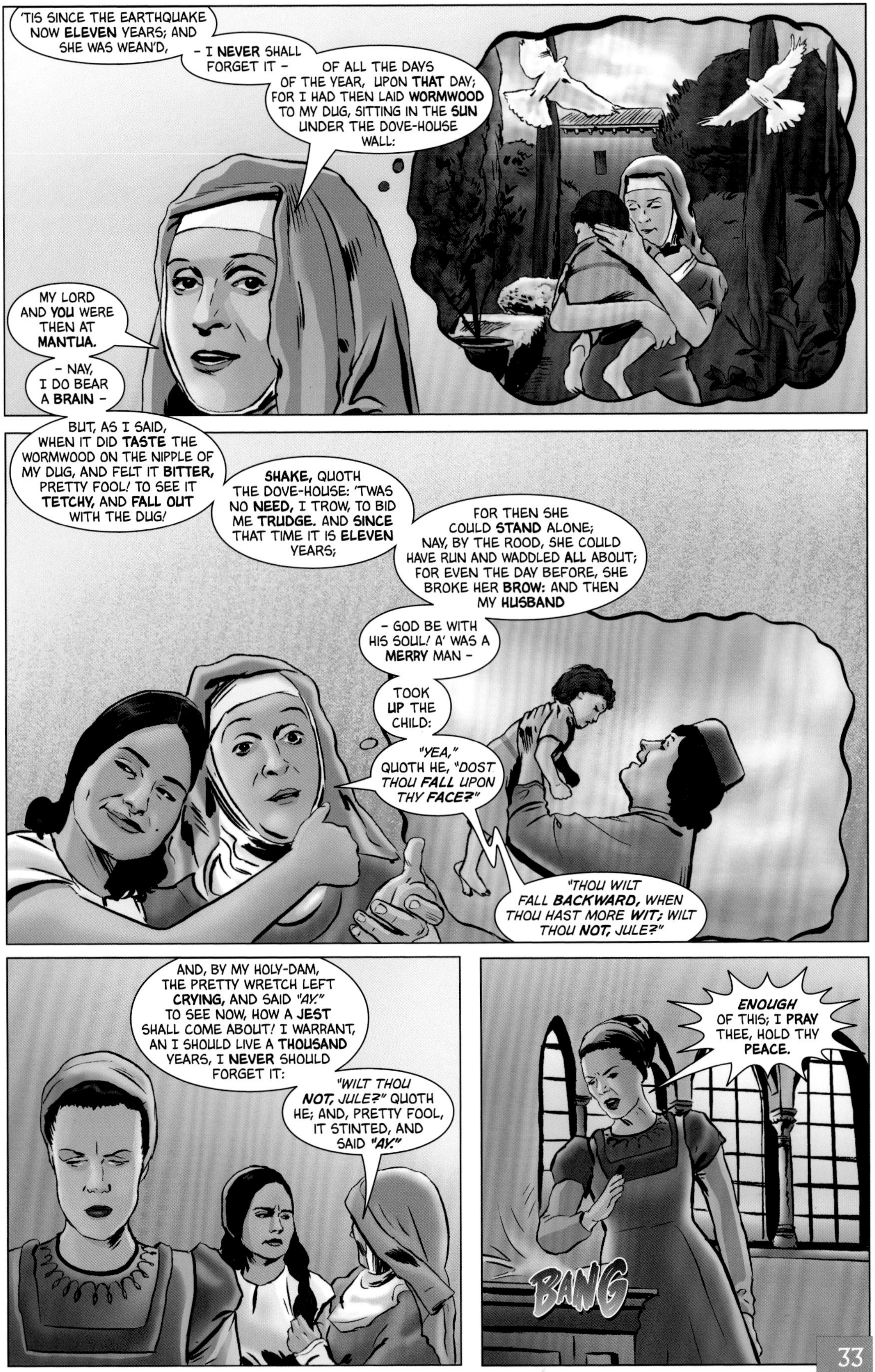
'TIS SINCE THE EARTHQUAKE NOW ELEVEN YEARS; AND SHE WAS WEAN'D,
- I NEVER SHALL FORGET IT -
OF ALL THE DAYS OF THE YEAR, UPON THAT DAY; FOR I HAD THEN LAID WORMWOOD TO MY DUG, SITTING IN THE SUN UNDER THE DOVE-HOUSE WALL:
MY LORD AND YOU WERE THEN AT MANTUA.
- NAY, I DO BEAR A BRAIN -
BUT, AS I SAID, WHEN IT DID TASTE THE WORMWOOD ON THE NIPPLE OF MY DUG, AND FELT IT BITTER, PRETTY FOOL! TO SEE IT TETCHY, AND FALL OUT WITH THE DUG!
SHAKE, QUOTH THE DOVE-HOUSE: 'TWAS NO NEED, I TROW, TO BID ME TRUDGE. AND SINCE THAT TIME IT IS ELEVEN YEARS;
FOR THEN SHE COULD STAND ALONE; NAY, BY THE ROOD, SHE COULD HAVE RUN AND WADDLED ALL ABOUT; FOR EVEN THE DAY BEFORE, SHE BROKE HER BROW: AND THEN MY HUSBAND
- GOD BE WITH HIS SOUL! A' WAS A MERRY MAN -
TOOK UP THE CHILD:
"YEA," QUOTH HE, "DOST THOU FALL UPON THY FACE?"
"THOU WILT FALL BACKWARD, WHEN THOU HAST MORE WIT; WILT THOU NOT, JULE?"
AND, BY MY HOLY-DAM, THE PRETTY WRETCH LEFT CRYING, AND SAID "AY." TO SEE NOW, HOW A JEST SHALL COME ABOUT! I WARRANT, AN I SHOULD LIVE A THOUSAND YEARS, I NEVER SHOULD FORGET IT:
"WILT THOU NOT, JULE?" QUOTH HE; AND, PRETTY FOOL, IT STINTED, AND SAID "AY."
ENOUGH OF THIS; I PRAY THEE, HOLD THY PEACE.
BANG

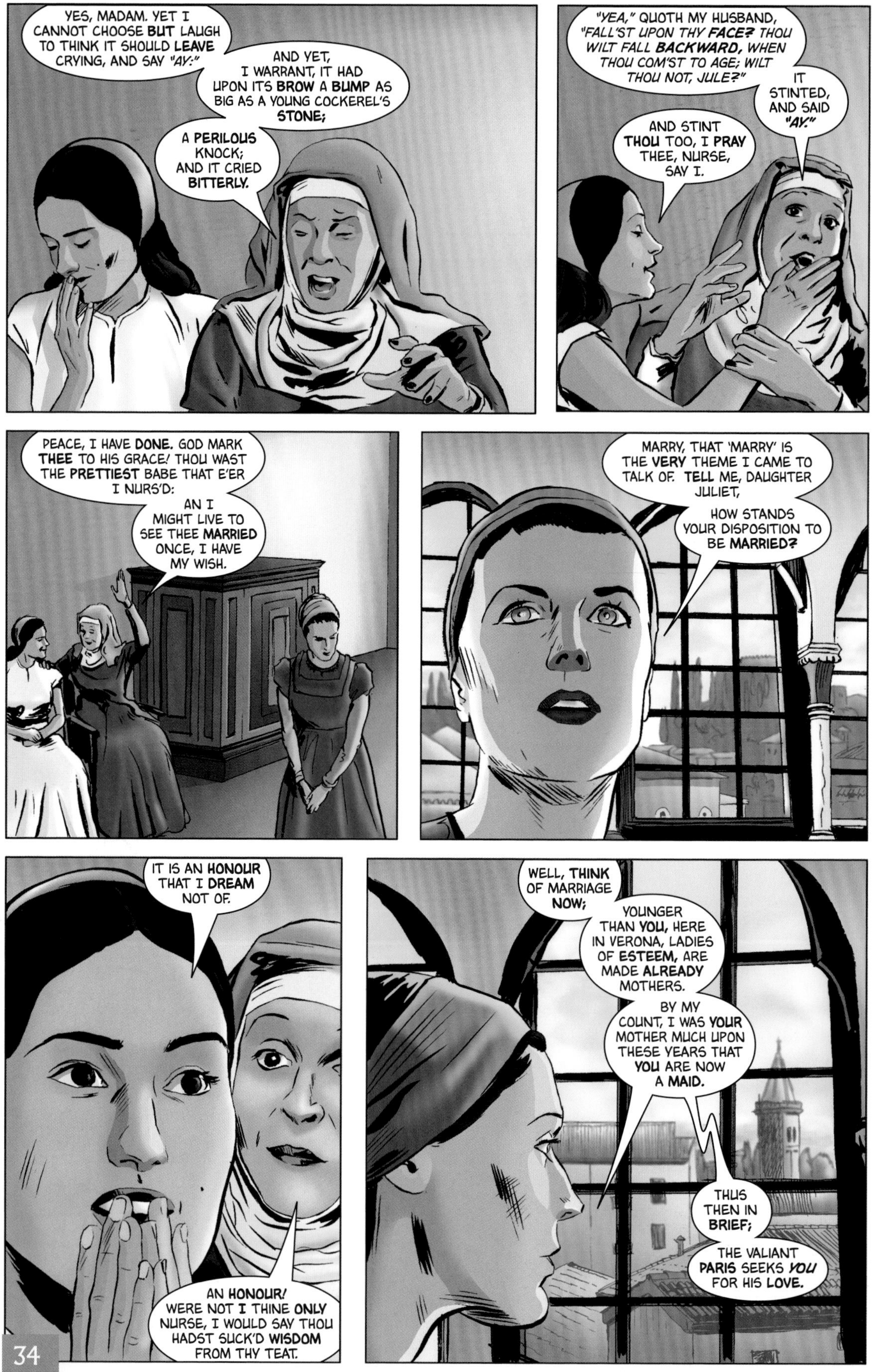
YES, MADAM. YET I CANNOT CHOOSE BUT LAUGH TO THINK IT SHOULD LEAVE CRYING, AND SAY "AY:"
AND YET, I WARRANT, IT HAD UPON ITS BROW A BUMP AS BIG AS A YOUNG COCKEREL'S STONE;
A PERILOUS KNOCK; AND IT CRIED BITTERLY.
"YEA," QUOTH MY HUSBAND, "FALL'ST UPON THY FACE? THOU WILT FALL BACKWARD, WHEN THOU COM'ST TO AGE; WILT THOU NOT, JULE?"
IT STINTED, AND SAID "AY."
AND STINT THOU TOO, I PRAY THEE, NURSE, SAY I.
PEACE, I HAVE DONE. GOD MARK THEE TO HIS GRACE! THOU WAST THE PRETTIEST BABE THAT E'ER I NURS'D:
AN I MIGHT LIVE TO SEE THEE MARRIED ONCE, I HAVE MY WISH.
MARRY, THAT 'MARRY' IS THE VERY THEME I CAME TO TALK OF. TELL ME, DAUGHTER JULIET,
HOW STANDS YOUR DISPOSITION TO BE MARRIED?
IT IS AN HONOUR THAT I DREAM NOT OF.
AN HONOUR! WERE NOT I THINE ONLY NURSE, I WOULD SAY THOU HADST SUCK'D WISDOM FROM THY TEAT.
WELL, THINK OF MARRIAGE NOW;
YOUNGER THAN YOU, HERE IN VERONA, LADIES OF ESTEEM, ARE MADE ALREADY MOTHERS.
BY MY COUNT, I WAS YOUR MOTHER MUCH UPON THESE YEARS THAT YOU ARE NOW A MAID.
THUS THEN IN BRIEF;
THE VALIANT PARIS SEEKS YOU FOR HIS LOVE.

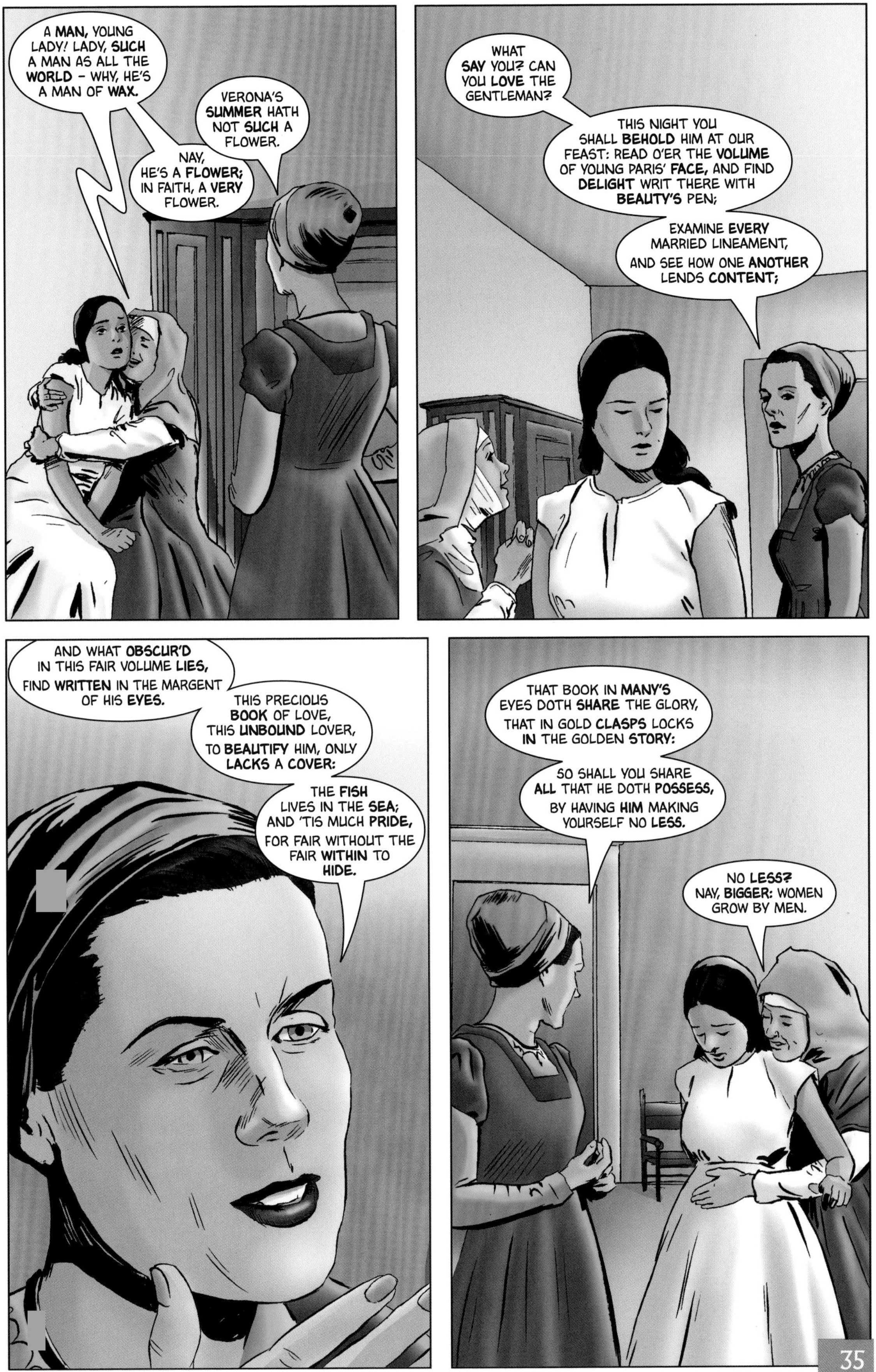
A MAN, YOUNG LADY! LADY, SUCH A MAN AS ALL THE WORLD – WHY, HE'S A MAN OF WAX.
VERONA'S SUMMER HATH NOT SUCH A FLOWER.
NAY, HE'S A FLOWER; IN FAITH, A VERY FLOWER.
WHAT SAY YOU? CAN YOU LOVE THE GENTLEMAN?
THIS NIGHT YOU SHALL BEHOLD HIM AT OUR FEAST: READ O'ER THE VOLUME OF YOUNG PARIS' FACE, AND FIND DELIGHT WRIT THERE WITH BEAUTY'S PEN;
EXAMINE EVERY MARRIED LINEAMENT, AND SEE HOW ONE ANOTHER LENDS CONTENT;
AND WHAT OBSCUR'D IN THIS FAIR VOLUME LIES, FIND WRITTEN IN THE MARGENT OF HIS EYES.
THIS PRECIOUS BOOK OF LOVE, THIS UNBOUND LOVER, TO BEAUTIFY HIM, ONLY LACKS A COVER:
THE FISH LIVES IN THE SEA; AND 'TIS MUCH PRIDE, FOR FAIR WITHOUT THE FAIR WITHIN TO HIDE.
THAT BOOK IN MANY'S EYES DOTH SHARE THE GLORY, THAT IN GOLD CLASPS LOCKS IN THE GOLDEN STORY:
SO SHALL YOU SHARE ALL THAT HE DOTH POSSESS, BY HAVING HIM MAKING YOURSELF NO LESS.
NO LESS? NAY, BIGGER: WOMEN GROW BY MEN.

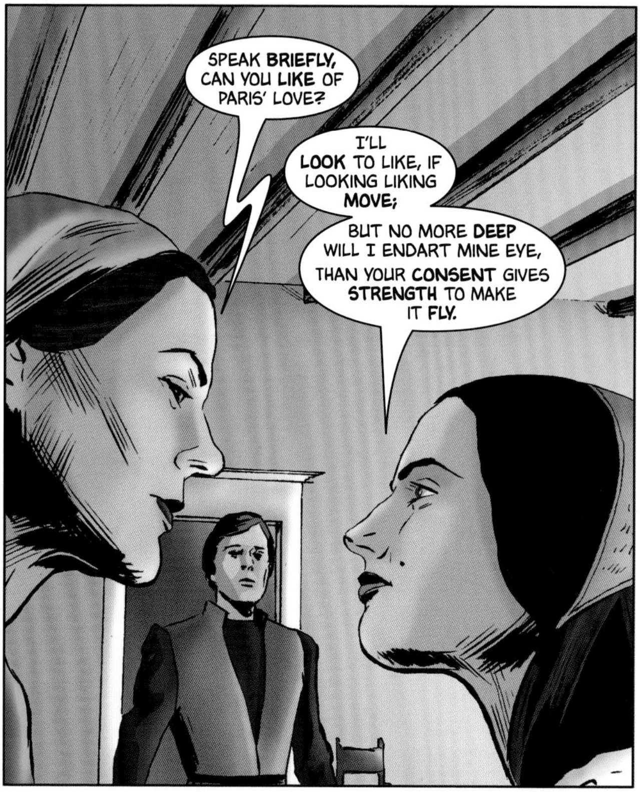
SPEAK BRIEFLY, CAN YOU LIKE OF PARIS' LOVE?
I'LL LOOK TO LIKE, IF LOOKING LIKING MOVE;
BUT NO MORE DEEP WILL I ENDART MINE EYE, THAN YOUR CONSENT GIVES STRENGTH TO MAKE IT FLY.
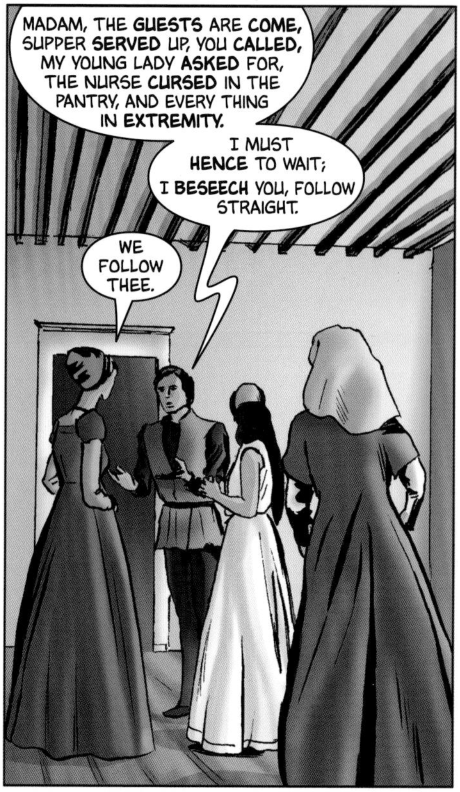
MADAM, THE GUESTS ARE COME, SUPPER SERVED UP, YOU CALLED, MY YOUNG LADY ASKED FOR, THE NURSE CURSED IN THE PANTRY, AND EVERY THING IN EXTREMITY.
I MUST HENCE TO WAIT; I BESEECH YOU, FOLLOW STRAIGHT.
WE FOLLOW THEE.
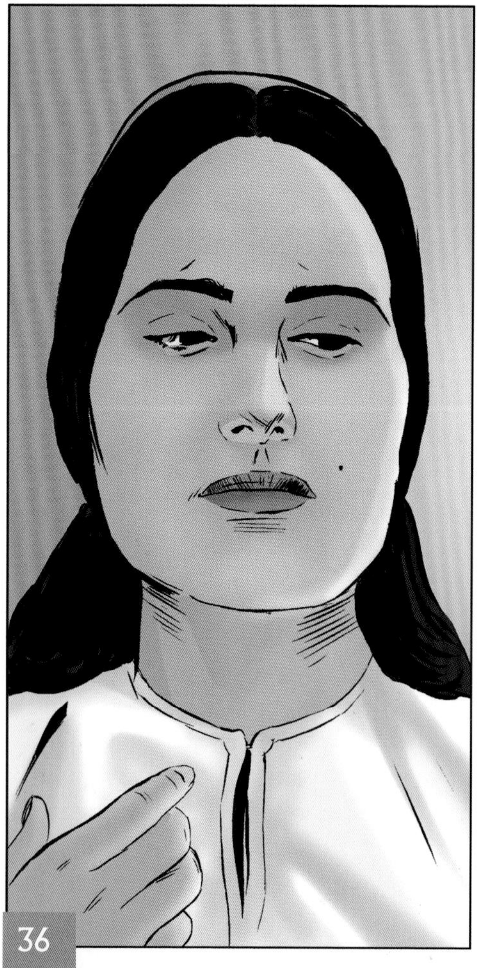
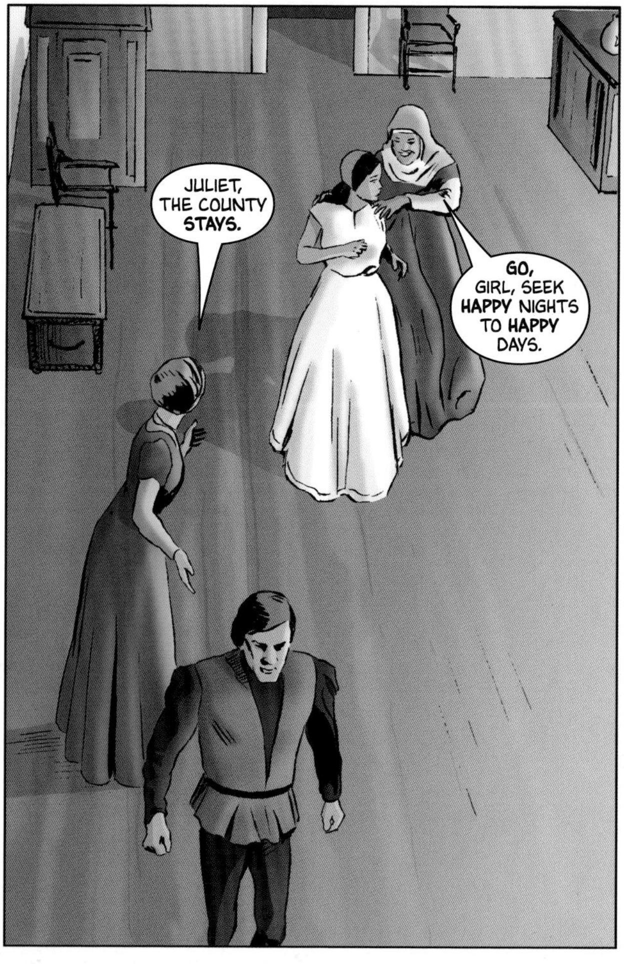
JULIET, THE COUNTY STAYS.
GO, GIRL, SEEK HAPPY NIGHTS TO HAPPY DAYS.

Act I - Scene IV

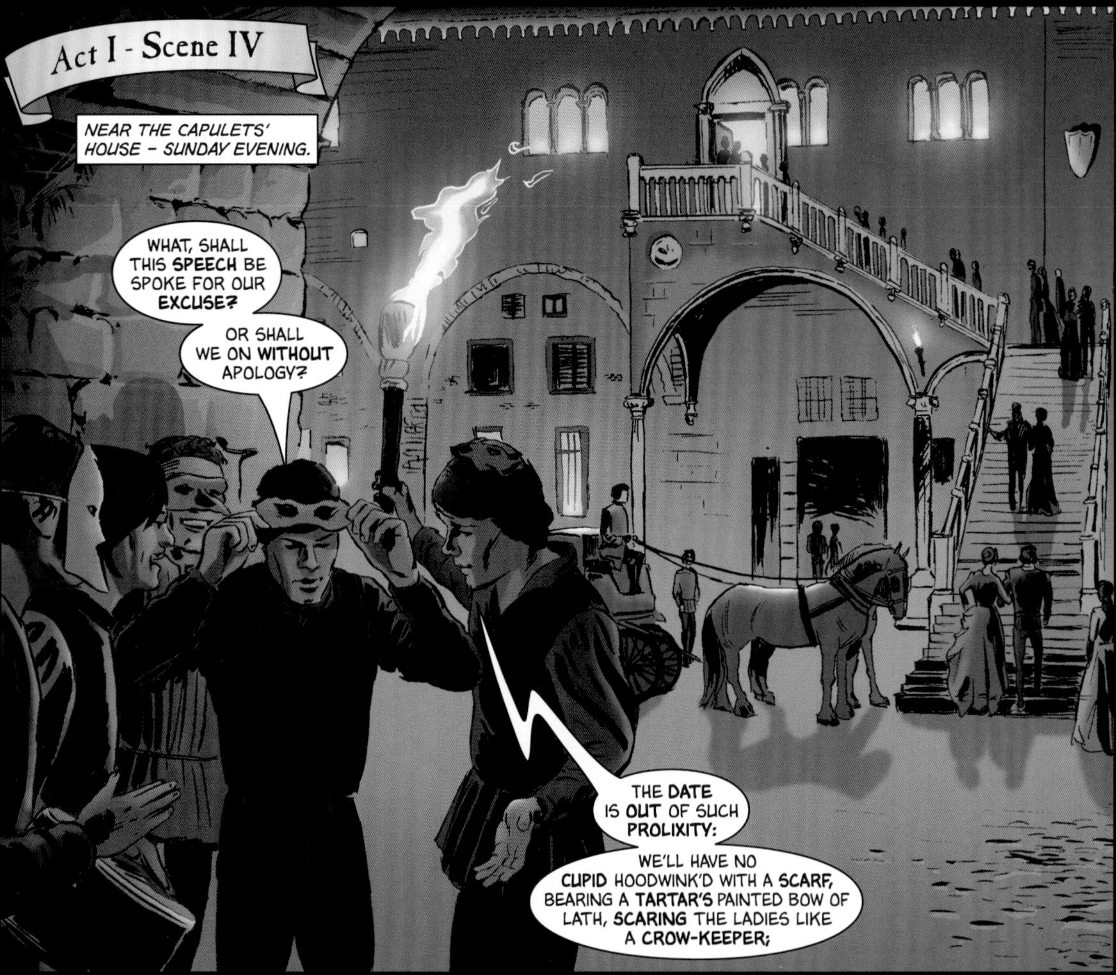
NEAR THE CAPULETS' HOUSE – SUNDAY EVENING.
WHAT, SHALL THIS SPEECH BE SPOKE FOR OUR EXCUSE?
OR SHALL WE ON WITHOUT APOLOGY?
THE DATE IS OUT OF SUCH PROLIXITY:
WE'LL HAVE NO CUPID HOODWINK'D WITH A SCARF, BEARING A TARTAR'S PAINTED BOW OF LATH, SCARING THE LADIES LIKE A CROW-KEEPER;

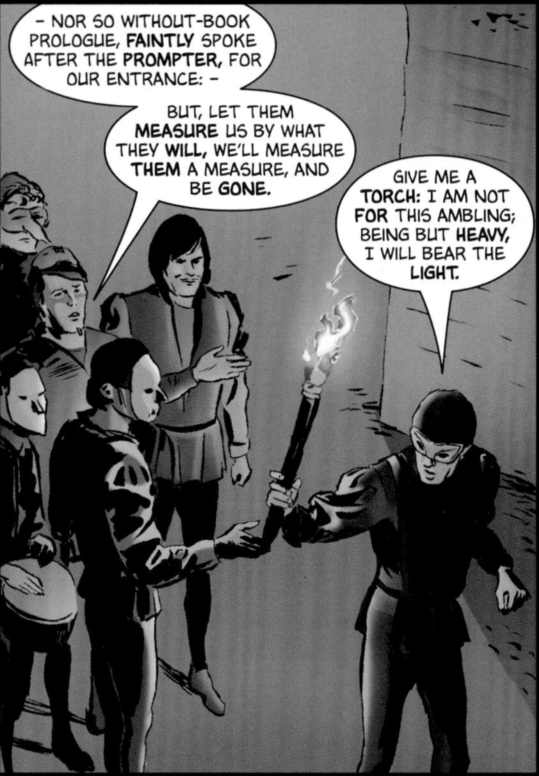
– NOR SO WITHOUT-BOOK PROLOGUE, FAINTLY SPOKE AFTER THE PROMPTER, FOR OUR ENTRANCE: –
BUT, LET THEM MEASURE US BY WHAT THEY WILL, WE'LL MEASURE THEM A MEASURE, AND BE GONE.
GIVE ME A TORCH: I AM NOT FOR THIS AMBLING; BEING BUT HEAVY, I WILL BEAR THE LIGHT.

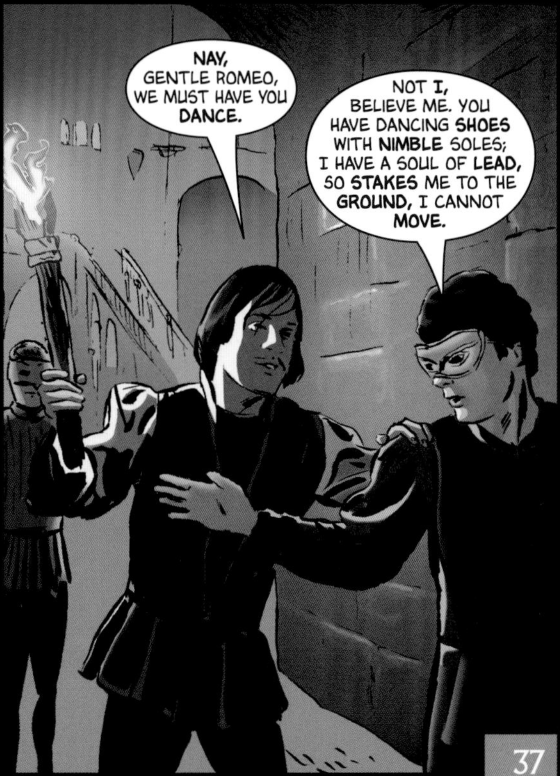
NAY, GENTLE ROMEO, WE MUST HAVE YOU DANCE.
NOT I, BELIEVE ME. YOU HAVE DANCING SHOES WITH NIMBLE SOLES; I HAVE A SOUL OF LEAD, SO STAKES ME TO THE GROUND, I CANNOT MOVE.

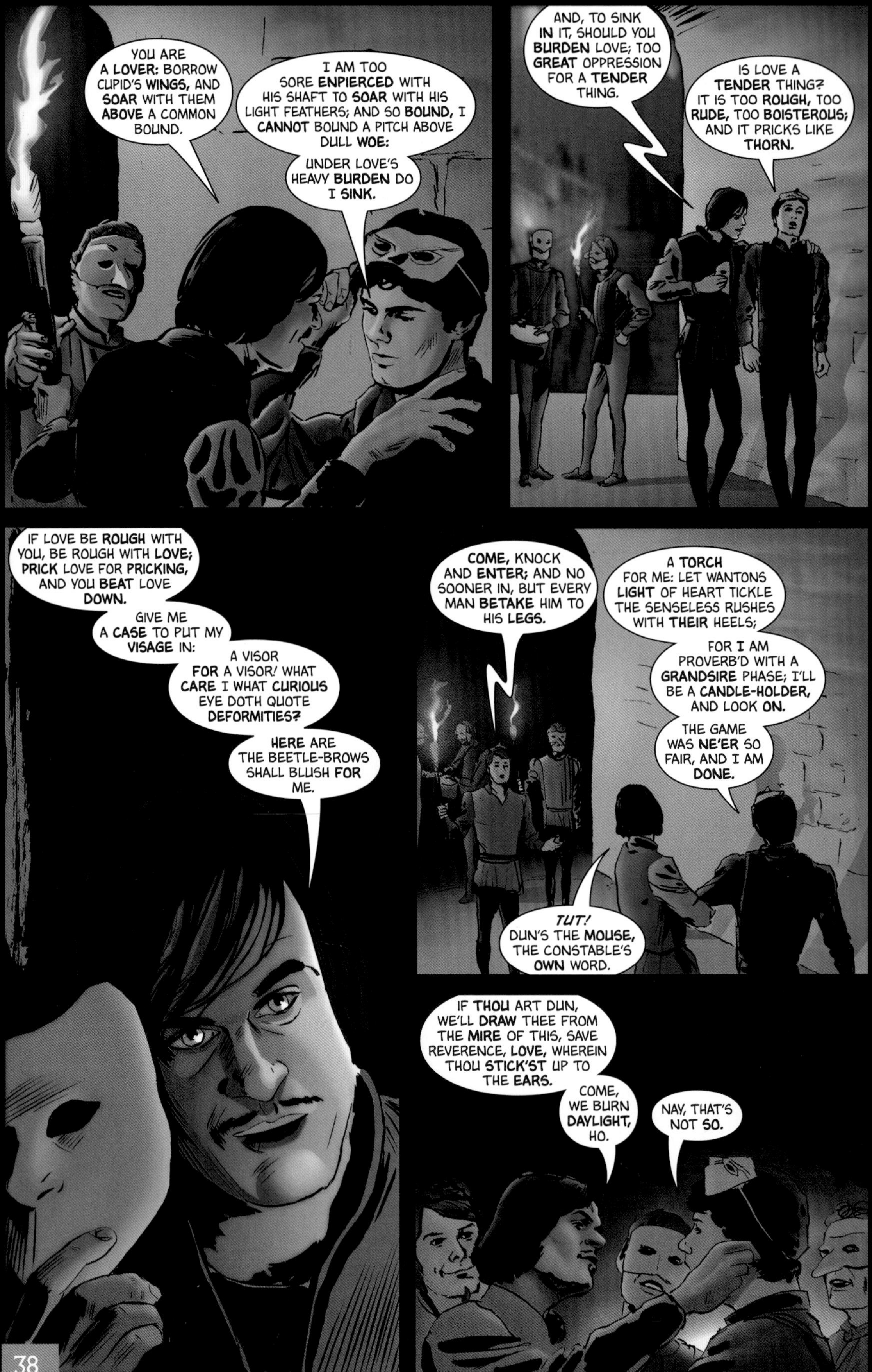
YOU ARE A LOVER: BORROW CUPID'S WINGS, AND SOAR WITH THEM ABOVE A COMMON BOUND.
I AM TOO SORE ENPIERCED WITH HIS SHAFT TO SOAR WITH HIS LIGHT FEATHERS; AND SO BOUND, I CANNOT BOUND A PITCH ABOVE DULL WOE:
UNDER LOVE'S HEAVY BURDEN DO I SINK.
AND, TO SINK IN IT, SHOULD YOU BURDEN LOVE; TOO GREAT OPPRESSION FOR A TENDER THING.
IS LOVE A TENDER THING? IT IS TOO ROUGH, TOO RUDE, TOO BOISTEROUS; AND IT PRICKS LIKE THORN.
IF LOVE BE ROUGH WITH YOU, BE ROUGH WITH LOVE; PRICK LOVE FOR PRICKING, AND YOU BEAT LOVE DOWN.
GIVE ME A CASE TO PUT MY VISAGE IN:
A VISOR FOR A VISOR! WHAT CARE I WHAT CURIOUS EYE DOTH QUOTE DEFORMITIES?
HERE ARE THE BEETLE-BROWS SHALL BLUSH FOR ME.
COME, KNOCK AND ENTER; AND NO SOONER IN, BUT EVERY MAN BETAKE HIM TO HIS LEGS.
A TORCH FOR ME: LET WANTONS LIGHT OF HEART TICKLE THE SENSELESS RUSHES WITH THEIR HEELS;
FOR I AM PROVERB'D WITH A GRANDSIRE PHASE; I'LL BE A CANDLE-HOLDER, AND LOOK ON.
THE GAME WAS NE'ER SO FAIR, AND I AM DONE.
TUT! DUN'S THE MOUSE, THE CONSTABLE'S OWN WORD.
IF THOU ART DUN, WE'LL DRAW THEE FROM THE MIRE OF THIS, SAVE REVERENCE, LOVE, WHEREIN THOU STICK'ST UP TO THE EARS.
COME, WE BURN DAYLIGHT, HO.
NAY, THAT'S NOT SO.

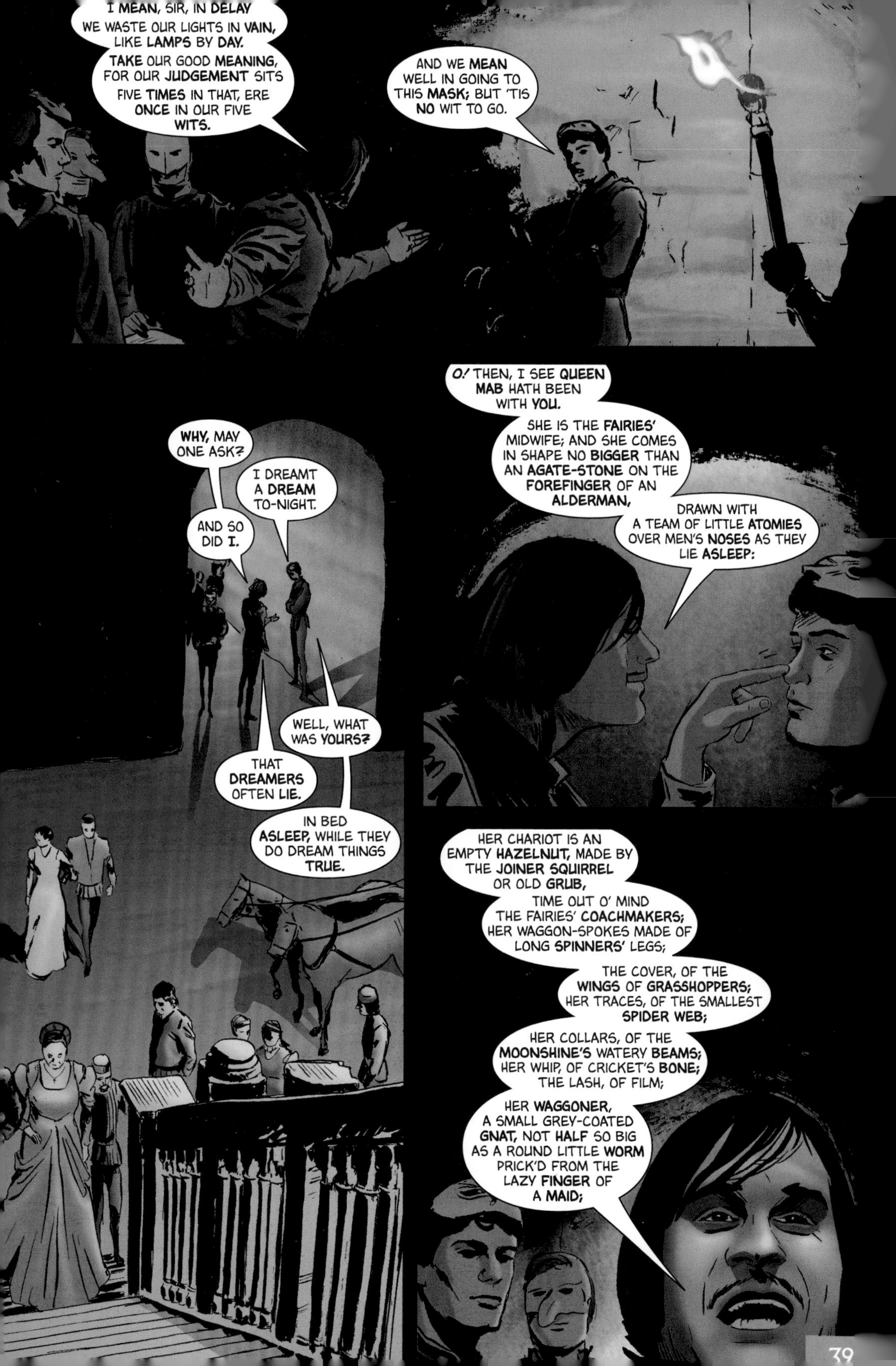
I MEAN, SIR, IN DELAY
WE WASTE OUR LIGHTS IN VAIN, LIKE LAMPS BY DAY.
TAKE OUR GOOD MEANING, FOR OUR JUDGEMENT SITS FIVE TIMES IN THAT, ERE ONCE IN OUR FIVE WITS.
AND WE MEAN WELL IN GOING TO THIS MASK; BUT 'TIS NO WIT TO GO.
WHY, MAY ONE ASK?
I DREAMT A DREAM TO-NIGHT.
AND SO DID I.
WELL, WHAT WAS YOURS?
THAT DREAMERS OFTEN LIE.
IN BED ASLEEP, WHILE THEY DO DREAM THINGS TRUE.
O! THEN, I SEE QUEEN MAB HATH BEEN WITH YOU.
SHE IS THE FAIRIES' MIDWIFE; AND SHE COMES IN SHAPE NO BIGGER THAN AN AGATE-STONE ON THE FOREFINGER OF AN ALDERMAN,
DRAWN WITH A TEAM OF LITTLE ATOMIES OVER MEN'S NOSES AS THEY LIE ASLEEP:
HER CHARIOT IS AN EMPTY HAZELNUT, MADE BY THE JOINER SQUIRREL OR OLD GRUB,
TIME OUT O' MIND THE FAIRIES' COACHMAKERS; HER WAGGON-SPOKES MADE OF LONG SPINNERS' LEGS;
THE COVER, OF THE WINGS OF GRASSHOPPERS; HER TRACES, OF THE SMALLEST SPIDER WEB;
HER COLLARS, OF THE MOONSHINE'S WATERY BEAMS; HER WHIP, OF CRICKET'S BONE; THE LASH, OF FILM;
HER WAGGONER, A SMALL GREY-COATED GNAT, NOT HALF SO BIG AS A ROUND LITTLE WORM PRICK'D FROM THE LAZY FINGER OF A MAID;

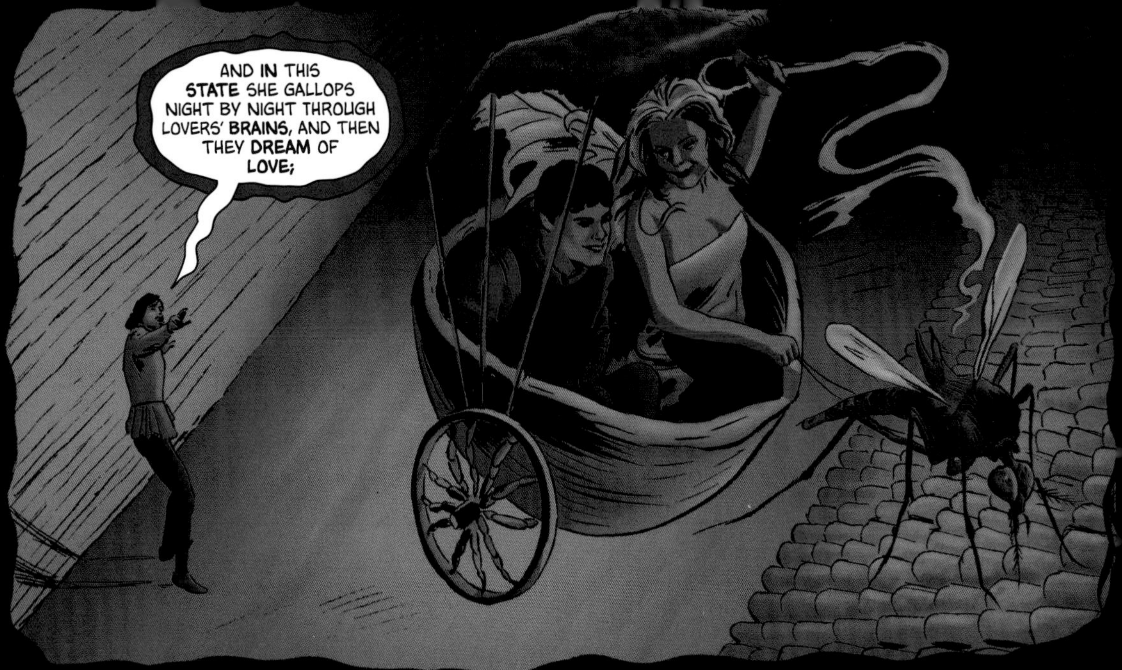
AND IN THIS STATE SHE GALLOPS NIGHT BY NIGHT THROUGH LOVERS' BRAINS, AND THEN THEY DREAM OF LOVE;

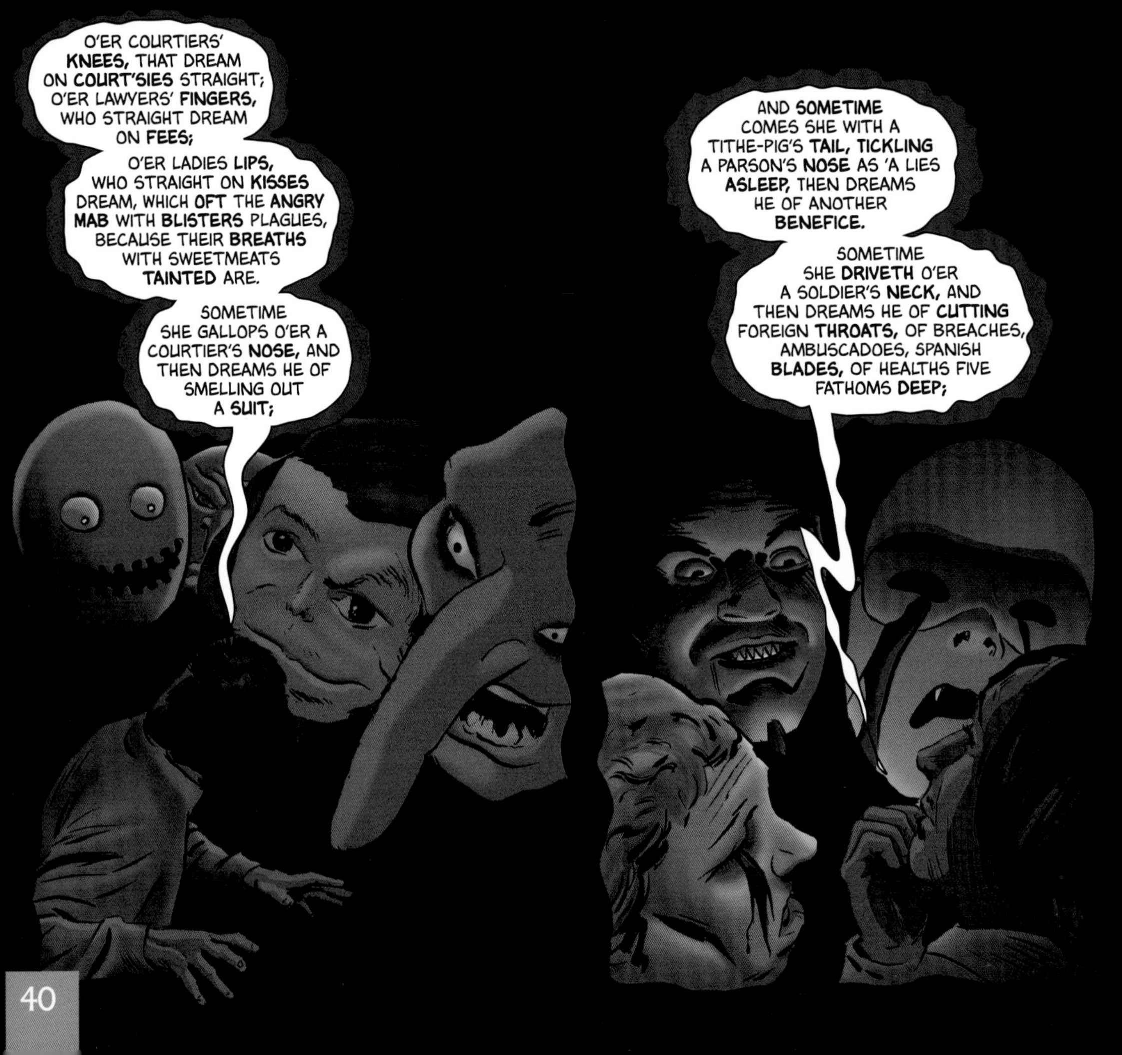
O'ER COURTIERS' KNEES, THAT DREAM ON COURT'SIES STRAIGHT; O'ER LAWYERS' FINGERS, WHO STRAIGHT DREAM ON FEES;
O'ER LADIES LIPS, WHO STRAIGHT ON KISSES DREAM, WHICH OFT THE ANGRY MAB WITH BLISTERS PLAGUES, BECAUSE THEIR BREATHS WITH SWEETMEATS TAINTED ARE.
SOMETIME SHE GALLOPS O'ER A COURTIER'S NOSE, AND THEN DREAMS HE OF SMELLING OUT A SUIT;
AND SOMETIME COMES SHE WITH A TITHE-PIG'S TAIL, TICKLING A PARSON'S NOSE AS 'A LIES ASLEEP, THEN DREAMS HE OF ANOTHER BENEFICE.
SOMETIME SHE DRIVETH O'ER A SOLDIER'S NECK, AND THEN DREAMS HE OF CUTTING FOREIGN THROATS, OF BREACHES, AMBUSCADOES, SPANISH BLADES, OF HEALTHS FIVE FATHOMS DEEP;

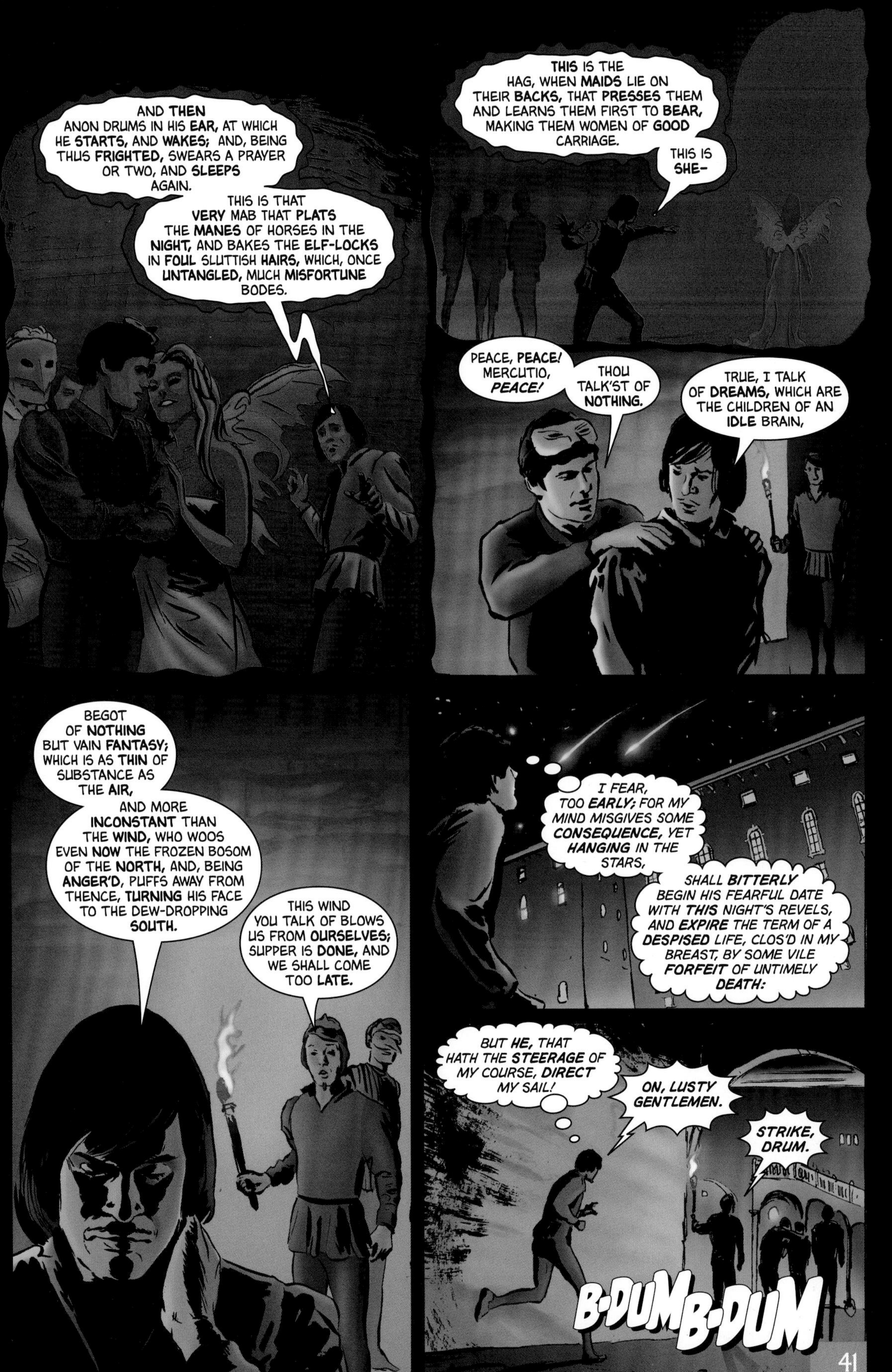
AND THEN ANON DRUMS IN HIS EAR, AT WHICH HE STARTS, AND WAKES; AND, BEING THUS FRIGHTED, SWEARS A PRAYER OR TWO, AND SLEEPS AGAIN.
THIS IS THAT VERY MAB THAT PLATS THE MANES OF HORSES IN THE NIGHT, AND BAKES THE ELF-LOCKS IN FOUL SLUTTISH HAIRS, WHICH, ONCE UNTANGLED, MUCH MISFORTUNE BODES.
THIS IS THE HAG, WHEN MAIDS LIE ON THEIR BACKS, THAT PRESSES THEM AND LEARNS THEM FIRST TO BEAR, MAKING THEM WOMEN OF GOOD CARRIAGE.
THIS IS SHE-
PEACE, PEACE! MERCUTIO, PEACE!
THOU TALK'ST OF NOTHING.
TRUE, I TALK OF DREAMS, WHICH ARE THE CHILDREN OF AN IDLE BRAIN,
BEGOT OF NOTHING BUT VAIN FANTASY; WHICH IS AS THIN OF SUBSTANCE AS THE AIR,
AND MORE INCONSTANT THAN THE WIND, WHO WOOS EVEN NOW THE FROZEN BOSOM OF THE NORTH, AND, BEING ANGER'D, PUFFS AWAY FROM THENCE, TURNING HIS FACE TO THE DEW-DROPPING SOUTH.
THIS WIND YOU TALK OF BLOWS US FROM OURSELVES; SUPPER IS DONE, AND WE SHALL COME TOO LATE.
I FEAR, TOO EARLY; FOR MY MIND MISGIVES SOME CONSEQUENCE, YET HANGING IN THE STARS,
SHALL BITTERLY BEGIN HIS FEARFUL DATE WITH THIS NIGHT'S REVELS, AND EXPIRE THE TERM OF A DESPISED LIFE, CLOS'D IN MY BREAST, BY SOME VILE FORFEIT OF UNTIMELY DEATH:
BUT HE, THAT HATH THE STEERAGE OF MY COURSE, DIRECT MY SAIL!
ON, LUSTY GENTLEMEN.
STRIKE, DRUM.
B-DUM B-DUM

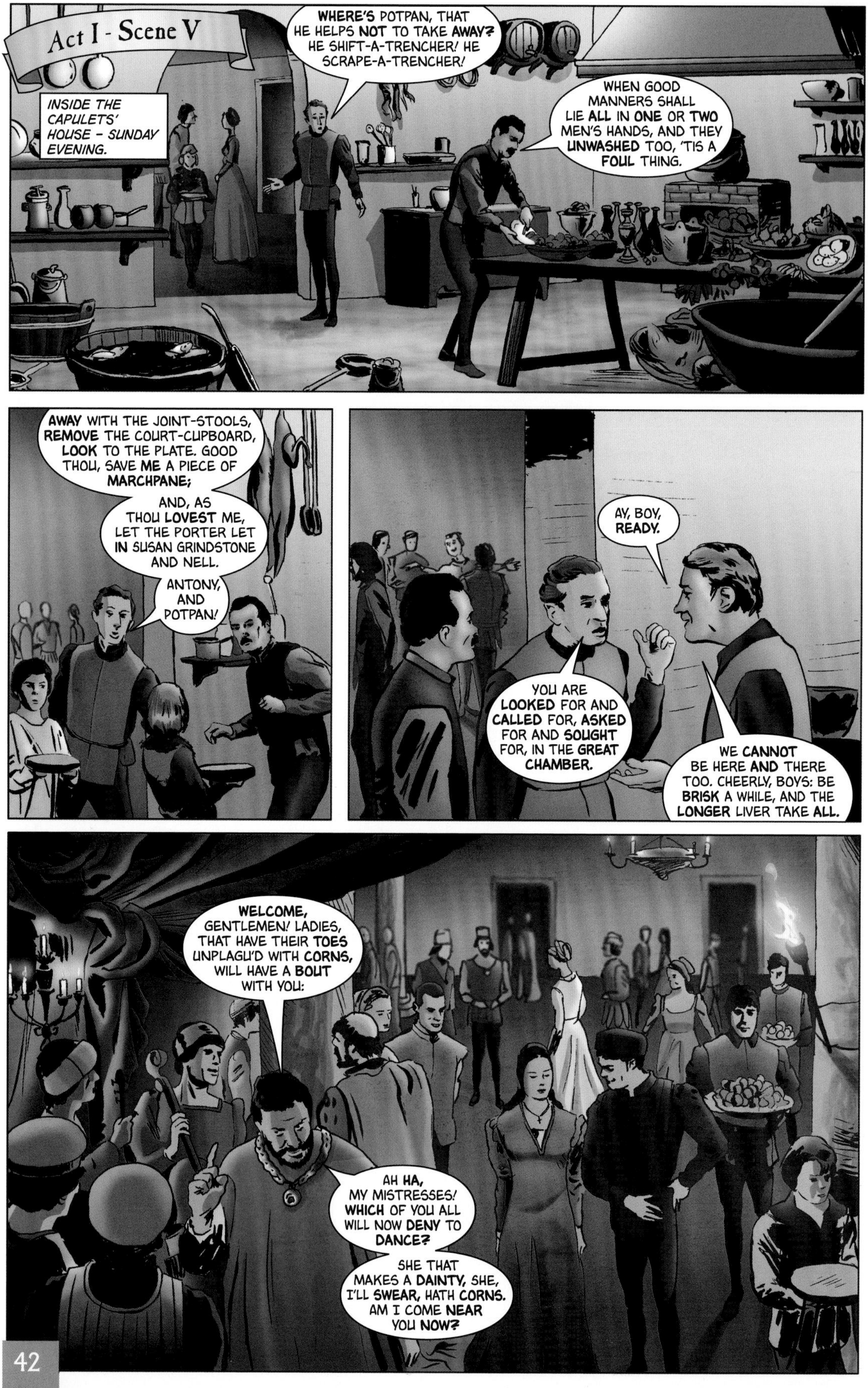
Act I - Scene V
INSIDE THE CAPULETS' HOUSE - SUNDAY EVENING.
WHERE'S POTPAN, THAT HE HELPS NOT TO TAKE AWAY? HE SHIFT-A-TRENCHER! HE SCRAPE-A-TRENCHER!
WHEN GOOD MANNERS SHALL LIE ALL IN ONE OR TWO MEN'S HANDS, AND THEY UNWASHED TOO, 'TIS A FOUL THING.
AWAY WITH THE JOINT-STOOLS, REMOVE THE COURT-CUPBOARD, LOOK TO THE PLATE. GOOD THOU, SAVE ME A PIECE OF MARCHPANE;
AND, AS THOU LOVEST ME, LET THE PORTER LET IN SUSAN GRINDSTONE AND NELL.
ANTONY, AND POTPAN!
AY, BOY, READY.
YOU ARE LOOKED FOR AND CALLED FOR, ASKED FOR AND SOUGHT FOR, IN THE GREAT CHAMBER.
WE CANNOT BE HERE AND THERE TOO. CHEERLY, BOYS: BE BRISK A WHILE, AND THE LONGER LIVER TAKE ALL.
WELCOME, GENTLEMEN! LADIES, THAT HAVE THEIR TOES UNPLAGU'D WITH CORNS, WILL HAVE A BOUT WITH YOU:
AH HA, MY MISTRESSES! WHICH OF YOU ALL WILL NOW DENY TO DANCE?
SHE THAT MAKES A DAINTY, SHE, I'LL SWEAR, HATH CORNS. AM I COME NEAR YOU NOW?

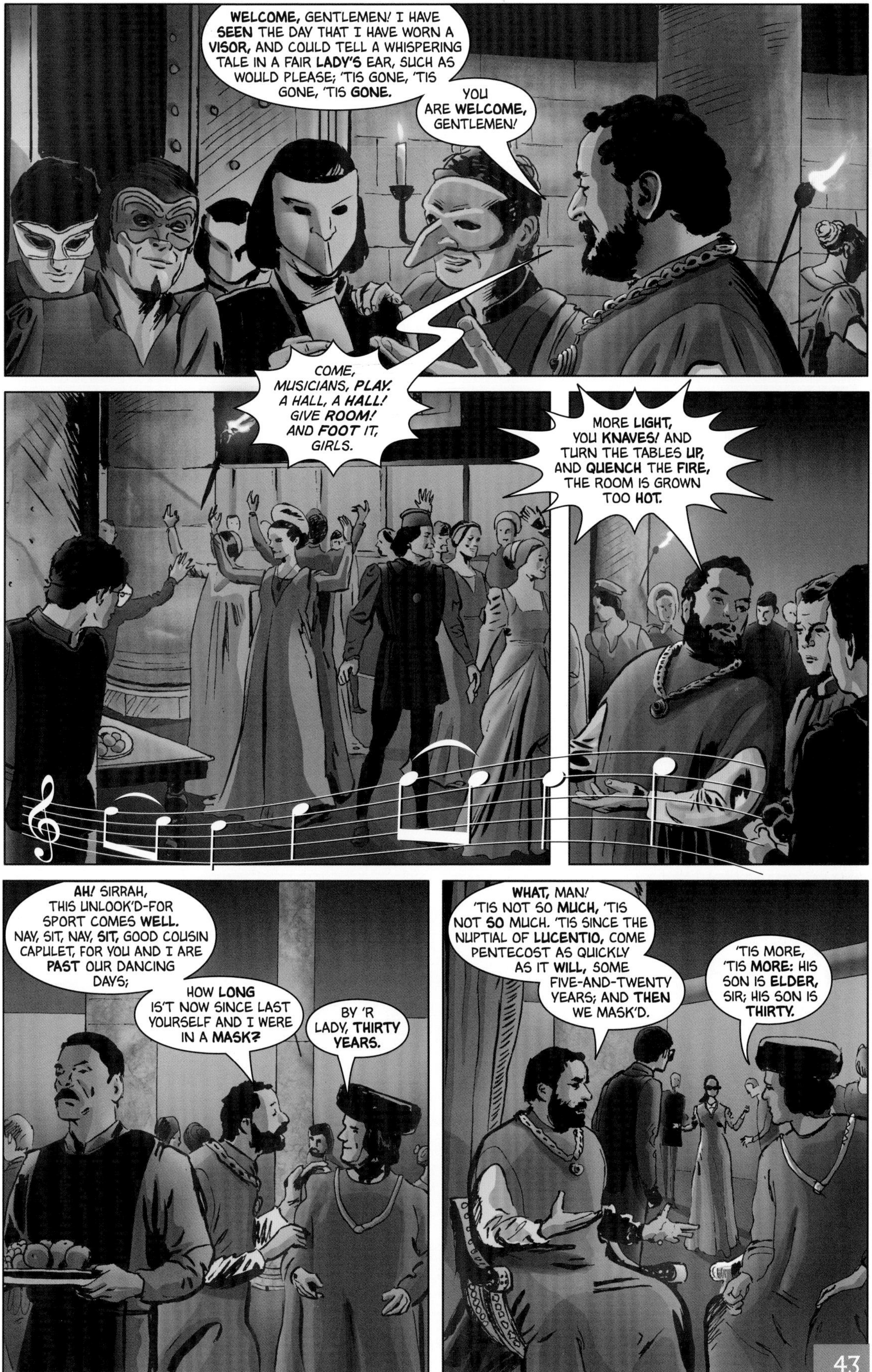
WELCOME, GENTLEMEN! I HAVE SEEN THE DAY THAT I HAVE WORN A VISOR, AND COULD TELL A WHISPERING TALE IN A FAIR LADY'S EAR, SUCH AS WOULD PLEASE; 'TIS GONE, 'TIS GONE, 'TIS GONE.
YOU ARE WELCOME, GENTLEMEN!
COME, MUSICIANS, PLAY. A HALL, A HALL! GIVE ROOM! AND FOOT IT, GIRLS.
MORE LIGHT, YOU KNAVES! AND TURN THE TABLES UP, AND QUENCH THE FIRE, THE ROOM IS GROWN TOO HOT.
AH! SIRRAH, THIS UNLOOK'D-FOR SPORT COMES WELL. NAY, SIT, NAY, SIT, GOOD COUSIN CAPULET, FOR YOU AND I ARE PAST OUR DANCING DAYS;
HOW LONG IS'T NOW SINCE LAST YOURSELF AND I WERE IN A MASK?
BY 'R LADY, THIRTY YEARS.
WHAT, MAN! 'TIS NOT SO MUCH, 'TIS NOT SO MUCH. 'TIS SINCE THE NUPTIAL OF LUCENTIO, COME PENTECOST AS QUICKLY AS IT WILL, SOME FIVE-AND-TWENTY YEARS; AND THEN WE MASK'D.
'TIS MORE, 'TIS MORE: HIS SON IS ELDER, SIR; HIS SON IS THIRTY.

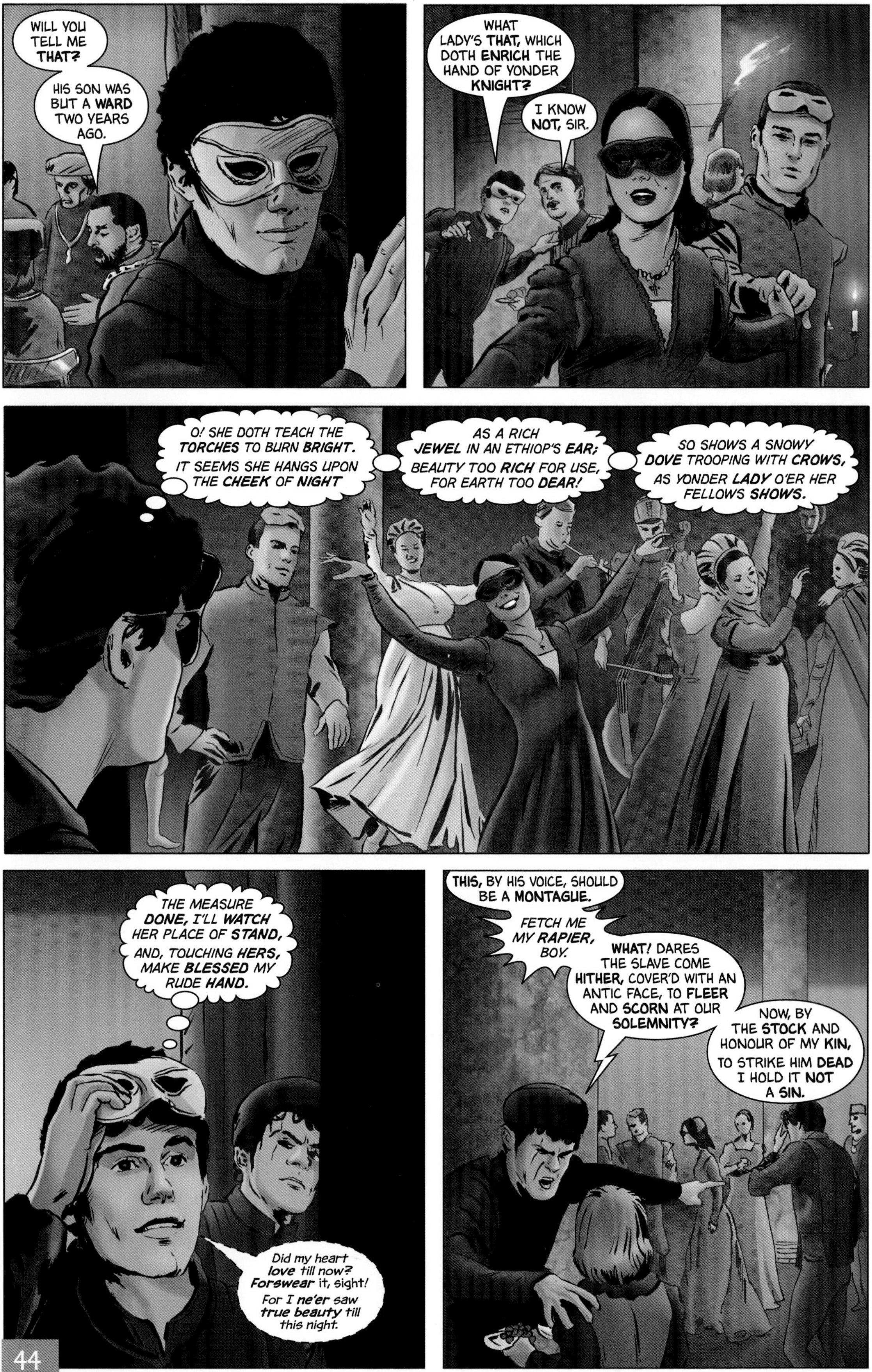

WILL YOU TELL ME THAT?
HIS SON WAS BUT A WARD TWO YEARS AGO.
WHAT LADY'S THAT, WHICH DOTH ENRICH THE HAND OF YONDER KNIGHT?
I KNOW NOT, SIR.
O! SHE DOTH TEACH THE TORCHES TO BURN BRIGHT. IT SEEMS SHE HANGS UPON THE CHEEK OF NIGHT
AS A RICH JEWEL IN AN ETHIOP'S EAR; BEAUTY TOO RICH FOR USE, FOR EARTH TOO DEAR!
SO SHOWS A SNOWY DOVE TROOPING WITH CROWS, AS YONDER LADY O'ER HER FELLOWS SHOWS.
THE MEASURE DONE, I'LL WATCH HER PLACE OF STAND, AND, TOUCHING HERS, MAKE BLESSED MY RUDE HAND.
Did my heart love till now? Forswear it, sight! For I ne'er saw true beauty till this night.
THIS, BY HIS VOICE, SHOULD BE A MONTAGUE.
FETCH ME MY RAPIER, BOY.
WHAT! DARES THE SLAVE COME HITHER, COVER'D WITH AN ANTIC FACE, TO FLEER AND SCORN AT OUR SOLEMNITY?
NOW, BY THE STOCK AND HONOUR OF MY KIN, TO STRIKE HIM DEAD I HOLD IT NOT A SIN.

WHY! HOW NOW, KINSMAN? WHEREFORE **STORM** YOU SO?

UNCLE, THIS IS A **MONTAGUE**, OUR **FOE**;

A **VILLAIN**, THAT IS HITHER COME IN **SPITE**, TO **SCORN** AT OUR **SOLEMNITY** THIS NIGHT.

YOUNG **ROMEO**, IS 'T?

'TIS **HE**, THAT VILLAIN **ROMEO**.

CONTENT THEE, GENTLE COZ, LET HIM **ALONE**: HE BEARS HIM LIKE A PORTLY **GENTLEMAN**;

AND, TO SAY TRUTH, VERONA **BRAGS** OF HIM TO BE A **VIRTUOUS** AND WELL-GOVERN'D YOUTH.

I WOULD **NOT** FOR THE WEALTH OF **ALL** THIS TOWN HERE, IN **MY** HOUSE, DO HIM **DISPARAGEMENT**; THEREFORE BE **PATIENT**, TAKE **NO** NOTE OF HIM:

IT IS **MY WILL**; THE WHICH IF THOU **RESPECT**, SHOW A **FAIR** PRESENCE AND PUT OFF THESE **FROWNS**, AN **ILL-BESEEMING** SEMBLANCE FOR A **FEAST**.

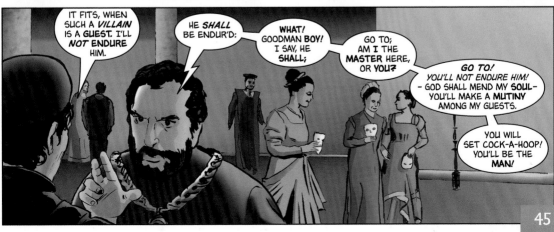

IT FITS, WHEN SUCH A **VILLAIN** IS A **GUEST**. I'LL **NOT** ENDURE HIM.

HE **SHALL** BE ENDUR'D:

WHAT! GOODMAN **BOY!** I SAY, HE **SHALL**;

GO TO; AM I THE **MASTER** HERE, OR **YOU?**

GO TO! YOU'LL NOT ENDURE HIM! – GOD SHALL MEND MY **SOUL** – YOU'LL MAKE A **MUTINY** AMONG MY GUESTS.

YOU WILL SET COCK-A-HOOP! YOU'LL BE THE **MAN!**

WHY, UNCLE, 'TIS A SHAME.

GO TO, GO TO; YOU ARE A SAUCY BOY.

— IS'T SO, INDEED? —

THIS TRICK MAY CHANCE TO SCATHE YOU; I KNOW WHAT. YOU MUST CONTRARY ME! MARRY, 'TIS TIME.

WELL SAID, MY HEARTS!

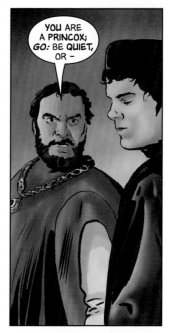

YOU ARE A PRINCOX; GO: BE QUIET, OR —

MORE LIGHT, MORE LIGHT!

FOR SHAME! I'LL MAKE YOU QUIET.

WHAT! CHEERLY, MY HEARTS!

PATIENCE PERFORCE WITH WILFUL CHOLER MEETING MAKES MY FLESH TREMBLE IN THEIR DIFFERENT GREETING.

I WILL WITHDRAW: BUT THIS INTRUSION SHALL, NOW SEEMING SWEET, CONVERT TO BITTEREST GALL.

46

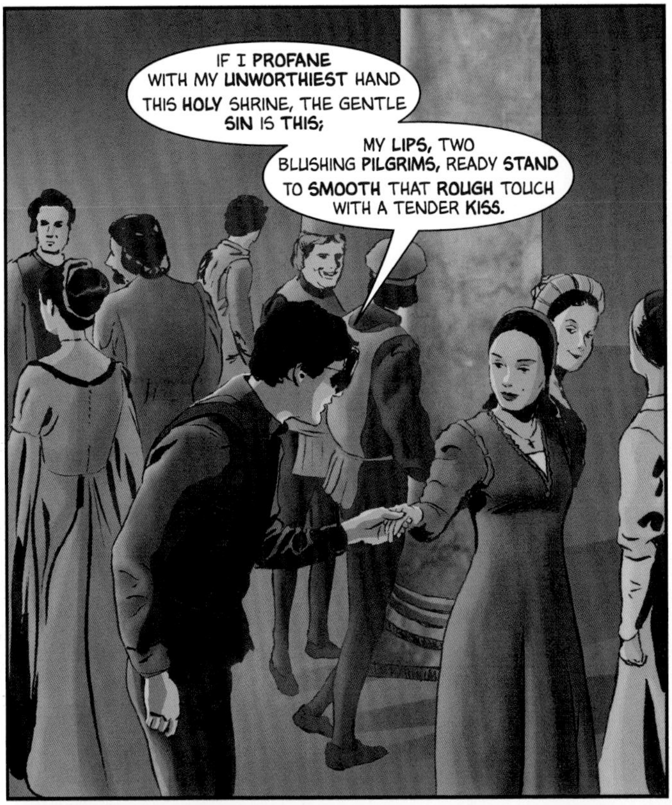
IF I PROFANE WITH MY UNWORTHIEST HAND THIS HOLY SHRINE, THE GENTLE SIN IS THIS;
MY LIPS, TWO BLUSHING PILGRIMS, READY STAND TO SMOOTH THAT ROUGH TOUCH WITH A TENDER KISS.

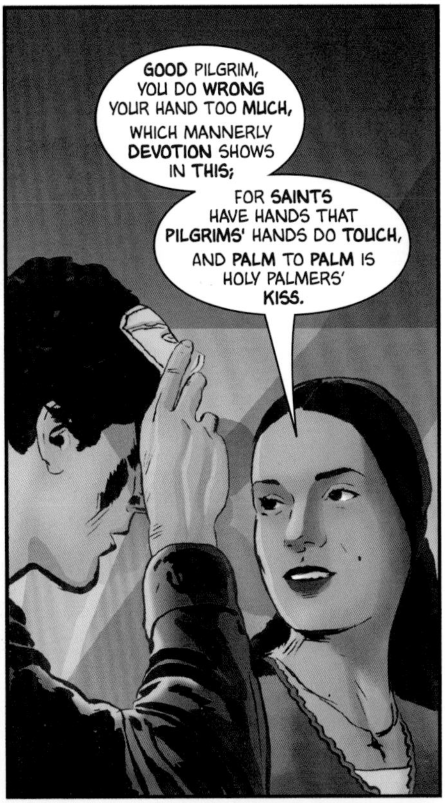
GOOD PILGRIM, YOU DO WRONG YOUR HAND TOO MUCH, WHICH MANNERLY DEVOTION SHOWS IN THIS;
FOR SAINTS HAVE HANDS THAT PILGRIMS' HANDS DO TOUCH, AND PALM TO PALM IS HOLY PALMERS' KISS.

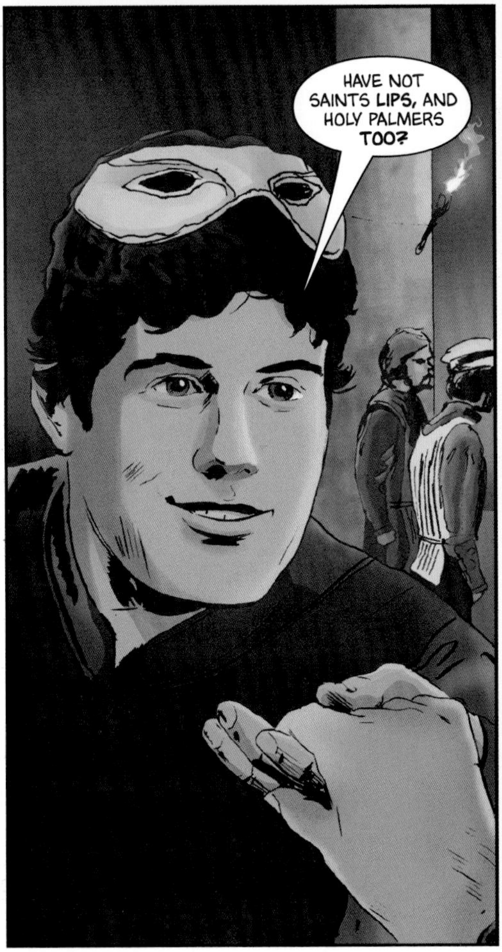
HAVE NOT SAINTS LIPS, AND HOLY PALMERS TOO?

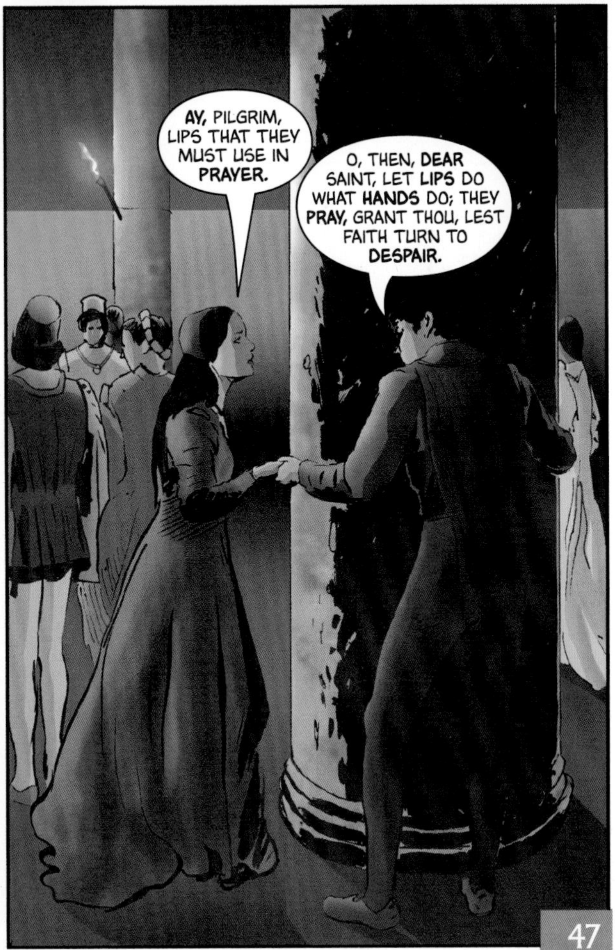
AY, PILGRIM, LIPS THAT THEY MUST USE IN PRAYER.
O, THEN, DEAR SAINT, LET LIPS DO WHAT HANDS DO; THEY PRAY, GRANT THOU, LEST FAITH TURN TO DESPAIR.

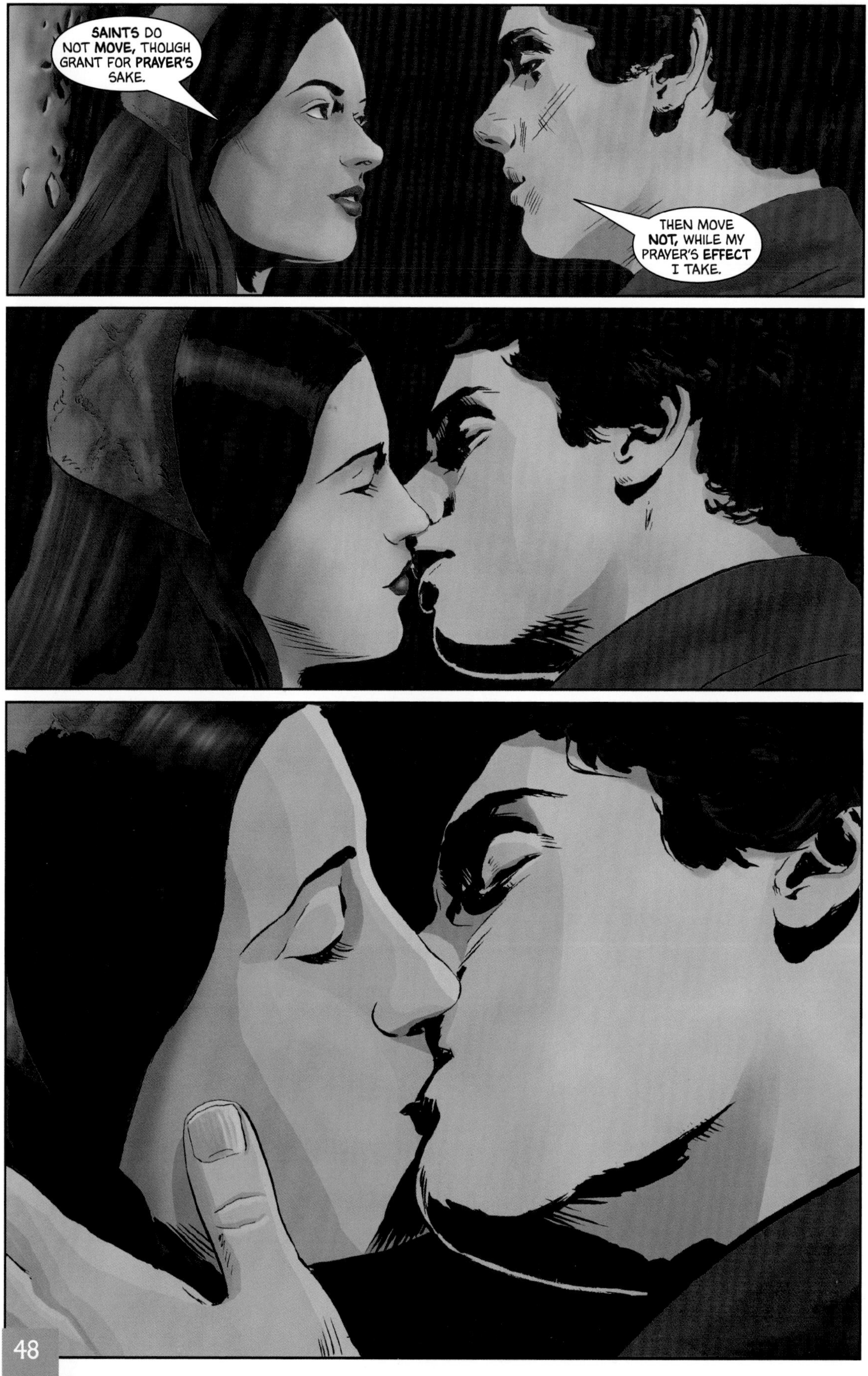
SAINTS DO NOT MOVE, THOUGH GRANT FOR PRAYER'S SAKE.
THEN MOVE NOT, WHILE MY PRAYER'S EFFECT I TAKE.

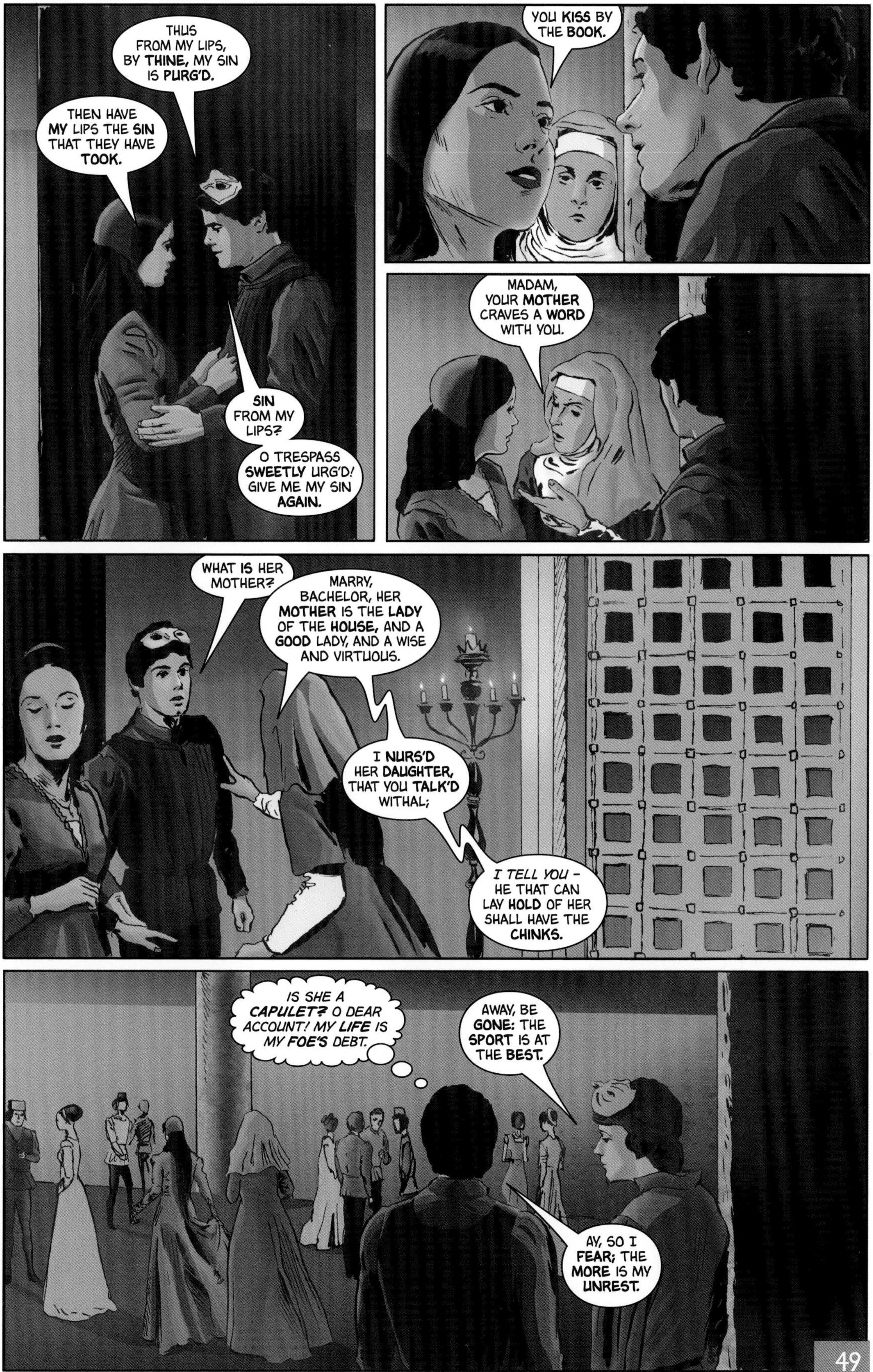
THUS FROM MY LIPS, BY THINE, MY SIN IS PURG'D.
THEN HAVE MY LIPS THE SIN THAT THEY HAVE TOOK.
SIN FROM MY LIPS?
O TRESPASS SWEETLY URG'D! GIVE ME MY SIN AGAIN.
YOU KISS BY THE BOOK.
MADAM, YOUR MOTHER CRAVES A WORD WITH YOU.
WHAT IS HER MOTHER?
MARRY, BACHELOR, HER MOTHER IS THE LADY OF THE HOUSE, AND A GOOD LADY, AND A WISE AND VIRTUOUS.
I NURS'D HER DAUGHTER, THAT YOU TALK'D WITHAL;
I TELL YOU - HE THAT CAN LAY HOLD OF HER SHALL HAVE THE CHINKS.
IS SHE A CAPULET? O DEAR ACCOUNT! MY LIFE IS MY FOE'S DEBT.
AWAY, BE GONE: THE SPORT IS AT THE BEST.
AY, SO I FEAR; THE MORE IS MY UNREST.

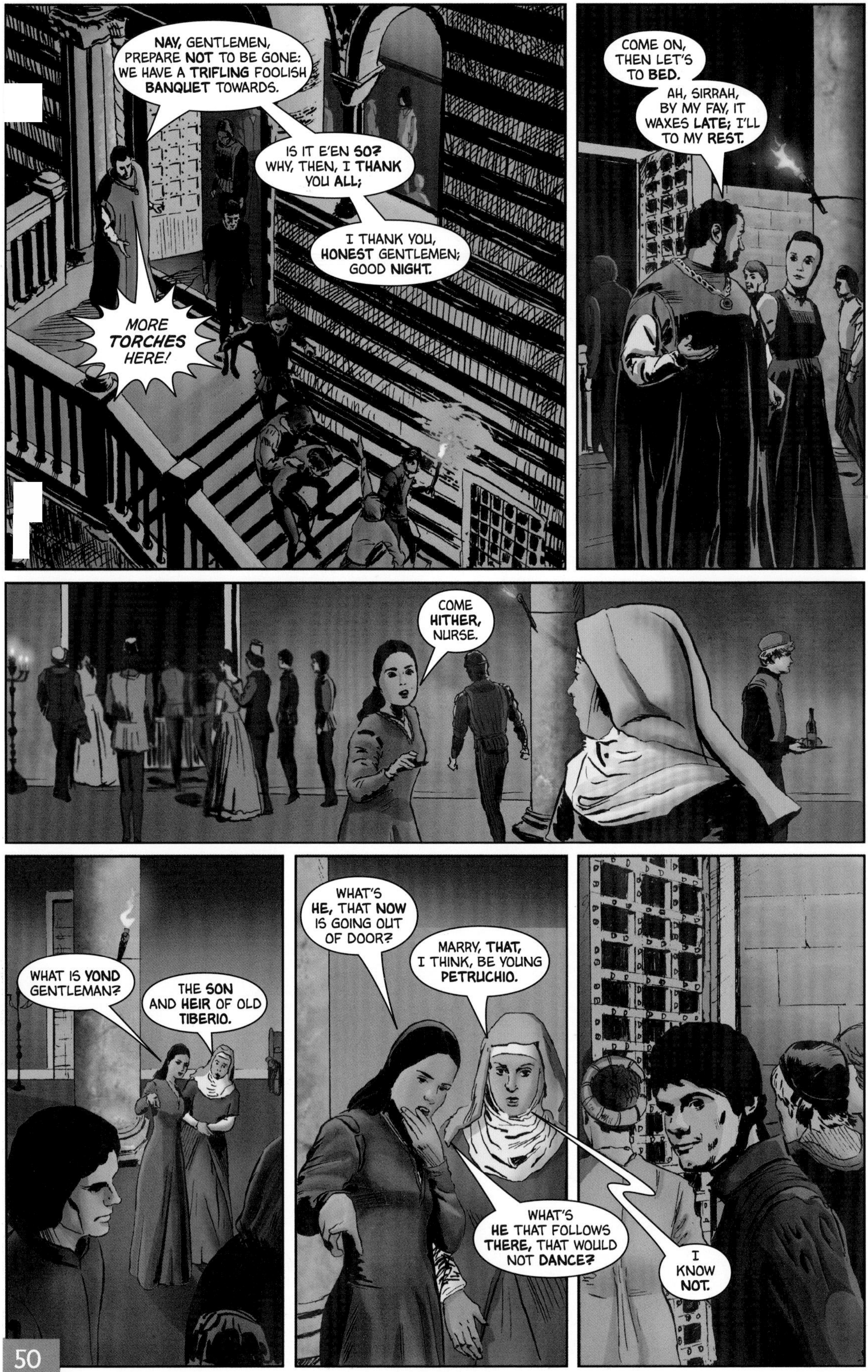
NAY, GENTLEMEN, PREPARE NOT TO BE GONE: WE HAVE A TRIFLING FOOLISH BANQUET TOWARDS.
IS IT E'EN SO? WHY, THEN, I THANK YOU ALL;
I THANK YOU, HONEST GENTLEMEN; GOOD NIGHT.
MORE TORCHES HERE!
COME ON, THEN LET'S TO BED.
AH, SIRRAH, BY MY FAY, IT WAXES LATE; I'LL TO MY REST.
COME HITHER, NURSE.
WHAT IS YOND GENTLEMAN?
THE SON AND HEIR OF OLD TIBERIO.
WHAT'S HE, THAT NOW IS GOING OUT OF DOOR?
MARRY, THAT, I THINK, BE YOUNG PETRUCHIO.
WHAT'S HE THAT FOLLOWS THERE, THAT WOULD NOT DANCE?
I KNOW NOT.

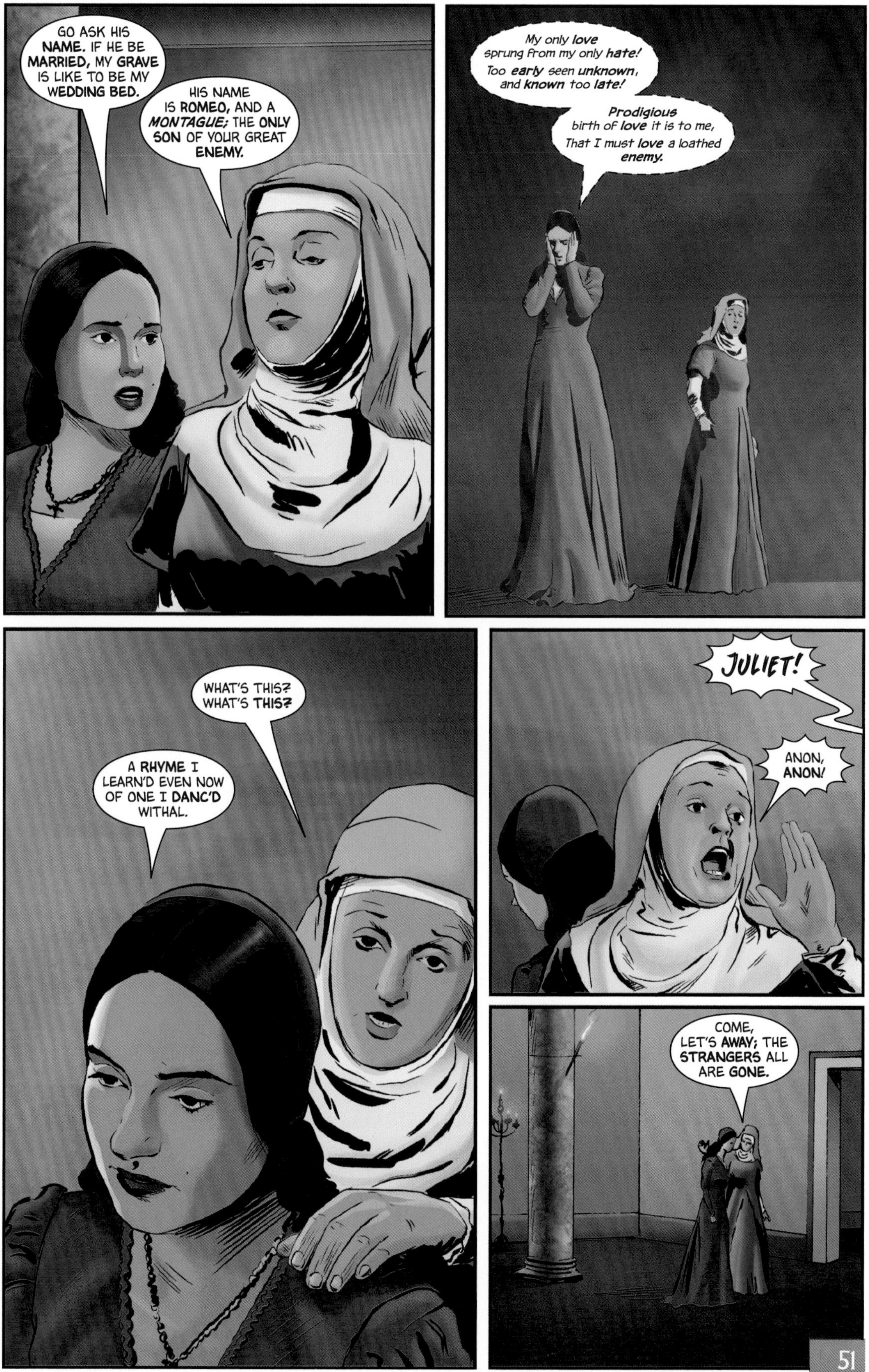
GO ASK HIS NAME. IF HE BE MARRIED, MY GRAVE IS LIKE TO BE MY WEDDING BED.
HIS NAME IS ROMEO, AND A MONTAGUE; THE ONLY SON OF YOUR GREAT ENEMY.
My only love sprung from my only hate! Too early seen unknown, and known too late!
Prodigious birth of love it is to me, That I must love a loathed enemy.
WHAT'S THIS? WHAT'S THIS?
A RHYME I LEARN'D EVEN NOW OF ONE I DANC'D WITHAL.
JULIET!
ANON, ANON!
COME, LET'S AWAY; THE STRANGERS ALL ARE GONE.

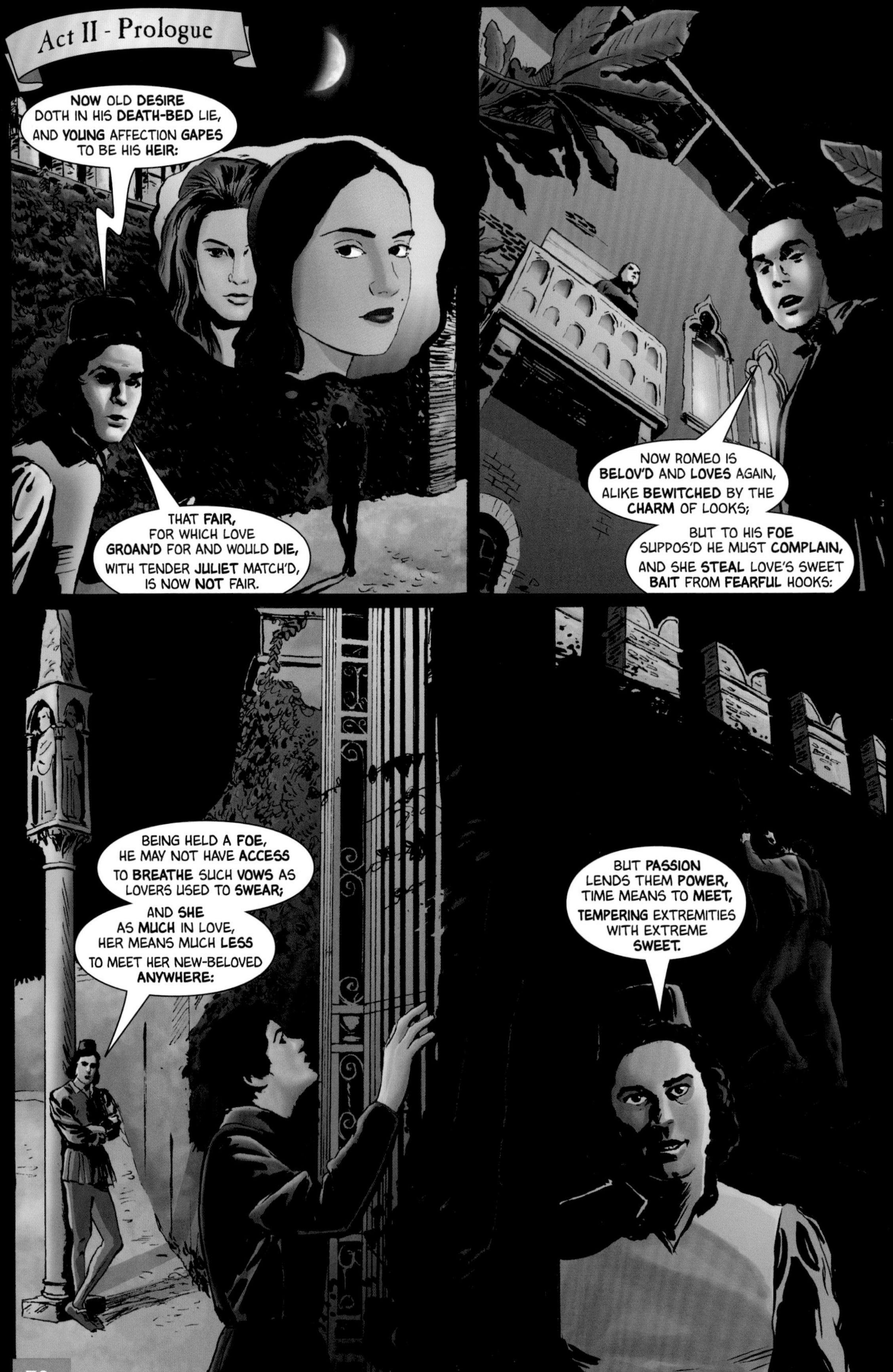
Act II - Prologue
NOW OLD DESIRE DOTH IN HIS DEATH-BED LIE, AND YOUNG AFFECTION GAPES TO BE HIS HEIR:
THAT FAIR, FOR WHICH LOVE GROAN'D FOR AND WOULD DIE, WITH TENDER JULIET MATCH'D, IS NOW NOT FAIR.
NOW ROMEO IS BELOV'D AND LOVES AGAIN, ALIKE BEWITCHED BY THE CHARM OF LOOKS;
BUT TO HIS FOE SUPPOS'D HE MUST COMPLAIN, AND SHE STEAL LOVE'S SWEET BAIT FROM FEARFUL HOOKS:
BEING HELD A FOE, HE MAY NOT HAVE ACCESS TO BREATHE SUCH VOWS AS LOVERS USED TO SWEAR;
AND SHE AS MUCH IN LOVE, HER MEANS MUCH LESS TO MEET HER NEW-BELOVED ANYWHERE:
BUT PASSION LENDS THEM POWER, TIME MEANS TO MEET, TEMPERING EXTREMITIES WITH EXTREME SWEET.

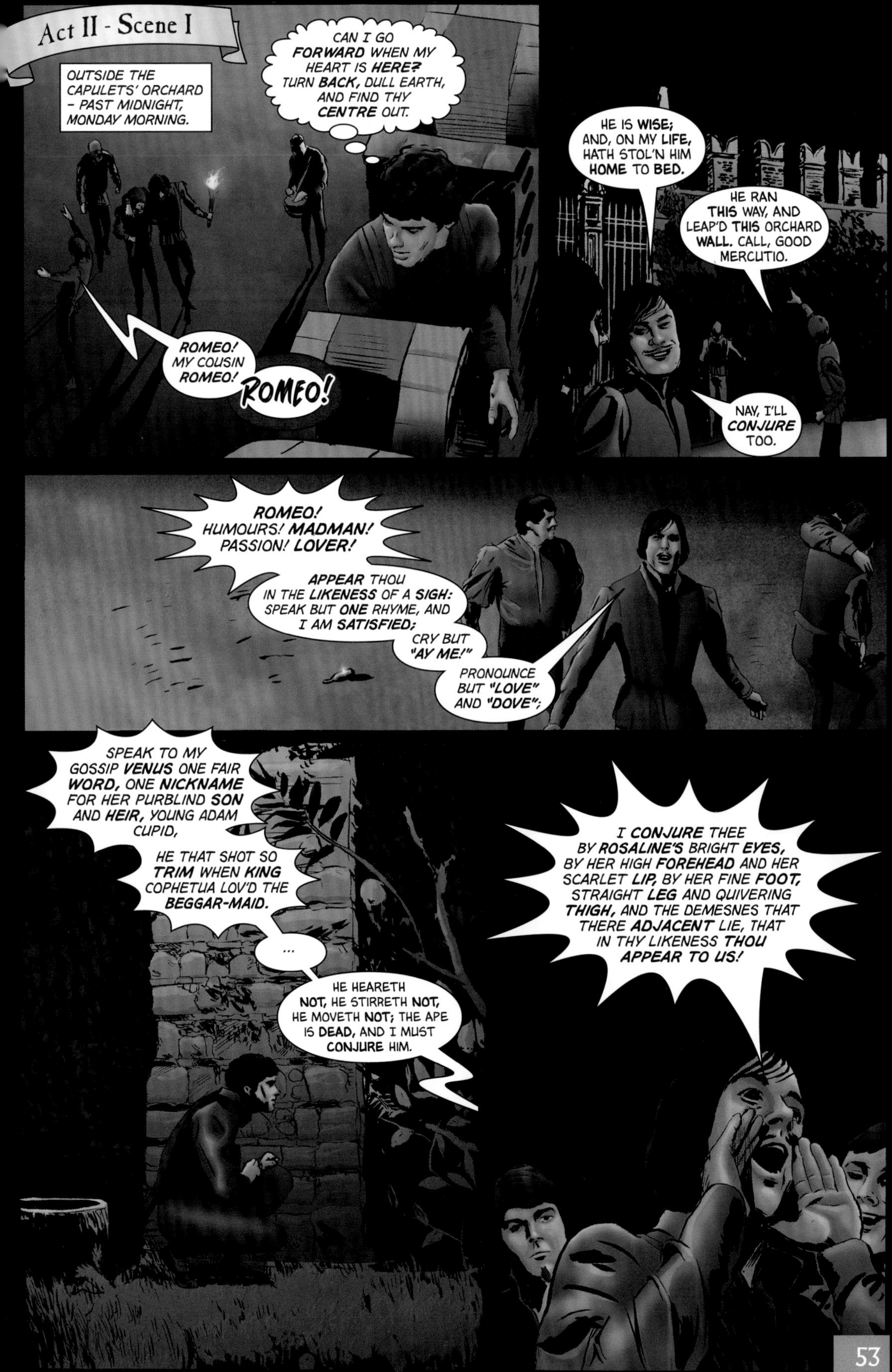
Act II - Scene I
OUTSIDE THE CAPULETS' ORCHARD – PAST MIDNIGHT, MONDAY MORNING.
CAN I GO FORWARD WHEN MY HEART IS HERE? TURN BACK, DULL EARTH, AND FIND THY CENTRE OUT.
ROMEO! MY COUSIN ROMEO!
ROMEO!
HE IS WISE; AND, ON MY LIFE, HATH STOL'N HIM HOME TO BED.
HE RAN THIS WAY, AND LEAP'D THIS ORCHARD WALL. CALL, GOOD MERCUTIO.
NAY, I'LL CONJURE TOO.
ROMEO! HUMOURS! MADMAN! PASSION! LOVER!
APPEAR THOU IN THE LIKENESS OF A SIGH: SPEAK BUT ONE RHYME, AND I AM SATISFIED;
CRY BUT "AY ME!"
PRONOUNCE BUT "LOVE" AND "DOVE";
SPEAK TO MY GOSSIP VENUS ONE FAIR WORD, ONE NICKNAME FOR HER PURBLIND SON AND HEIR, YOUNG ADAM CUPID,
HE THAT SHOT SO TRIM WHEN KING COPHETUA LOV'D THE BEGGAR-MAID.
...
HE HEARETH NOT, HE STIRRETH NOT, HE MOVETH NOT; THE APE IS DEAD, AND I MUST CONJURE HIM.
I CONJURE THEE BY ROSALINE'S BRIGHT EYES, BY HER HIGH FOREHEAD AND HER SCARLET LIP, BY HER FINE FOOT, STRAIGHT LEG AND QUIVERING THIGH, AND THE DEMESNES THAT THERE ADJACENT LIE, THAT IN THY LIKENESS THOU APPEAR TO US!

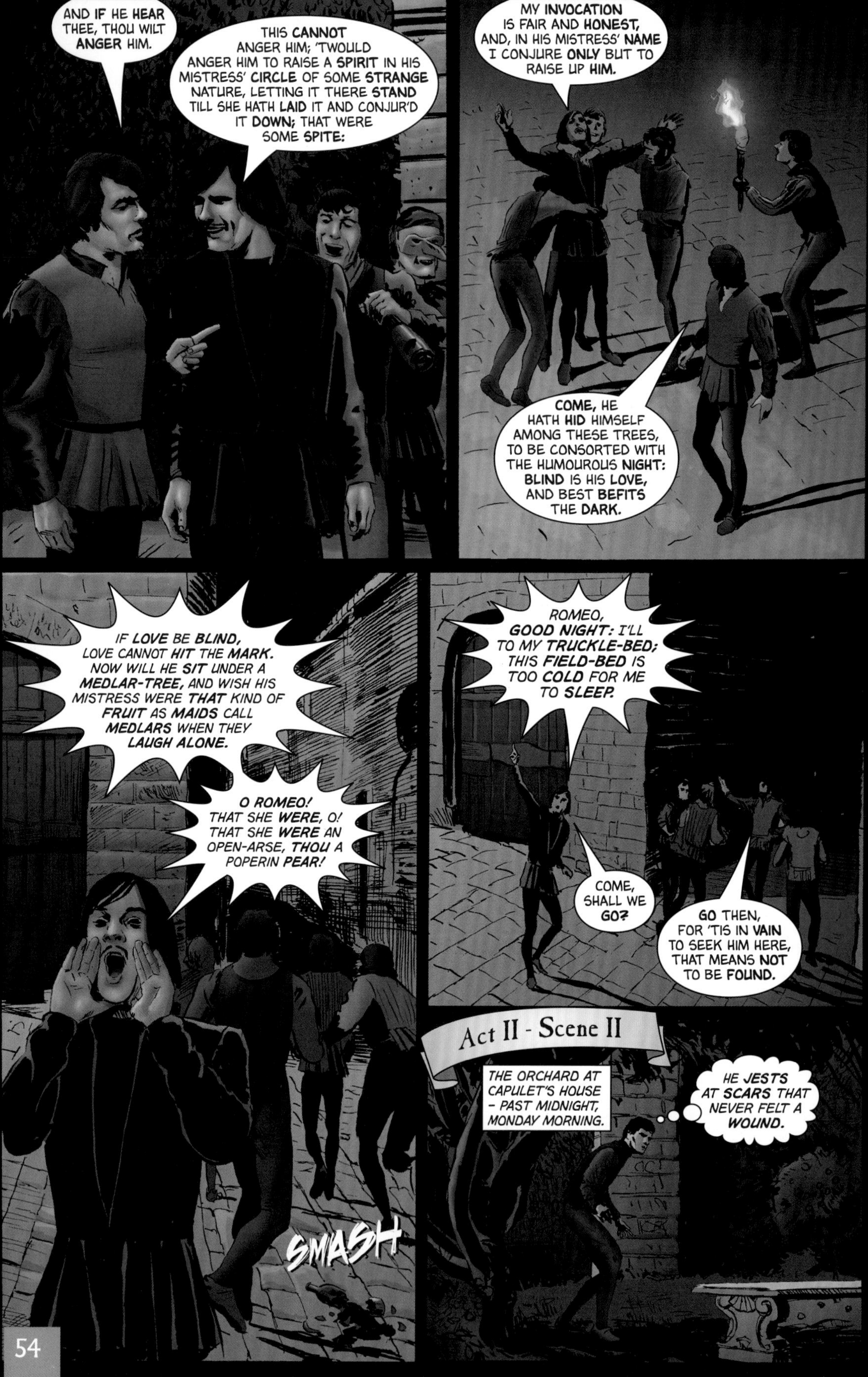
AND IF HE HEAR THEE, THOU WILT ANGER HIM.
THIS CANNOT ANGER HIM; 'TWOULD ANGER HIM TO RAISE A SPIRIT IN HIS MISTRESS' CIRCLE OF SOME STRANGE NATURE, LETTING IT THERE STAND TILL SHE HATH LAID IT AND CONJUR'D IT DOWN; THAT WERE SOME SPITE:
MY INVOCATION IS FAIR AND HONEST, AND, IN HIS MISTRESS' NAME I CONJURE ONLY BUT TO RAISE UP HIM.
COME, HE HATH HID HIMSELF AMONG THESE TREES, TO BE CONSORTED WITH THE HUMOUROUS NIGHT: BLIND IS HIS LOVE, AND BEST BEFITS THE DARK.
IF LOVE BE BLIND, LOVE CANNOT HIT THE MARK. NOW WILL HE SIT UNDER A MEDLAR-TREE, AND WISH HIS MISTRESS WERE THAT KIND OF FRUIT AS MAIDS CALL MEDLARS WHEN THEY LAUGH ALONE.
O ROMEO! THAT SHE WERE, O! THAT SHE WERE AN OPEN-ARSE, THOU A POPERIN PEAR!
SMASH
ROMEO, GOOD NIGHT: I'LL TO MY TRUCKLE-BED; THIS FIELD-BED IS TOO COLD FOR ME TO SLEEP.
COME, SHALL WE GO?
GO THEN, FOR 'TIS IN VAIN TO SEEK HIM HERE, THAT MEANS NOT TO BE FOUND.
Act II - Scene II
THE ORCHARD AT CAPULET'S HOUSE - PAST MIDNIGHT, MONDAY MORNING.
HE JESTS AT SCARS THAT NEVER FELT A WOUND.

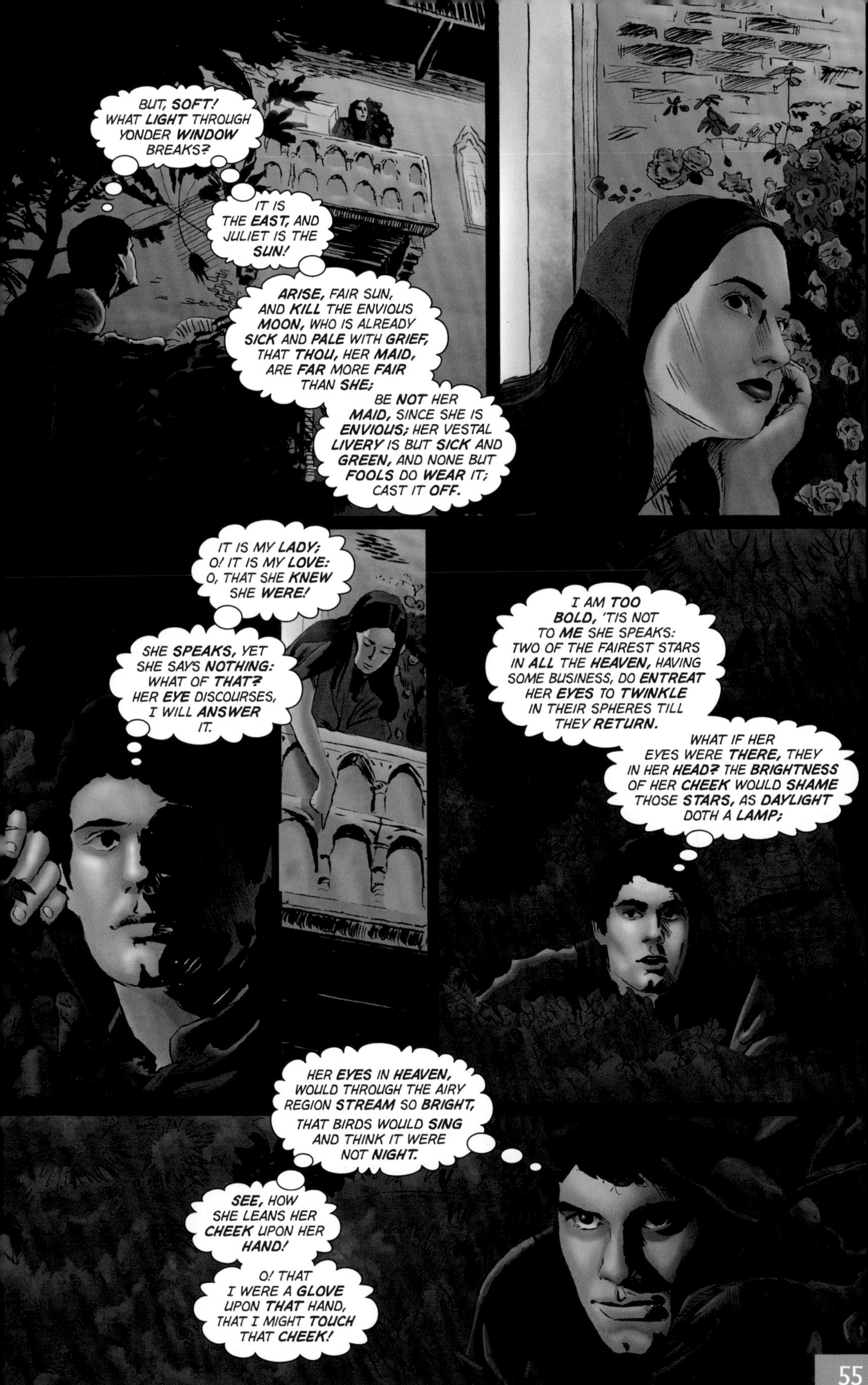
BUT, SOFT! WHAT LIGHT THROUGH YONDER WINDOW BREAKS?
IT IS THE EAST, AND JULIET IS THE SUN!
ARISE, FAIR SUN, AND KILL THE ENVIOUS MOON, WHO IS ALREADY SICK AND PALE WITH GRIEF, THAT THOU, HER MAID, ARE FAR MORE FAIR THAN SHE;
BE NOT HER MAID, SINCE SHE IS ENVIOUS; HER VESTAL LIVERY IS BUT SICK AND GREEN, AND NONE BUT FOOLS DO WEAR IT; CAST IT OFF.
IT IS MY LADY; O! IT IS MY LOVE: O, THAT SHE KNEW SHE WERE!
SHE SPEAKS, YET SHE SAYS NOTHING: WHAT OF THAT? HER EYE DISCOURSES, I WILL ANSWER IT.
I AM TOO BOLD, 'TIS NOT TO ME SHE SPEAKS: TWO OF THE FAIREST STARS IN ALL THE HEAVEN, HAVING SOME BUSINESS, DO ENTREAT HER EYES TO TWINKLE IN THEIR SPHERES TILL THEY RETURN.
WHAT IF HER EYES WERE THERE, THEY IN HER HEAD? THE BRIGHTNESS OF HER CHEEK WOULD SHAME THOSE STARS, AS DAYLIGHT DOTH A LAMP;
HER EYES IN HEAVEN, WOULD THROUGH THE AIRY REGION STREAM SO BRIGHT, THAT BIRDS WOULD SING AND THINK IT WERE NOT NIGHT.
SEE, HOW SHE LEANS HER CHEEK UPON HER HAND!
O! THAT I WERE A GLOVE UPON THAT HAND, THAT I MIGHT TOUCH THAT CHEEK!

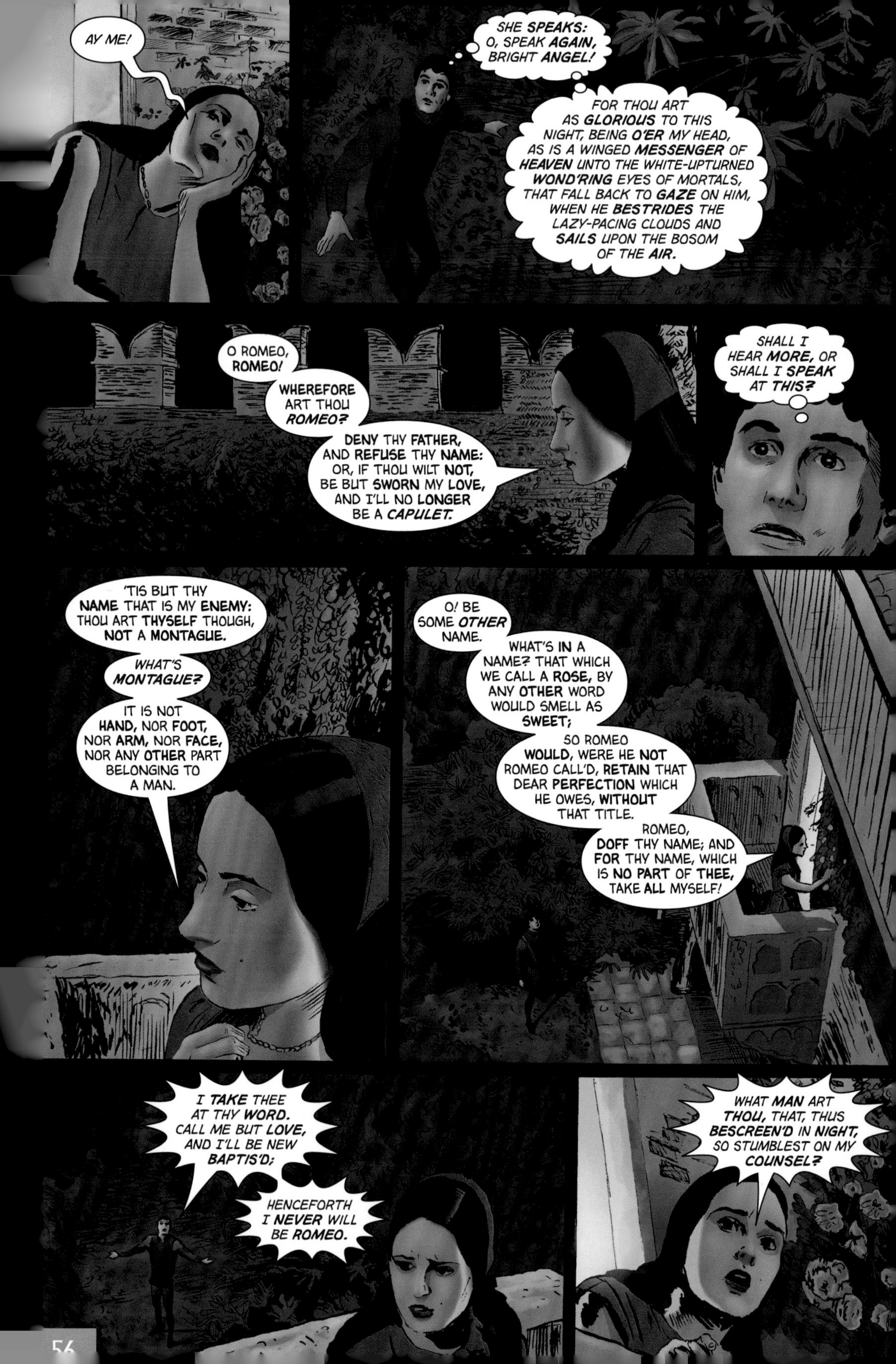
AY ME!
SHE SPEAKS: O, SPEAK AGAIN, BRIGHT ANGEL!
FOR THOU ART AS GLORIOUS TO THIS NIGHT, BEING O'ER MY HEAD, AS IS A WINGED MESSENGER OF HEAVEN UNTO THE WHITE-UPTURNED WOND'RING EYES OF MORTALS, THAT FALL BACK TO GAZE ON HIM, WHEN HE BESTRIDES THE LAZY-PACING CLOUDS AND SAILS UPON THE BOSOM OF THE AIR.
O ROMEO, ROMEO!
WHEREFORE ART THOU ROMEO?
DENY THY FATHER, AND REFUSE THY NAME: OR, IF THOU WILT NOT, BE BUT SWORN MY LOVE, AND I'LL NO LONGER BE A CAPULET.
SHALL I HEAR MORE, OR SHALL I SPEAK AT THIS?
'TIS BUT THY NAME THAT IS MY ENEMY: THOU ART THYSELF THOUGH, NOT A MONTAGUE.
WHAT'S MONTAGUE?
IT IS NOT HAND, NOR FOOT, NOR ARM, NOR FACE, NOR ANY OTHER PART BELONGING TO A MAN.
O! BE SOME OTHER NAME.
WHAT'S IN A NAME? THAT WHICH WE CALL A ROSE, BY ANY OTHER WORD WOULD SMELL AS SWEET;
SO ROMEO WOULD, WERE HE NOT ROMEO CALL'D, RETAIN THAT DEAR PERFECTION WHICH HE OWES, WITHOUT THAT TITLE.
ROMEO, DOFF THY NAME; AND FOR THY NAME, WHICH IS NO PART OF THEE, TAKE ALL MYSELF!
I TAKE THEE AT THY WORD. CALL ME BUT LOVE, AND I'LL BE NEW BAPTIS'D;
HENCEFORTH I NEVER WILL BE ROMEO.
WHAT MAN ART THOU, THAT, THUS BESCREEN'D IN NIGHT, SO STUMBLEST ON MY COUNSEL?

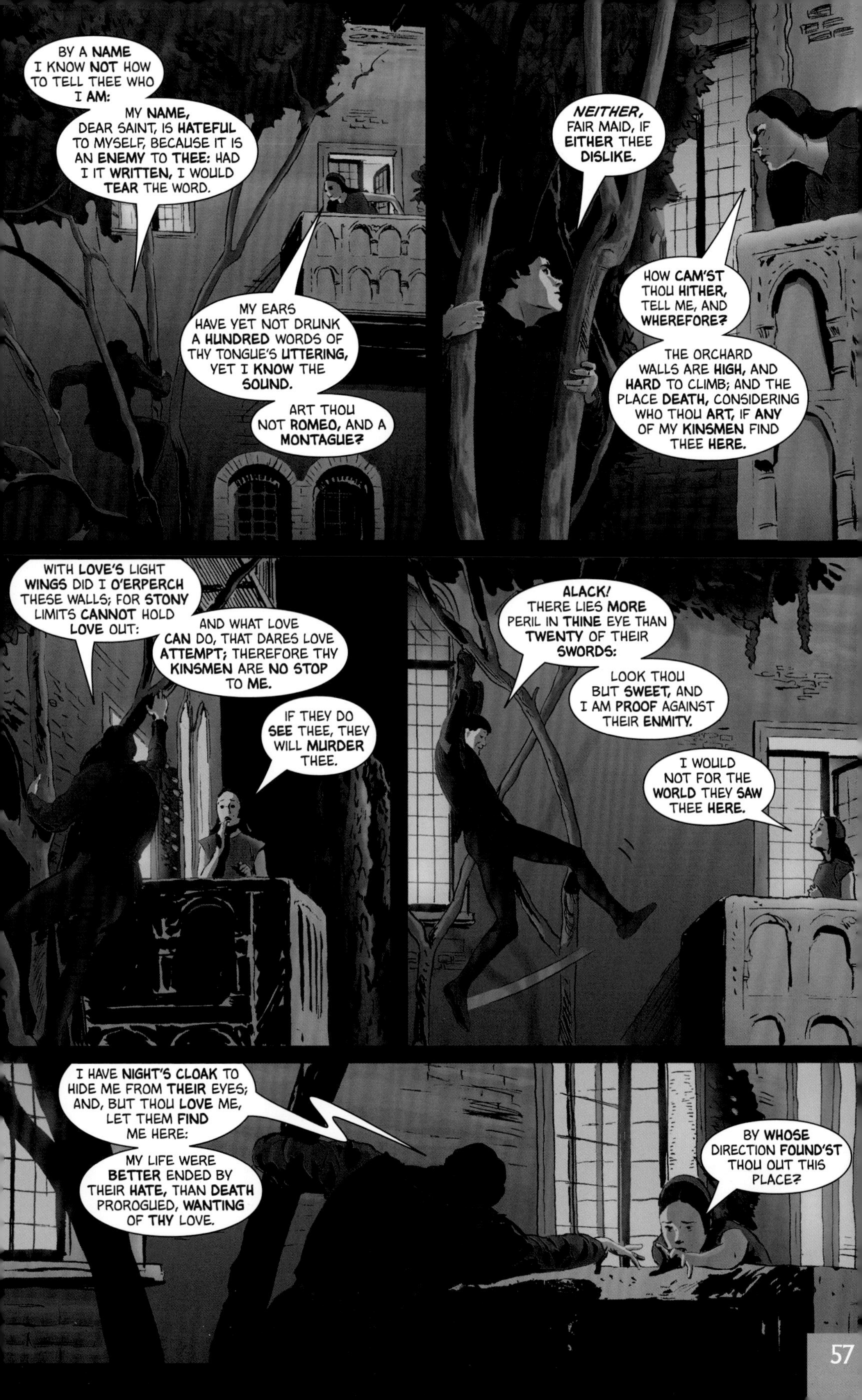
BY A NAME I KNOW NOT HOW TO TELL THEE WHO I AM:
MY NAME, DEAR SAINT, IS HATEFUL TO MYSELF, BECAUSE IT IS AN ENEMY TO THEE: HAD I IT WRITTEN, I WOULD TEAR THE WORD.
MY EARS HAVE YET NOT DRUNK A HUNDRED WORDS OF THY TONGUE'S UTTERING, YET I KNOW THE SOUND.
ART THOU NOT ROMEO, AND A MONTAGUE?
NEITHER, FAIR MAID, IF EITHER THEE DISLIKE.
HOW CAM'ST THOU HITHER, TELL ME, AND WHEREFORE?
THE ORCHARD WALLS ARE HIGH, AND HARD TO CLIMB; AND THE PLACE DEATH, CONSIDERING WHO THOU ART, IF ANY OF MY KINSMEN FIND THEE HERE.
WITH LOVE'S LIGHT WINGS DID I O'ERPERCH THESE WALLS; FOR STONY LIMITS CANNOT HOLD LOVE OUT:
AND WHAT LOVE CAN DO, THAT DARES LOVE ATTEMPT; THEREFORE THY KINSMEN ARE NO STOP TO ME.
IF THEY DO SEE THEE, THEY WILL MURDER THEE.
ALACK! THERE LIES MORE PERIL IN THINE EYE THAN TWENTY OF THEIR SWORDS:
LOOK THOU BUT SWEET, AND I AM PROOF AGAINST THEIR ENMITY.
I WOULD NOT FOR THE WORLD THEY SAW THEE HERE.
I HAVE NIGHT'S CLOAK TO HIDE ME FROM THEIR EYES; AND, BUT THOU LOVE ME, LET THEM FIND ME HERE:
MY LIFE WERE BETTER ENDED BY THEIR HATE, THAN DEATH PROROGUED, WANTING OF THY LOVE.
BY WHOSE DIRECTION FOUND'ST THOU OUT THIS PLACE?

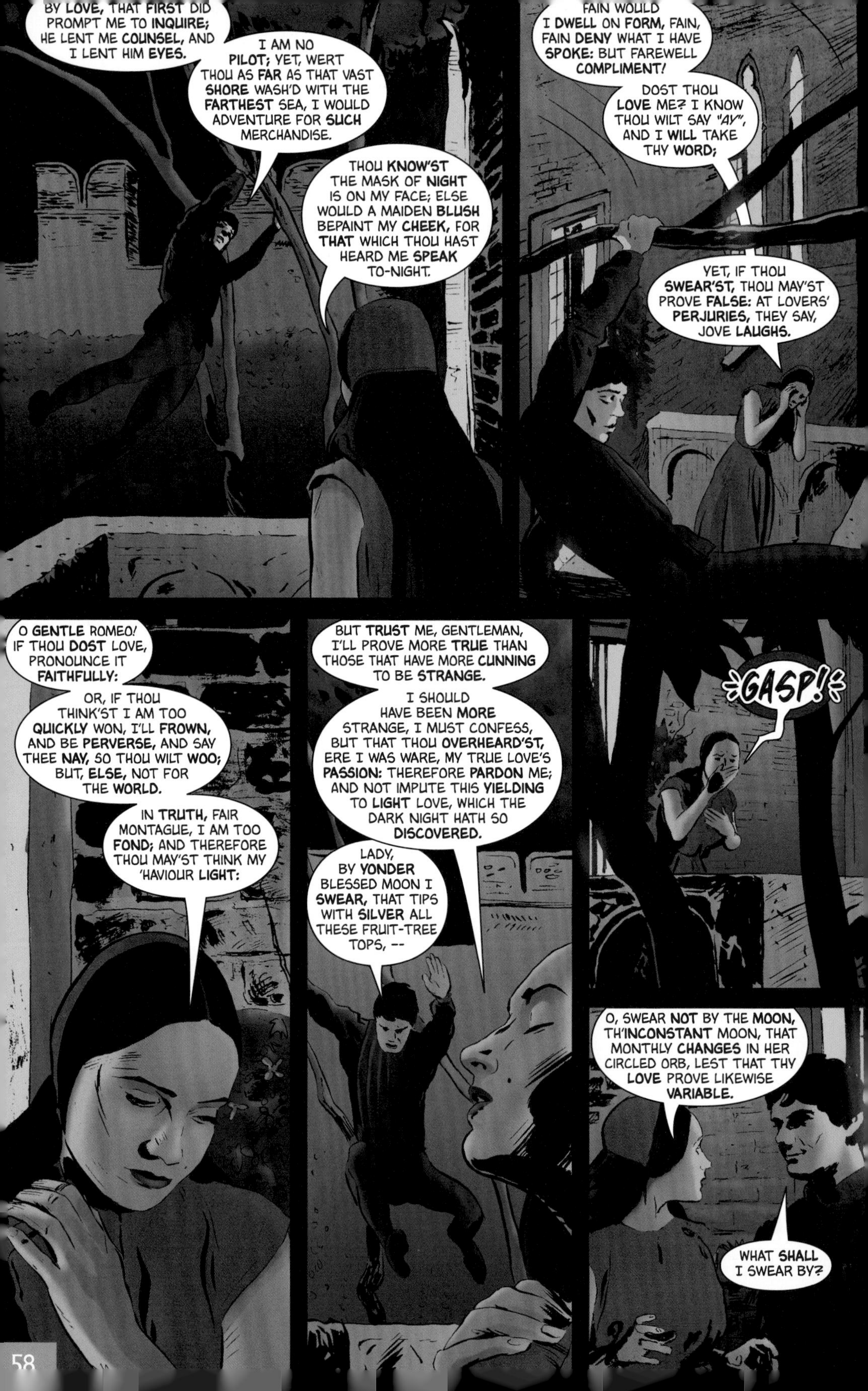

BY LOVE, THAT FIRST DID PROMPT ME TO INQUIRE; HE LENT ME COUNSEL, AND I LENT HIM EYES.
I AM NO PILOT; YET, WERT THOU AS FAR AS THAT VAST SHORE WASH'D WITH THE FARTHEST SEA, I WOULD ADVENTURE FOR SUCH MERCHANDISE.
THOU KNOW'ST THE MASK OF NIGHT IS ON MY FACE; ELSE WOULD A MAIDEN BLUSH BEPAINT MY CHEEK, FOR THAT WHICH THOU HAST HEARD ME SPEAK TO-NIGHT.
FAIN WOULD I DWELL ON FORM, FAIN, FAIN DENY WHAT I HAVE SPOKE: BUT FAREWELL COMPLIMENT!
DOST THOU LOVE ME? I KNOW THOU WILT SAY "AY", AND I WILL TAKE THY WORD;
YET, IF THOU SWEAR'ST, THOU MAY'ST PROVE FALSE: AT LOVERS' PERJURIES, THEY SAY, JOVE LAUGHS.
O GENTLE ROMEO! IF THOU DOST LOVE, PRONOUNCE IT FAITHFULLY:
OR, IF THOU THINK'ST I AM TOO QUICKLY WON, I'LL FROWN, AND BE PERVERSE, AND SAY THEE NAY, SO THOU WILT WOO; BUT, ELSE, NOT FOR THE WORLD.
IN TRUTH, FAIR MONTAGUE, I AM TOO FOND; AND THEREFORE THOU MAY'ST THINK MY 'HAVIOUR LIGHT:
BUT TRUST ME, GENTLEMAN, I'LL PROVE MORE TRUE THAN THOSE THAT HAVE MORE CUNNING TO BE STRANGE.
I SHOULD HAVE BEEN MORE STRANGE, I MUST CONFESS, BUT THAT THOU OVERHEARD'ST, ERE I WAS WARE, MY TRUE LOVE'S PASSION: THEREFORE PARDON ME; AND NOT IMPUTE THIS YIELDING TO LIGHT LOVE, WHICH THE DARK NIGHT HATH SO DISCOVERED.
LADY, BY YONDER BLESSED MOON I SWEAR, THAT TIPS WITH SILVER ALL THESE FRUIT-TREE TOPS, --
GASP!
O, SWEAR NOT BY THE MOON, TH'INCONSTANT MOON, THAT MONTHLY CHANGES IN HER CIRCLED ORB, LEST THAT THY LOVE PROVE LIKEWISE VARIABLE.
WHAT SHALL I SWEAR BY?

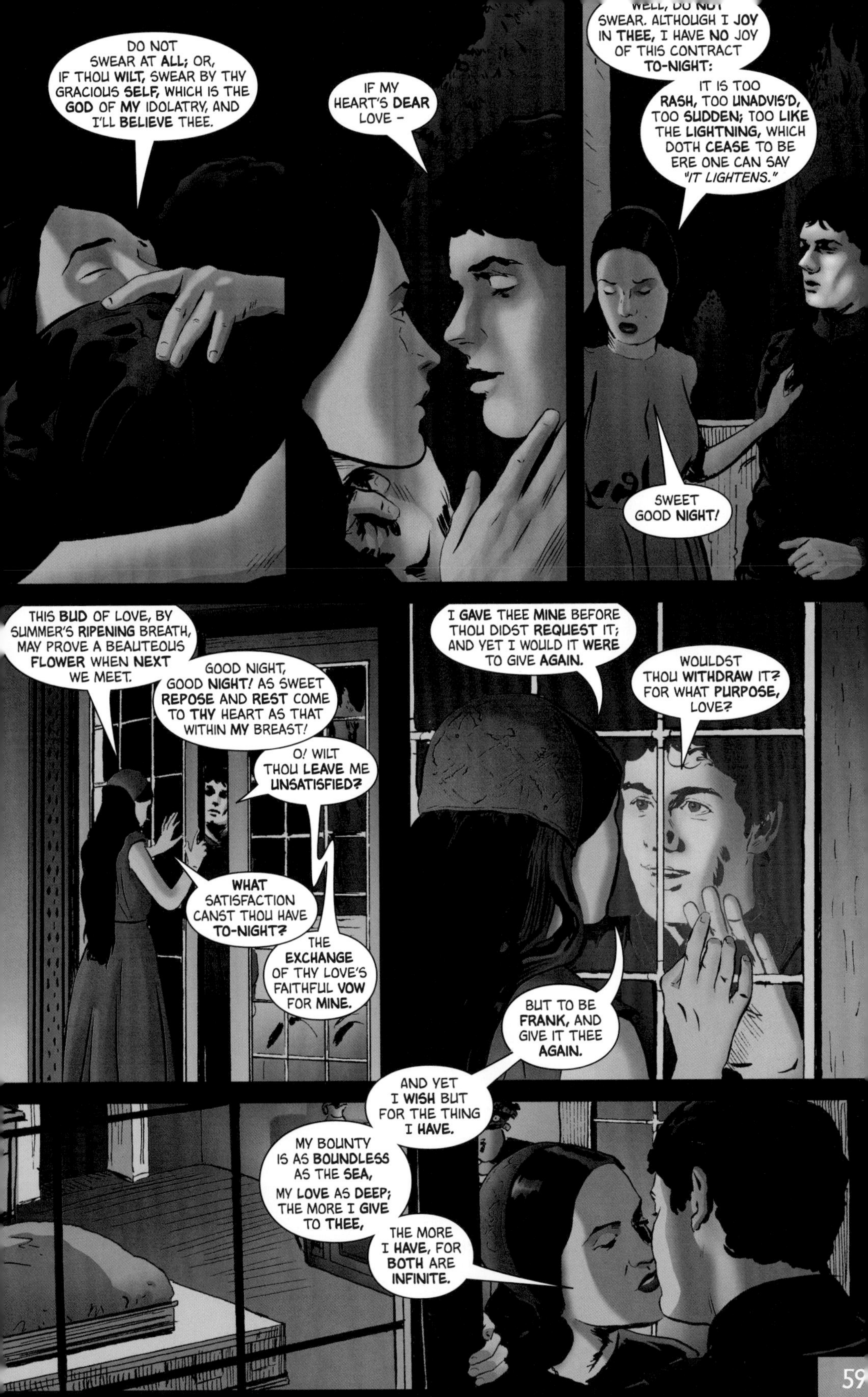

DO NOT SWEAR AT ALL; OR, IF THOU WILT, SWEAR BY THY GRACIOUS SELF, WHICH IS THE GOD OF MY IDOLATRY, AND I'LL BELIEVE THEE.
IF MY HEART'S DEAR LOVE –
WELL, DO NOT SWEAR. ALTHOUGH I JOY IN THEE, I HAVE NO JOY OF THIS CONTRACT TO-NIGHT:
IT IS TOO RASH, TOO UNADVIS'D, TOO SUDDEN; TOO LIKE THE LIGHTNING, WHICH DOTH CEASE TO BE ERE ONE CAN SAY "IT LIGHTENS."
SWEET GOOD NIGHT!
THIS BUD OF LOVE, BY SUMMER'S RIPENING BREATH, MAY PROVE A BEAUTEOUS FLOWER WHEN NEXT WE MEET.
GOOD NIGHT, GOOD NIGHT! AS SWEET REPOSE AND REST COME TO THY HEART AS THAT WITHIN MY BREAST!
O! WILT THOU LEAVE ME UNSATISFIED?
WHAT SATISFACTION CANST THOU HAVE TO-NIGHT?
THE EXCHANGE OF THY LOVE'S FAITHFUL VOW FOR MINE.
I GAVE THEE MINE BEFORE THOU DIDST REQUEST IT; AND YET I WOULD IT WERE TO GIVE AGAIN.
WOULDST THOU WITHDRAW IT? FOR WHAT PURPOSE, LOVE?
BUT TO BE FRANK, AND GIVE IT THEE AGAIN.
AND YET I WISH BUT FOR THE THING I HAVE.
MY BOUNTY IS AS BOUNDLESS AS THE SEA, MY LOVE AS DEEP; THE MORE I GIVE TO THEE,
THE MORE I HAVE, FOR BOTH ARE INFINITE.

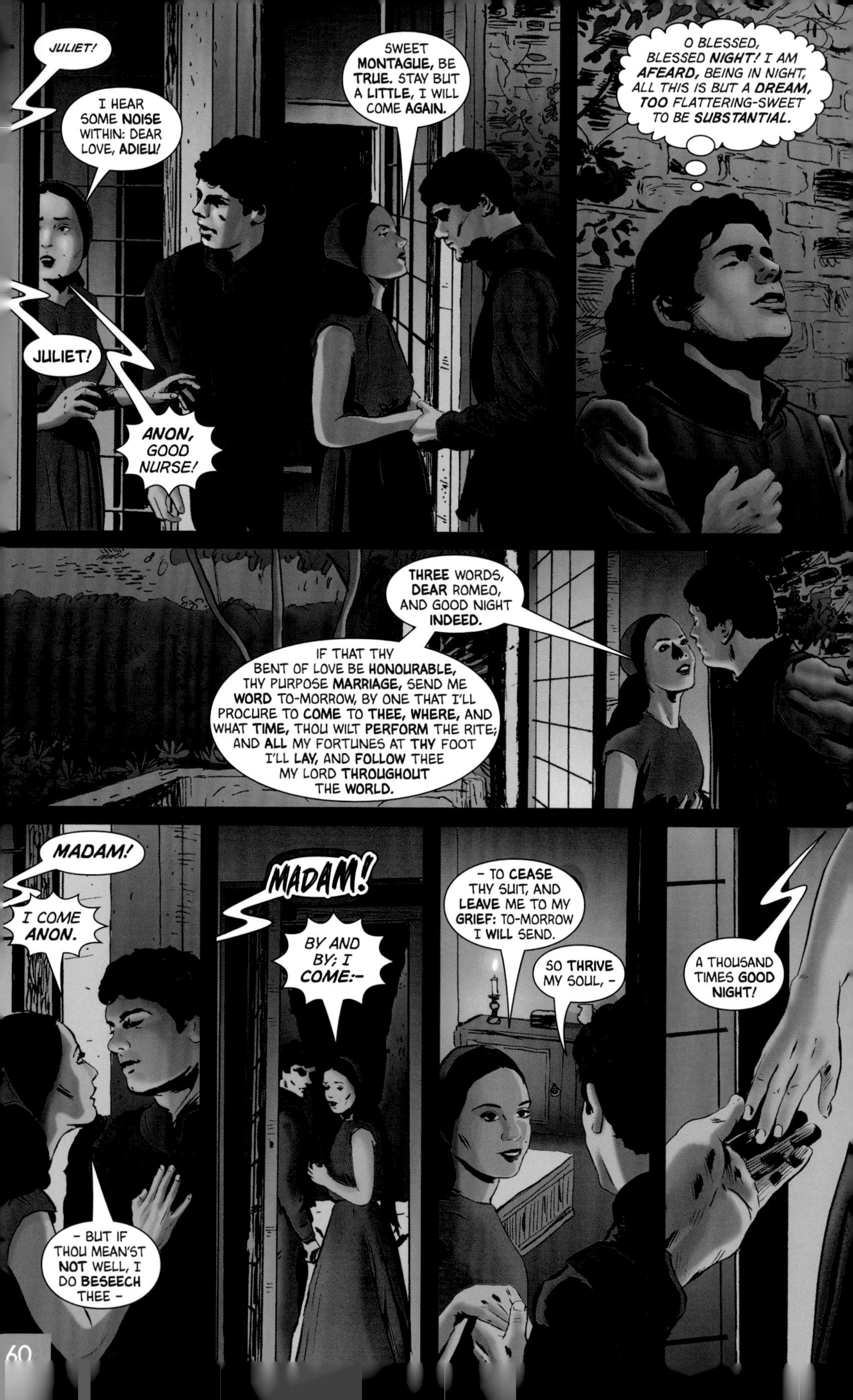
JULIET!
I HEAR SOME NOISE WITHIN: DEAR LOVE, ADIEU!
JULIET!
ANON, GOOD NURSE!
SWEET MONTAGUE, BE TRUE. STAY BUT A LITTLE, I WILL COME AGAIN.
O BLESSED, BLESSED NIGHT! I AM AFEARD, BEING IN NIGHT, ALL THIS IS BUT A DREAM, TOO FLATTERING-SWEET TO BE SUBSTANTIAL.
THREE WORDS, DEAR ROMEO, AND GOOD NIGHT INDEED.
IF THAT THY BENT OF LOVE BE HONOURABLE, THY PURPOSE MARRIAGE, SEND ME WORD TO-MORROW, BY ONE THAT I'LL PROCURE TO COME TO THEE, WHERE, AND WHAT TIME, THOU WILT PERFORM THE RITE; AND ALL MY FORTUNES AT THY FOOT I'LL LAY, AND FOLLOW THEE MY LORD THROUGHOUT THE WORLD.
MADAM!
I COME ANON.
- BUT IF THOU MEAN'ST NOT WELL, I DO BESEECH THEE -
MADAM!
BY AND BY; I COME:-
- TO CEASE THY SUIT, AND LEAVE ME TO MY GRIEF: TO-MORROW I WILL SEND.
SO THRIVE MY SOUL, -
A THOUSAND TIMES GOOD NIGHT!

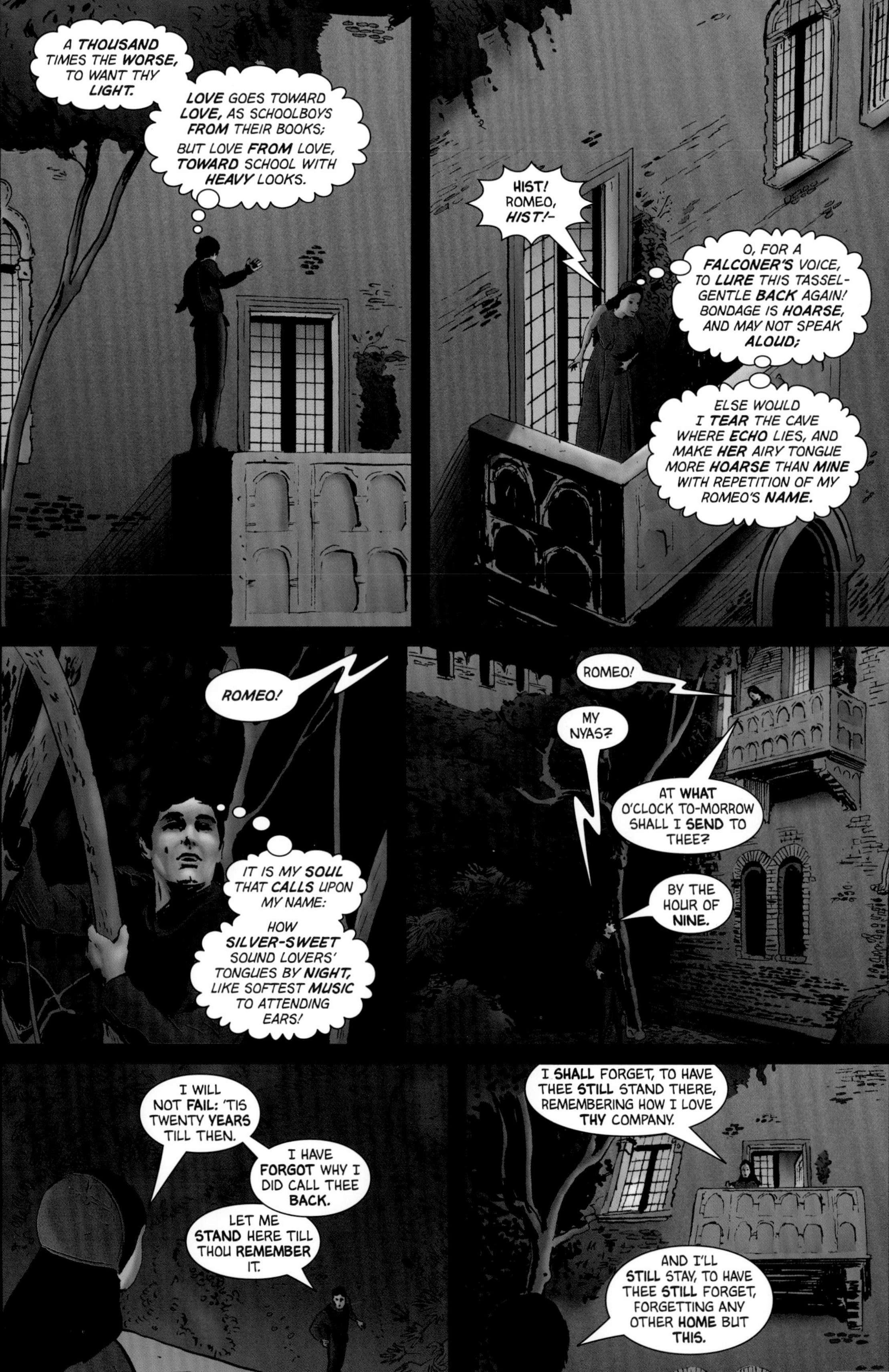
A THOUSAND TIMES THE WORSE, TO WANT THY LIGHT.
LOVE GOES TOWARD LOVE, AS SCHOOLBOYS FROM THEIR BOOKS;
BUT LOVE FROM LOVE, TOWARD SCHOOL WITH HEAVY LOOKS.
HIST! ROMEO, HIST!-
O, FOR A FALCONER'S VOICE, TO LURE THIS TASSEL-GENTLE BACK AGAIN! BONDAGE IS HOARSE, AND MAY NOT SPEAK ALOUD;
ELSE WOULD I TEAR THE CAVE WHERE ECHO LIES, AND MAKE HER AIRY TONGUE MORE HOARSE THAN MINE WITH REPETITION OF MY ROMEO'S NAME.
ROMEO!
IT IS MY SOUL THAT CALLS UPON MY NAME:
HOW SILVER-SWEET SOUND LOVERS' TONGUES BY NIGHT, LIKE SOFTEST MUSIC TO ATTENDING EARS!
ROMEO!
MY NYAS?
AT WHAT O'CLOCK TO-MORROW SHALL I SEND TO THEE?
BY THE HOUR OF NINE.
I WILL NOT FAIL: 'TIS TWENTY YEARS TILL THEN.
I HAVE FORGOT WHY I DID CALL THEE BACK.
LET ME STAND HERE TILL THOU REMEMBER IT.
I SHALL FORGET, TO HAVE THEE STILL STAND THERE, REMEMBERING HOW I LOVE THY COMPANY.
AND I'LL STILL STAY, TO HAVE THEE STILL FORGET, FORGETTING ANY OTHER HOME BUT THIS.

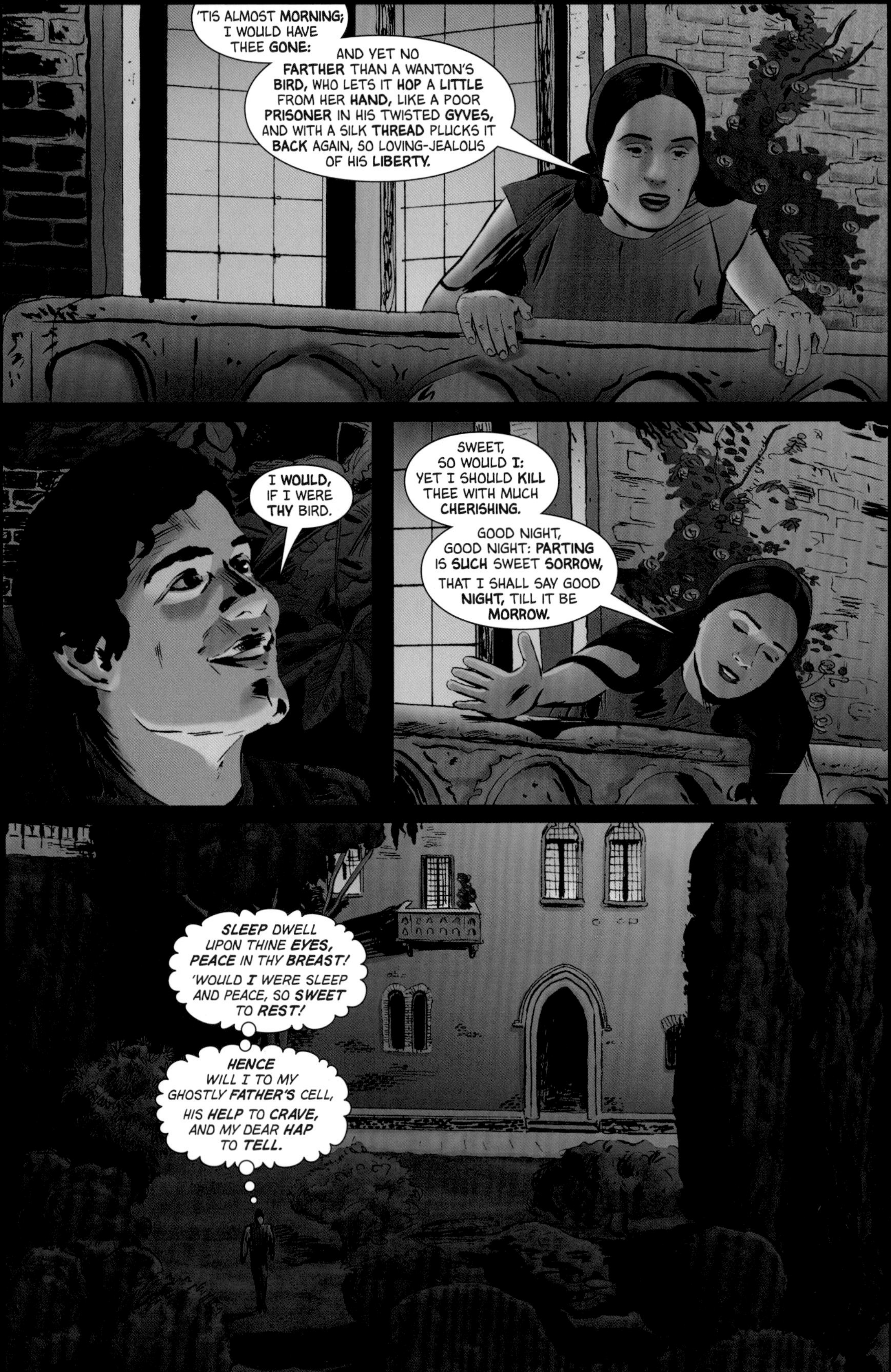
'TIS ALMOST MORNING; I WOULD HAVE THEE GONE:
AND YET NO FARTHER THAN A WANTON'S BIRD, WHO LETS IT HOP A LITTLE FROM HER HAND, LIKE A POOR PRISONER IN HIS TWISTED GYVES, AND WITH A SILK THREAD PLUCKS IT BACK AGAIN, SO LOVING-JEALOUS OF HIS LIBERTY.
I WOULD, IF I WERE THY BIRD.
SWEET, SO WOULD I: YET I SHOULD KILL THEE WITH MUCH CHERISHING.
GOOD NIGHT, GOOD NIGHT: PARTING IS SUCH SWEET SORROW, THAT I SHALL SAY GOOD NIGHT, TILL IT BE MORROW.
SLEEP DWELL UPON THINE EYES, PEACE IN THY BREAST!
'WOULD I WERE SLEEP AND PEACE, SO SWEET TO REST!
HENCE WILL I TO MY GHOSTLY FATHER'S CELL, HIS HELP TO CRAVE, AND MY DEAR HAP TO TELL.

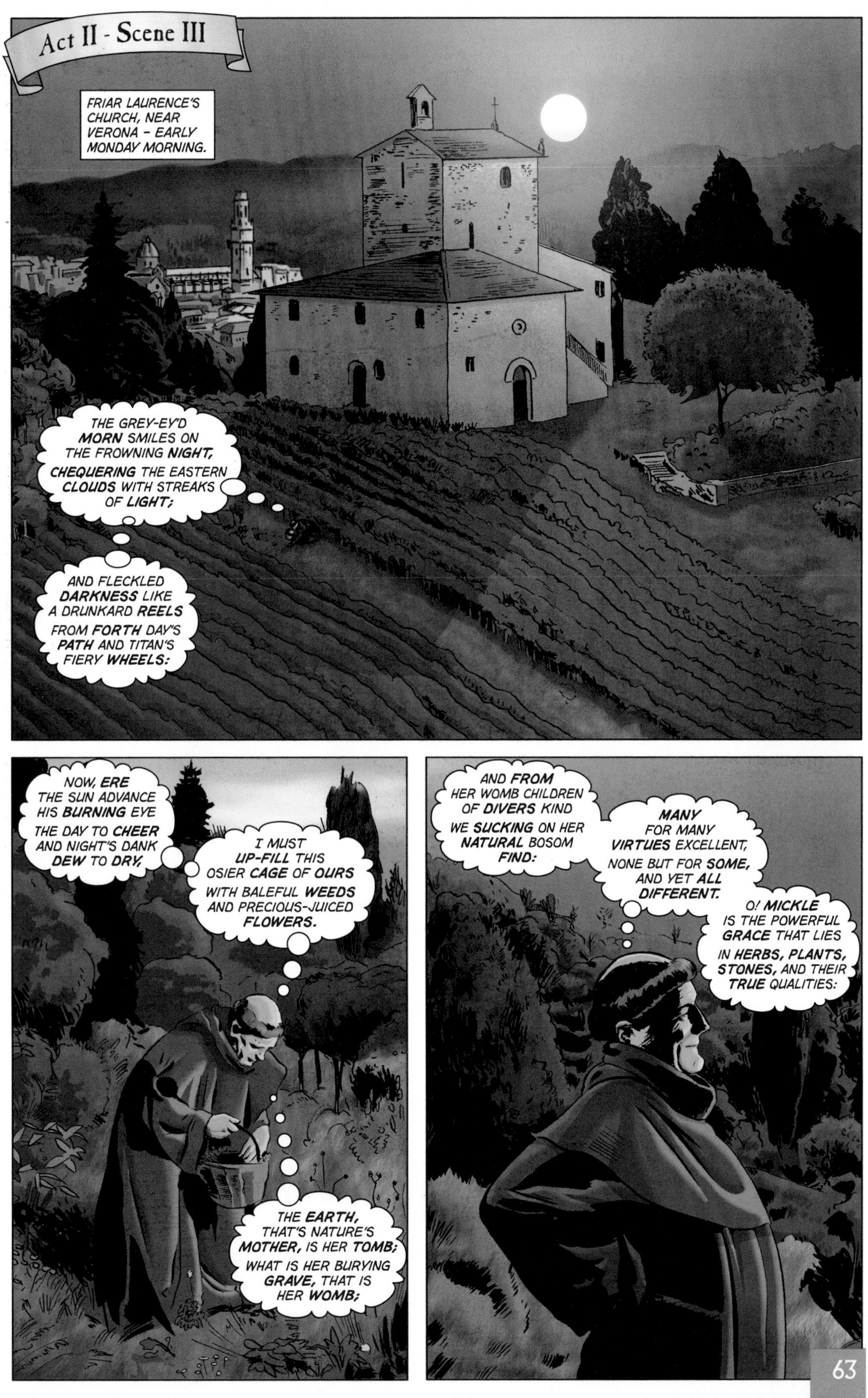
Act II - Scene III
FRIAR LAURENCE'S CHURCH, NEAR VERONA – EARLY MONDAY MORNING.
THE GREY-EY'D MORN SMILES ON THE FROWNING NIGHT, CHEQUERING THE EASTERN CLOUDS WITH STREAKS OF LIGHT;
AND FLECKLED DARKNESS LIKE A DRUNKARD REELS FROM FORTH DAY'S PATH AND TITAN'S FIERY WHEELS:
NOW, ERE THE SUN ADVANCE HIS BURNING EYE THE DAY TO CHEER AND NIGHT'S DANK DEW TO DRY,
I MUST UP-FILL THIS OSIER CAGE OF OURS WITH BALEFUL WEEDS AND PRECIOUS-JUICED FLOWERS.
THE EARTH, THAT'S NATURE'S MOTHER, IS HER TOMB; WHAT IS HER BURYING GRAVE, THAT IS HER WOMB;
AND FROM HER WOMB CHILDREN OF DIVERS KIND WE SUCKING ON HER NATURAL BOSOM FIND:
MANY FOR MANY VIRTUES EXCELLENT, NONE BUT FOR SOME, AND YET ALL DIFFERENT.
O! MICKLE IS THE POWERFUL GRACE THAT LIES IN HERBS, PLANTS, STONES, AND THEIR TRUE QUALITIES:

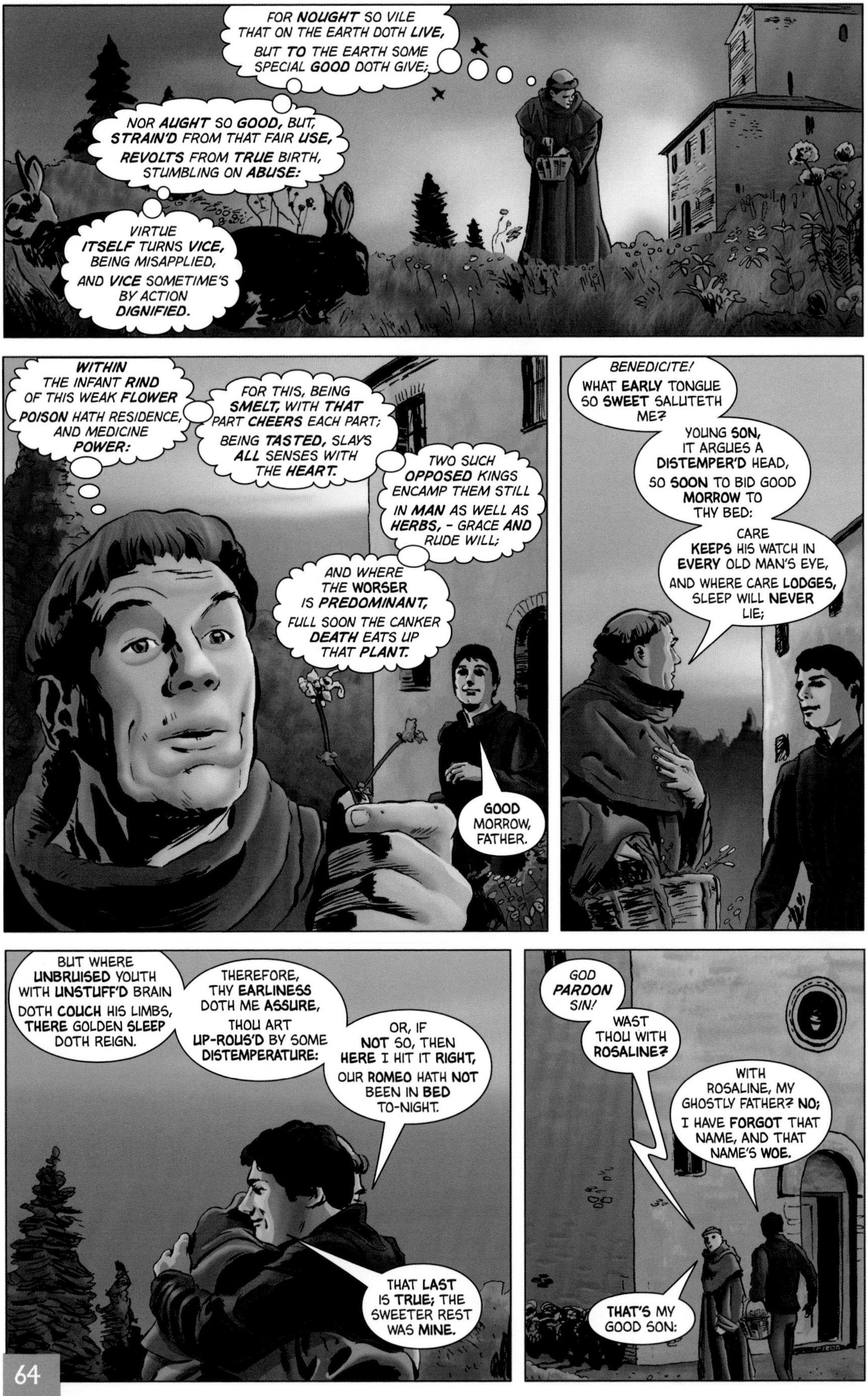
FOR NOUGHT SO VILE THAT ON THE EARTH DOTH LIVE, BUT TO THE EARTH SOME SPECIAL GOOD DOTH GIVE;
NOR AUGHT SO GOOD, BUT, STRAIN'D FROM THAT FAIR USE, REVOLTS FROM TRUE BIRTH, STUMBLING ON ABUSE:
VIRTUE ITSELF TURNS VICE, BEING MISAPPLIED, AND VICE SOMETIME'S BY ACTION DIGNIFIED.
WITHIN THE INFANT RIND OF THIS WEAK FLOWER POISON HATH RESIDENCE, AND MEDICINE POWER:
FOR THIS, BEING SMELT, WITH THAT PART CHEERS EACH PART; BEING TASTED, SLAYS ALL SENSES WITH THE HEART.
TWO SUCH OPPOSED KINGS ENCAMP THEM STILL IN MAN AS WELL AS HERBS, - GRACE AND RUDE WILL;
AND WHERE THE WORSER IS PREDOMINANT, FULL SOON THE CANKER DEATH EATS UP THAT PLANT.
GOOD MORROW, FATHER.
BENEDICITE! WHAT EARLY TONGUE SO SWEET SALUTETH ME?
YOUNG SON, IT ARGUES A DISTEMPER'D HEAD, SO SOON TO BID GOOD MORROW TO THY BED:
CARE KEEPS HIS WATCH IN EVERY OLD MAN'S EYE, AND WHERE CARE LODGES, SLEEP WILL NEVER LIE;
BUT WHERE UNBRUISED YOUTH WITH UNSTUFF'D BRAIN DOTH COUCH HIS LIMBS, THERE GOLDEN SLEEP DOTH REIGN.
THEREFORE, THY EARLINESS DOTH ME ASSURE, THOU ART UP-ROUS'D BY SOME DISTEMPERATURE:
OR, IF NOT SO, THEN HERE I HIT IT RIGHT, OUR ROMEO HATH NOT BEEN IN BED TO-NIGHT.
THAT LAST IS TRUE; THE SWEETER REST WAS MINE.
GOD PARDON SIN!
WAST THOU WITH ROSALINE?
WITH ROSALINE, MY GHOSTLY FATHER? NO; I HAVE FORGOT THAT NAME, AND THAT NAME'S WOE.
THAT'S MY GOOD SON:

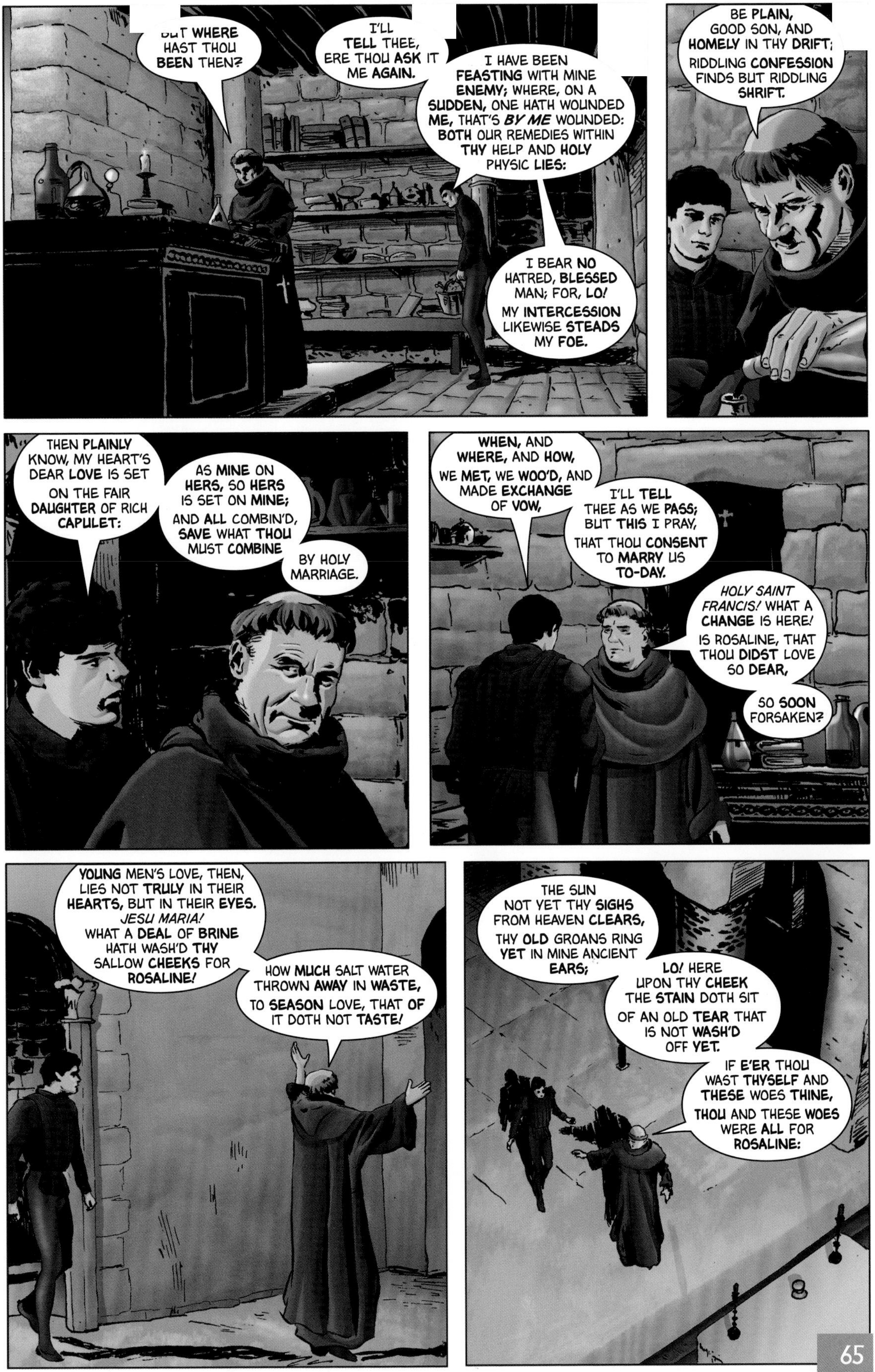
BUT WHERE HAST THOU BEEN THEN?
I'LL TELL THEE, ERE THOU ASK IT ME AGAIN.
I HAVE BEEN FEASTING WITH MINE ENEMY; WHERE, ON A SUDDEN, ONE HATH WOUNDED ME, THAT'S BY ME WOUNDED: BOTH OUR REMEDIES WITHIN THY HELP AND HOLY PHYSIC LIES:
I BEAR NO HATRED, BLESSED MAN; FOR, LO! MY INTERCESSION LIKEWISE STEADS MY FOE.
BE PLAIN, GOOD SON, AND HOMELY IN THY DRIFT; RIDDLING CONFESSION FINDS BUT RIDDLING SHRIFT.
THEN PLAINLY KNOW, MY HEART'S DEAR LOVE IS SET ON THE FAIR DAUGHTER OF RICH CAPULET:
AS MINE ON HERS, SO HERS IS SET ON MINE; AND ALL COMBIN'D, SAVE WHAT THOU MUST COMBINE
BY HOLY MARRIAGE.
WHEN, AND WHERE, AND HOW, WE MET, WE WOO'D, AND MADE EXCHANGE OF VOW,
I'LL TELL THEE AS WE PASS; BUT THIS I PRAY, THAT THOU CONSENT TO MARRY US TO-DAY.
HOLY SAINT FRANCIS! WHAT A CHANGE IS HERE! IS ROSALINE, THAT THOU DIDST LOVE SO DEAR,
SO SOON FORSAKEN?
YOUNG MEN'S LOVE, THEN, LIES NOT TRULY IN THEIR HEARTS, BUT IN THEIR EYES. JESU MARIA! WHAT A DEAL OF BRINE HATH WASH'D THY SALLOW CHEEKS FOR ROSALINE!
HOW MUCH SALT WATER THROWN AWAY IN WASTE, TO SEASON LOVE, THAT OF IT DOTH NOT TASTE!
THE SUN NOT YET THY SIGHS FROM HEAVEN CLEARS, THY OLD GROANS RING YET IN MINE ANCIENT EARS;
LO! HERE UPON THY CHEEK THE STAIN DOTH SIT OF AN OLD TEAR THAT IS NOT WASH'D OFF YET.
IF E'ER THOU WAST THYSELF AND THESE WOES THINE, THOU AND THESE WOES WERE ALL FOR ROSALINE:

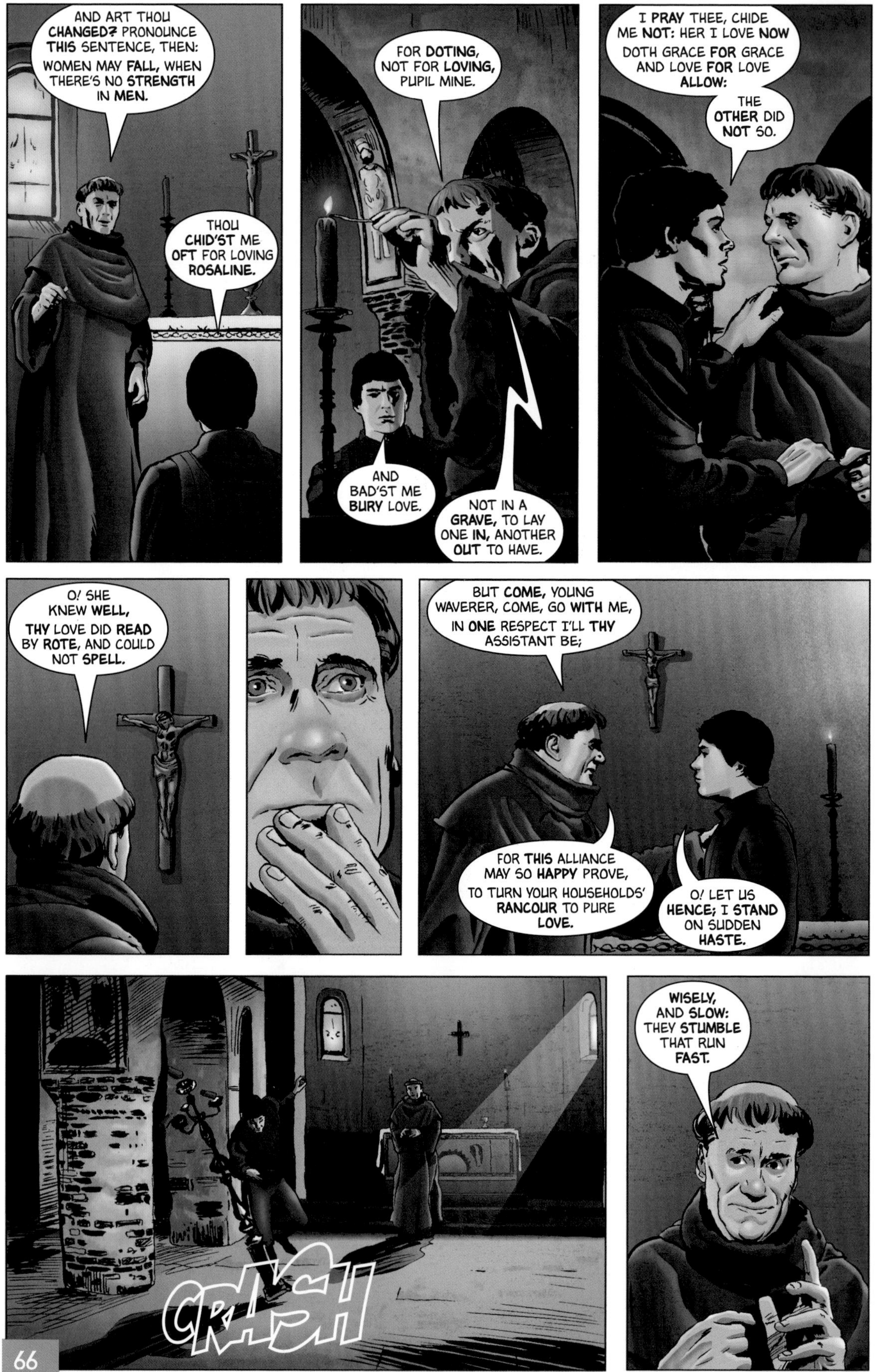
AND ART THOU CHANGED? PRONOUNCE THIS SENTENCE, THEN: WOMEN MAY FALL, WHEN THERE'S NO STRENGTH IN MEN.
THOU CHID'ST ME OFT FOR LOVING ROSALINE.
FOR DOTING, NOT FOR LOVING, PUPIL MINE.
AND BAD'ST ME BURY LOVE.
NOT IN A GRAVE, TO LAY ONE IN, ANOTHER OUT TO HAVE.
I PRAY THEE, CHIDE ME NOT: HER I LOVE NOW DOTH GRACE FOR GRACE AND LOVE FOR LOVE ALLOW:
THE OTHER DID NOT SO.
O! SHE KNEW WELL, THY LOVE DID READ BY ROTE, AND COULD NOT SPELL.
BUT COME, YOUNG WAVERER, COME, GO WITH ME, IN ONE RESPECT I'LL THY ASSISTANT BE;
FOR THIS ALLIANCE MAY SO HAPPY PROVE, TO TURN YOUR HOUSEHOLDS' RANCOUR TO PURE LOVE.
O! LET US HENCE; I STAND ON SUDDEN HASTE.
CRASH
WISELY, AND SLOW: THEY STUMBLE THAT RUN FAST.

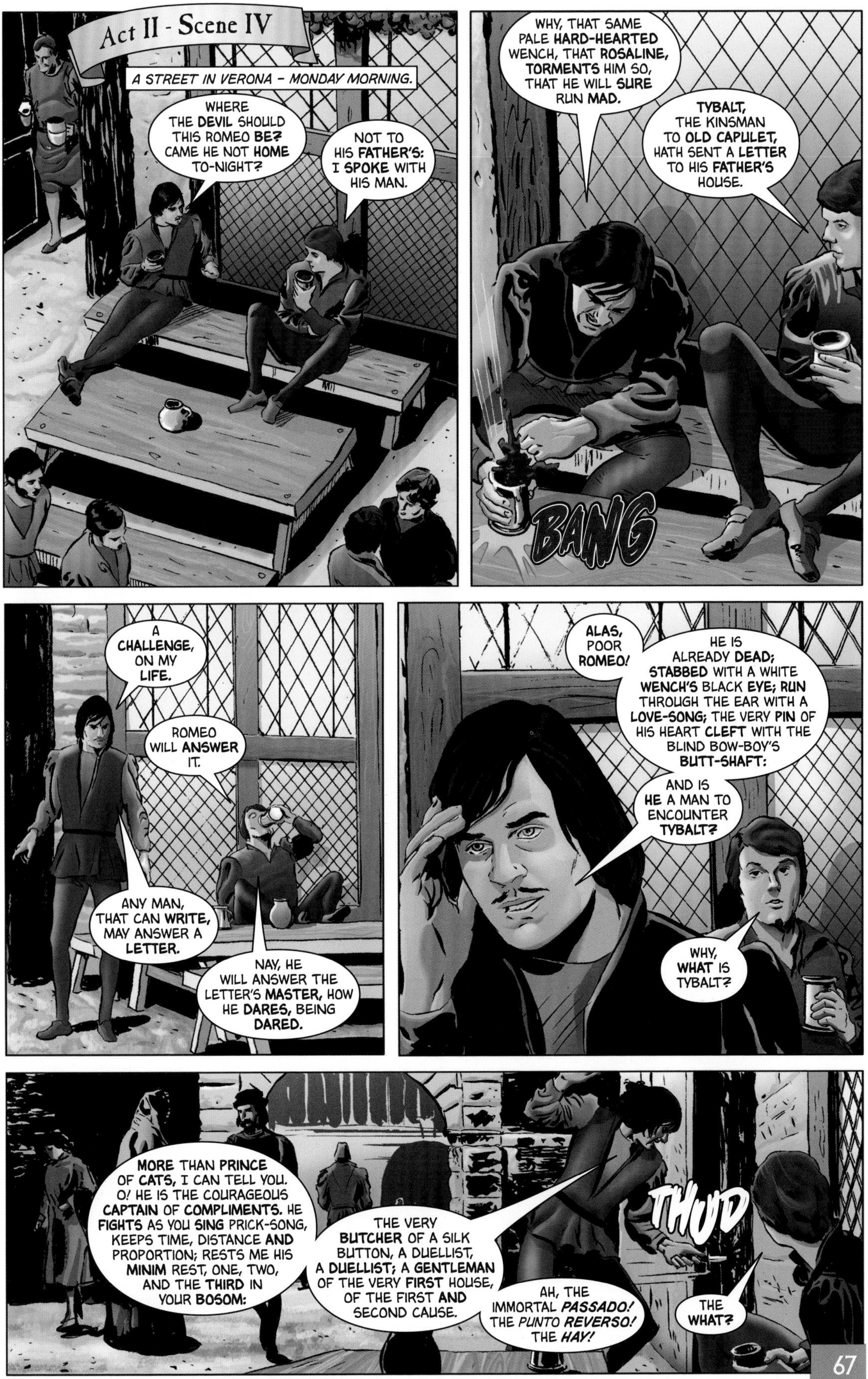
Act II - Scene IV
A STREET IN VERONA - MONDAY MORNING.
WHERE THE DEVIL SHOULD THIS ROMEO BE? CAME HE NOT HOME TO-NIGHT?
NOT TO HIS FATHER'S: I SPOKE WITH HIS MAN.
WHY, THAT SAME PALE HARD-HEARTED WENCH, THAT ROSALINE, TORMENTS HIM SO, THAT HE WILL SURE RUN MAD.
TYBALT, THE KINSMAN TO OLD CAPULET, HATH SENT A LETTER TO HIS FATHER'S HOUSE.
BANG
A CHALLENGE, ON MY LIFE.
ROMEO WILL ANSWER IT.
ANY MAN, THAT CAN WRITE, MAY ANSWER A LETTER.
NAY, HE WILL ANSWER THE LETTER'S MASTER, HOW HE DARES, BEING DARED.
ALAS, POOR ROMEO!
HE IS ALREADY DEAD; STABBED WITH A WHITE WENCH'S BLACK EYE; RUN THROUGH THE EAR WITH A LOVE-SONG; THE VERY PIN OF HIS HEART CLEFT WITH THE BLIND BOW-BOY'S BUTT-SHAFT:
AND IS HE A MAN TO ENCOUNTER TYBALT?
WHY, WHAT IS TYBALT?
MORE THAN PRINCE OF CATS, I CAN TELL YOU. O! HE IS THE COURAGEOUS CAPTAIN OF COMPLIMENTS. HE FIGHTS AS YOU SING PRICK-SONG, KEEPS TIME, DISTANCE AND PROPORTION; RESTS ME HIS MINIM REST, ONE, TWO, AND THE THIRD IN YOUR BOSOM:
THE VERY BUTCHER OF A SILK BUTTON, A DUELLIST, A DUELLIST; A GENTLEMAN OF THE VERY FIRST HOUSE, OF THE FIRST AND SECOND CAUSE.
THUD
AH, THE IMMORTAL *PASSADO!* THE *PUNTO REVERSO!* THE *HAY!*
THE WHAT?

THE POX OF SUCH ANTIC, LISPING, AFFECTING FANTASTICOES;

THESE NEW TUNERS OF ACCENTS! "BY JESU, A *VERY* GOOD BLADE! A *VERY* TALL MAN! A *VERY* GOOD WHORE!"

WHY, IS NOT THIS A LAMENTABLE THING, GRANDSIRE, THAT WE SHOULD BE THUS AFFLICTED WITH THESE STRANGE FLIES, THESE FASHION-MONGERS, THESE *PARDONNEZ-MOIS*,

WHO STAND SO MUCH ON THE NEW FORM, THAT THEY CANNOT SIT AT EASE ON THE OLD BENCH?

O, THEIR BONES, THEIR BONES!

HERE COMES ROMEO, HERE COMES ROMEO.

WITHOUT HIS ROE, LIKE A DRIED HERRING. O FLESH, FLESH, HOW ART THOU FISHIFIED!

NOW IS HE FOR THE NUMBERS THAT PETRARCH FLOWED IN: LAURA, TO HIS LADY, WAS BUT A KITCHEN-WENCH;

MARRY, SHE HAD A BETTER LOVE TO BE-RHYME HER; DIDO, A DOWDY; CLEOPATRA, A GIPSY; HELEN AND HERO, HILDINGS AND HARLOTS; THISBE, A GREY EYE OR SO, BUT NOT TO THE PURPOSE.

SIGNIOR ROMEO, BON JOUR! THERE'S A FRENCH SALUTATION TO YOUR FRENCH SLOP. YOU GAVE US THE COUNTERFEIT FAIRLY LAST NIGHT.

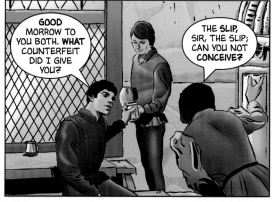

GOOD MORROW TO YOU BOTH. WHAT COUNTERFEIT DID I GIVE YOU?

THE SLIP, SIR, THE SLIP; CAN YOU NOT CONCEIVE?

PARDON, GOOD MERCUTIO, MY BUSINESS WAS GREAT; AND IN SUCH A CASE AS MINE, A MAN MAY STRAIN COURTESY.

THAT'S AS MUCH AS TO SAY, SUCH A CASE AS YOURS CONSTRAINS A MAN TO BOW IN THE HAMS.

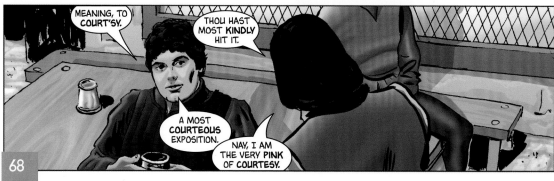

MEANING, TO COURT'SY.

THOU HAST MOST KINDLY HIT IT.

A MOST COURTEOUS EXPOSITION.

NAY, I AM THE VERY PINK OF COURTESY.

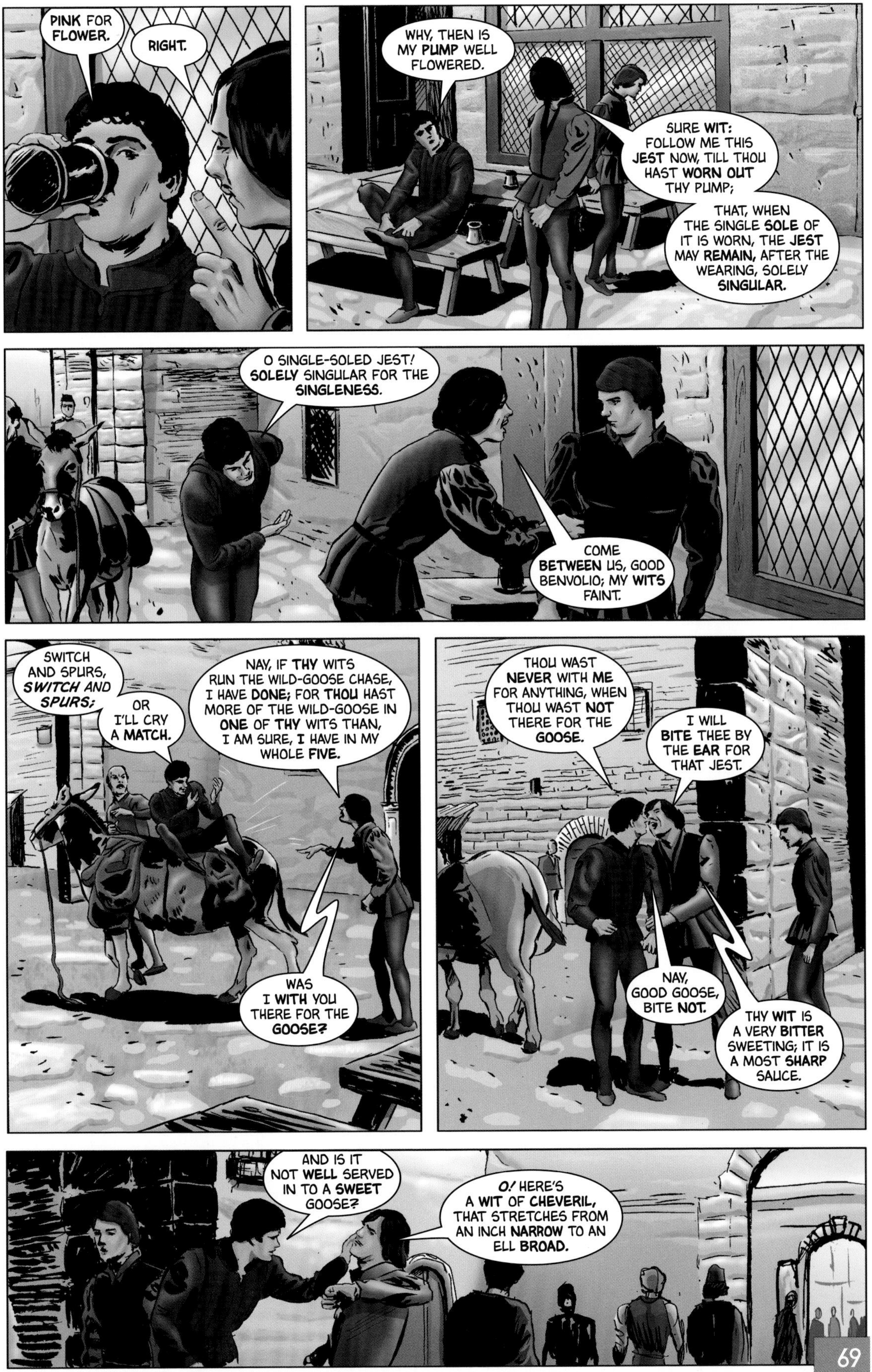
PINK FOR FLOWER.
RIGHT.
WHY, THEN IS MY PUMP WELL FLOWERED.
SURE WIT: FOLLOW ME THIS JEST NOW, TILL THOU HAST WORN OUT THY PUMP;
THAT, WHEN THE SINGLE SOLE OF IT IS WORN, THE JEST MAY REMAIN, AFTER THE WEARING, SOLELY SINGULAR.
O SINGLE-SOLED JEST! SOLELY SINGULAR FOR THE SINGLENESS.
COME BETWEEN US, GOOD BENVOLIO; MY WITS FAINT.
SWITCH AND SPURS, SWITCH AND SPURS;
OR I'LL CRY A MATCH.
NAY, IF THY WITS RUN THE WILD-GOOSE CHASE, I HAVE DONE; FOR THOU HAST MORE OF THE WILD-GOOSE IN ONE OF THY WITS THAN, I AM SURE, I HAVE IN MY WHOLE FIVE.
WAS I WITH YOU THERE FOR THE GOOSE?
THOU WAST NEVER WITH ME FOR ANYTHING, WHEN THOU WAST NOT THERE FOR THE GOOSE.
I WILL BITE THEE BY THE EAR FOR THAT JEST.
NAY, GOOD GOOSE, BITE NOT.
THY WIT IS A VERY BITTER SWEETING; IT IS A MOST SHARP SAUCE.
AND IS IT NOT WELL SERVED IN TO A SWEET GOOSE?
O! HERE'S A WIT OF CHEVERIL, THAT STRETCHES FROM AN INCH NARROW TO AN ELL BROAD.

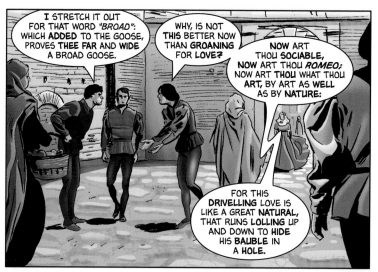

I STRETCH IT OUT FOR THAT WORD *"BROAD"*: WHICH **ADDED** TO THE GOOSE, PROVES **THEE** FAR AND **WIDE** A BROAD GOOSE.

WHY, IS NOT **THIS** BETTER NOW THAN **GROANING** FOR **LOVE**?

NOW ART THOU **SOCIABLE**, NOW ART THOU *ROMEO*; NOW ART THOU WHAT THOU **ART**, BY ART AS WELL AS BY **NATURE**:

FOR THIS **DRIVELLING** LOVE IS LIKE A GREAT **NATURAL**, THAT RUNS **LOLLING** UP AND DOWN TO HIDE HIS **BAUBLE** IN A HOLE.

STOP THERE, *STOP THERE.*

THOU **DESIREST** ME TO **STOP** IN MY TALE AGAINST THE **HAIR**.

THOU **WOULDST ELSE** HAVE MADE THY TALE **LARGE**.

O, THOU ART **DECEIVED**; I WOULD HAVE MADE IT **SHORT**: FOR I WAS **COME** TO THE WHOLE **DEPTH** OF MY TALE AND **MEANT**, INDEED, TO **OCCUPY** THE **ARGUMENT** NO **LONGER**.

HERE'S **GOODLY** GEAR!

A **SAIL**, A **SAIL**!

TWO, **TWO**; A **SHIRT AND** A SMOCK.

PETER!

ANON?

MY **FAN**, PETER.

GOOD PETER, TO HIDE HER **FACE**; FOR HER **FAN'S** THE **FAIRER** FACE.

GOD YE **GOOD** MORROW, GENTLEMEN.

GOD YE **GOOD DEN**, FAIR **GENTLEWOMAN**.

IS IT **GOOD DEN**?

'TIS NO **LESS**, I TELL YOU; FOR THE **BAWDY HAND** OF THE **DIAL** IS NOW UPON THE **PRICK** OF NOON.

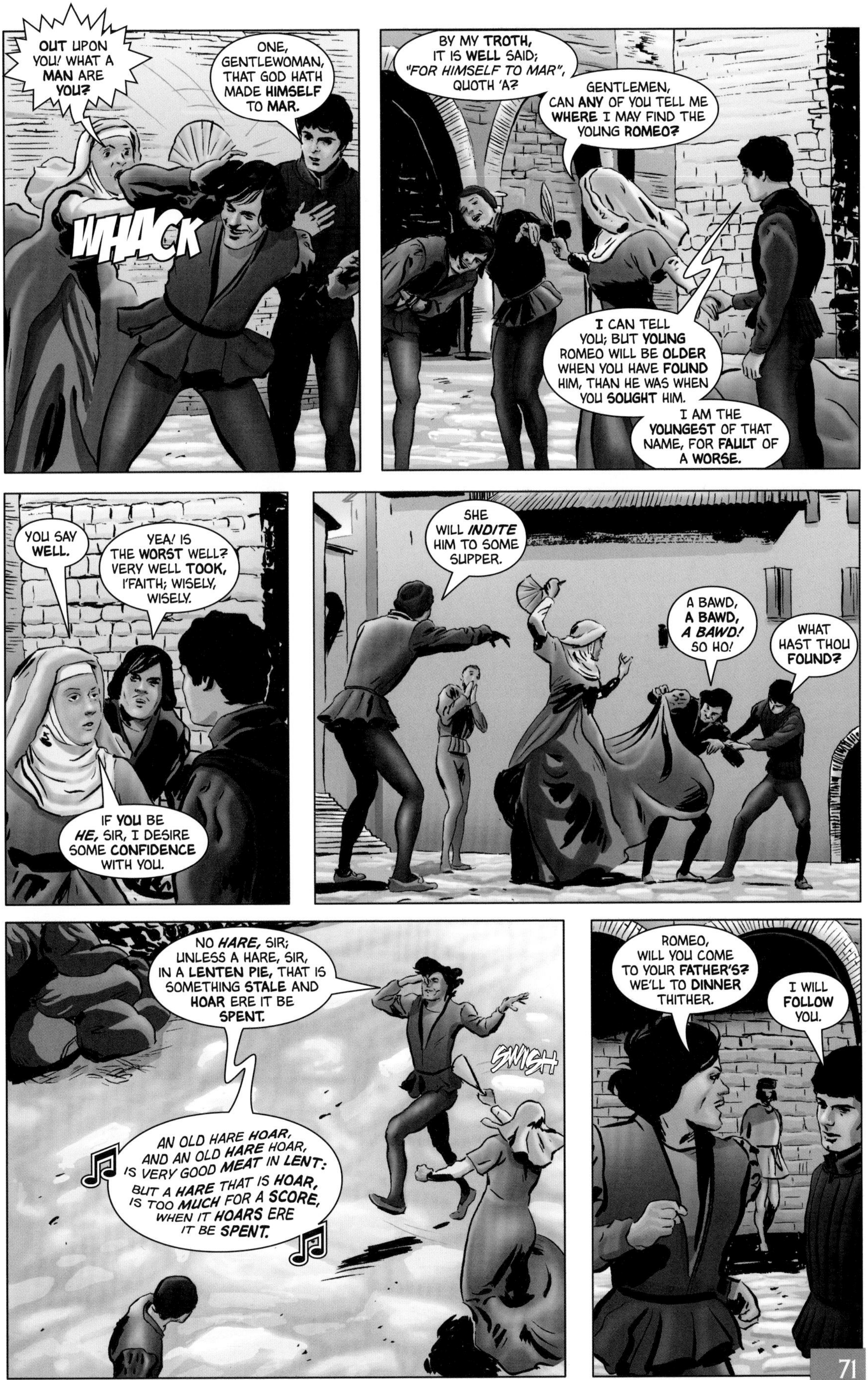
OUT UPON YOU! WHAT A MAN ARE YOU?
ONE, GENTLEWOMAN, THAT GOD HATH MADE HIMSELF TO MAR.
WHACK
BY MY TROTH, IT IS WELL SAID; "FOR HIMSELF TO MAR", QUOTH 'A?
GENTLEMEN, CAN ANY OF YOU TELL ME WHERE I MAY FIND THE YOUNG ROMEO?
I CAN TELL YOU; BUT YOUNG ROMEO WILL BE OLDER WHEN YOU HAVE FOUND HIM, THAN HE WAS WHEN YOU SOUGHT HIM.
I AM THE YOUNGEST OF THAT NAME, FOR FAULT OF A WORSE.
YOU SAY WELL.
YEA! IS THE WORST WELL? VERY WELL TOOK, I'FAITH; WISELY, WISELY.
IF YOU BE HE, SIR, I DESIRE SOME CONFIDENCE WITH YOU.
SHE WILL INDITE HIM TO SOME SUPPER.
A BAWD, A BAWD, A BAWD! SO HO!
WHAT HAST THOU FOUND?
NO HARE, SIR; UNLESS A HARE, SIR, IN A LENTEN PIE, THAT IS SOMETHING STALE AND HOAR ERE IT BE SPENT.
SWISH
AN OLD HARE HOAR, AND AN OLD HARE HOAR, IS VERY GOOD MEAT IN LENT: BUT A HARE THAT IS HOAR, IS TOO MUCH FOR A SCORE, WHEN IT HOARS ERE IT BE SPENT.
ROMEO, WILL YOU COME TO YOUR FATHER'S? WE'LL TO DINNER THITHER.
I WILL FOLLOW YOU.

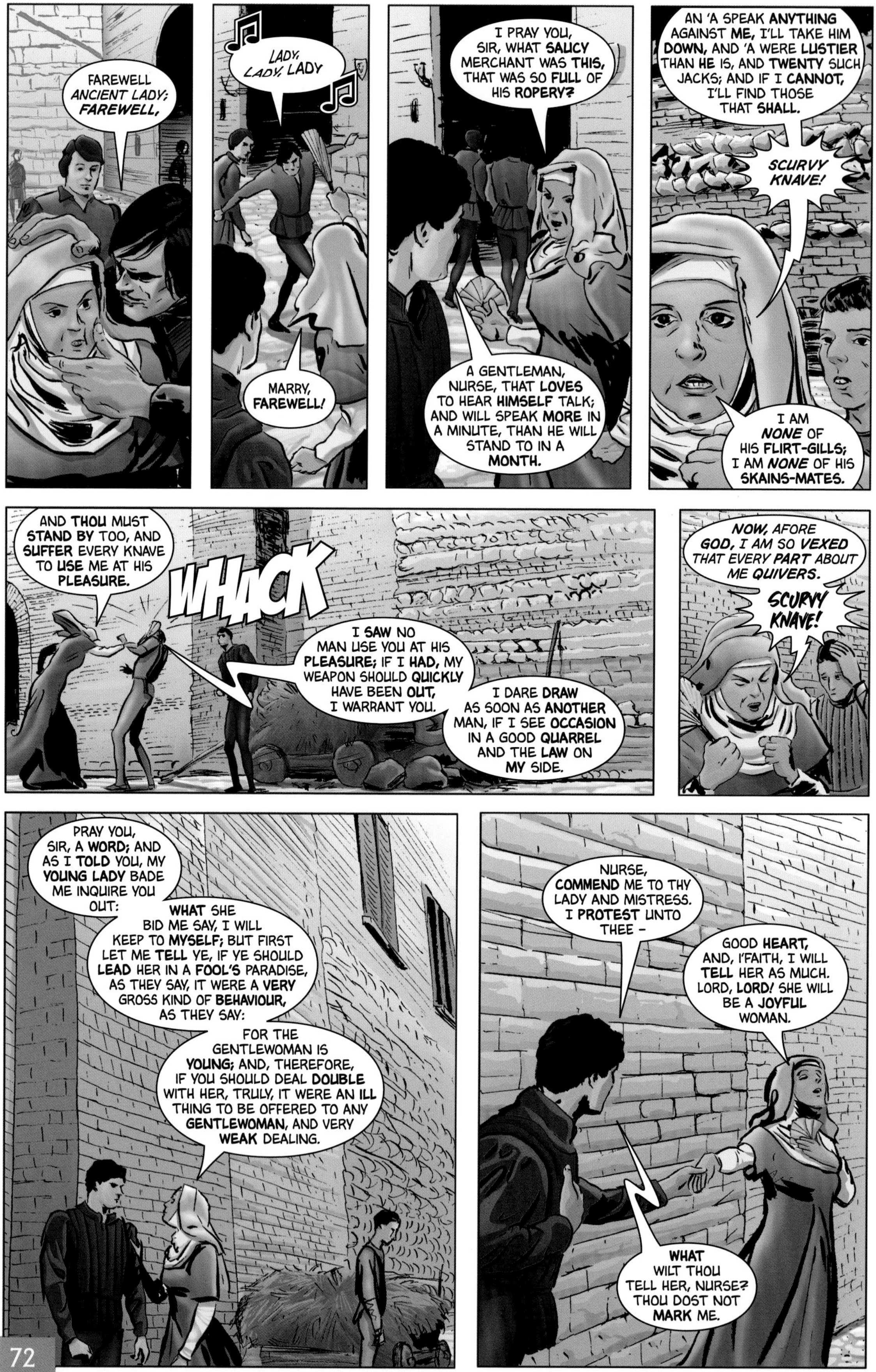
FAREWELL ANCIENT LADY; FAREWELL,
LADY, LADY, LADY
MARRY, FAREWELL!
I PRAY YOU, SIR, WHAT SAUCY MERCHANT WAS THIS, THAT WAS SO FULL OF HIS ROPERY?
A GENTLEMAN, NURSE, THAT LOVES TO HEAR HIMSELF TALK; AND WILL SPEAK MORE IN A MINUTE, THAN HE WILL STAND TO IN A MONTH.
AN 'A SPEAK ANYTHING AGAINST ME, I'LL TAKE HIM DOWN, AND 'A WERE LUSTIER THAN HE IS, AND TWENTY SUCH JACKS; AND IF I CANNOT, I'LL FIND THOSE THAT SHALL.
SCURVY KNAVE!
I AM NONE OF HIS FLIRT-GILLS; I AM NONE OF HIS SKAINS-MATES.
AND THOU MUST STAND BY TOO, AND SUFFER EVERY KNAVE TO USE ME AT HIS PLEASURE.
WHACK
I SAW NO MAN USE YOU AT HIS PLEASURE; IF I HAD, MY WEAPON SHOULD QUICKLY HAVE BEEN OUT, I WARRANT YOU.
I DARE DRAW AS SOON AS ANOTHER MAN, IF I SEE OCCASION IN A GOOD QUARREL AND THE LAW ON MY SIDE.
NOW, AFORE GOD, I AM SO VEXED THAT EVERY PART ABOUT ME QUIVERS.
SCURVY KNAVE!
PRAY YOU, SIR, A WORD; AND AS I TOLD YOU, MY YOUNG LADY BADE ME INQUIRE YOU OUT:
WHAT SHE BID ME SAY, I WILL KEEP TO MYSELF; BUT FIRST LET ME TELL YE, IF YE SHOULD LEAD HER IN A FOOL'S PARADISE, AS THEY SAY, IT WERE A VERY GROSS KIND OF BEHAVIOUR, AS THEY SAY:
FOR THE GENTLEWOMAN IS YOUNG; AND, THEREFORE, IF YOU SHOULD DEAL DOUBLE WITH HER, TRULY, IT WERE AN ILL THING TO BE OFFERED TO ANY GENTLEWOMAN, AND VERY WEAK DEALING.
NURSE, COMMEND ME TO THY LADY AND MISTRESS. I PROTEST UNTO THEE –
GOOD HEART, AND, I'FAITH, I WILL TELL HER AS MUCH. LORD, LORD! SHE WILL BE A JOYFUL WOMAN.
WHAT WILT THOU TELL HER, NURSE? THOU DOST NOT MARK ME.

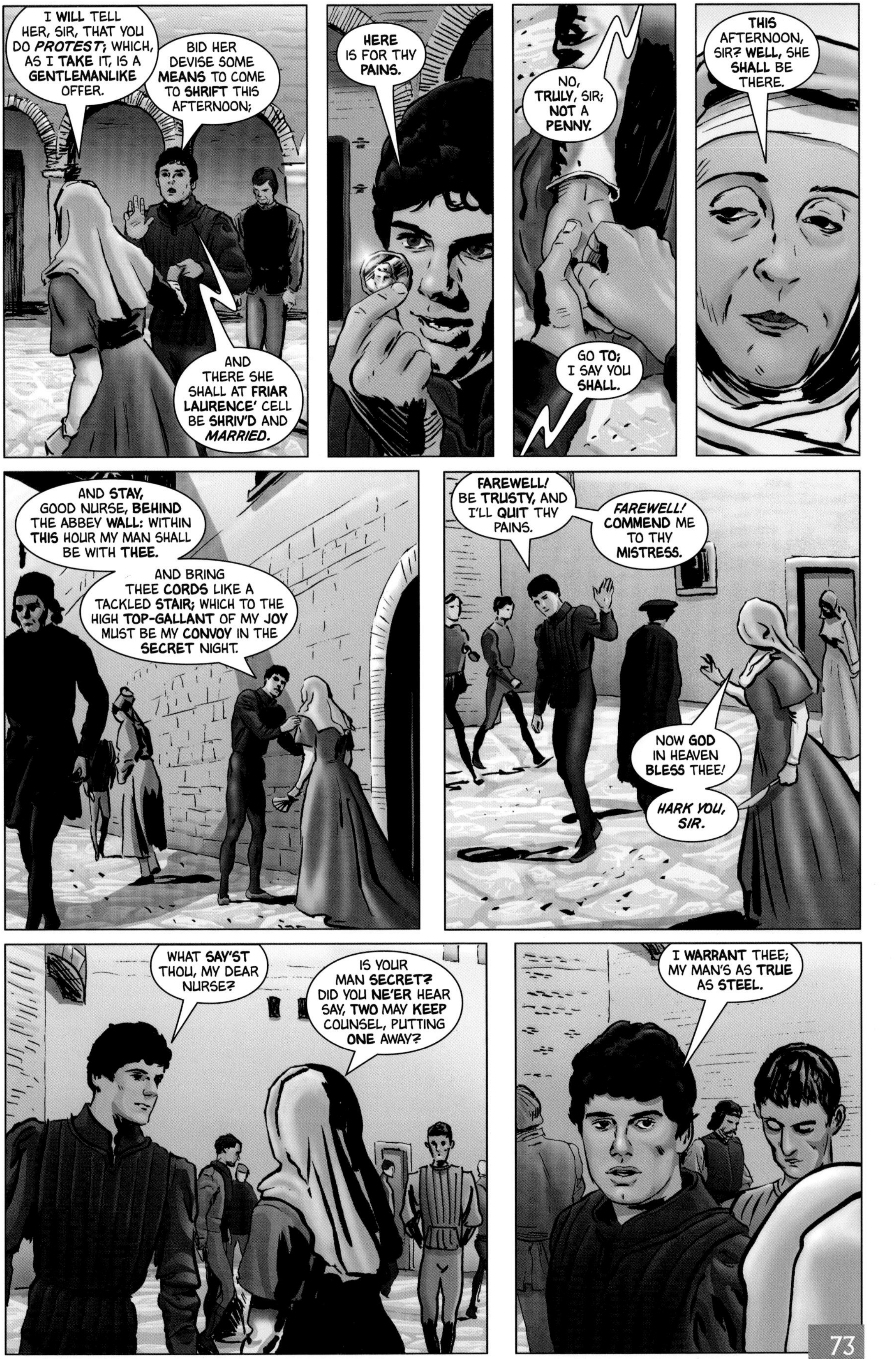
I WILL TELL HER, SIR, THAT YOU DO PROTEST; WHICH, AS I TAKE IT, IS A GENTLEMANLIKE OFFER.
BID HER DEVISE SOME MEANS TO COME TO SHRIFT THIS AFTERNOON;
AND THERE SHE SHALL AT FRIAR LAURENCE' CELL BE SHRIV'D AND MARRIED.
HERE IS FOR THY PAINS.
NO, TRULY, SIR; NOT A PENNY.
GO TO; I SAY YOU SHALL.
THIS AFTERNOON, SIR? WELL, SHE SHALL BE THERE.
AND STAY, GOOD NURSE, BEHIND THE ABBEY WALL: WITHIN THIS HOUR MY MAN SHALL BE WITH THEE.
AND BRING THEE CORDS LIKE A TACKLED STAIR; WHICH TO THE HIGH TOP-GALLANT OF MY JOY MUST BE MY CONVOY IN THE SECRET NIGHT.
FAREWELL! BE TRUSTY, AND I'LL QUIT THY PAINS.
FAREWELL! COMMEND ME TO THY MISTRESS.
NOW GOD IN HEAVEN BLESS THEE!
HARK YOU, SIR.
WHAT SAY'ST THOU, MY DEAR NURSE?
IS YOUR MAN SECRET? DID YOU NE'ER HEAR SAY, TWO MAY KEEP COUNSEL, PUTTING ONE AWAY?
I WARRANT THEE; MY MAN'S AS TRUE AS STEEL.

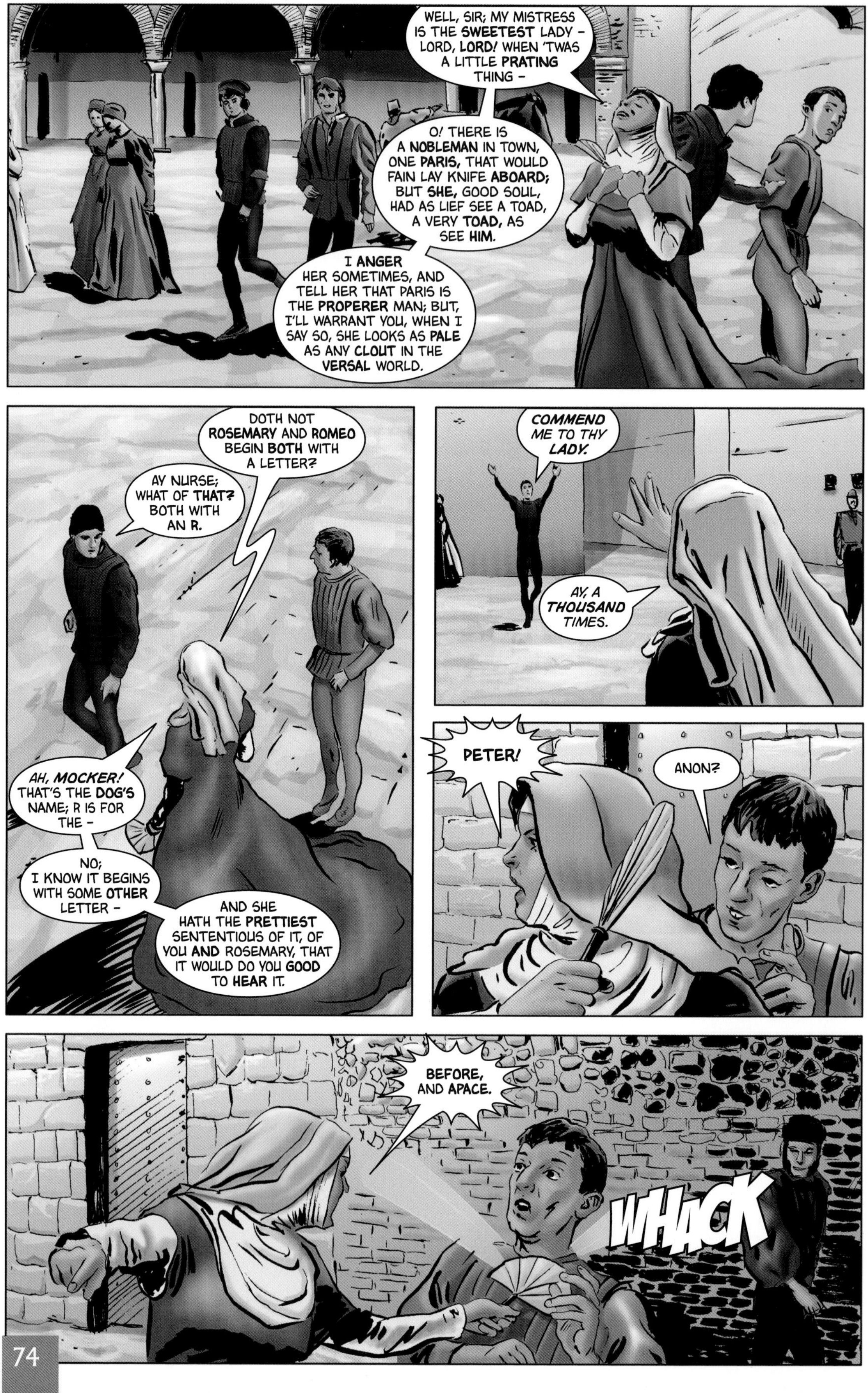
WELL, SIR; MY MISTRESS IS THE SWEETEST LADY – LORD, LORD! WHEN 'TWAS A LITTLE PRATING THING –
O! THERE IS A NOBLEMAN IN TOWN, ONE PARIS, THAT WOULD FAIN LAY KNIFE ABOARD; BUT SHE, GOOD SOUL, HAD AS LIEF SEE A TOAD, A VERY TOAD, AS SEE HIM.
I ANGER HER SOMETIMES, AND TELL HER THAT PARIS IS THE PROPERER MAN; BUT, I'LL WARRANT YOU, WHEN I SAY SO, SHE LOOKS AS PALE AS ANY CLOUT IN THE VERSAL WORLD.
DOTH NOT ROSEMARY AND ROMEO BEGIN BOTH WITH A LETTER?
AY NURSE; WHAT OF THAT? BOTH WITH AN R.
AH, MOCKER! THAT'S THE DOG'S NAME; R IS FOR THE –
NO; I KNOW IT BEGINS WITH SOME OTHER LETTER –
AND SHE HATH THE PRETTIEST SENTENTIOUS OF IT, OF YOU AND ROSEMARY, THAT IT WOULD DO YOU GOOD TO HEAR IT.
COMMEND ME TO THY LADY.
AY, A THOUSAND TIMES.
PETER!
ANON?
BEFORE, AND APACE.
WHACK

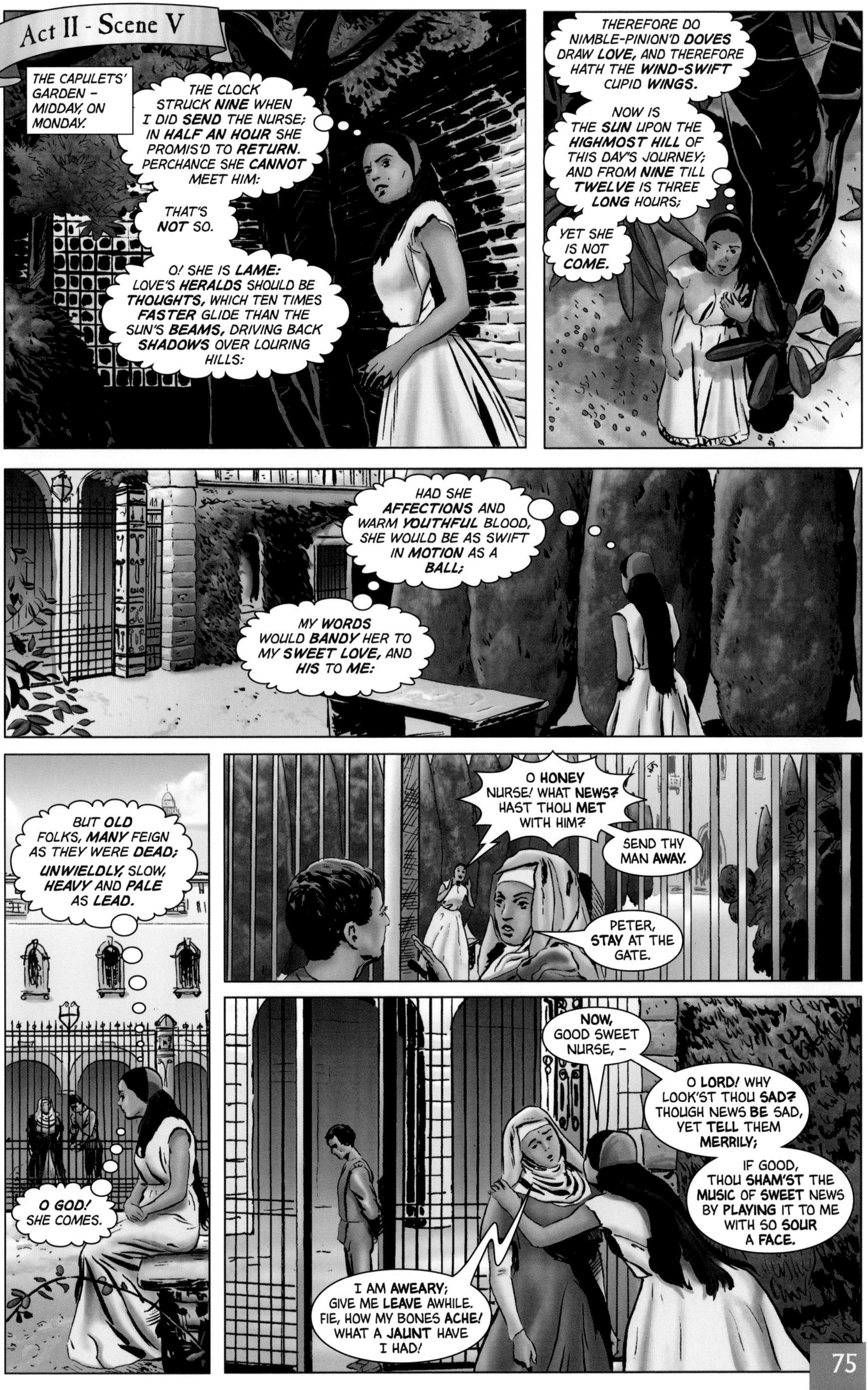
Act II - Scene V
THE CAPULETS' GARDEN – MIDDAY, ON MONDAY.
THE CLOCK STRUCK NINE WHEN I DID SEND THE NURSE; IN HALF AN HOUR SHE PROMIS'D TO RETURN. PERCHANCE SHE CANNOT MEET HIM:
THAT'S NOT SO.
O! SHE IS LAME: LOVE'S HERALDS SHOULD BE THOUGHTS, WHICH TEN TIMES FASTER GLIDE THAN THE SUN'S BEAMS, DRIVING BACK SHADOWS OVER LOURING HILLS:
THEREFORE DO NIMBLE-PINION'D DOVES DRAW LOVE, AND THEREFORE HATH THE WIND-SWIFT CUPID WINGS.
NOW IS THE SUN UPON THE HIGHMOST HILL OF THIS DAY'S JOURNEY; AND FROM NINE TILL TWELVE IS THREE LONG HOURS;
YET SHE IS NOT COME.
HAD SHE AFFECTIONS AND WARM YOUTHFUL BLOOD, SHE WOULD BE AS SWIFT IN MOTION AS A BALL;
MY WORDS WOULD BANDY HER TO MY SWEET LOVE, AND HIS TO ME:
BUT OLD FOLKS, MANY FEIGN AS THEY WERE DEAD; UNWIELDLY, SLOW, HEAVY AND PALE AS LEAD.
O GOD! SHE COMES.
O HONEY NURSE! WHAT NEWS? HAST THOU MET WITH HIM?
SEND THY MAN AWAY.
PETER, STAY AT THE GATE.
NOW, GOOD SWEET NURSE, –
O LORD! WHY LOOK'ST THOU SAD? THOUGH NEWS BE SAD, YET TELL THEM MERRILY;
IF GOOD, THOU SHAM'ST THE MUSIC OF SWEET NEWS BY PLAYING IT TO ME WITH SO SOUR A FACE.
I AM AWEARY; GIVE ME LEAVE AWHILE. FIE, HOW MY BONES ACHE! WHAT A JAUNT HAVE I HAD!

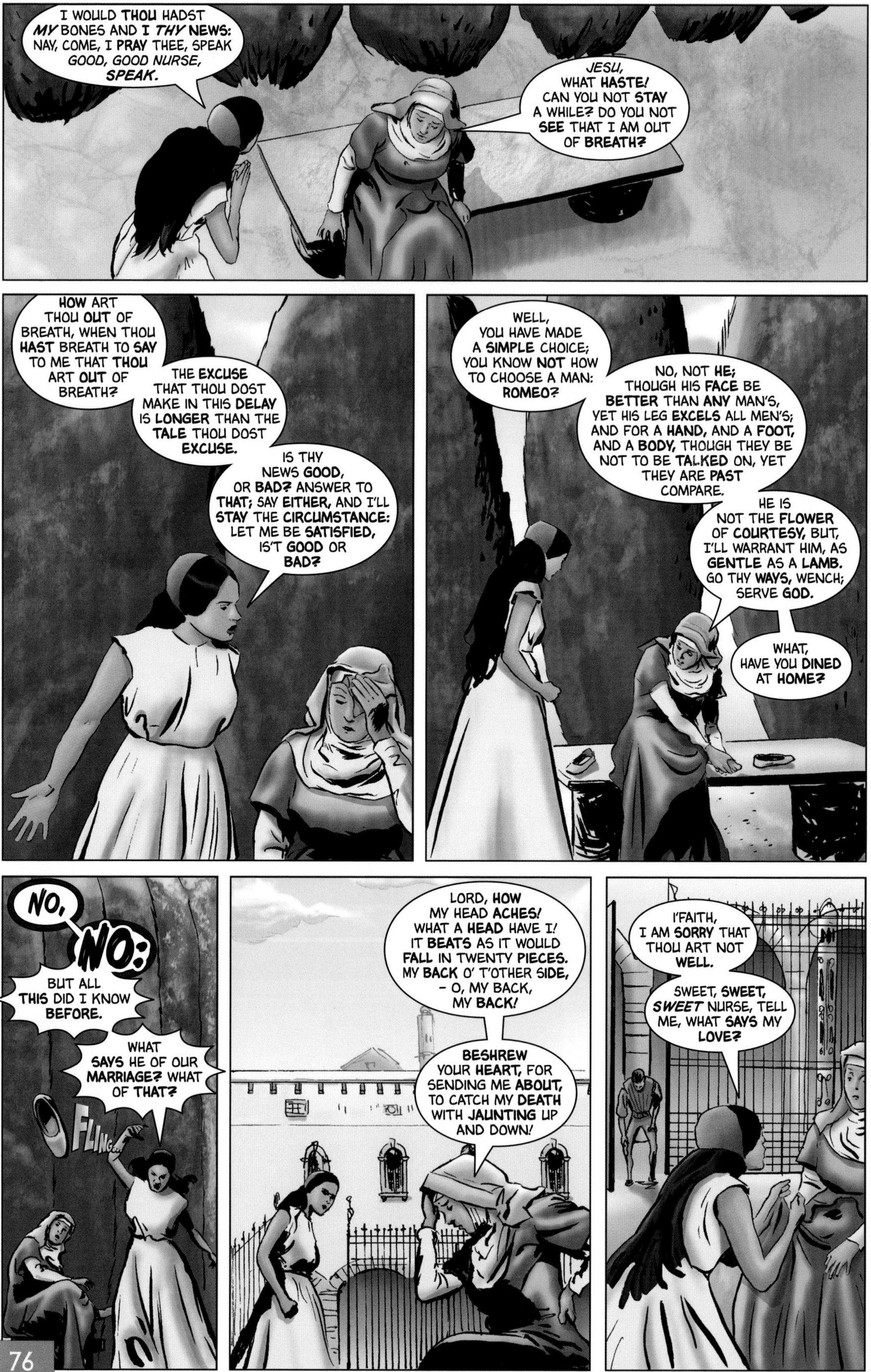
I WOULD THOU HADST MY BONES AND I THY NEWS: NAY, COME, I PRAY THEE, SPEAK GOOD, GOOD NURSE, SPEAK.
JESU, WHAT HASTE! CAN YOU NOT STAY A WHILE? DO YOU NOT SEE THAT I AM OUT OF BREATH?
HOW ART THOU OUT OF BREATH, WHEN THOU HAST BREATH TO SAY TO ME THAT THOU ART OUT OF BREATH?
THE EXCUSE THAT THOU DOST MAKE IN THIS DELAY IS LONGER THAN THE TALE THOU DOST EXCUSE.
IS THY NEWS GOOD, OR BAD? ANSWER TO THAT; SAY EITHER, AND I'LL STAY THE CIRCUMSTANCE: LET ME BE SATISFIED, IS'T GOOD OR BAD?
WELL, YOU HAVE MADE A SIMPLE CHOICE; YOU KNOW NOT HOW TO CHOOSE A MAN: ROMEO?
NO, NOT HE; THOUGH HIS FACE BE BETTER THAN ANY MAN'S, YET HIS LEG EXCELS ALL MEN'S; AND FOR A HAND, AND A FOOT, AND A BODY, THOUGH THEY BE NOT TO BE TALKED ON, YET THEY ARE PAST COMPARE.
HE IS NOT THE FLOWER OF COURTESY, BUT, I'LL WARRANT HIM, AS GENTLE AS A LAMB. GO THY WAYS, WENCH; SERVE GOD.
WHAT, HAVE YOU DINED AT HOME?
NO, NO:
BUT ALL THIS DID I KNOW BEFORE.
WHAT SAYS HE OF OUR MARRIAGE? WHAT OF THAT?
FLING...
LORD, HOW MY HEAD ACHES! WHAT A HEAD HAVE I! IT BEATS AS IT WOULD FALL IN TWENTY PIECES. MY BACK O' T'OTHER SIDE, – O, MY BACK, MY BACK!
BESHREW YOUR HEART, FOR SENDING ME ABOUT, TO CATCH MY DEATH WITH JAUNTING UP AND DOWN!
I'FAITH, I AM SORRY THAT THOU ART NOT WELL.
SWEET, SWEET, SWEET NURSE, TELL ME, WHAT SAYS MY LOVE?

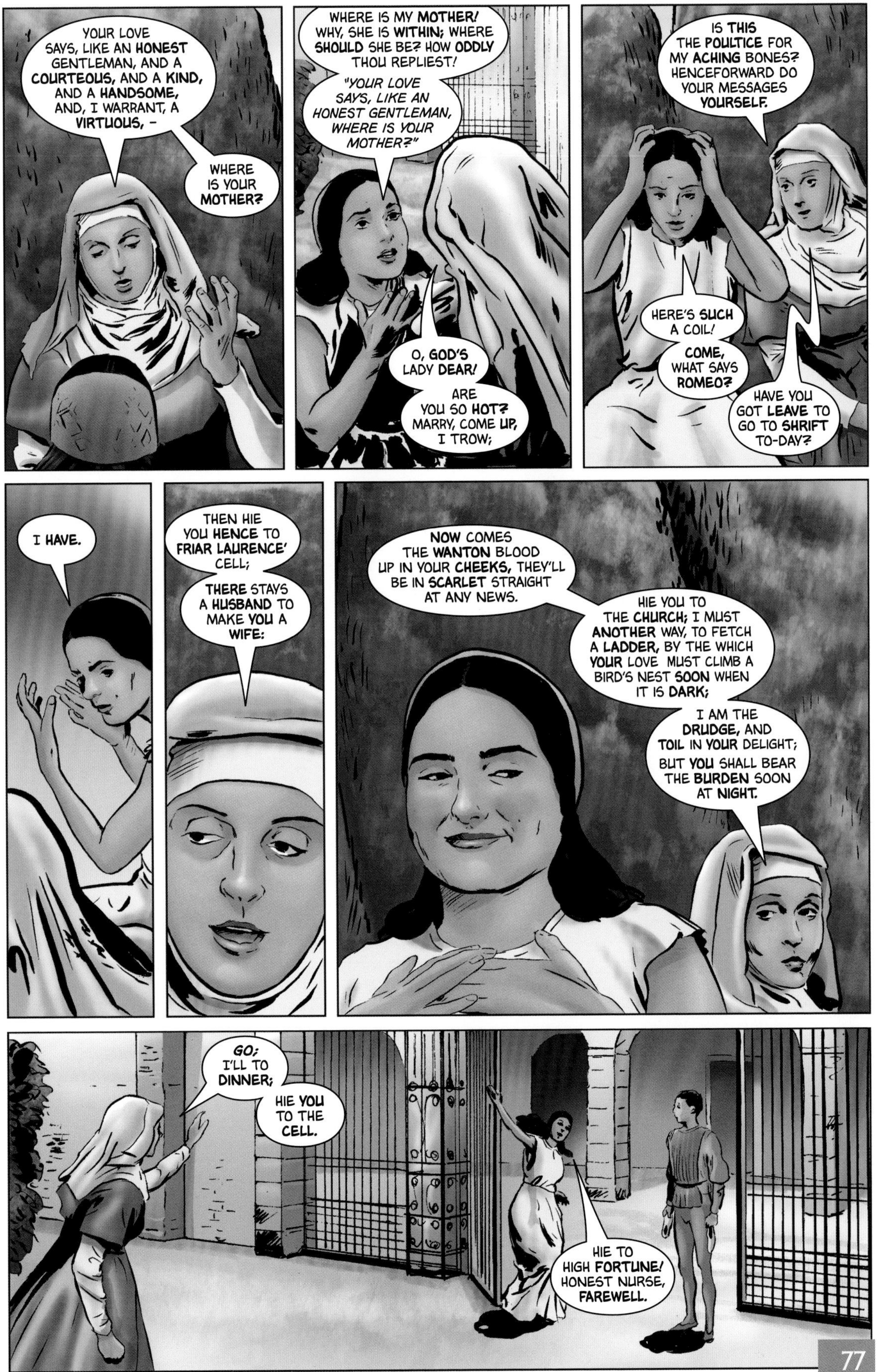
YOUR LOVE SAYS, LIKE AN HONEST GENTLEMAN, AND A COURTEOUS, AND A KIND, AND A HANDSOME, AND, I WARRANT, A VIRTUOUS, –
WHERE IS YOUR MOTHER?
WHERE IS MY MOTHER! WHY, SHE IS WITHIN; WHERE SHOULD SHE BE? HOW ODDLY THOU REPLIEST!
"YOUR LOVE SAYS, LIKE AN HONEST GENTLEMAN, WHERE IS YOUR MOTHER?"
O, GOD'S LADY DEAR!
ARE YOU SO HOT? MARRY, COME UP, I TROW;
IS THIS THE POULTICE FOR MY ACHING BONES? HENCEFORWARD DO YOUR MESSAGES YOURSELF.
HERE'S SUCH A COIL!
COME, WHAT SAYS ROMEO?
HAVE YOU GOT LEAVE TO GO TO SHRIFT TO-DAY?
I HAVE.
THEN HIE YOU HENCE TO FRIAR LAURENCE' CELL;
THERE STAYS A HUSBAND TO MAKE YOU A WIFE:
NOW COMES THE WANTON BLOOD UP IN YOUR CHEEKS, THEY'LL BE IN SCARLET STRAIGHT AT ANY NEWS.
HIE YOU TO THE CHURCH; I MUST ANOTHER WAY, TO FETCH A LADDER, BY THE WHICH YOUR LOVE MUST CLIMB A BIRD'S NEST SOON WHEN IT IS DARK;
I AM THE DRUDGE, AND TOIL IN YOUR DELIGHT;
BUT YOU SHALL BEAR THE BURDEN SOON AT NIGHT.
GO; I'LL TO DINNER;
HIE YOU TO THE CELL.
HIE TO HIGH FORTUNE! HONEST NURSE, FAREWELL.

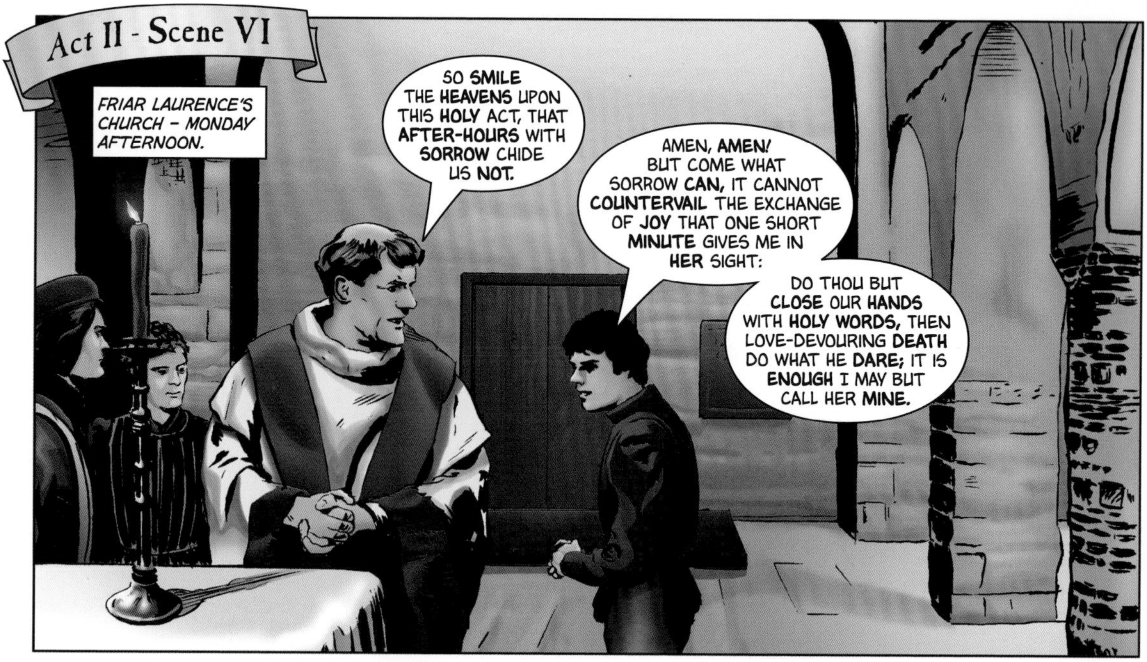
Act II - Scene VI
FRIAR LAURENCE'S CHURCH – MONDAY AFTERNOON.
SO SMILE THE HEAVENS UPON THIS HOLY ACT, THAT AFTER-HOURS WITH SORROW CHIDE US NOT.
AMEN, AMEN! BUT COME WHAT SORROW CAN, IT CANNOT COUNTERVAIL THE EXCHANGE OF JOY THAT ONE SHORT MINUTE GIVES ME IN HER SIGHT:
DO THOU BUT CLOSE OUR HANDS WITH HOLY WORDS, THEN LOVE-DEVOURING DEATH DO WHAT HE DARE; IT IS ENOUGH I MAY BUT CALL HER MINE.

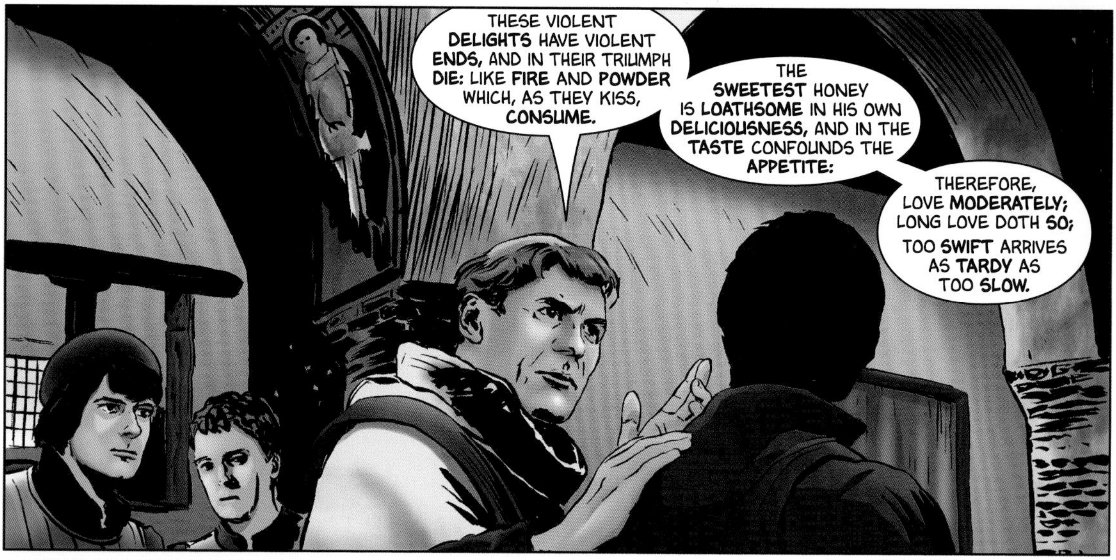
THESE VIOLENT DELIGHTS HAVE VIOLENT ENDS, AND IN THEIR TRIUMPH DIE: LIKE FIRE AND POWDER WHICH, AS THEY KISS, CONSUME.
THE SWEETEST HONEY IS LOATHSOME IN HIS OWN DELICIOUSNESS, AND IN THE TASTE CONFOUNDS THE APPETITE:
THEREFORE, LOVE MODERATELY; LONG LOVE DOTH SO;
TOO SWIFT ARRIVES AS TARDY AS TOO SLOW.

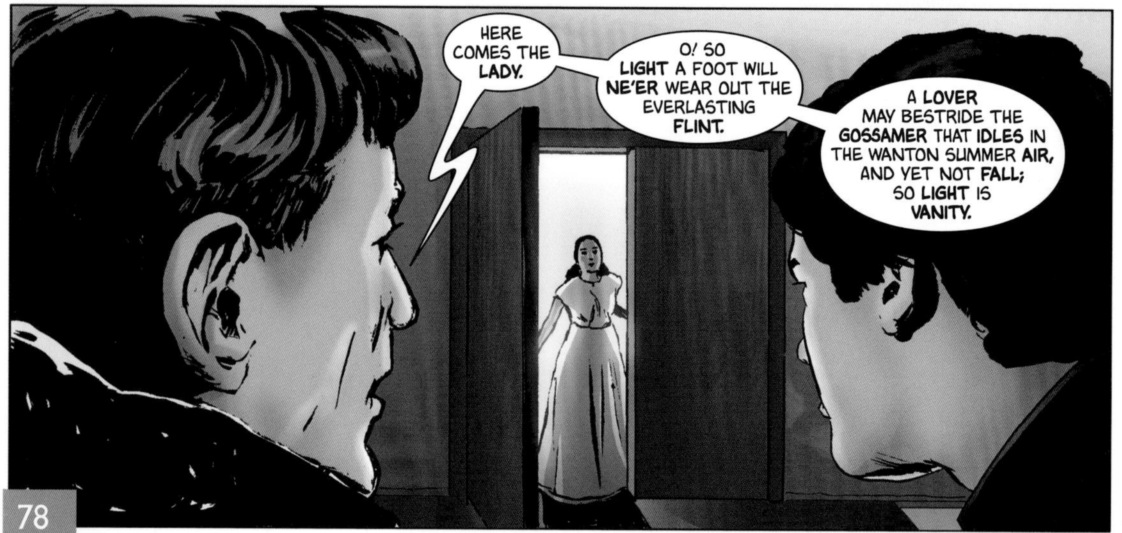
HERE COMES THE LADY.
O! SO LIGHT A FOOT WILL NE'ER WEAR OUT THE EVERLASTING FLINT.
A LOVER MAY BESTRIDE THE GOSSAMER THAT IDLES IN THE WANTON SUMMER AIR, AND YET NOT FALL; SO LIGHT IS VANITY.

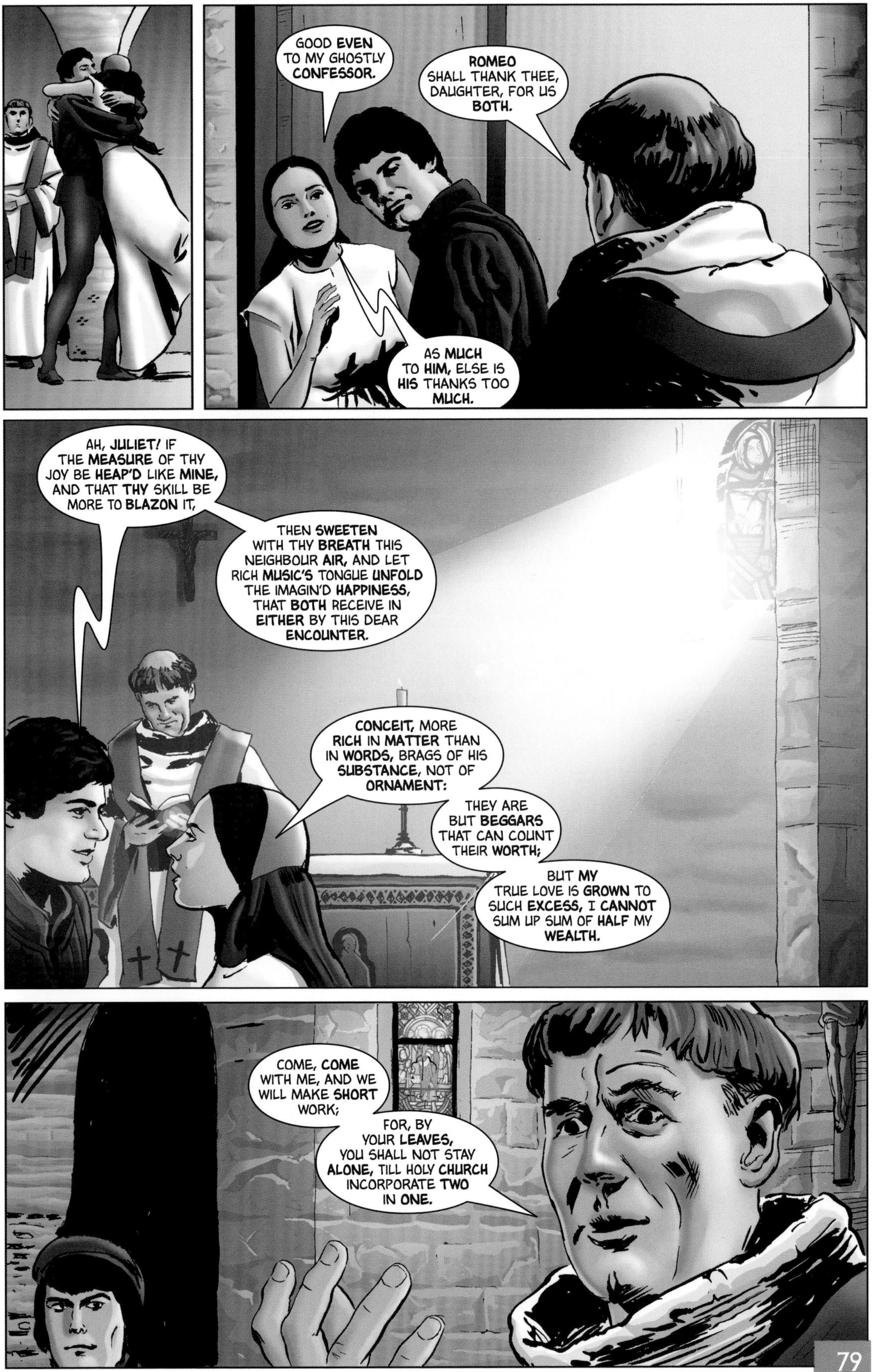
GOOD EVEN TO MY GHOSTLY CONFESSOR.
ROMEO SHALL THANK THEE, DAUGHTER, FOR US BOTH.
AS MUCH TO HIM, ELSE IS HIS THANKS TOO MUCH.
AH, JULIET! IF THE MEASURE OF THY JOY BE HEAP'D LIKE MINE, AND THAT THY SKILL BE MORE TO BLAZON IT,
THEN SWEETEN WITH THY BREATH THIS NEIGHBOUR AIR, AND LET RICH MUSIC'S TONGUE UNFOLD THE IMAGIN'D HAPPINESS, THAT BOTH RECEIVE IN EITHER BY THIS DEAR ENCOUNTER.
CONCEIT, MORE RICH IN MATTER THAN IN WORDS, BRAGS OF HIS SUBSTANCE, NOT OF ORNAMENT:
THEY ARE BUT BEGGARS THAT CAN COUNT THEIR WORTH;
BUT MY TRUE LOVE IS GROWN TO SUCH EXCESS, I CANNOT SUM UP SUM OF HALF MY WEALTH.
COME, COME WITH ME, AND WE WILL MAKE SHORT WORK;
FOR, BY YOUR LEAVES, YOU SHALL NOT STAY ALONE, TILL HOLY CHURCH INCORPORATE TWO IN ONE.

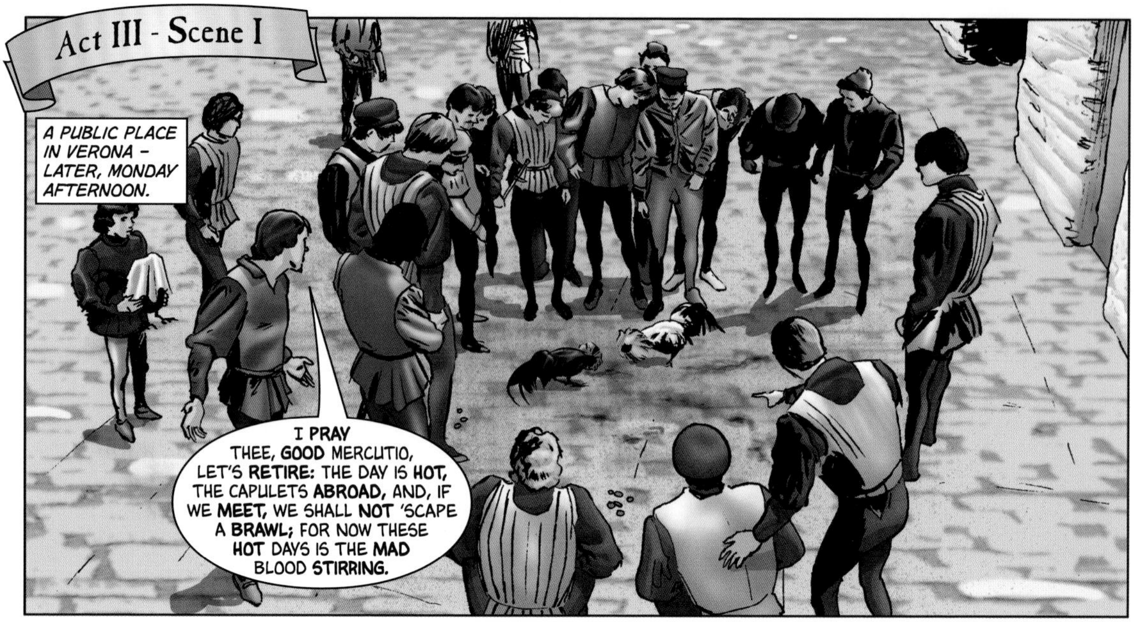
Act III - Scene I
A PUBLIC PLACE IN VERONA – LATER, MONDAY AFTERNOON.
I PRAY THEE, GOOD MERCUTIO, LET'S RETIRE: THE DAY IS HOT, THE CAPULETS ABROAD, AND, IF WE MEET, WE SHALL NOT 'SCAPE A BRAWL; FOR NOW THESE HOT DAYS IS THE MAD BLOOD STIRRING.

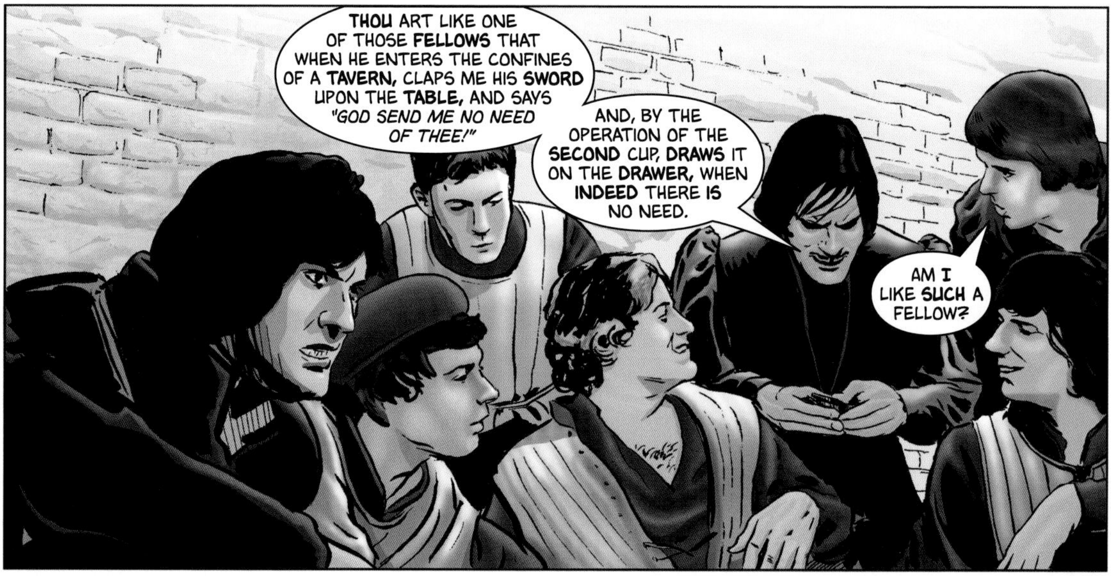
THOU ART LIKE ONE OF THOSE FELLOWS THAT WHEN HE ENTERS THE CONFINES OF A TAVERN, CLAPS ME HIS SWORD UPON THE TABLE, AND SAYS "GOD SEND ME NO NEED OF THEE!"
AND, BY THE OPERATION OF THE SECOND CUP, DRAWS IT ON THE DRAWER, WHEN INDEED THERE IS NO NEED.
AM I LIKE SUCH A FELLOW?

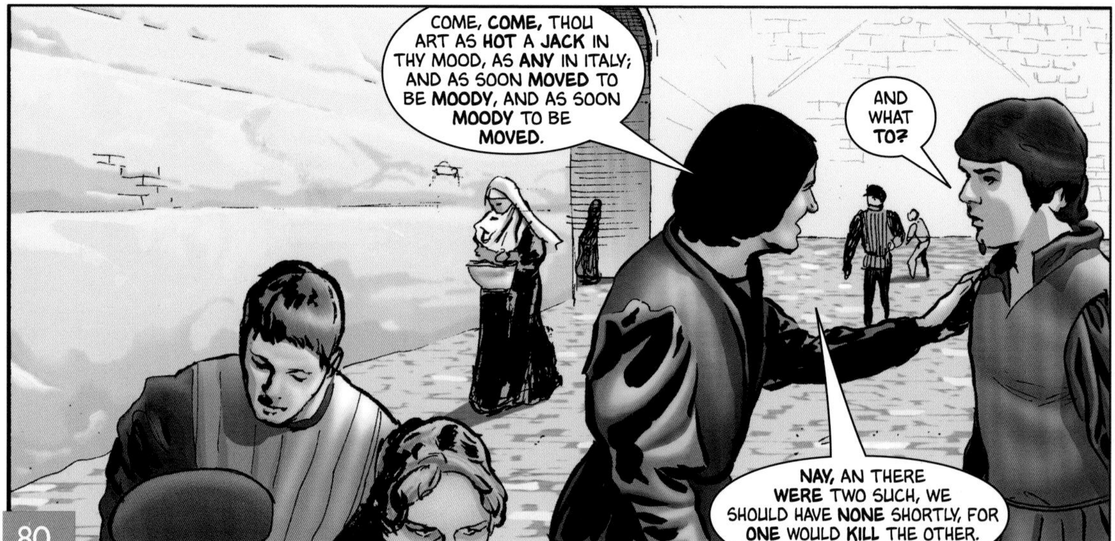
COME, COME, THOU ART AS HOT A JACK IN THY MOOD, AS ANY IN ITALY; AND AS SOON MOVED TO BE MOODY, AND AS SOON MOODY TO BE MOVED.
AND WHAT TO?
NAY, AN THERE WERE TWO SUCH, WE SHOULD HAVE NONE SHORTLY, FOR ONE WOULD KILL THE OTHER.

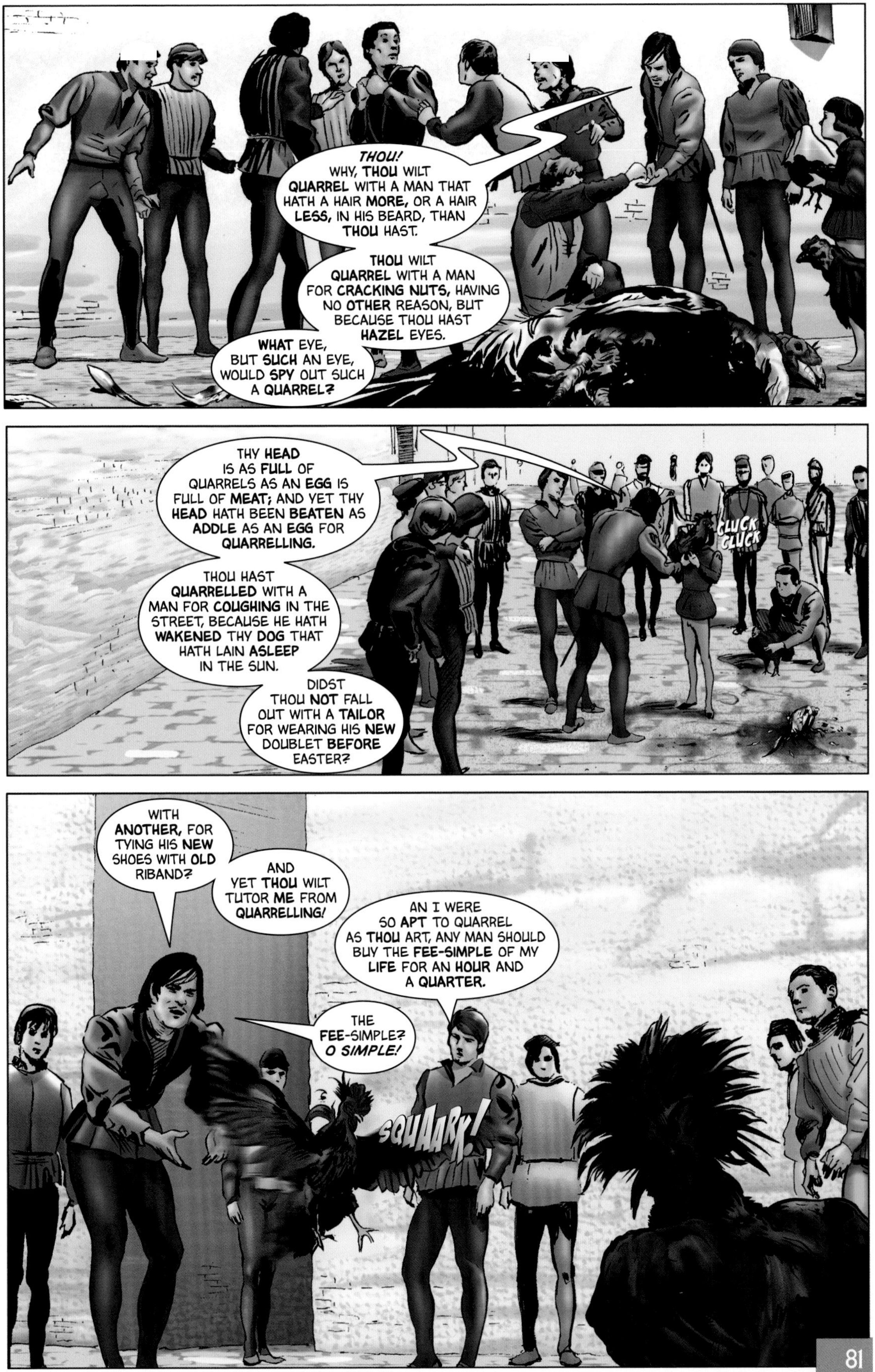
THOU! WHY, THOU WILT QUARREL WITH A MAN THAT HATH A HAIR MORE, OR A HAIR LESS, IN HIS BEARD, THAN THOU HAST.
THOU WILT QUARREL WITH A MAN FOR CRACKING NUTS, HAVING NO OTHER REASON, BUT BECAUSE THOU HAST HAZEL EYES.
WHAT EYE, BUT SUCH AN EYE, WOULD SPY OUT SUCH A QUARREL?
THY HEAD IS AS FULL OF QUARRELS AS AN EGG IS FULL OF MEAT; AND YET THY HEAD HATH BEEN BEATEN AS ADDLE AS AN EGG FOR QUARRELLING.
THOU HAST QUARRELLED WITH A MAN FOR COUGHING IN THE STREET, BECAUSE HE HATH WAKENED THY DOG THAT HATH LAIN ASLEEP IN THE SUN.
DIDST THOU NOT FALL OUT WITH A TAILOR FOR WEARING HIS NEW DOUBLET BEFORE EASTER?
CLUCK CLUCK
WITH ANOTHER, FOR TYING HIS NEW SHOES WITH OLD RIBAND?
AND YET THOU WILT TUTOR ME FROM QUARRELLING!
AN I WERE SO APT TO QUARREL AS THOU ART, ANY MAN SHOULD BUY THE FEE-SIMPLE OF MY LIFE FOR AN HOUR AND A QUARTER.
THE FEE-SIMPLE? O SIMPLE!
SQUAAARK!

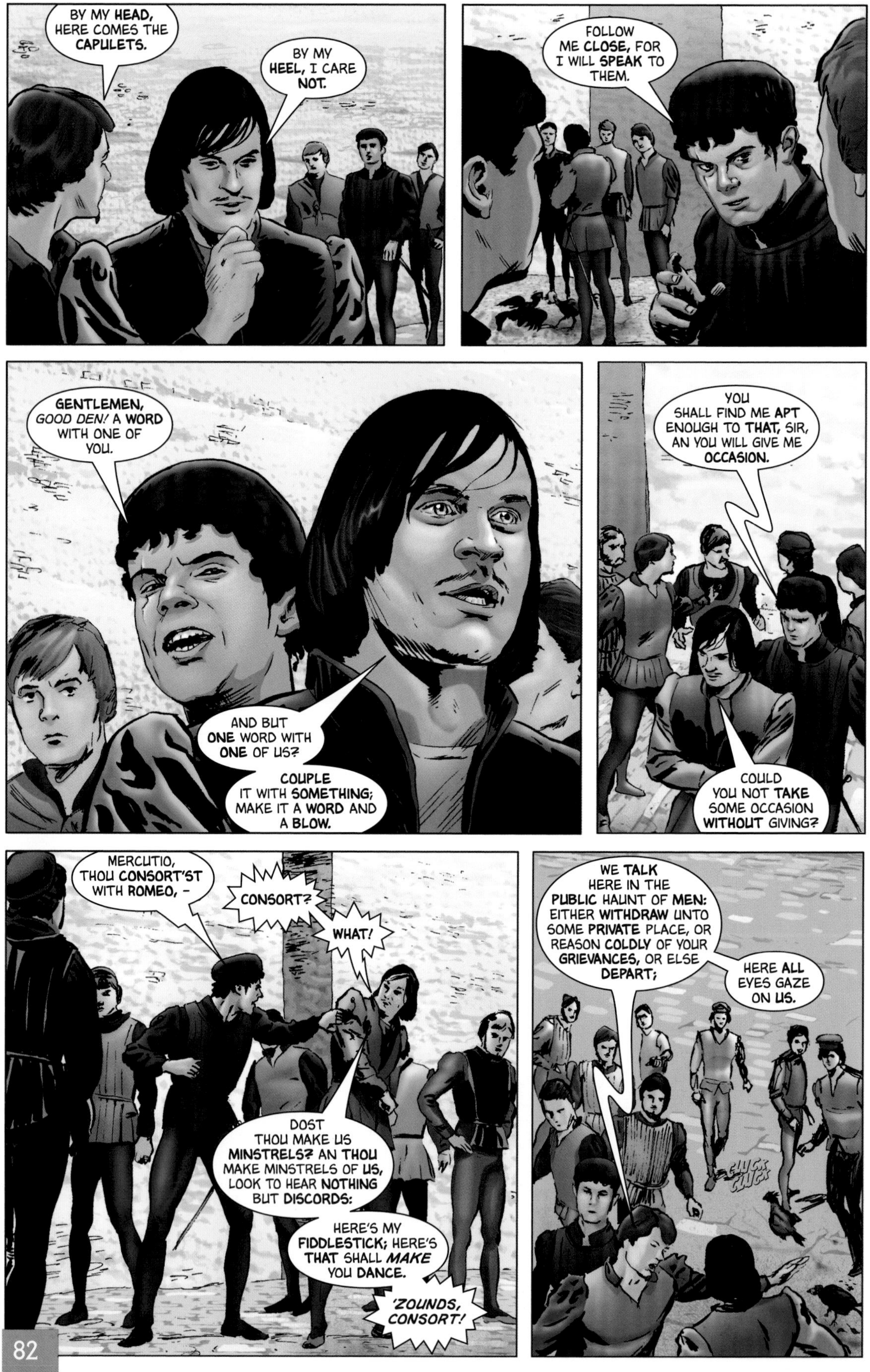
BY MY HEAD, HERE COMES THE CAPULETS.
BY MY HEEL, I CARE NOT.
FOLLOW ME CLOSE, FOR I WILL SPEAK TO THEM.
GENTLEMEN, GOOD DEN! A WORD WITH ONE OF YOU.
AND BUT ONE WORD WITH ONE OF US?
COUPLE IT WITH SOMETHING; MAKE IT A WORD AND A BLOW.
YOU SHALL FIND ME APT ENOUGH TO THAT, SIR, AN YOU WILL GIVE ME OCCASION.
COULD YOU NOT TAKE SOME OCCASION WITHOUT GIVING?
MERCUTIO, THOU CONSORT'ST WITH ROMEO, –
CONSORT?
WHAT!
DOST THOU MAKE US MINSTRELS? AN THOU MAKE MINSTRELS OF US, LOOK TO HEAR NOTHING BUT DISCORDS:
HERE'S MY FIDDLESTICK; HERE'S THAT SHALL MAKE YOU DANCE.
'ZOUNDS, CONSORT!
WE TALK HERE IN THE PUBLIC HAUNT OF MEN: EITHER WITHDRAW UNTO SOME PRIVATE PLACE, OR REASON COLDLY OF YOUR GRIEVANCES, OR ELSE DEPART;
HERE ALL EYES GAZE ON US.
CLUCK CLUCK

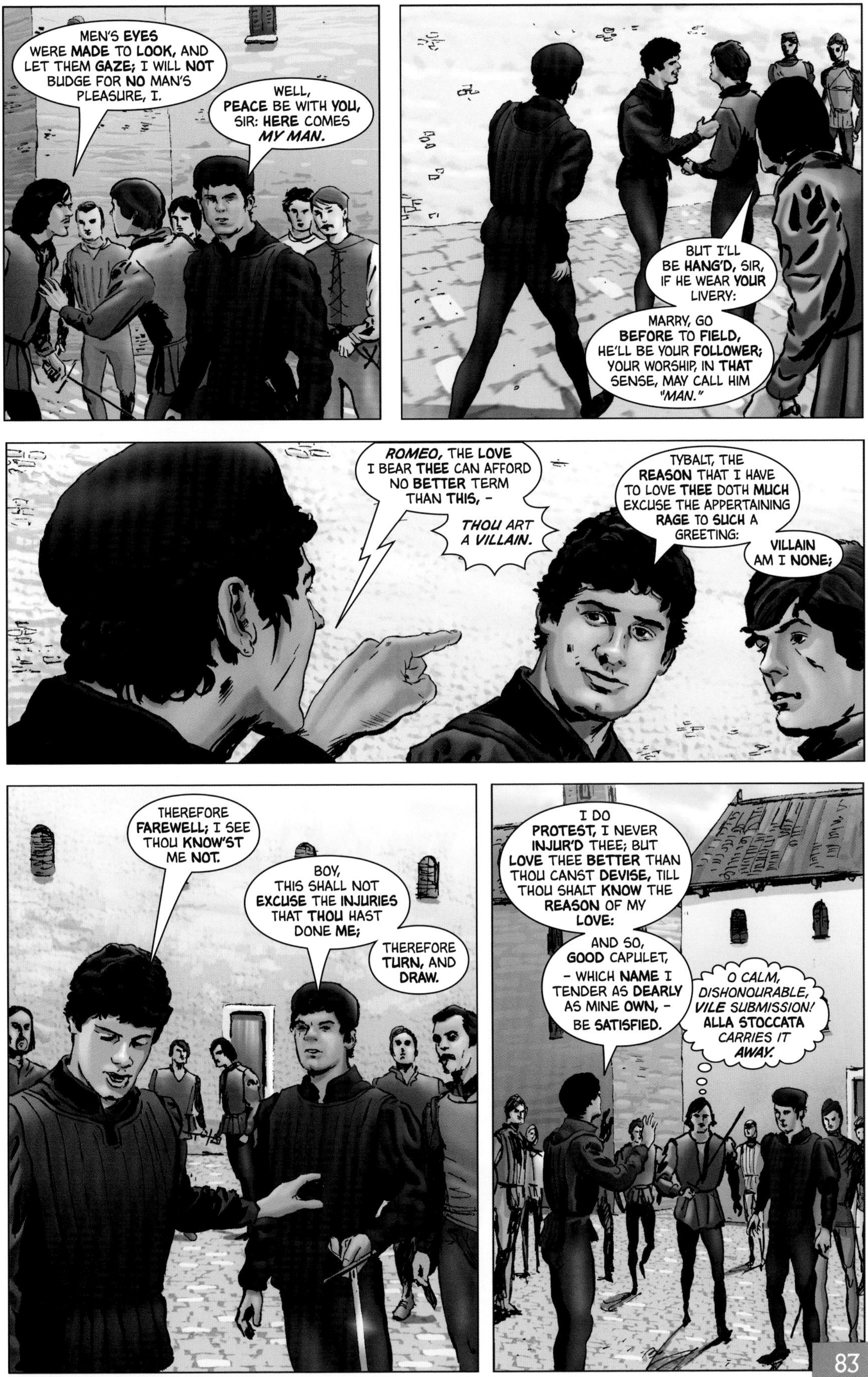
MEN'S EYES WERE MADE TO LOOK, AND LET THEM GAZE; I WILL NOT BUDGE FOR NO MAN'S PLEASURE, I.
WELL, PEACE BE WITH YOU, SIR: HERE COMES MY MAN.
BUT I'LL BE HANG'D, SIR, IF HE WEAR YOUR LIVERY:
MARRY, GO BEFORE TO FIELD, HE'LL BE YOUR FOLLOWER; YOUR WORSHIP, IN THAT SENSE, MAY CALL HIM "MAN."
ROMEO, THE LOVE I BEAR THEE CAN AFFORD NO BETTER TERM THAN THIS, –
THOU ART A VILLAIN.
TYBALT, THE REASON THAT I HAVE TO LOVE THEE DOTH MUCH EXCUSE THE APPERTAINING RAGE TO SUCH A GREETING:
VILLAIN AM I NONE;
THEREFORE FAREWELL; I SEE THOU KNOW'ST ME NOT.
BOY, THIS SHALL NOT EXCUSE THE INJURIES THAT THOU HAST DONE ME;
THEREFORE TURN, AND DRAW.
I DO PROTEST, I NEVER INJUR'D THEE; BUT LOVE THEE BETTER THAN THOU CANST DEVISE, TILL THOU SHALT KNOW THE REASON OF MY LOVE:
AND SO, GOOD CAPULET, – WHICH NAME I TENDER AS DEARLY AS MINE OWN, – BE SATISFIED.
O CALM, DISHONOURABLE, VILE SUBMISSION! ALLA STOCCATA CARRIES IT AWAY.

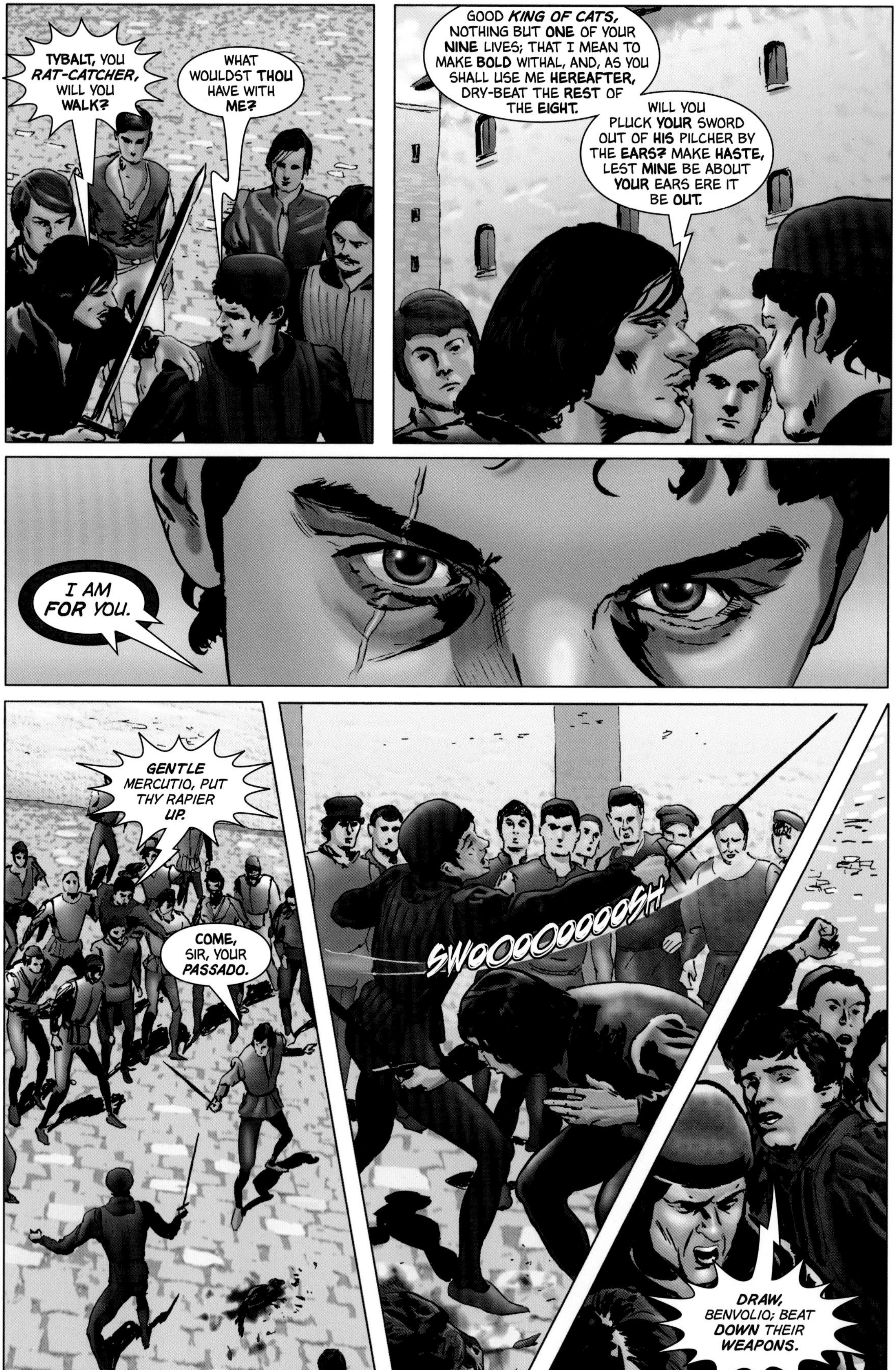
TYBALT, YOU RAT-CATCHER, WILL YOU WALK?
WHAT WOULDST THOU HAVE WITH ME?
GOOD KING OF CATS, NOTHING BUT ONE OF YOUR NINE LIVES; THAT I MEAN TO MAKE BOLD WITHAL, AND, AS YOU SHALL USE ME HEREAFTER, DRY-BEAT THE REST OF THE EIGHT.
WILL YOU PLUCK YOUR SWORD OUT OF HIS PILCHER BY THE EARS? MAKE HASTE, LEST MINE BE ABOUT YOUR EARS ERE IT BE OUT.
I AM FOR YOU.
GENTLE MERCUTIO, PUT THY RAPIER UP.
COME, SIR, YOUR PASSADO.
SWOOOOOOOOOSH
DRAW, BENVOLIO; BEAT DOWN THEIR WEAPONS.

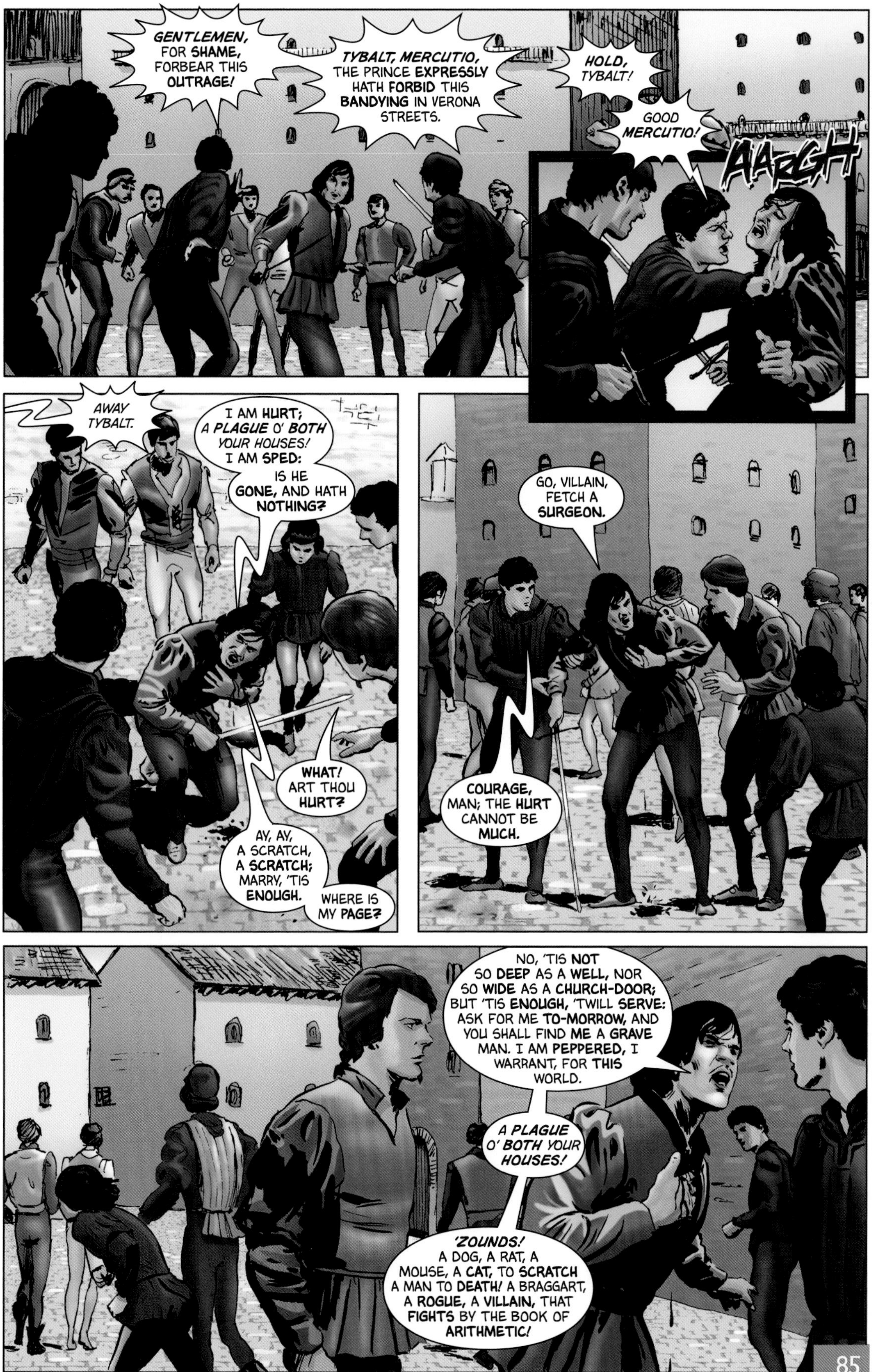
GENTLEMEN, FOR SHAME, FORBEAR THIS OUTRAGE!
TYBALT, MERCUTIO, THE PRINCE EXPRESSLY HATH FORBID THIS BANDYING IN VERONA STREETS.
HOLD, TYBALT!
GOOD MERCUTIO!
AARGH
AWAY TYBALT.
I AM HURT; A PLAGUE O' BOTH YOUR HOUSES! I AM SPED:
IS HE GONE, AND HATH NOTHING?
WHAT! ART THOU HURT?
AY, AY, A SCRATCH, A SCRATCH; MARRY, 'TIS ENOUGH.
WHERE IS MY PAGE?
GO, VILLAIN, FETCH A SURGEON.
COURAGE, MAN; THE HURT CANNOT BE MUCH.
NO, 'TIS NOT SO DEEP AS A WELL, NOR SO WIDE AS A CHURCH-DOOR; BUT 'TIS ENOUGH, 'TWILL SERVE: ASK FOR ME TO-MORROW, AND YOU SHALL FIND ME A GRAVE MAN. I AM PEPPERED, I WARRANT, FOR THIS WORLD.
A PLAGUE O' BOTH YOUR HOUSES!
'ZOUNDS! A DOG, A RAT, A MOUSE, A CAT, TO SCRATCH A MAN TO DEATH! A BRAGGART, A ROGUE, A VILLAIN, THAT FIGHTS BY THE BOOK OF ARITHMETIC!

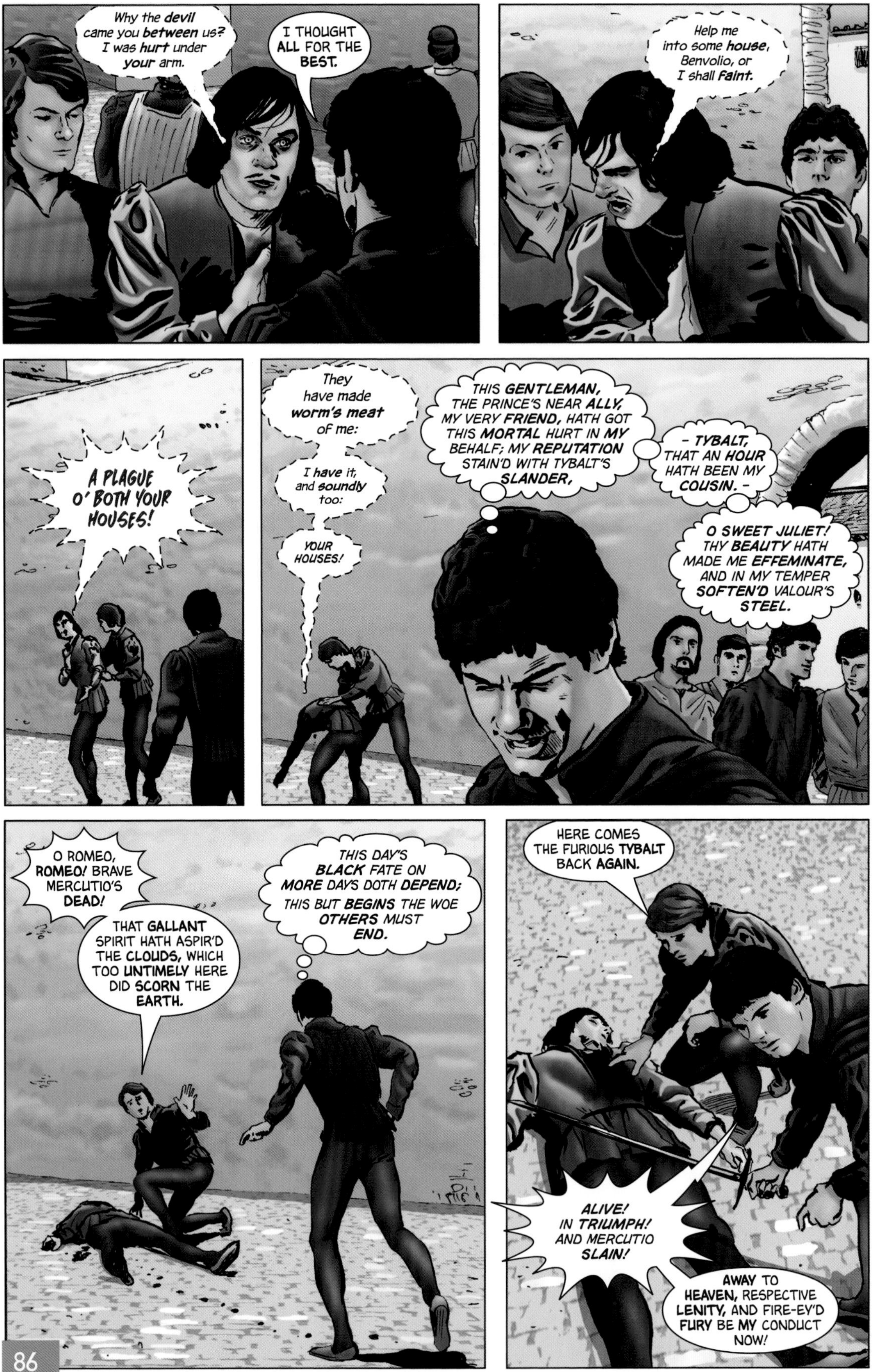
Why the devil came you between us? I was hurt under your arm.
I THOUGHT ALL FOR THE BEST.
Help me into some house, Benvolio, or I shall faint.
A PLAGUE O' BOTH YOUR HOUSES!
They have made worm's meat of me:
I have it, and soundly too:
YOUR HOUSES!
THIS GENTLEMAN, THE PRINCE'S NEAR ALLY, MY VERY FRIEND, HATH GOT THIS MORTAL HURT IN MY BEHALF; MY REPUTATION STAIN'D WITH TYBALT'S SLANDER,
- TYBALT, THAT AN HOUR HATH BEEN MY COUSIN. -
O SWEET JULIET! THY BEAUTY HATH MADE ME EFFEMINATE, AND IN MY TEMPER SOFTEN'D VALOUR'S STEEL.
O ROMEO, ROMEO! BRAVE MERCUTIO'S DEAD!
THAT GALLANT SPIRIT HATH ASPIR'D THE CLOUDS, WHICH TOO UNTIMELY HERE DID SCORN THE EARTH.
THIS DAY'S BLACK FATE ON MORE DAYS DOTH DEPEND; THIS BUT BEGINS THE WOE OTHERS MUST END.
HERE COMES THE FURIOUS TYBALT BACK AGAIN.
ALIVE! IN TRIUMPH! AND MERCUTIO SLAIN!
AWAY TO HEAVEN, RESPECTIVE LENITY, AND FIRE-EY'D FURY BE MY CONDUCT NOW!

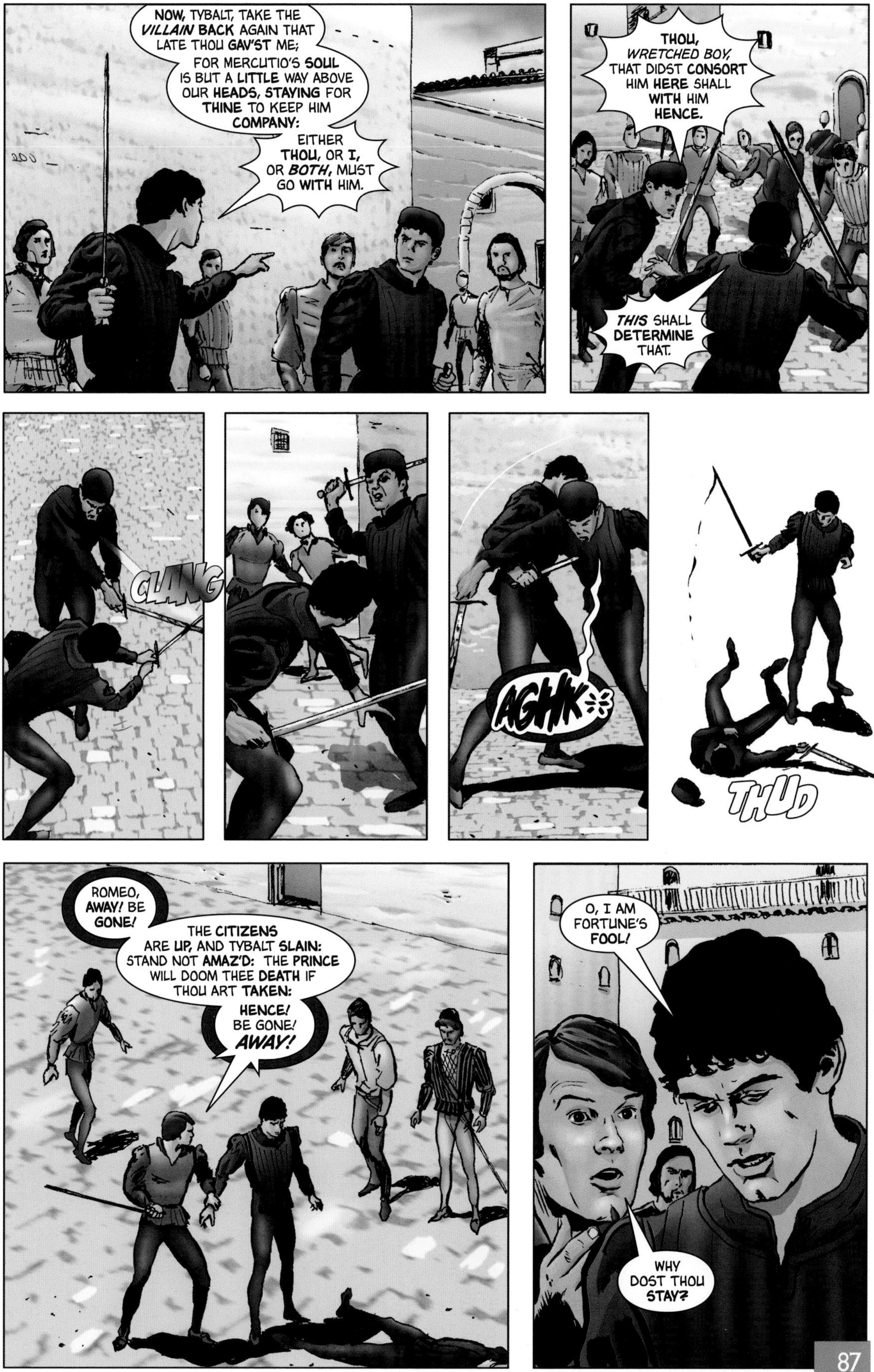

NOW, TYBALT, TAKE THE *VILLAIN* **BACK** AGAIN THAT LATE THOU **GAV'ST** ME;
FOR MERCUTIO'S **SOUL** IS BUT A **LITTLE** WAY ABOVE OUR **HEADS, STAYING** FOR **THINE** TO KEEP HIM **COMPANY:**
EITHER **THOU,** OR **I,** OR ***BOTH,*** MUST GO **WITH** HIM.
THOU, *WRETCHED BOY,* THAT DIDST **CONSORT** HIM **HERE** SHALL **WITH** HIM **HENCE.**
THIS SHALL **DETERMINE** THAT.
CLANG
AGHK
THUD
ROMEO, **AWAY!** BE **GONE!**
THE **CITIZENS** ARE **UP,** AND TYBALT **SLAIN:** STAND NOT **AMAZ'D:** THE **PRINCE** WILL DOOM THEE **DEATH** IF THOU ART **TAKEN:**
HENCE! BE GONE! ***AWAY!***
O, I AM FORTUNE'S **FOOL!**
WHY DOST THOU **STAY?**

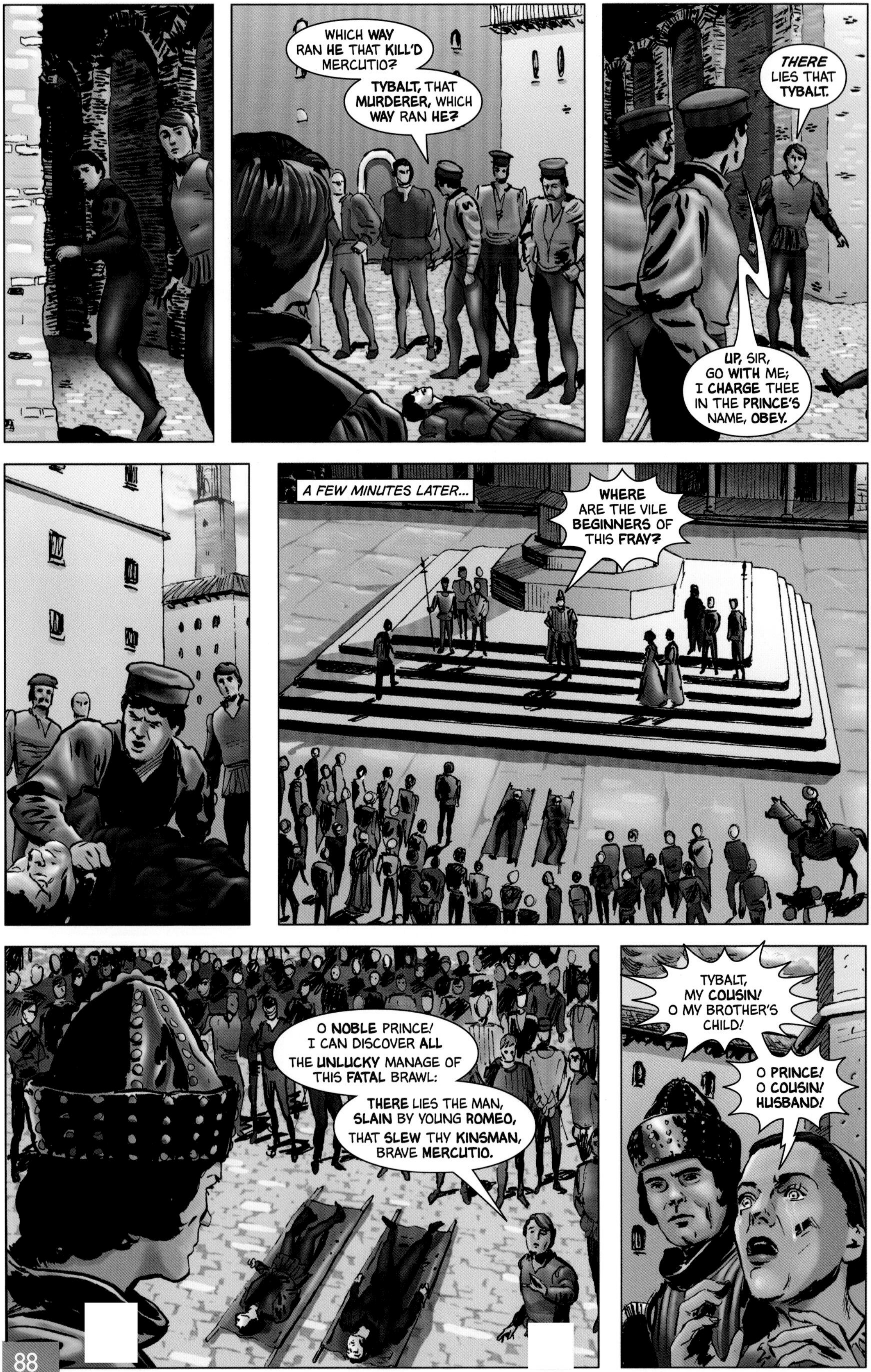
WHICH WAY RAN HE THAT KILL'D MERCUTIO?
TYBALT, THAT MURDERER, WHICH WAY RAN HE?
THERE LIES THAT TYBALT.
UP, SIR, GO WITH ME; I CHARGE THEE IN THE PRINCE'S NAME, OBEY.
A FEW MINUTES LATER...
WHERE ARE THE VILE BEGINNERS OF THIS FRAY?
O NOBLE PRINCE! I CAN DISCOVER ALL THE UNLUCKY MANAGE OF THIS FATAL BRAWL:
THERE LIES THE MAN, SLAIN BY YOUNG ROMEO, THAT SLEW THY KINSMAN, BRAVE MERCUTIO.
TYBALT, MY COUSIN! O MY BROTHER'S CHILD!
O PRINCE! O COUSIN! HUSBAND!

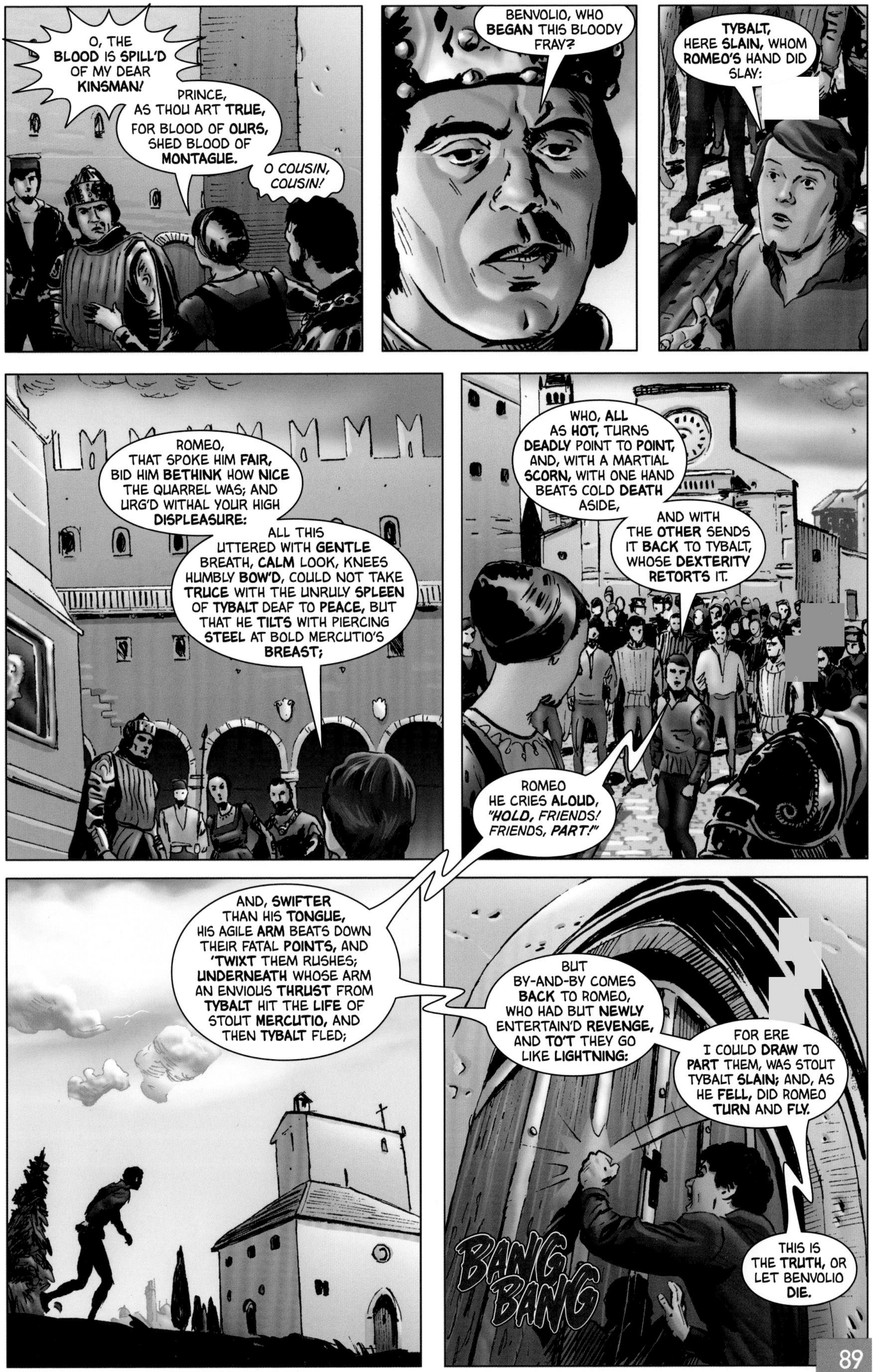
O, THE BLOOD IS SPILL'D OF MY DEAR KINSMAN!
PRINCE, AS THOU ART TRUE, FOR BLOOD OF OURS, SHED BLOOD OF MONTAGUE.
O COUSIN, COUSIN!
BENVOLIO, WHO BEGAN THIS BLOODY FRAY?
TYBALT, HERE SLAIN, WHOM ROMEO'S HAND DID SLAY:
ROMEO, THAT SPOKE HIM FAIR, BID HIM BETHINK HOW NICE THE QUARREL WAS; AND URG'D WITHAL YOUR HIGH DISPLEASURE:
ALL THIS UTTERED WITH GENTLE BREATH, CALM LOOK, KNEES HUMBLY BOW'D, COULD NOT TAKE TRUCE WITH THE UNRULY SPLEEN OF TYBALT DEAF TO PEACE, BUT THAT HE TILTS WITH PIERCING STEEL AT BOLD MERCUTIO'S BREAST;
WHO, ALL AS HOT, TURNS DEADLY POINT TO POINT, AND, WITH A MARTIAL SCORN, WITH ONE HAND BEATS COLD DEATH ASIDE,
AND WITH THE OTHER SENDS IT BACK TO TYBALT, WHOSE DEXTERITY RETORTS IT.
ROMEO HE CRIES ALOUD, "HOLD, FRIENDS! FRIENDS, PART!"
AND, SWIFTER THAN HIS TONGUE, HIS AGILE ARM BEATS DOWN THEIR FATAL POINTS, AND 'TWIXT THEM RUSHES; UNDERNEATH WHOSE ARM AN ENVIOUS THRUST FROM TYBALT HIT THE LIFE OF STOUT MERCUTIO, AND THEN TYBALT FLED;
BUT BY-AND-BY COMES BACK TO ROMEO, WHO HAD BUT NEWLY ENTERTAIN'D REVENGE, AND TO'T THEY GO LIKE LIGHTNING:
FOR ERE I COULD DRAW TO PART THEM, WAS STOUT TYBALT SLAIN; AND, AS HE FELL, DID ROMEO TURN AND FLY.
BANG BANG
THIS IS THE TRUTH, OR LET BENVOLIO DIE.

HE IS A KINSMAN TO THE MONTAGUE, AFFECTION MAKES HIM FALSE, HE SPEAKS NOT TRUE:

SOME TWENTY OF THEM FOUGHT IN THIS BLACK STRIFE, AND ALL THOSE TWENTY COULD BUT KILL ONE LIFE.

I BEG FOR JUSTICE, WHICH THOU, PRINCE, MUST GIVE: ROMEO SLEW TYBALT, ROMEO MUST NOT LIVE.

ROMEO SLEW HIM, HE SLEW MERCUTIO; WHO NOW THE PRICE OF HIS DEAR BLOOD DOTH OWE?

NOT ROMEO, PRINCE, HE WAS MERCUTIO'S FRIEND; HIS FAULT CONCLUDES BUT WHAT THE LAW SHOULD END,

THE LIFE OF TYBALT.

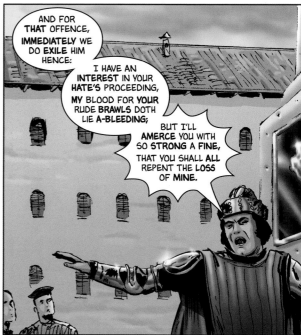

AND FOR THAT OFFENCE, IMMEDIATELY WE DO EXILE HIM HENCE:

I HAVE AN INTEREST IN YOUR HATE'S PROCEEDING, MY BLOOD FOR YOUR RUDE BRAWLS DOTH LIE A-BLEEDING;

BUT I'LL AMERCE YOU WITH SO STRONG A FINE, THAT YOU SHALL ALL REPENT THE LOSS OF MINE.

I WILL BE DEAF TO PLEADING AND EXCUSES; NOR TEARS NOR PRAYERS SHALL PURCHASE OUT ABUSES;

THEREFORE USE NONE: LET ROMEO HENCE IN HASTE, ELSE, WHEN HE'S FOUND, THAT HOUR IS HIS LAST.

BEAR HENCE THIS BODY, AND ATTEND OUR WILL: MERCY BUT MURDERS, PARDONING THOSE THAT KILL.

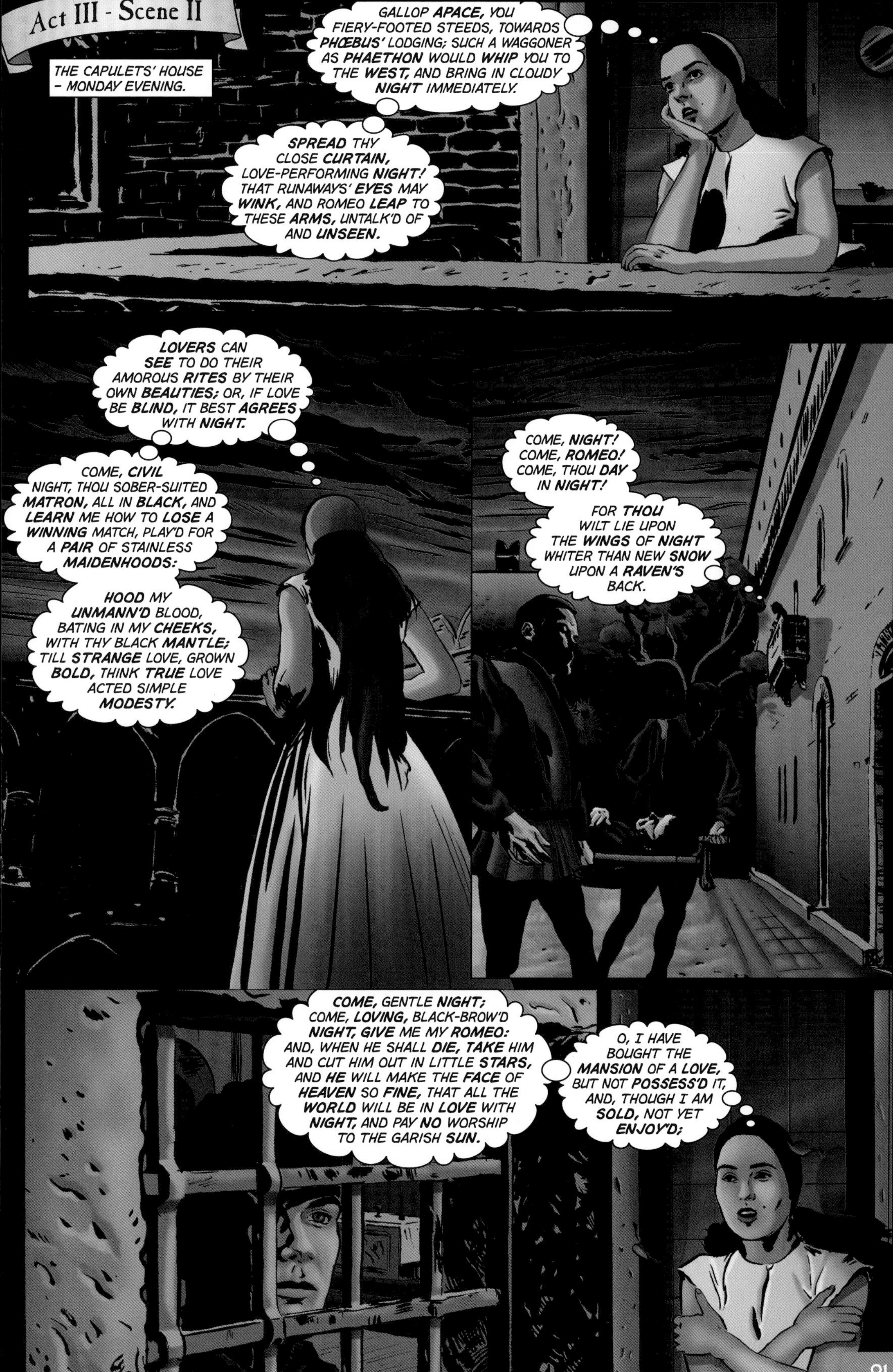
Act III - Scene II
THE CAPULETS' HOUSE - MONDAY EVENING.
GALLOP APACE, YOU FIERY-FOOTED STEEDS, TOWARDS PHŒBUS' LODGING; SUCH A WAGGONER AS PHAETHON WOULD WHIP YOU TO THE WEST, AND BRING IN CLOUDY NIGHT IMMEDIATELY.
SPREAD THY CLOSE CURTAIN, LOVE-PERFORMING NIGHT! THAT RUNAWAYS' EYES MAY WINK, AND ROMEO LEAP TO THESE ARMS, UNTALK'D OF AND UNSEEN.
LOVERS CAN SEE TO DO THEIR AMOROUS RITES BY THEIR OWN BEAUTIES; OR, IF LOVE BE BLIND, IT BEST AGREES WITH NIGHT.
COME, CIVIL NIGHT, THOU SOBER-SUITED MATRON, ALL IN BLACK, AND LEARN ME HOW TO LOSE A WINNING MATCH, PLAY'D FOR A PAIR OF STAINLESS MAIDENHOODS:
HOOD MY UNMANN'D BLOOD, BATING IN MY CHEEKS, WITH THY BLACK MANTLE; TILL STRANGE LOVE, GROWN BOLD, THINK TRUE LOVE ACTED SIMPLE MODESTY.
COME, NIGHT! COME, ROMEO! COME, THOU DAY IN NIGHT!
FOR THOU WILT LIE UPON THE WINGS OF NIGHT WHITER THAN NEW SNOW UPON A RAVEN'S BACK.
COME, GENTLE NIGHT; COME, LOVING, BLACK-BROW'D NIGHT, GIVE ME MY ROMEO: AND, WHEN HE SHALL DIE, TAKE HIM AND CUT HIM OUT IN LITTLE STARS, AND HE WILL MAKE THE FACE OF HEAVEN SO FINE, THAT ALL THE WORLD WILL BE IN LOVE WITH NIGHT, AND PAY NO WORSHIP TO THE GARISH SUN.
O, I HAVE BOUGHT THE MANSION OF A LOVE, BUT NOT POSSESS'D IT, AND, THOUGH I AM SOLD, NOT YET ENJOY'D;

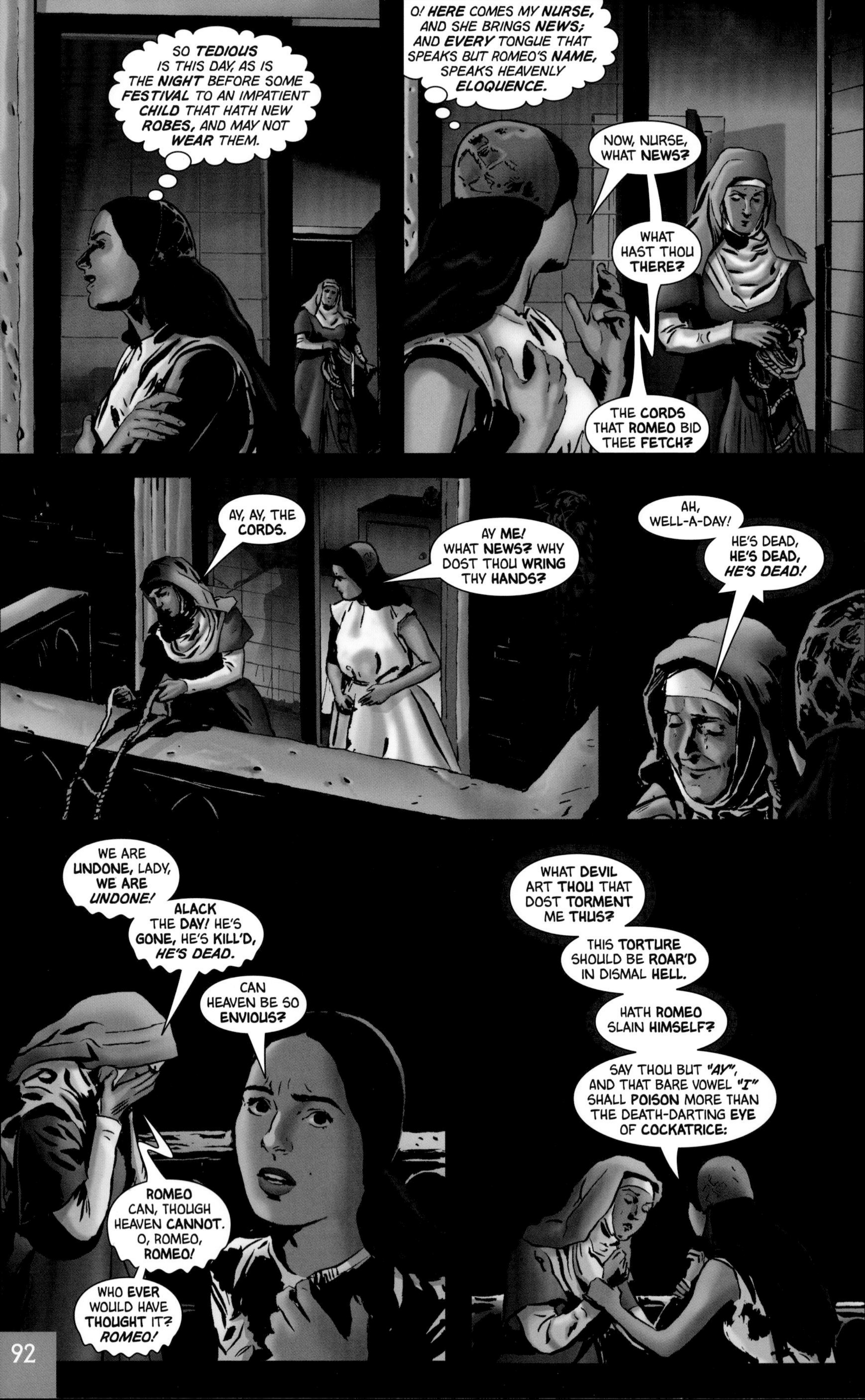

SO TEDIOUS IS THIS DAY, AS IS THE NIGHT BEFORE SOME FESTIVAL TO AN IMPATIENT CHILD THAT HATH NEW ROBES, AND MAY NOT WEAR THEM.
O! HERE COMES MY NURSE, AND SHE BRINGS NEWS; AND EVERY TONGUE THAT SPEAKS BUT ROMEO'S NAME, SPEAKS HEAVENLY ELOQUENCE.
NOW, NURSE, WHAT NEWS?
WHAT HAST THOU THERE?
THE CORDS THAT ROMEO BID THEE FETCH?
AY, AY, THE CORDS.
AY ME! WHAT NEWS? WHY DOST THOU WRING THY HANDS?
AH, WELL-A-DAY!
HE'S DEAD, HE'S DEAD, HE'S DEAD!
WE ARE UNDONE, LADY, WE ARE UNDONE!
ALACK THE DAY! HE'S GONE, HE'S KILL'D, HE'S DEAD.
CAN HEAVEN BE SO ENVIOUS?
ROMEO CAN, THOUGH HEAVEN CANNOT. O, ROMEO, ROMEO!
WHO EVER WOULD HAVE THOUGHT IT? ROMEO!
WHAT DEVIL ART THOU THAT DOST TORMENT ME THUS?
THIS TORTURE SHOULD BE ROAR'D IN DISMAL HELL.
HATH ROMEO SLAIN HIMSELF?
SAY THOU BUT "AY", AND THAT BARE VOWEL "I" SHALL POISON MORE THAN THE DEATH-DARTING EYE OF COCKATRICE:

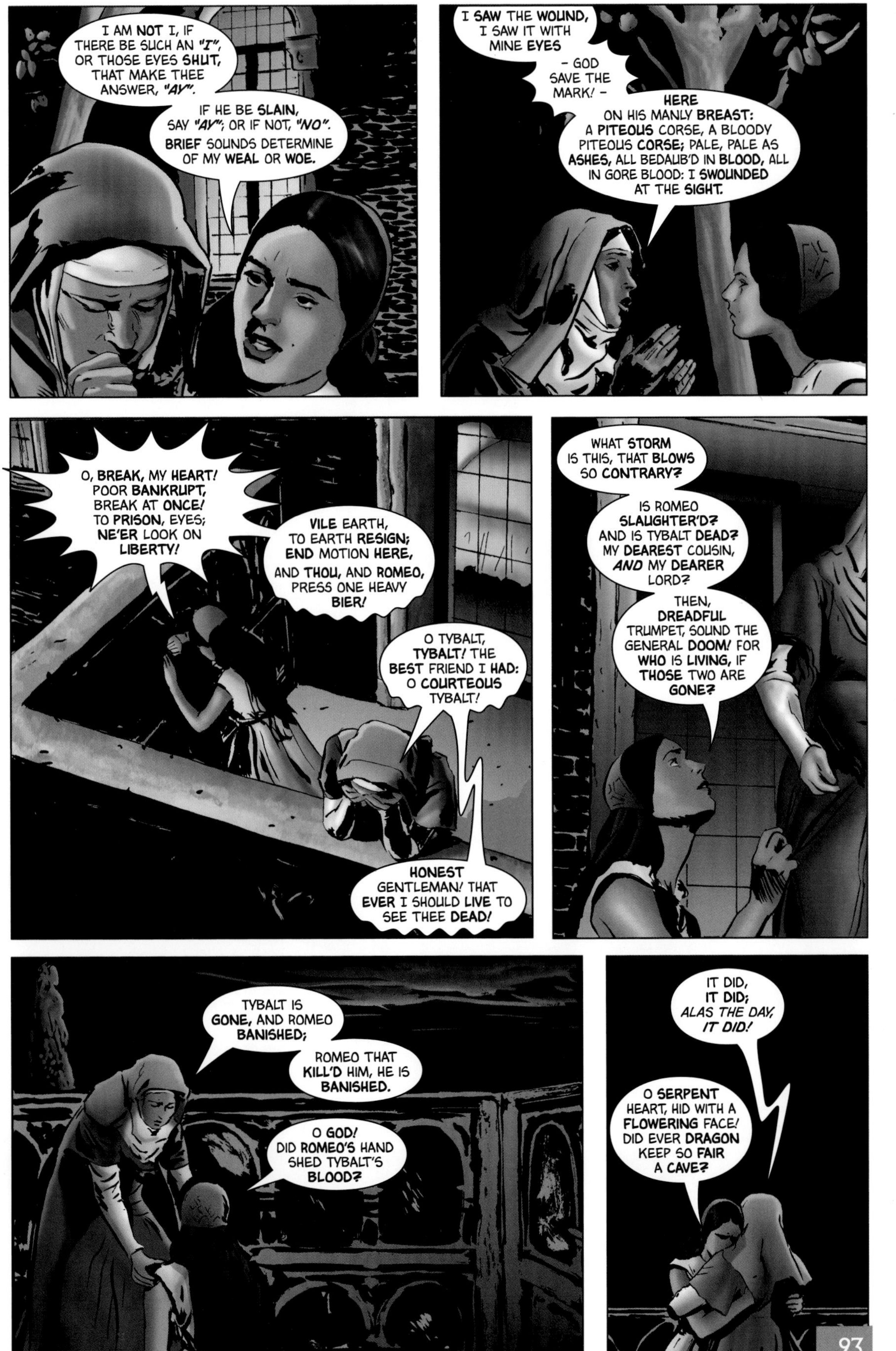
I AM NOT I, IF THERE BE SUCH AN "I", OR THOSE EYES SHUT, THAT MAKE THEE ANSWER, "AY".
IF HE BE SLAIN, SAY "AY"; OR IF NOT, "NO". BRIEF SOUNDS DETERMINE OF MY WEAL OR WOE.
I SAW THE WOUND, I SAW IT WITH MINE EYES
- GOD SAVE THE MARK! -
HERE ON HIS MANLY BREAST: A PITEOUS CORSE, A BLOODY PITEOUS CORSE; PALE, PALE AS ASHES, ALL BEDAUB'D IN BLOOD, ALL IN GORE BLOOD: I SWOUNDED AT THE SIGHT.
O, BREAK, MY HEART! POOR BANKRUPT, BREAK AT ONCE! TO PRISON, EYES; NE'ER LOOK ON LIBERTY!
VILE EARTH, TO EARTH RESIGN; END MOTION HERE,
AND THOU, AND ROMEO, PRESS ONE HEAVY BIER!
O TYBALT, TYBALT! THE BEST FRIEND I HAD: O COURTEOUS TYBALT!
HONEST GENTLEMAN! THAT EVER I SHOULD LIVE TO SEE THEE DEAD!
WHAT STORM IS THIS, THAT BLOWS SO CONTRARY?
IS ROMEO SLAUGHTER'D? AND IS TYBALT DEAD? MY DEAREST COUSIN, AND MY DEARER LORD?
THEN, DREADFUL TRUMPET, SOUND THE GENERAL DOOM! FOR WHO IS LIVING, IF THOSE TWO ARE GONE?
TYBALT IS GONE, AND ROMEO BANISHED;
ROMEO THAT KILL'D HIM, HE IS BANISHED.
O GOD! DID ROMEO'S HAND SHED TYBALT'S BLOOD?
IT DID, IT DID; ALAS THE DAY, IT DID!
O SERPENT HEART, HID WITH A FLOWERING FACE! DID EVER DRAGON KEEP SO FAIR A CAVE?

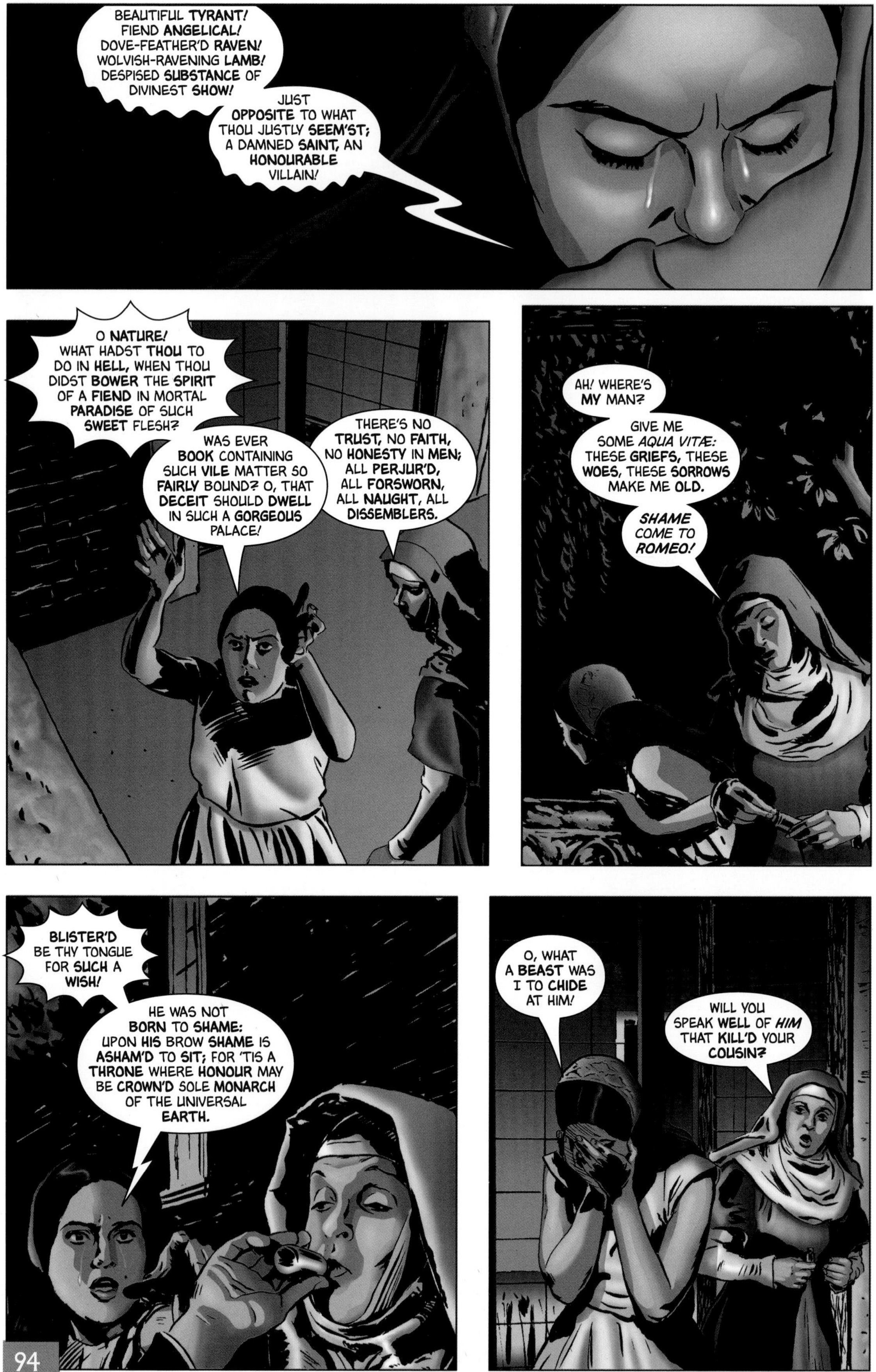

BEAUTIFUL TYRANT! FIEND ANGELICAL! DOVE-FEATHER'D RAVEN! WOLVISH-RAVENING LAMB! DESPISED SUBSTANCE OF DIVINEST SHOW!
JUST OPPOSITE TO WHAT THOU JUSTLY SEEM'ST; A DAMNED SAINT, AN HONOURABLE VILLAIN!
O NATURE! WHAT HADST THOU TO DO IN HELL, WHEN THOU DIDST BOWER THE SPIRIT OF A FIEND IN MORTAL PARADISE OF SUCH SWEET FLESH?
WAS EVER BOOK CONTAINING SUCH VILE MATTER SO FAIRLY BOUND? O, THAT DECEIT SHOULD DWELL IN SUCH A GORGEOUS PALACE!
THERE'S NO TRUST, NO FAITH, NO HONESTY IN MEN; ALL PERJUR'D, ALL FORSWORN, ALL NAUGHT, ALL DISSEMBLERS.
AH! WHERE'S MY MAN?
GIVE ME SOME AQUA VITÆ: THESE GRIEFS, THESE WOES, THESE SORROWS MAKE ME OLD.
SHAME COME TO ROMEO!
BLISTER'D BE THY TONGUE FOR SUCH A WISH!
HE WAS NOT BORN TO SHAME: UPON HIS BROW SHAME IS ASHAM'D TO SIT; FOR 'TIS A THRONE WHERE HONOUR MAY BE CROWN'D SOLE MONARCH OF THE UNIVERSAL EARTH.
O, WHAT A BEAST WAS I TO CHIDE AT HIM!
WILL YOU SPEAK WELL OF HIM THAT KILL'D YOUR COUSIN?

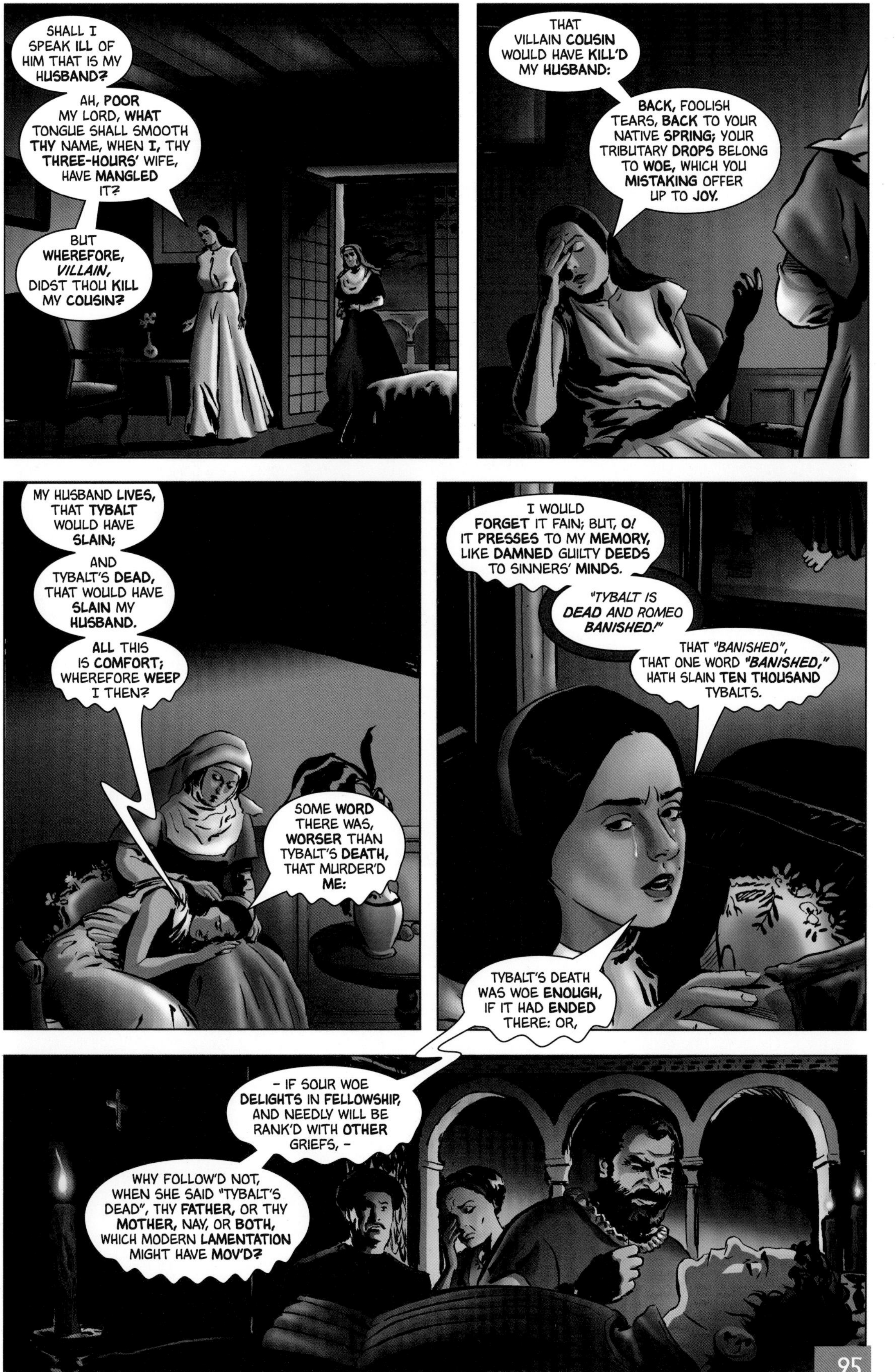
SHALL I SPEAK ILL OF HIM THAT IS MY HUSBAND?
AH, POOR MY LORD, WHAT TONGUE SHALL SMOOTH THY NAME, WHEN I, THY THREE-HOURS' WIFE, HAVE MANGLED IT?
BUT WHEREFORE, VILLAIN, DIDST THOU KILL MY COUSIN?
THAT VILLAIN COUSIN WOULD HAVE KILL'D MY HUSBAND:
BACK, FOOLISH TEARS, BACK TO YOUR NATIVE SPRING; YOUR TRIBUTARY DROPS BELONG TO WOE, WHICH YOU MISTAKING OFFER UP TO JOY.
MY HUSBAND LIVES, THAT TYBALT WOULD HAVE SLAIN;
AND TYBALT'S DEAD, THAT WOULD HAVE SLAIN MY HUSBAND.
ALL THIS IS COMFORT; WHEREFORE WEEP I THEN?
SOME WORD THERE WAS, WORSER THAN TYBALT'S DEATH, THAT MURDER'D ME:
I WOULD FORGET IT FAIN; BUT, O! IT PRESSES TO MY MEMORY, LIKE DAMNED GUILTY DEEDS TO SINNERS' MINDS.
"TYBALT IS DEAD AND ROMEO BANISHED!"
THAT "BANISHED", THAT ONE WORD "BANISHED," HATH SLAIN TEN THOUSAND TYBALTS.
TYBALT'S DEATH WAS WOE ENOUGH, IF IT HAD ENDED THERE: OR,
– IF SOUR WOE DELIGHTS IN FELLOWSHIP, AND NEEDLY WILL BE RANK'D WITH OTHER GRIEFS, –
WHY FOLLOW'D NOT, WHEN SHE SAID "TYBALT'S DEAD", THY FATHER, OR THY MOTHER, NAY, OR BOTH, WHICH MODERN LAMENTATION MIGHT HAVE MOV'D?

BUT, WITH A REARWARD FOLLOWING TYBALT'S DEATH, "ROMEO IS BANISHED!"

– TO SPEAK THAT WORD, IS FATHER, MOTHER, TYBALT, ROMEO, JULIET, ALL SLAIN, ALL DEAD. "ROMEO IS *BANISHED!*" –

THERE IS NO END, NO LIMIT, MEASURE, BOUND, IN THAT WORD'S DEATH; NO WORDS CAN THAT WOE SOUND.

WHERE IS MY FATHER, AND MY MOTHER, NURSE?

WEEPING AND WAILING OVER TYBALT'S CORSE: WILL YOU GO TO THEM? I WILL BRING YOU THITHER.

WASH THEY HIS WOUNDS WITH TEARS: MINE SHALL BE SPENT, WHEN THEIRS ARE DRY, FOR ROMEO'S BANISHMENT.

TAKE UP THOSE CORDS:

POOR ROPES, YOU ARE BEGUIL'D, BOTH YOU AND I; FOR ROMEO IS EXIL'D:

HE MADE YOU FOR A HIGHWAY TO MY BED; BUT I, A MAID, DIE MAIDEN-WIDOWED.

COME, CORDS; COME, NURSE; I'LL TO MY WEDDING BED; AND DEATH, NOT ROMEO, TAKE MY MAIDENHEAD!

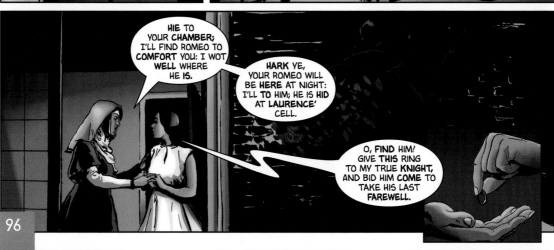

HIE TO YOUR CHAMBER; I'LL FIND ROMEO TO COMFORT YOU: I WOT WELL WHERE HE IS.

HARK YE, YOUR ROMEO WILL BE HERE AT NIGHT: I'LL TO HIM; HE IS HID AT LAURENCE' CELL.

O, FIND HIM! GIVE THIS RING TO MY TRUE KNIGHT, AND BID HIM COME TO TAKE HIS LAST FAREWELL.

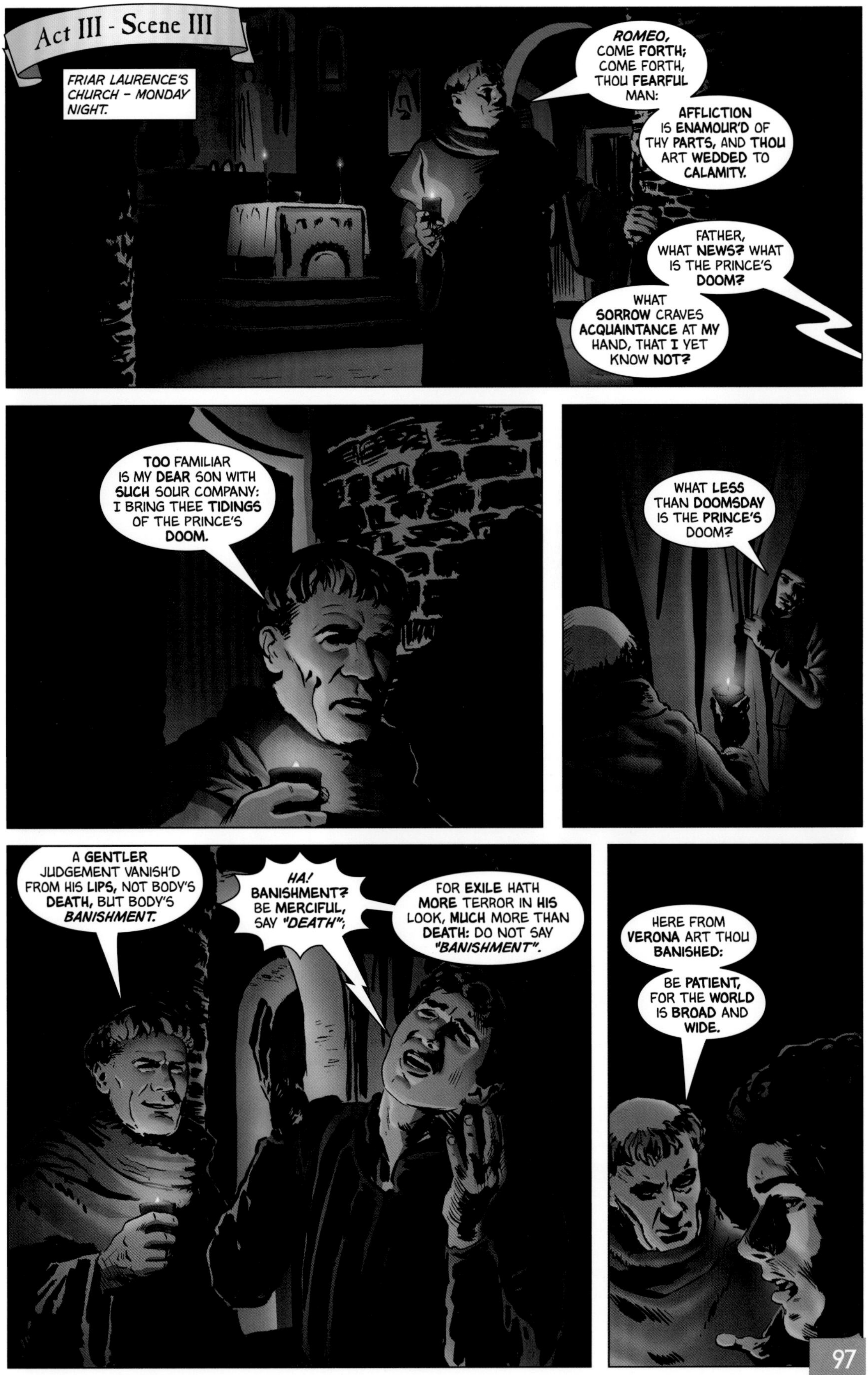
Act III - Scene III
FRIAR LAURENCE'S CHURCH – MONDAY NIGHT.
ROMEO, COME FORTH; COME FORTH, THOU FEARFUL MAN:
AFFLICTION IS ENAMOUR'D OF THY PARTS, AND THOU ART WEDDED TO CALAMITY.
FATHER, WHAT NEWS? WHAT IS THE PRINCE'S DOOM?
WHAT SORROW CRAVES ACQUAINTANCE AT MY HAND, THAT I YET KNOW NOT?
TOO FAMILIAR IS MY DEAR SON WITH SUCH SOUR COMPANY: I BRING THEE TIDINGS OF THE PRINCE'S DOOM.
WHAT LESS THAN DOOMSDAY IS THE PRINCE'S DOOM?
A GENTLER JUDGEMENT VANISH'D FROM HIS LIPS, NOT BODY'S DEATH, BUT BODY'S BANISHMENT.
HA! BANISHMENT? BE MERCIFUL, SAY "DEATH";
FOR EXILE HATH MORE TERROR IN HIS LOOK, MUCH MORE THAN DEATH: DO NOT SAY "BANISHMENT".
HERE FROM VERONA ART THOU BANISHED:
BE PATIENT, FOR THE WORLD IS BROAD AND WIDE.

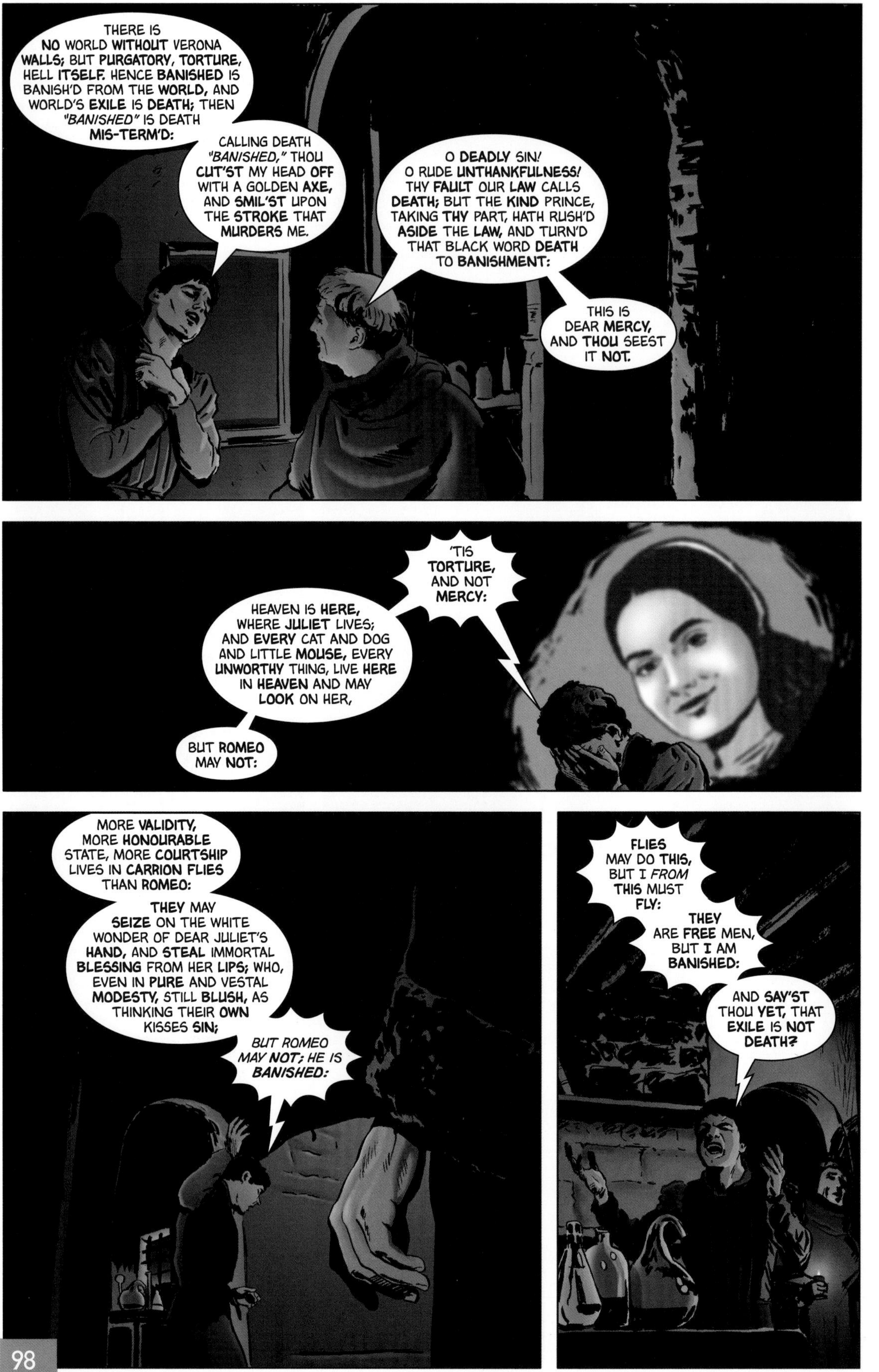
THERE IS NO WORLD WITHOUT VERONA WALLS; BUT PURGATORY, TORTURE, HELL ITSELF. HENCE BANISHED IS BANISH'D FROM THE WORLD, AND WORLD'S EXILE IS DEATH; THEN "BANISHED" IS DEATH MIS-TERM'D:
CALLING DEATH "BANISHED," THOU CUT'ST MY HEAD OFF WITH A GOLDEN AXE, AND SMIL'ST UPON THE STROKE THAT MURDERS ME.
O DEADLY SIN! O RUDE UNTHANKFULNESS! THY FAULT OUR LAW CALLS DEATH; BUT THE KIND PRINCE, TAKING THY PART, HATH RUSH'D ASIDE THE LAW, AND TURN'D THAT BLACK WORD DEATH TO BANISHMENT:
THIS IS DEAR MERCY, AND THOU SEEST IT NOT.
'TIS TORTURE, AND NOT MERCY:
HEAVEN IS HERE, WHERE JULIET LIVES; AND EVERY CAT AND DOG AND LITTLE MOUSE, EVERY UNWORTHY THING, LIVE HERE IN HEAVEN AND MAY LOOK ON HER,
BUT ROMEO MAY NOT:
MORE VALIDITY, MORE HONOURABLE STATE, MORE COURTSHIP LIVES IN CARRION FLIES THAN ROMEO:
THEY MAY SEIZE ON THE WHITE WONDER OF DEAR JULIET'S HAND, AND STEAL IMMORTAL BLESSING FROM HER LIPS; WHO, EVEN IN PURE AND VESTAL MODESTY, STILL BLUSH, AS THINKING THEIR OWN KISSES SIN;
BUT ROMEO MAY NOT; HE IS BANISHED:
FLIES MAY DO THIS, BUT I FROM THIS MUST FLY:
THEY ARE FREE MEN, BUT I AM BANISHED:
AND SAY'ST THOU YET, THAT EXILE IS NOT DEATH?

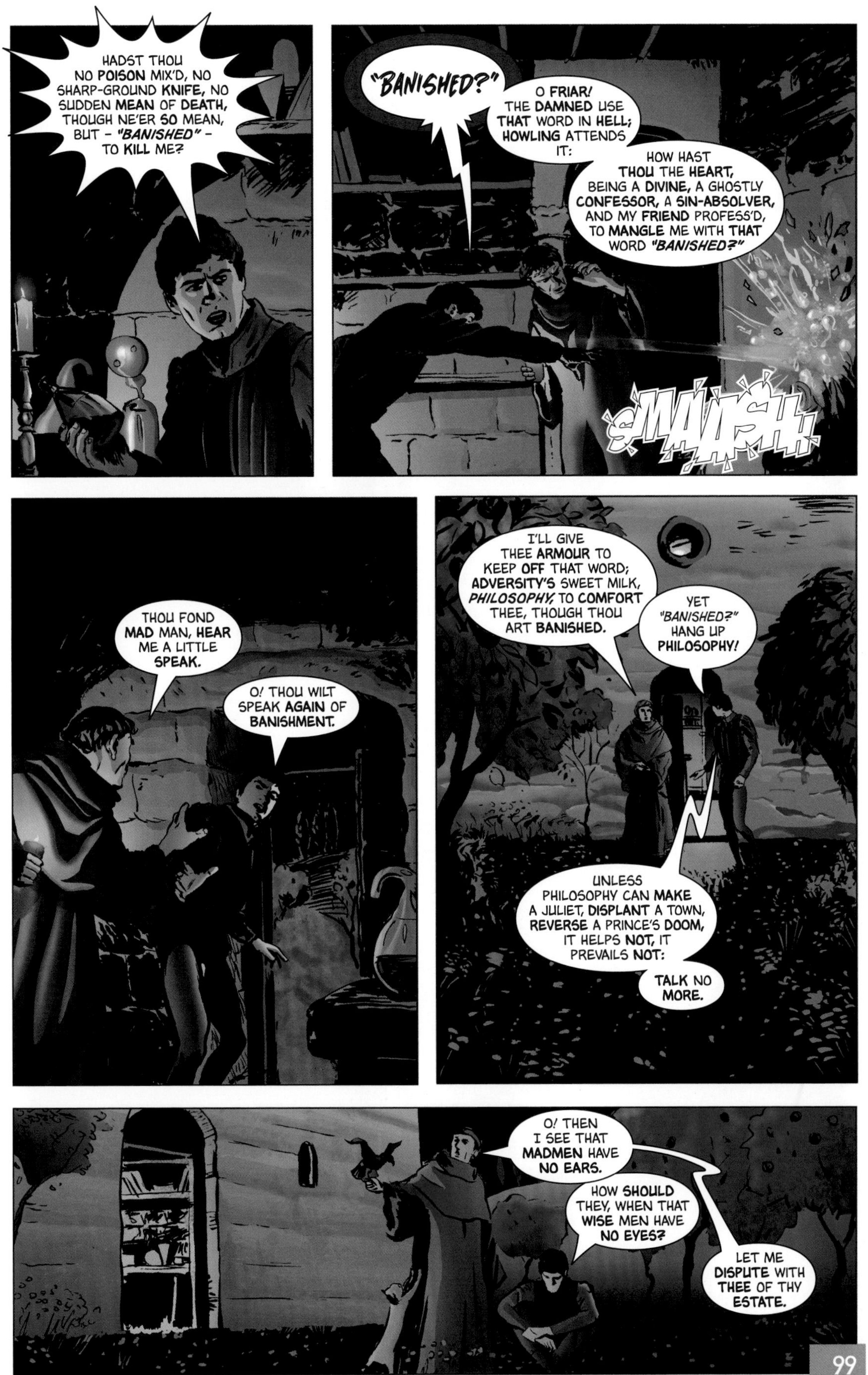
HADST THOU NO POISON MIX'D, NO SHARP-GROUND KNIFE, NO SUDDEN MEAN OF DEATH, THOUGH NE'ER SO MEAN, BUT – "BANISHED" – TO KILL ME?
"BANISHED?"
O FRIAR! THE DAMNED USE THAT WORD IN HELL; HOWLING ATTENDS IT:
HOW HAST THOU THE HEART, BEING A DIVINE, A GHOSTLY CONFESSOR, A SIN-ABSOLVER, AND MY FRIEND PROFESS'D, TO MANGLE ME WITH THAT WORD "BANISHED?"
SMAAASH
THOU FOND MAD MAN, HEAR ME A LITTLE SPEAK.
O! THOU WILT SPEAK AGAIN OF BANISHMENT.
I'LL GIVE THEE ARMOUR TO KEEP OFF THAT WORD; ADVERSITY'S SWEET MILK, PHILOSOPHY, TO COMFORT THEE, THOUGH THOU ART BANISHED.
YET "BANISHED?" HANG UP PHILOSOPHY!
UNLESS PHILOSOPHY CAN MAKE A JULIET, DISPLANT A TOWN, REVERSE A PRINCE'S DOOM, IT HELPS NOT, IT PREVAILS NOT:
TALK NO MORE.
O! THEN I SEE THAT MADMEN HAVE NO EARS.
HOW SHOULD THEY, WHEN THAT WISE MEN HAVE NO EYES?
LET ME DISPUTE WITH THEE OF THY ESTATE.

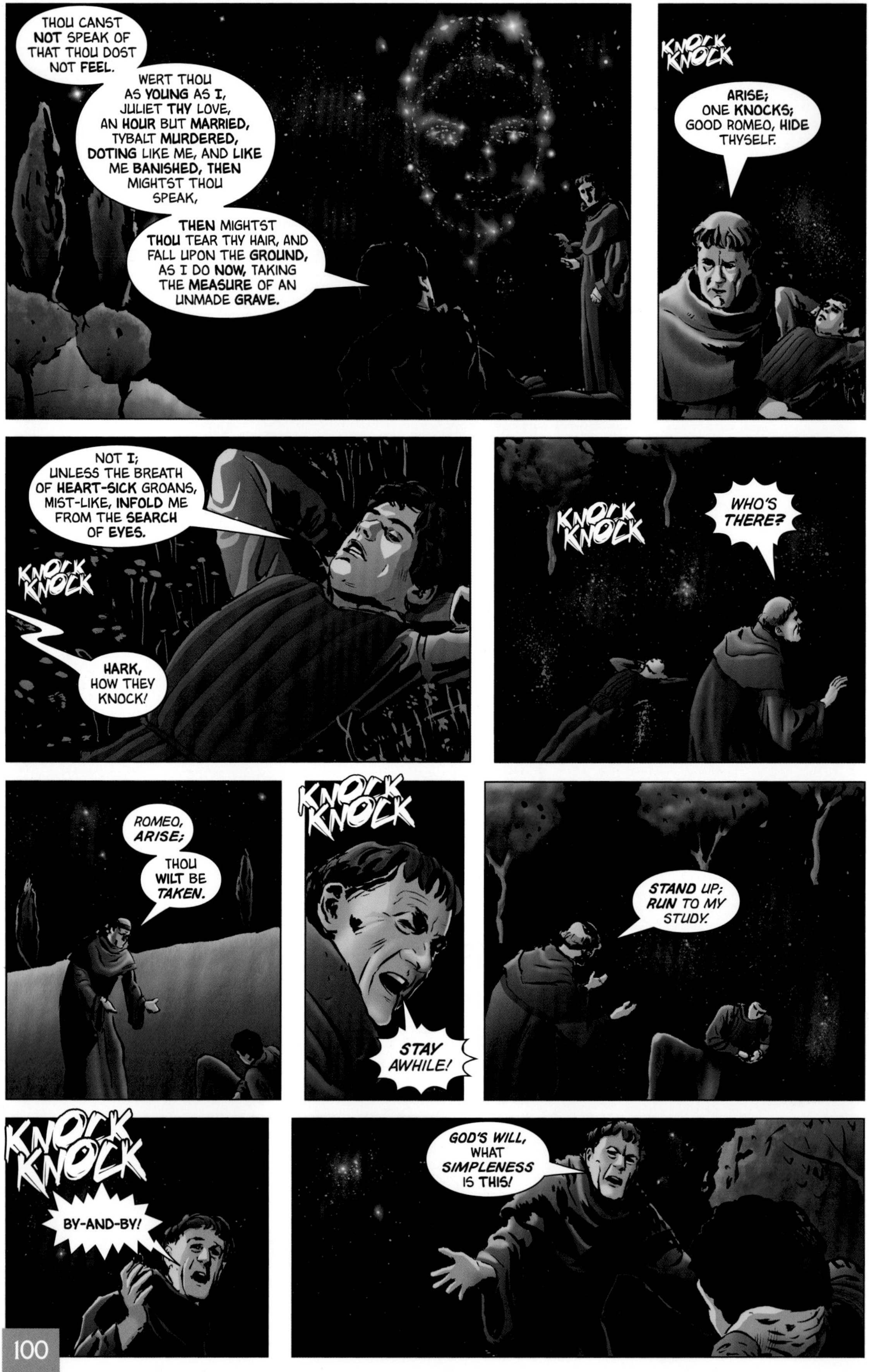
THOU CANST NOT SPEAK OF THAT THOU DOST NOT FEEL.
WERT THOU AS YOUNG AS I, JULIET THY LOVE, AN HOUR BUT MARRIED, TYBALT MURDERED, DOTING LIKE ME, AND LIKE ME BANISHED, THEN MIGHTST THOU SPEAK,
THEN MIGHTST THOU TEAR THY HAIR, AND FALL UPON THE GROUND, AS I DO NOW, TAKING THE MEASURE OF AN UNMADE GRAVE.
KNOCK KNOCK
ARISE; ONE KNOCKS; GOOD ROMEO, HIDE THYSELF.
NOT I; UNLESS THE BREATH OF HEART-SICK GROANS, MIST-LIKE, INFOLD ME FROM THE SEARCH OF EYES.
KNOCK KNOCK
HARK, HOW THEY KNOCK!
KNOCK KNOCK
WHO'S THERE?
ROMEO, ARISE;
THOU WILT BE TAKEN.
KNOCK KNOCK
STAY AWHILE!
STAND UP; RUN TO MY STUDY.
KNOCK KNOCK
BY-AND-BY!
GOD'S WILL, WHAT SIMPLENESS IS THIS!

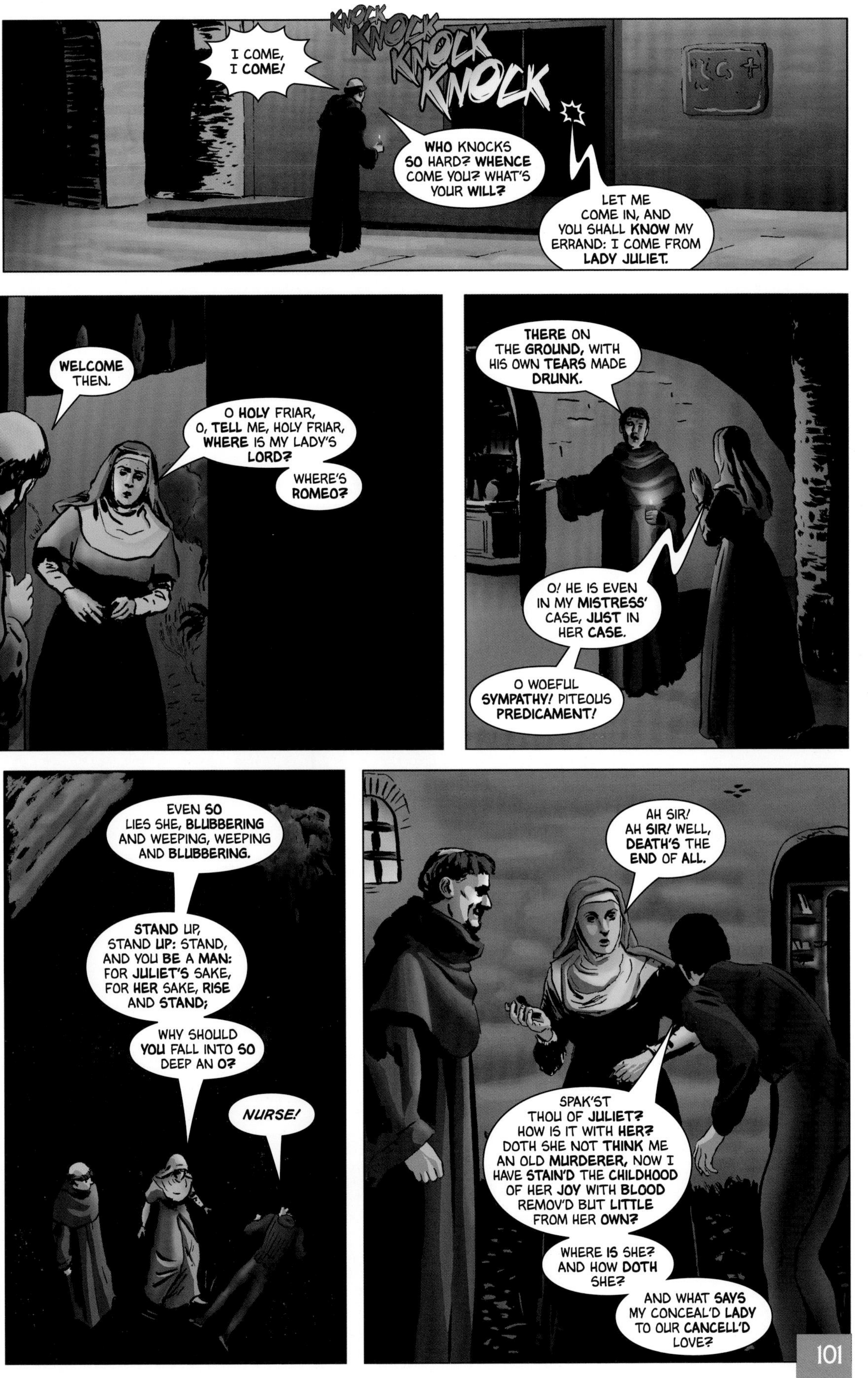

KNOCK KNOCK KNOCK KNOCK
I COME, I COME!
WHO KNOCKS SO HARD? WHENCE COME YOU? WHAT'S YOUR WILL?
LET ME COME IN, AND YOU SHALL KNOW MY ERRAND: I COME FROM LADY JULIET.
WELCOME THEN.
O HOLY FRIAR, O, TELL ME, HOLY FRIAR, WHERE IS MY LADY'S LORD?
WHERE'S ROMEO?
THERE ON THE GROUND, WITH HIS OWN TEARS MADE DRUNK.
O! HE IS EVEN IN MY MISTRESS' CASE, JUST IN HER CASE.
O WOEFUL SYMPATHY! PITEOUS PREDICAMENT!
EVEN SO LIES SHE, BLUBBERING AND WEEPING, WEEPING AND BLUBBERING.
STAND UP, STAND UP: STAND, AND YOU BE A MAN: FOR JULIET'S SAKE, FOR HER SAKE, RISE AND STAND;
WHY SHOULD YOU FALL INTO SO DEEP AN O?
NURSE!
AH SIR! AH SIR! WELL, DEATH'S THE END OF ALL.
SPAK'ST THOU OF JULIET? HOW IS IT WITH HER? DOTH SHE NOT THINK ME AN OLD MURDERER, NOW I HAVE STAIN'D THE CHILDHOOD OF HER JOY WITH BLOOD REMOV'D BUT LITTLE FROM HER OWN?
WHERE IS SHE? AND HOW DOTH SHE?
AND WHAT SAYS MY CONCEAL'D LADY TO OUR CANCELL'D LOVE?

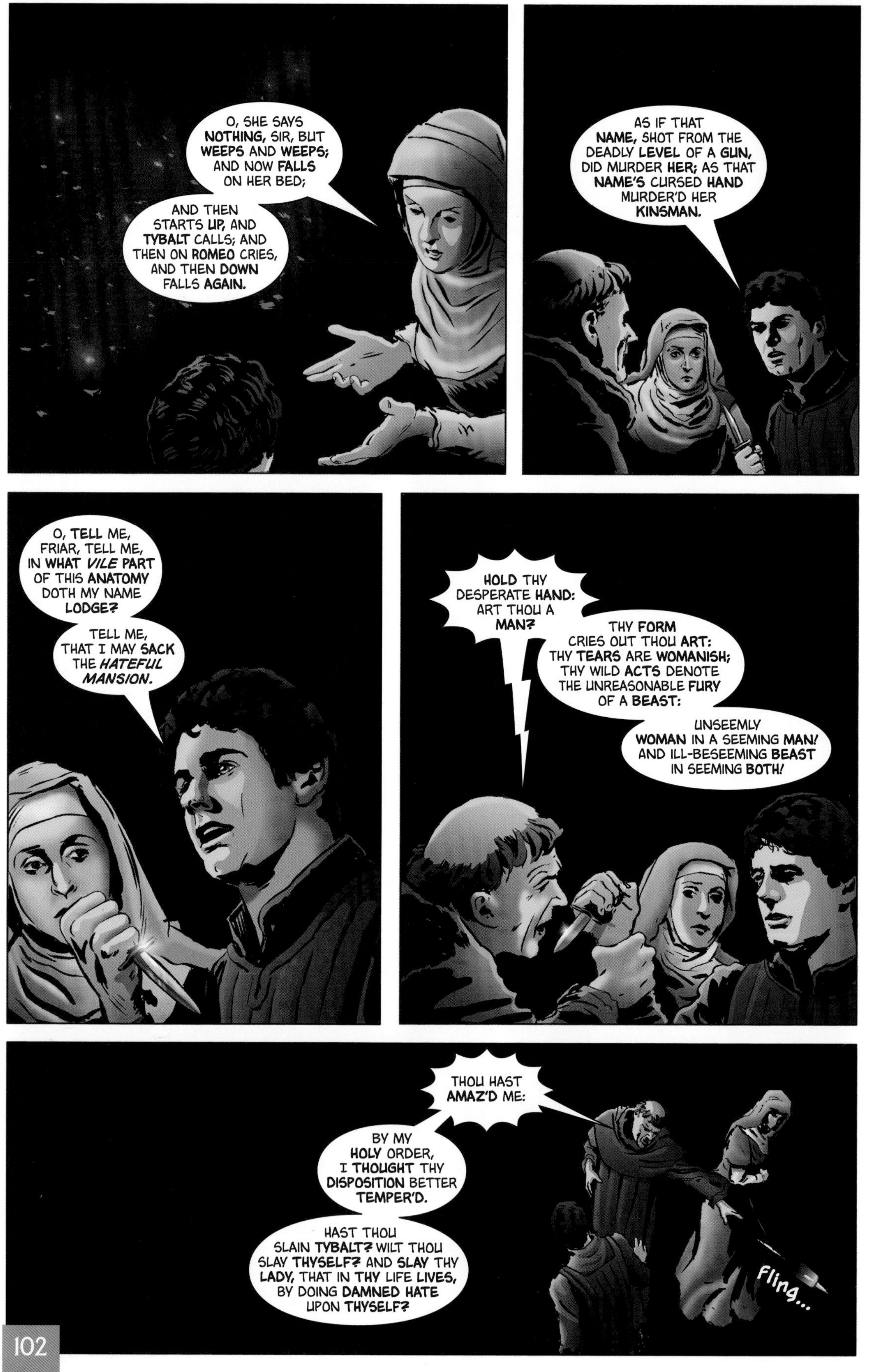
O, SHE SAYS NOTHING, SIR, BUT WEEPS AND WEEPS; AND NOW FALLS ON HER BED;
AND THEN STARTS UP, AND TYBALT CALLS; AND THEN ON ROMEO CRIES, AND THEN DOWN FALLS AGAIN.
AS IF THAT NAME, SHOT FROM THE DEADLY LEVEL OF A GUN, DID MURDER HER; AS THAT NAME'S CURSED HAND MURDER'D HER KINSMAN.
O, TELL ME, FRIAR, TELL ME, IN WHAT VILE PART OF THIS ANATOMY DOTH MY NAME LODGE?
TELL ME, THAT I MAY SACK THE HATEFUL MANSION.
HOLD THY DESPERATE HAND: ART THOU A MAN?
THY FORM CRIES OUT THOU ART: THY TEARS ARE WOMANISH; THY WILD ACTS DENOTE THE UNREASONABLE FURY OF A BEAST:
UNSEEMLY WOMAN IN A SEEMING MAN! AND ILL-BESEEMING BEAST IN SEEMING BOTH!
THOU HAST AMAZ'D ME:
BY MY HOLY ORDER, I THOUGHT THY DISPOSITION BETTER TEMPER'D.
HAST THOU SLAIN TYBALT? WILT THOU SLAY THYSELF? AND SLAY THY LADY, THAT IN THY LIFE LIVES, BY DOING DAMNED HATE UPON THYSELF?
Fling...

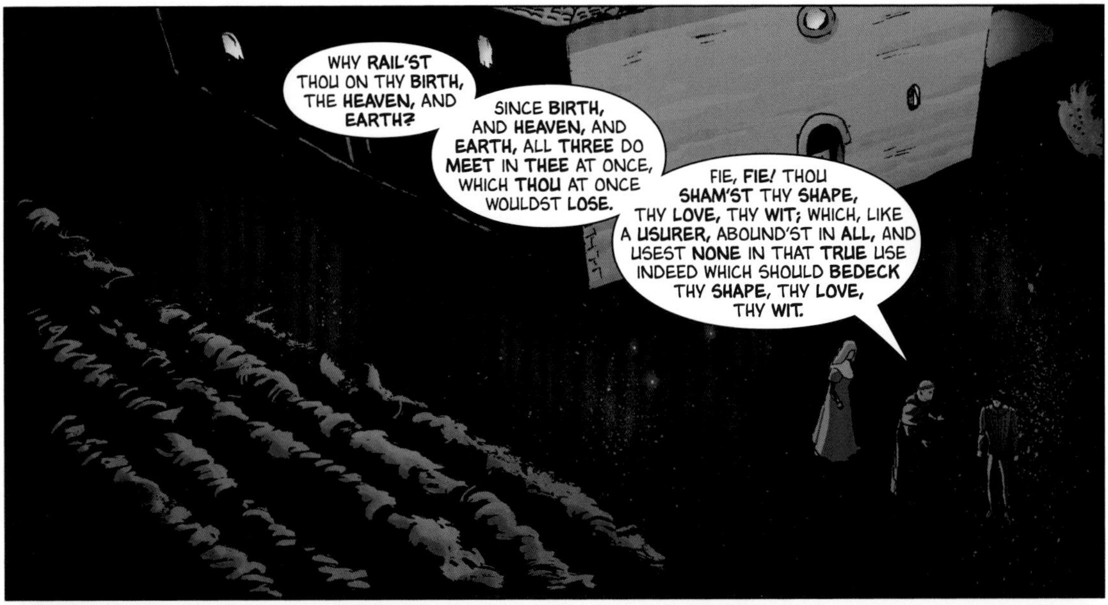
WHY RAIL'ST THOU ON THY BIRTH, THE HEAVEN, AND EARTH?
SINCE BIRTH, AND HEAVEN, AND EARTH, ALL THREE DO MEET IN THEE AT ONCE, WHICH THOU AT ONCE WOULDST LOSE.
FIE, FIE! THOU SHAM'ST THY SHAPE, THY LOVE, THY WIT; WHICH, LIKE A USURER, ABOUND'ST IN ALL, AND USEST NONE IN THAT TRUE USE INDEED WHICH SHOULD BEDECK THY SHAPE, THY LOVE, THY WIT.

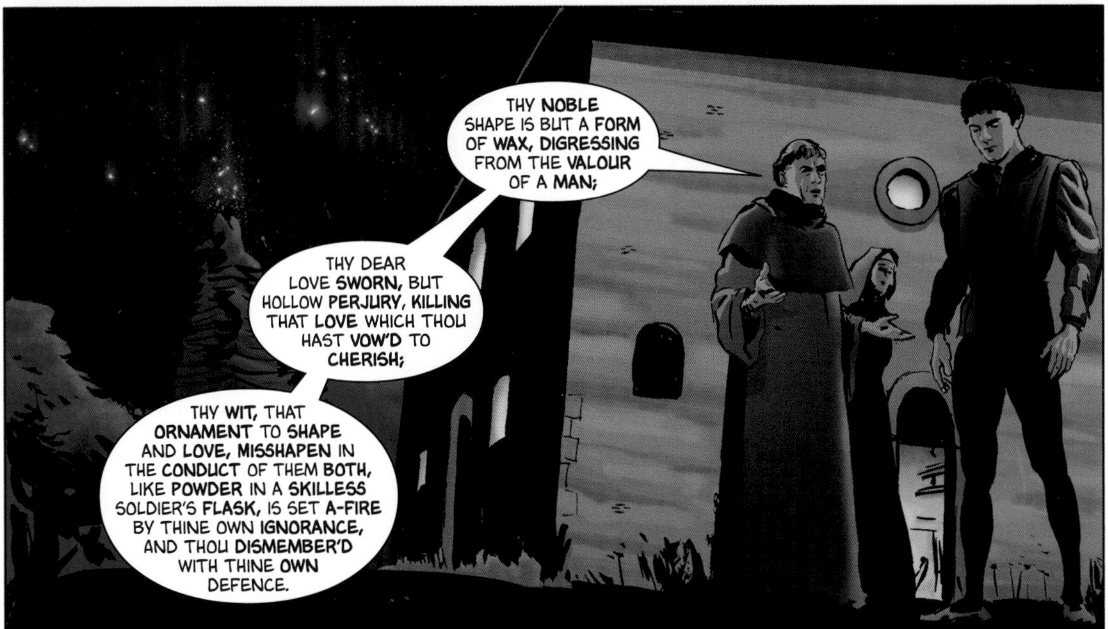
THY NOBLE SHAPE IS BUT A FORM OF WAX, DIGRESSING FROM THE VALOUR OF A MAN;
THY DEAR LOVE SWORN, BUT HOLLOW PERJURY, KILLING THAT LOVE WHICH THOU HAST VOW'D TO CHERISH;
THY WIT, THAT ORNAMENT TO SHAPE AND LOVE, MISSHAPEN IN THE CONDUCT OF THEM BOTH, LIKE POWDER IN A SKILLESS SOLDIER'S FLASK, IS SET A-FIRE BY THINE OWN IGNORANCE, AND THOU DISMEMBER'D WITH THINE OWN DEFENCE.

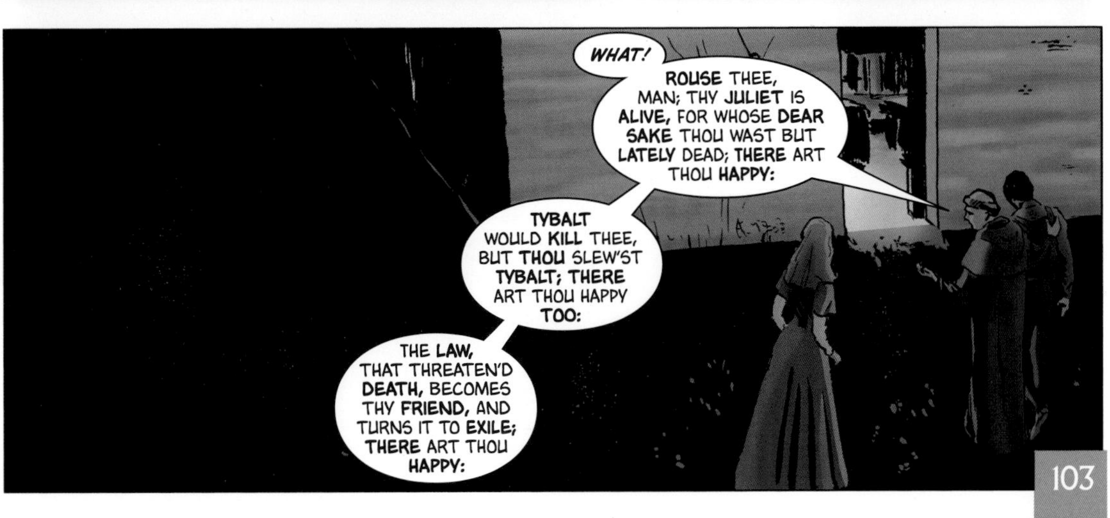
WHAT!
ROUSE THEE, MAN; THY JULIET IS ALIVE, FOR WHOSE DEAR SAKE THOU WAST BUT LATELY DEAD; THERE ART THOU HAPPY:
TYBALT WOULD KILL THEE, BUT THOU SLEW'ST TYBALT; THERE ART THOU HAPPY TOO:
THE LAW, THAT THREATEN'D DEATH, BECOMES THY FRIEND, AND TURNS IT TO EXILE; THERE ART THOU HAPPY:

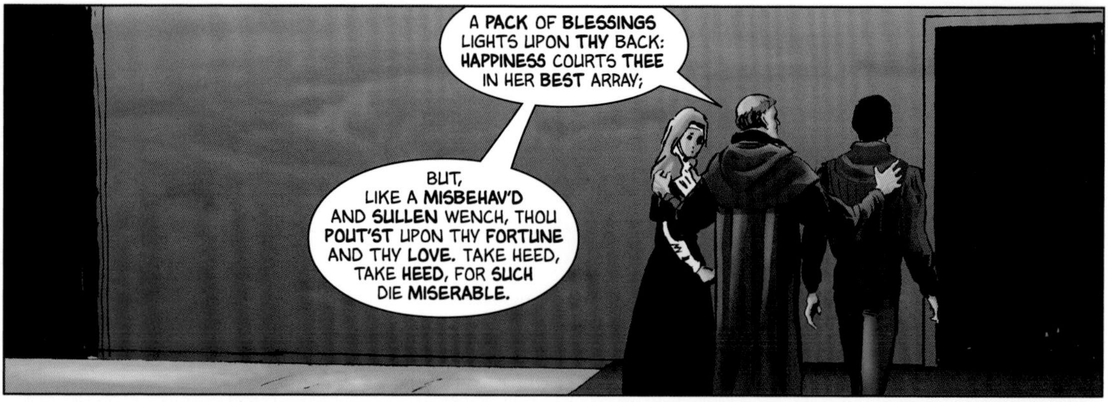
A PACK OF BLESSINGS LIGHTS UPON THY BACK: HAPPINESS COURTS THEE IN HER BEST ARRAY;
BUT, LIKE A MISBEHAV'D AND SULLEN WENCH, THOU POUT'ST UPON THY FORTUNE AND THY LOVE. TAKE HEED, TAKE HEED, FOR SUCH DIE MISERABLE.

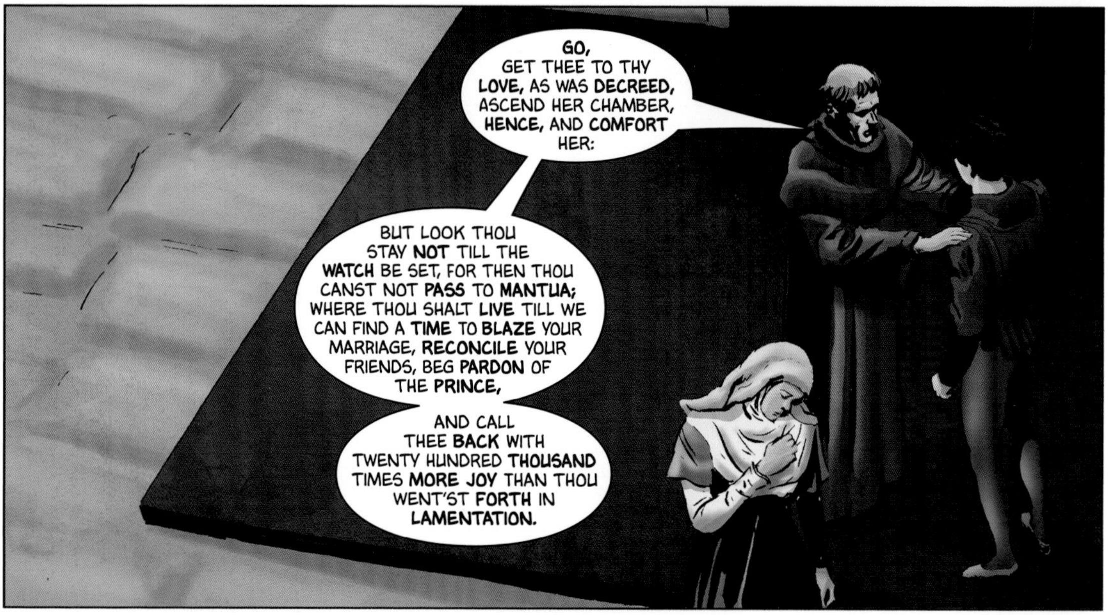
GO, GET THEE TO THY LOVE, AS WAS DECREED, ASCEND HER CHAMBER, HENCE, AND COMFORT HER:
BUT LOOK THOU STAY NOT TILL THE WATCH BE SET, FOR THEN THOU CANST NOT PASS TO MANTUA; WHERE THOU SHALT LIVE TILL WE CAN FIND A TIME TO BLAZE YOUR MARRIAGE, RECONCILE YOUR FRIENDS, BEG PARDON OF THE PRINCE,
AND CALL THEE BACK WITH TWENTY HUNDRED THOUSAND TIMES MORE JOY THAN THOU WENT'ST FORTH IN LAMENTATION.

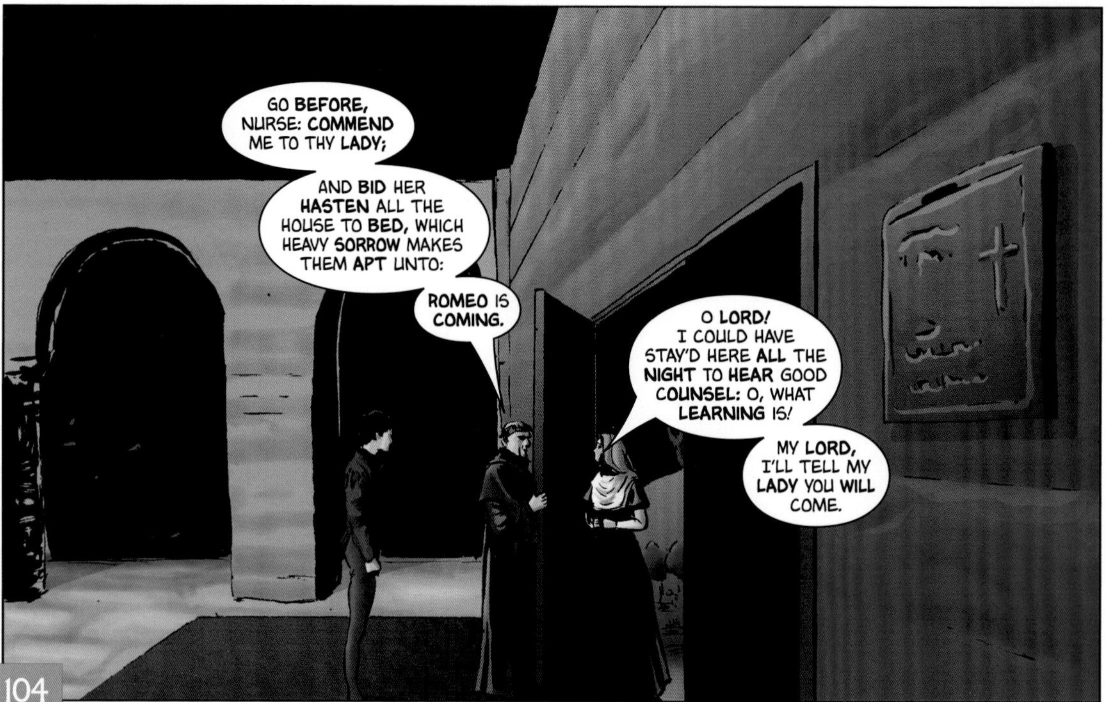
GO BEFORE, NURSE: COMMEND ME TO THY LADY;
AND BID HER HASTEN ALL THE HOUSE TO BED, WHICH HEAVY SORROW MAKES THEM APT UNTO:
ROMEO IS COMING.
O LORD! I COULD HAVE STAY'D HERE ALL THE NIGHT TO HEAR GOOD COUNSEL: O, WHAT LEARNING IS!
MY LORD, I'LL TELL MY LADY YOU WILL COME.

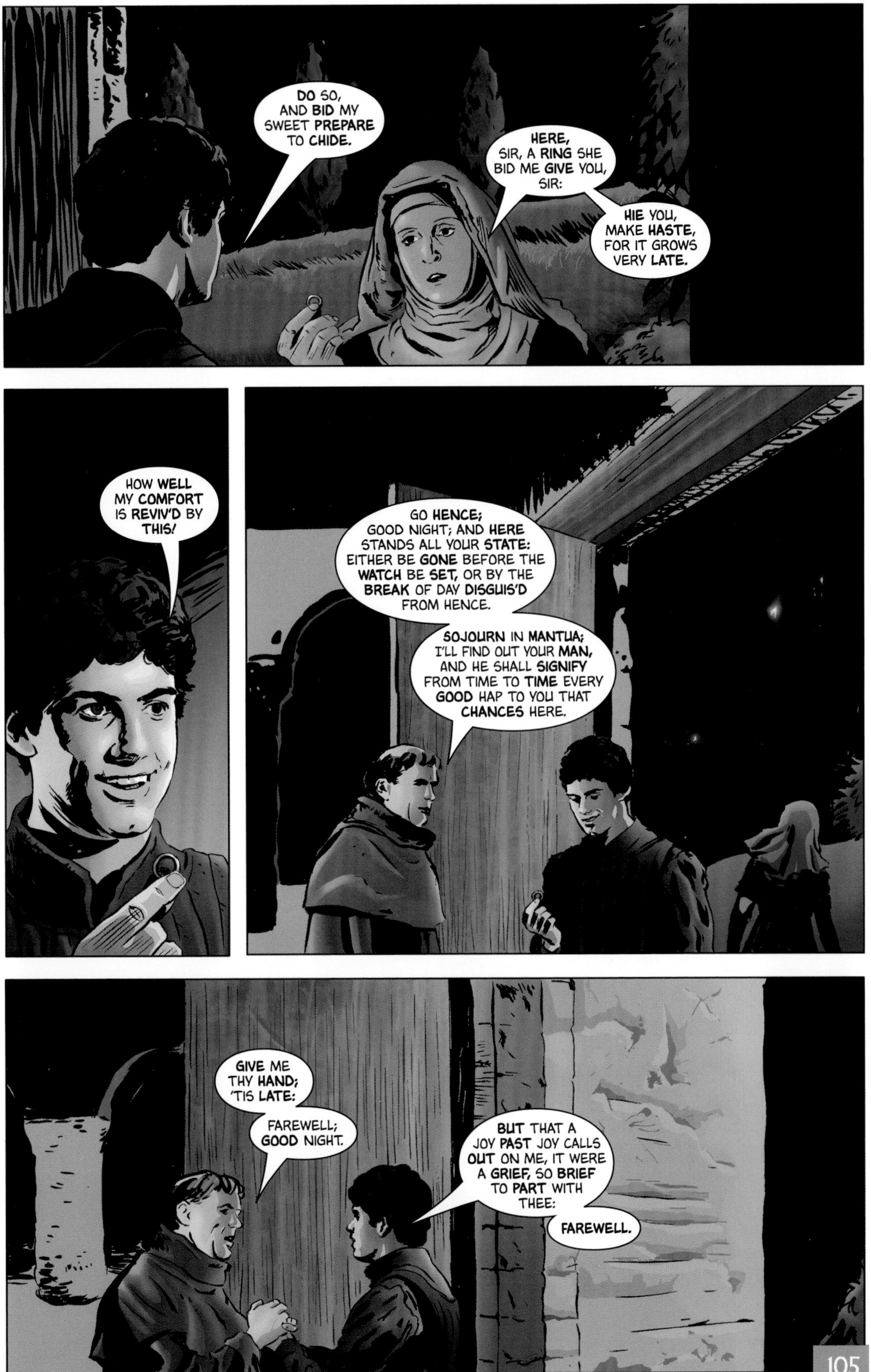
DO SO, AND BID MY SWEET PREPARE TO CHIDE.
HERE, SIR, A RING SHE BID ME GIVE YOU, SIR:
HIE YOU, MAKE HASTE, FOR IT GROWS VERY LATE.
HOW WELL MY COMFORT IS REVIV'D BY THIS!
GO HENCE; GOOD NIGHT; AND HERE STANDS ALL YOUR STATE: EITHER BE GONE BEFORE THE WATCH BE SET, OR BY THE BREAK OF DAY DISGUIS'D FROM HENCE.
SOJOURN IN MANTUA; I'LL FIND OUT YOUR MAN, AND HE SHALL SIGNIFY FROM TIME TO TIME EVERY GOOD HAP TO YOU THAT CHANCES HERE.
GIVE ME THY HAND; 'TIS LATE:
FAREWELL; GOOD NIGHT.
BUT THAT A JOY PAST JOY CALLS OUT ON ME, IT WERE A GRIEF, SO BRIEF TO PART WITH THEE:
FAREWELL.

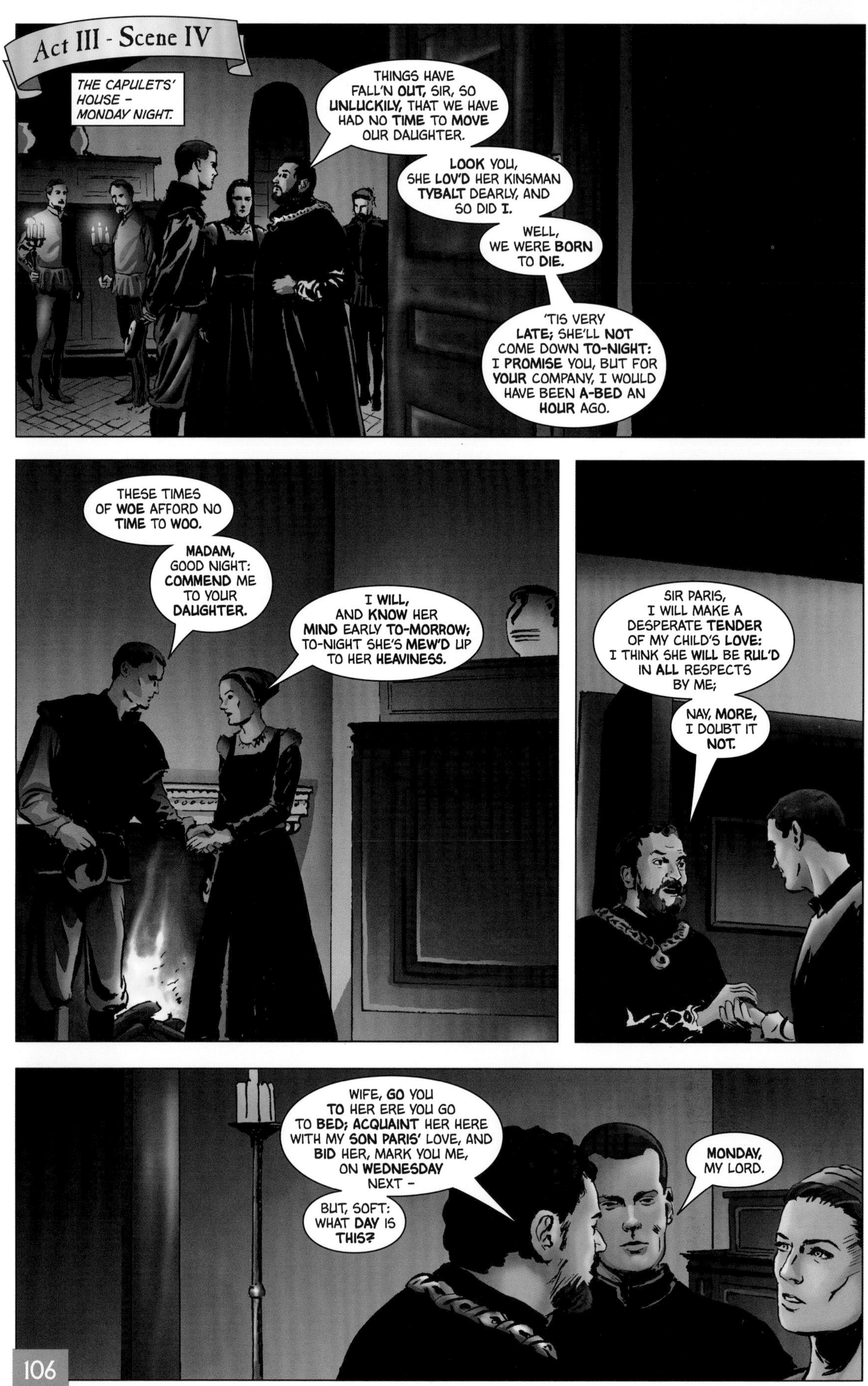
Act III - Scene IV
THE CAPULETS' HOUSE – MONDAY NIGHT.
THINGS HAVE FALL'N OUT, SIR, SO UNLUCKILY, THAT WE HAVE HAD NO TIME TO MOVE OUR DAUGHTER.
LOOK YOU, SHE LOV'D HER KINSMAN TYBALT DEARLY, AND SO DID I.
WELL, WE WERE BORN TO DIE.
'TIS VERY LATE; SHE'LL NOT COME DOWN TO-NIGHT: I PROMISE YOU, BUT FOR YOUR COMPANY, I WOULD HAVE BEEN A-BED AN HOUR AGO.
THESE TIMES OF WOE AFFORD NO TIME TO WOO.
MADAM, GOOD NIGHT: COMMEND ME TO YOUR DAUGHTER.
I WILL, AND KNOW HER MIND EARLY TO-MORROW; TO-NIGHT SHE'S MEW'D UP TO HER HEAVINESS.
SIR PARIS, I WILL MAKE A DESPERATE TENDER OF MY CHILD'S LOVE: I THINK SHE WILL BE RUL'D IN ALL RESPECTS BY ME;
NAY, MORE, I DOUBT IT NOT.
WIFE, GO YOU TO HER ERE YOU GO TO BED; ACQUAINT HER HERE WITH MY SON PARIS' LOVE, AND BID HER, MARK YOU ME, ON WEDNESDAY NEXT –
BUT, SOFT: WHAT DAY IS THIS?
MONDAY, MY LORD.

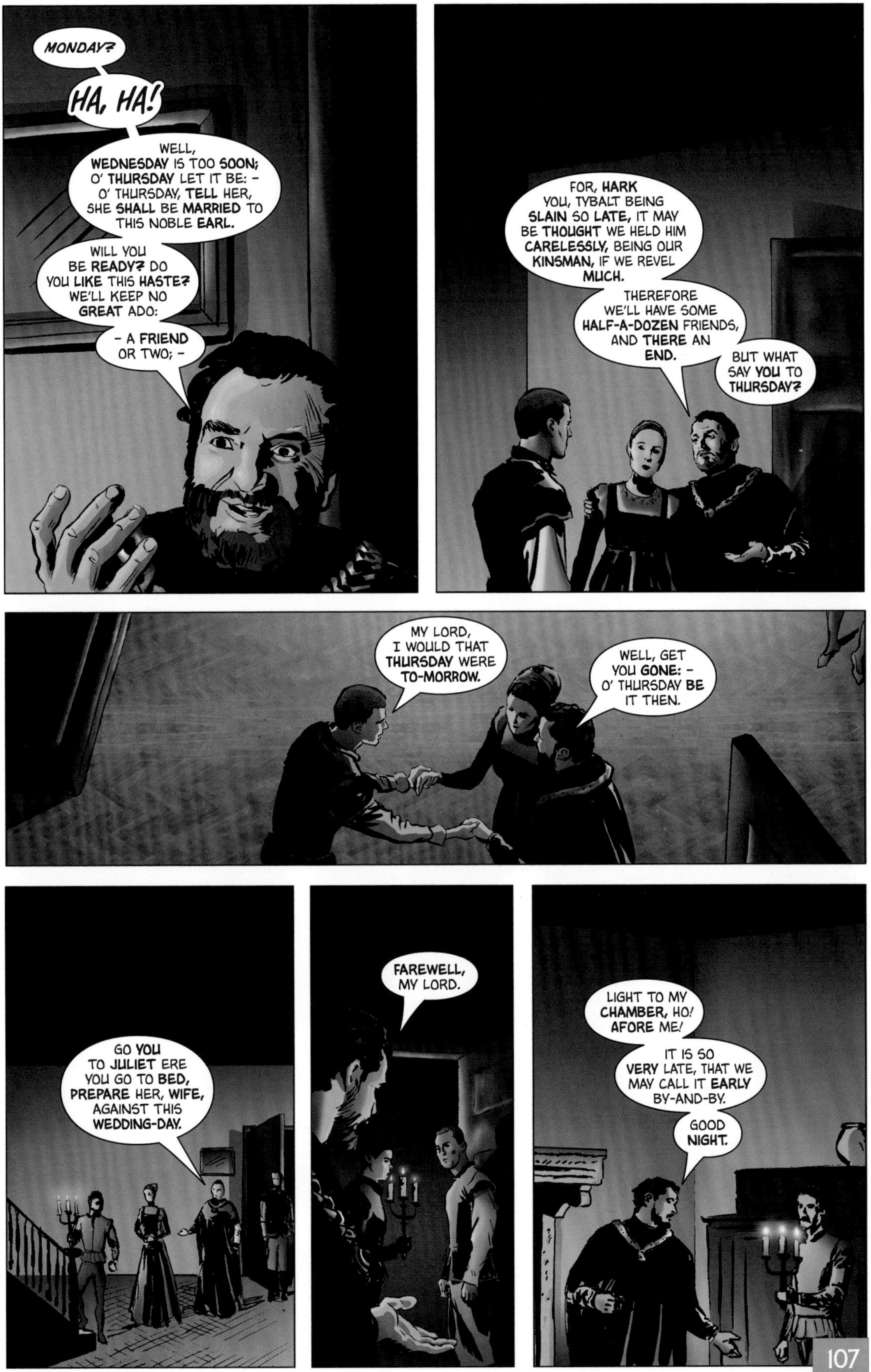
MONDAY?
HA, HA!
WELL, WEDNESDAY IS TOO SOON; O' THURSDAY LET IT BE: - O' THURSDAY, TELL HER, SHE SHALL BE MARRIED TO THIS NOBLE EARL.
WILL YOU BE READY? DO YOU LIKE THIS HASTE? WE'LL KEEP NO GREAT ADO:
- A FRIEND OR TWO; -
FOR, HARK YOU, TYBALT BEING SLAIN SO LATE, IT MAY BE THOUGHT WE HELD HIM CARELESSLY, BEING OUR KINSMAN, IF WE REVEL MUCH.
THEREFORE WE'LL HAVE SOME HALF-A-DOZEN FRIENDS, AND THERE AN END.
BUT WHAT SAY YOU TO THURSDAY?
MY LORD, I WOULD THAT THURSDAY WERE TO-MORROW.
WELL, GET YOU GONE: - O' THURSDAY BE IT THEN.
GO YOU TO JULIET ERE YOU GO TO BED, PREPARE HER, WIFE, AGAINST THIS WEDDING-DAY.
FAREWELL, MY LORD.
LIGHT TO MY CHAMBER, HO! AFORE ME!
IT IS SO VERY LATE, THAT WE MAY CALL IT EARLY BY-AND-BY.
GOOD NIGHT.

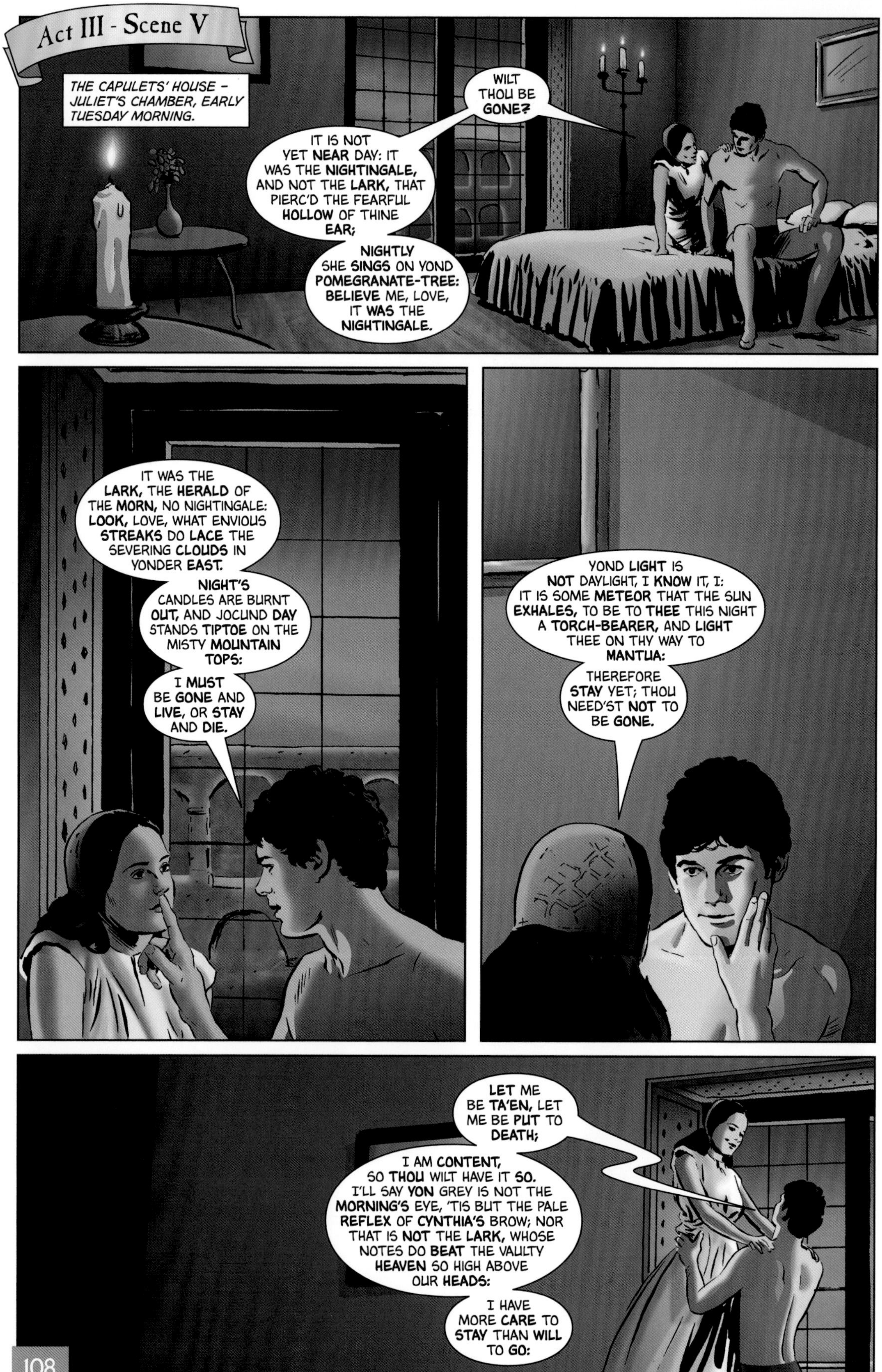
Act III - Scene V
THE CAPULETS' HOUSE – JULIET'S CHAMBER, EARLY TUESDAY MORNING.
WILT THOU BE GONE?
IT IS NOT YET NEAR DAY: IT WAS THE NIGHTINGALE, AND NOT THE LARK, THAT PIERC'D THE FEARFUL HOLLOW OF THINE EAR;
NIGHTLY SHE SINGS ON YOND POMEGRANATE-TREE: BELIEVE ME, LOVE, IT WAS THE NIGHTINGALE.
IT WAS THE LARK, THE HERALD OF THE MORN, NO NIGHTINGALE: LOOK, LOVE, WHAT ENVIOUS STREAKS DO LACE THE SEVERING CLOUDS IN YONDER EAST.
NIGHT'S CANDLES ARE BURNT OUT, AND JOCUND DAY STANDS TIPTOE ON THE MISTY MOUNTAIN TOPS:
I MUST BE GONE AND LIVE, OR STAY AND DIE.
YOND LIGHT IS NOT DAYLIGHT, I KNOW IT, I: IT IS SOME METEOR THAT THE SUN EXHALES, TO BE TO THEE THIS NIGHT A TORCH-BEARER, AND LIGHT THEE ON THY WAY TO MANTUA:
THEREFORE STAY YET; THOU NEED'ST NOT TO BE GONE.
LET ME BE TA'EN, LET ME BE PUT TO DEATH;
I AM CONTENT, SO THOU WILT HAVE IT SO. I'LL SAY YON GREY IS NOT THE MORNING'S EYE, 'TIS BUT THE PALE REFLEX OF CYNTHIA'S BROW; NOR THAT IS NOT THE LARK, WHOSE NOTES DO BEAT THE VAULTY HEAVEN SO HIGH ABOVE OUR HEADS:
I HAVE MORE CARE TO STAY THAN WILL TO GO:

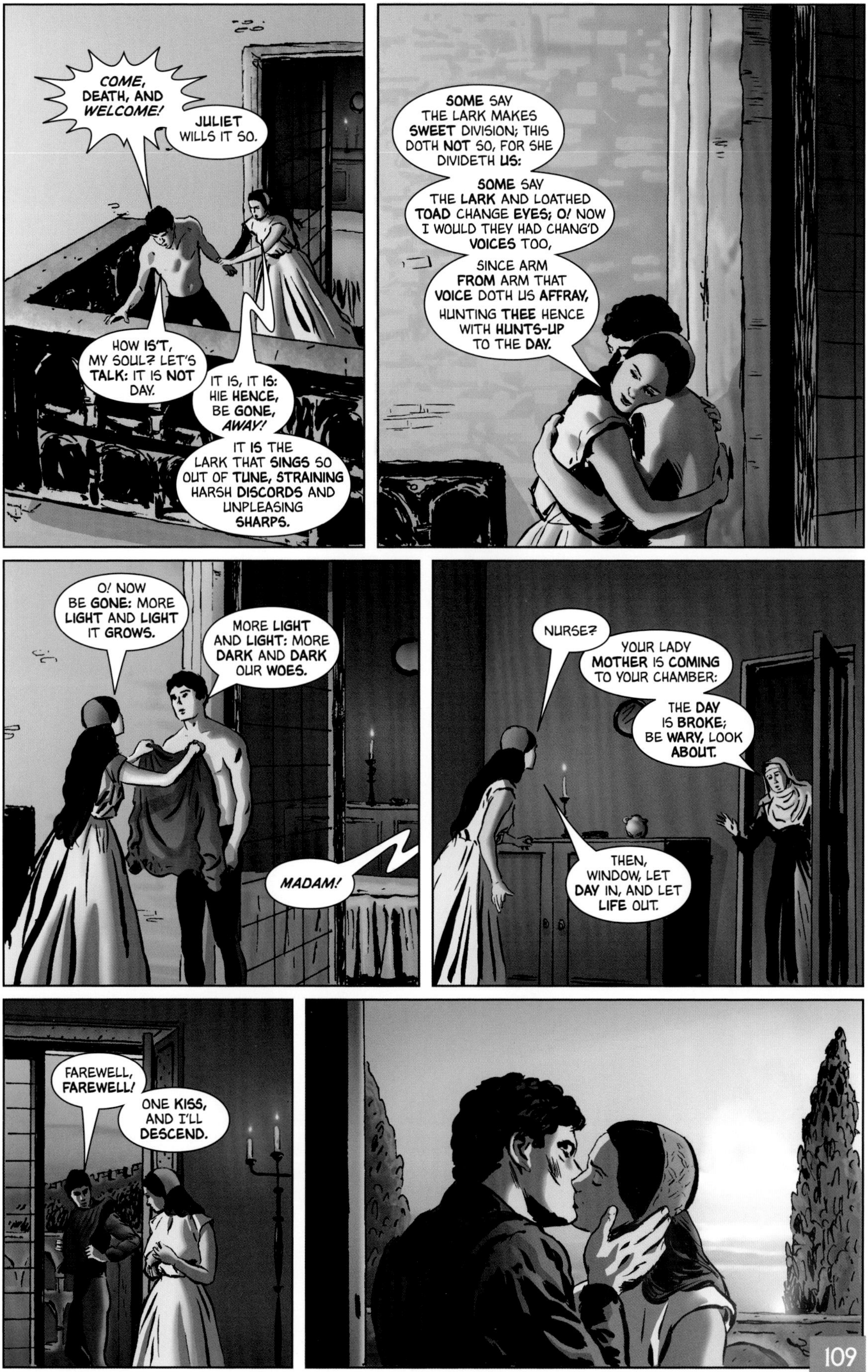
COME, DEATH, AND WELCOME!
JULIET WILLS IT SO.
HOW IS'T, MY SOUL? LET'S TALK: IT IS NOT DAY.
IT IS, IT IS: HIE HENCE, BE GONE, AWAY!
IT IS THE LARK THAT SINGS SO OUT OF TUNE, STRAINING HARSH DISCORDS AND UNPLEASING SHARPS.
SOME SAY THE LARK MAKES SWEET DIVISION; THIS DOTH NOT SO, FOR SHE DIVIDETH US:
SOME SAY THE LARK AND LOATHED TOAD CHANGE EYES; O! NOW I WOULD THEY HAD CHANG'D VOICES TOO,
SINCE ARM FROM ARM THAT VOICE DOTH US AFFRAY,
HUNTING THEE HENCE WITH HUNTS-UP TO THE DAY.
O! NOW BE GONE: MORE LIGHT AND LIGHT IT GROWS.
MORE LIGHT AND LIGHT: MORE DARK AND DARK OUR WOES.
MADAM!
NURSE?
YOUR LADY MOTHER IS COMING TO YOUR CHAMBER:
THE DAY IS BROKE; BE WARY, LOOK ABOUT.
THEN, WINDOW, LET DAY IN, AND LET LIFE OUT.
FAREWELL, FAREWELL!
ONE KISS, AND I'LL DESCEND.

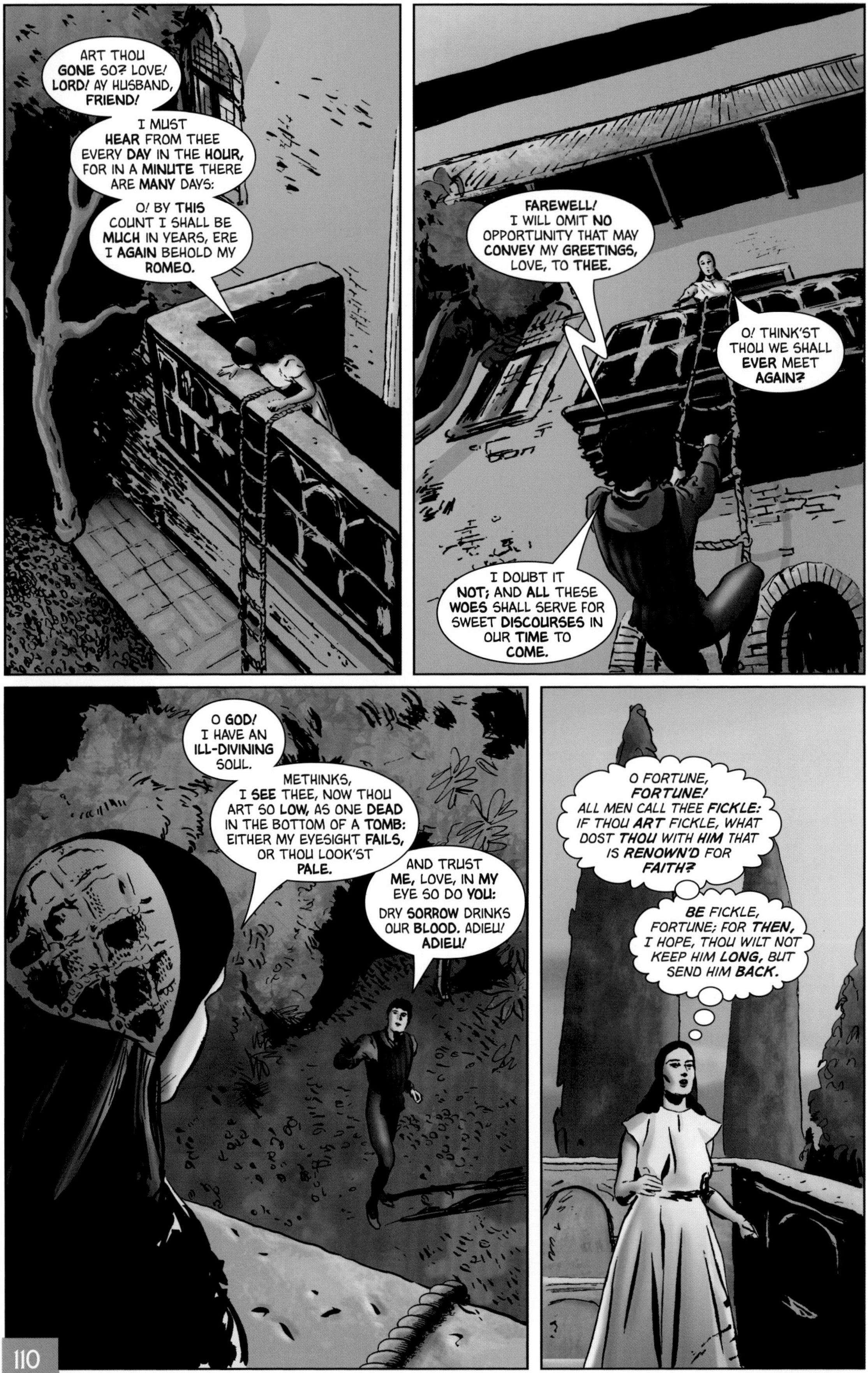
ART THOU GONE SO? LOVE! LORD! AY HUSBAND, FRIEND!
I MUST HEAR FROM THEE EVERY DAY IN THE HOUR, FOR IN A MINUTE THERE ARE MANY DAYS:
O! BY THIS COUNT I SHALL BE MUCH IN YEARS, ERE I AGAIN BEHOLD MY ROMEO.
FAREWELL! I WILL OMIT NO OPPORTUNITY THAT MAY CONVEY MY GREETINGS, LOVE, TO THEE.
O! THINK'ST THOU WE SHALL EVER MEET AGAIN?
I DOUBT IT NOT; AND ALL THESE WOES SHALL SERVE FOR SWEET DISCOURSES IN OUR TIME TO COME.
O GOD! I HAVE AN ILL-DIVINING SOUL.
METHINKS, I SEE THEE, NOW THOU ART SO LOW, AS ONE DEAD IN THE BOTTOM OF A TOMB: EITHER MY EYESIGHT FAILS, OR THOU LOOK'ST PALE.
AND TRUST ME, LOVE, IN MY EYE SO DO YOU: DRY SORROW DRINKS OUR BLOOD. ADIEU! ADIEU!
O FORTUNE, FORTUNE! ALL MEN CALL THEE FICKLE: IF THOU ART FICKLE, WHAT DOST THOU WITH HIM THAT IS RENOWN'D FOR FAITH?
BE FICKLE, FORTUNE; FOR THEN, I HOPE, THOU WILT NOT KEEP HIM LONG, BUT SEND HIM BACK.

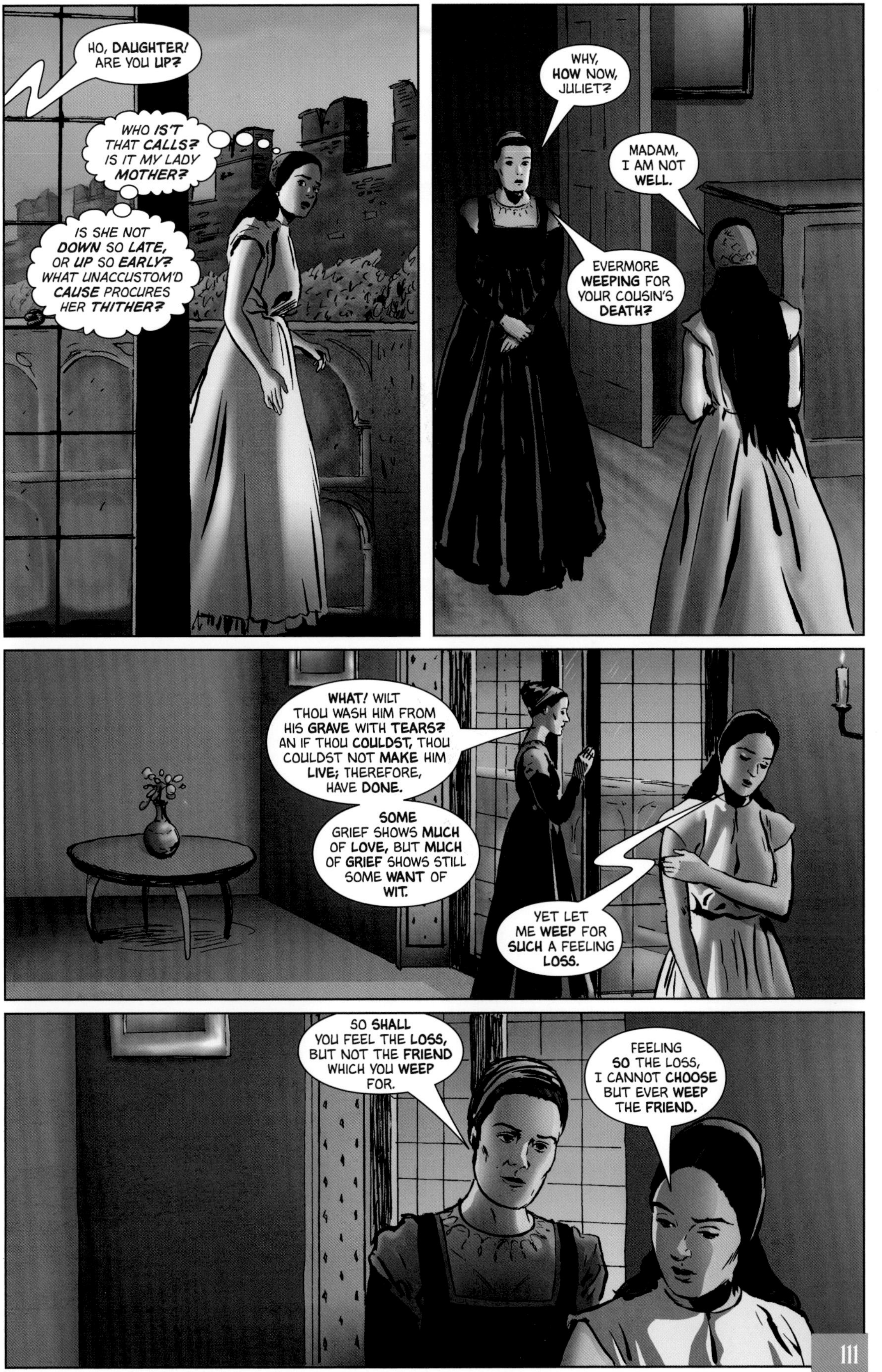

HO, DAUGHTER! ARE YOU UP?
WHO IS'T THAT CALLS? IS IT MY LADY MOTHER?
IS SHE NOT DOWN SO LATE, OR UP SO EARLY? WHAT UNACCUSTOM'D CAUSE PROCURES HER THITHER?
WHY, HOW NOW, JULIET?
MADAM, I AM NOT WELL.
EVERMORE WEEPING FOR YOUR COUSIN'S DEATH?
WHAT! WILT THOU WASH HIM FROM HIS GRAVE WITH TEARS? AN IF THOU COULDST, THOU COULDST NOT MAKE HIM LIVE; THEREFORE, HAVE DONE.
SOME GRIEF SHOWS MUCH OF LOVE, BUT MUCH OF GRIEF SHOWS STILL SOME WANT OF WIT.
YET LET ME WEEP FOR SUCH A FEELING LOSS.
SO SHALL YOU FEEL THE LOSS, BUT NOT THE FRIEND WHICH YOU WEEP FOR.
FEELING SO THE LOSS, I CANNOT CHOOSE BUT EVER WEEP THE FRIEND.

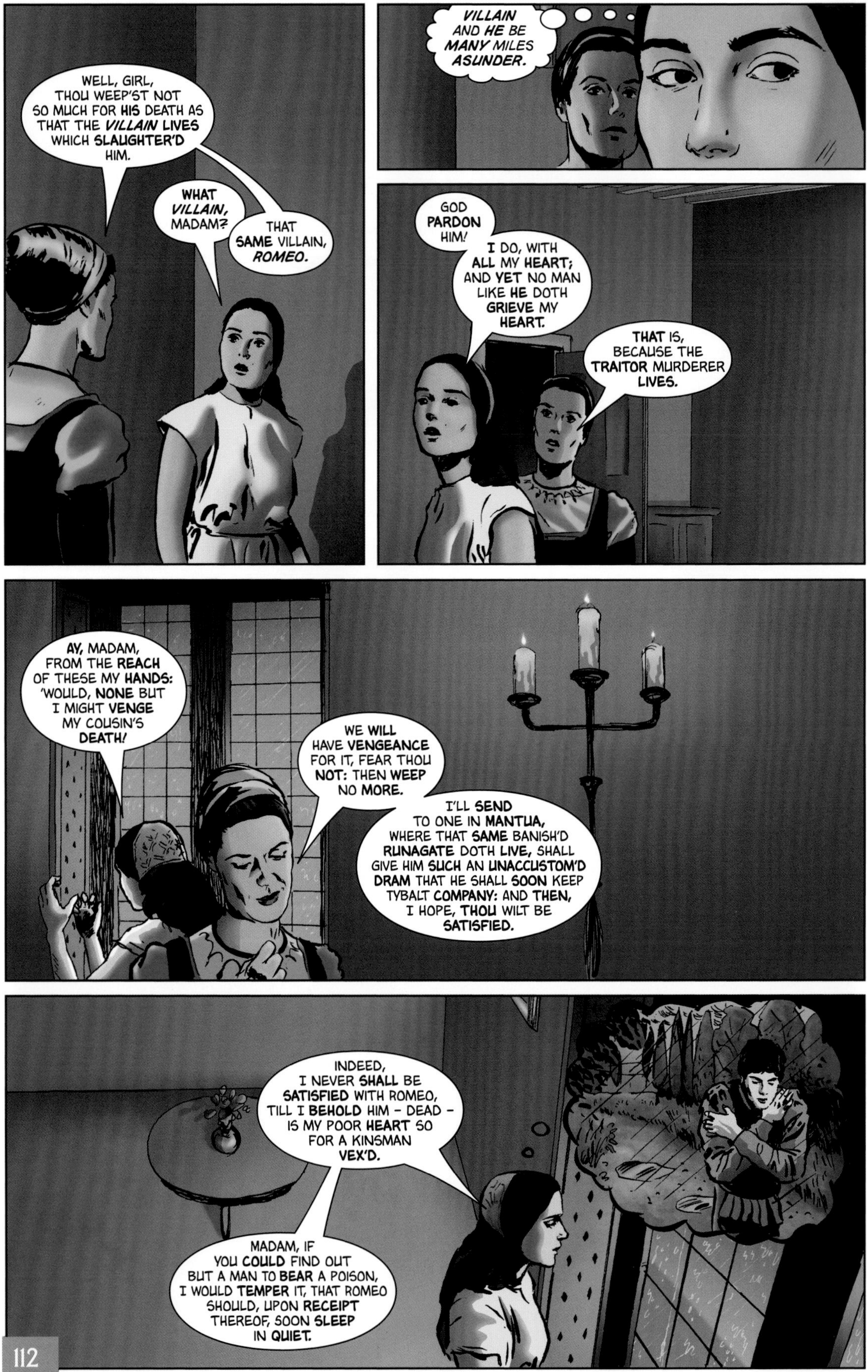
WELL, GIRL, THOU WEEP'ST NOT SO MUCH FOR HIS DEATH AS THAT THE VILLAIN LIVES WHICH SLAUGHTER'D HIM.
WHAT VILLAIN, MADAM?
THAT SAME VILLAIN, ROMEO.
VILLAIN AND HE BE MANY MILES ASUNDER.
GOD PARDON HIM!
I DO, WITH ALL MY HEART; AND YET NO MAN LIKE HE DOTH GRIEVE MY HEART.
THAT IS, BECAUSE THE TRAITOR MURDERER LIVES.
AY, MADAM, FROM THE REACH OF THESE MY HANDS: 'WOULD, NONE BUT I MIGHT VENGE MY COUSIN'S DEATH!
WE WILL HAVE VENGEANCE FOR IT, FEAR THOU NOT: THEN WEEP NO MORE.
I'LL SEND TO ONE IN MANTUA, WHERE THAT SAME BANISH'D RUNAGATE DOTH LIVE, SHALL GIVE HIM SUCH AN UNACCUSTOM'D DRAM THAT HE SHALL SOON KEEP TYBALT COMPANY: AND THEN, I HOPE, THOU WILT BE SATISFIED.
INDEED, I NEVER SHALL BE SATISFIED WITH ROMEO, TILL I BEHOLD HIM - DEAD - IS MY POOR HEART SO FOR A KINSMAN VEX'D.
MADAM, IF YOU COULD FIND OUT BUT A MAN TO BEAR A POISON, I WOULD TEMPER IT, THAT ROMEO SHOULD, UPON RECEIPT THEREOF, SOON SLEEP IN QUIET.

O! HOW MY HEART **ABHORS** TO HEAR HIM **NAM'D**, AND CANNOT **COME** TO HIM, TO **WREAK** THE LOVE I BORE MY COUSIN UPON HIS **BODY** THAT HATH SLAUGHTER'D HIM!

FIND **THOU** THE **MEANS**, AND I'LL FIND SUCH A **MAN**. BUT **NOW** I'LL TELL THEE **JOYFUL** TIDINGS, GIRL.

AND **JOY** COMES **WELL** IN SUCH A **NEEDY** TIME: WHAT **ARE** THEY, I **BESEECH** YOUR LADYSHIP?

WELL, WELL, THOU HAST A **CAREFUL** FATHER, CHILD:

ONE WHO, TO PUT THEE FROM THY **HEAVINESS**, HATH **SORTED** OUT A **SUDDEN** DAY OF JOY, THAT THOU **EXPECT'ST** NOT, NOR I **LOOK'D** NOT FOR.

MADAM, IN **HAPPY** TIME, WHAT **DAY** IS THAT?

MARRY, MY CHILD, **EARLY** NEXT **THURSDAY** MORN, THE **GALLANT**, YOUNG, AND **NOBLE** GENTLEMAN, THE **COUNTY PARIS**,

AT SAINT PETER'S CHURCH, SHALL **HAPPILY** MAKE THEE THERE A JOYFUL **BRIDE.**

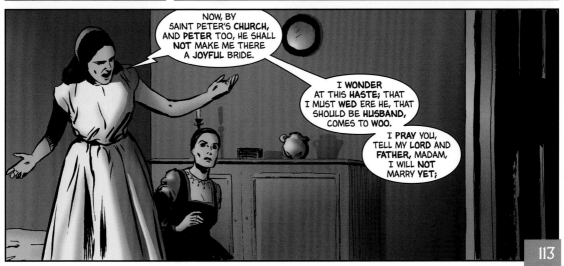

NOW, BY SAINT PETER'S **CHURCH**, AND **PETER** TOO, HE SHALL **NOT** MAKE ME THERE A **JOYFUL** BRIDE.

I **WONDER** AT THIS **HASTE**; THAT I MUST WED ERE HE, THAT SHOULD BE **HUSBAND**, COMES TO WOO.

I PRAY YOU, TELL MY **LORD** AND FATHER, MADAM, I WILL **NOT** MARRY YET;

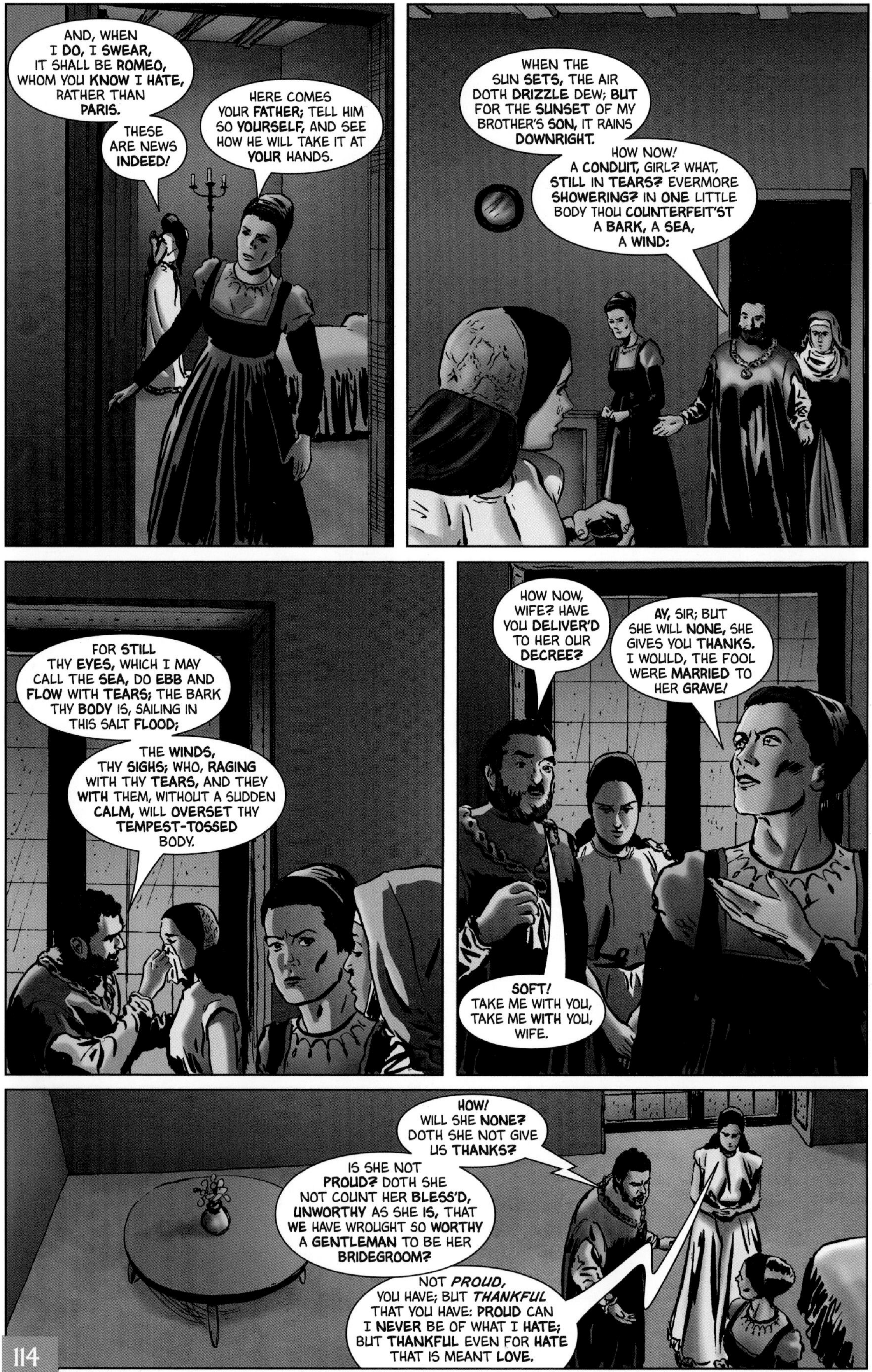
AND, WHEN I DO, I SWEAR, IT SHALL BE ROMEO, WHOM YOU KNOW I HATE, RATHER THAN PARIS.
THESE ARE NEWS INDEED!
HERE COMES YOUR FATHER; TELL HIM SO YOURSELF, AND SEE HOW HE WILL TAKE IT AT YOUR HANDS.
WHEN THE SUN SETS, THE AIR DOTH DRIZZLE DEW; BUT FOR THE SUNSET OF MY BROTHER'S SON, IT RAINS DOWNRIGHT.
HOW NOW! A CONDUIT, GIRL? WHAT, STILL IN TEARS? EVERMORE SHOWERING? IN ONE LITTLE BODY THOU COUNTERFEIT'ST A BARK, A SEA, A WIND:
FOR STILL THY EYES, WHICH I MAY CALL THE SEA, DO EBB AND FLOW WITH TEARS; THE BARK THY BODY IS, SAILING IN THIS SALT FLOOD;
THE WINDS, THY SIGHS; WHO, RAGING WITH THY TEARS, AND THEY WITH THEM, WITHOUT A SUDDEN CALM, WILL OVERSET THY TEMPEST-TOSSED BODY.
HOW NOW, WIFE? HAVE YOU DELIVER'D TO HER OUR DECREE?
AY, SIR; BUT SHE WILL NONE, SHE GIVES YOU THANKS. I WOULD, THE FOOL WERE MARRIED TO HER GRAVE!
SOFT! TAKE ME WITH YOU, TAKE ME WITH YOU, WIFE.
HOW! WILL SHE NONE? DOTH SHE NOT GIVE US THANKS?
IS SHE NOT PROUD? DOTH SHE NOT COUNT HER BLESS'D, UNWORTHY AS SHE IS, THAT WE HAVE WROUGHT SO WORTHY A GENTLEMAN TO BE HER BRIDEGROOM?
NOT PROUD, YOU HAVE; BUT THANKFUL THAT YOU HAVE: PROUD CAN I NEVER BE OF WHAT I HATE; BUT THANKFUL EVEN FOR HATE THAT IS MEANT LOVE.

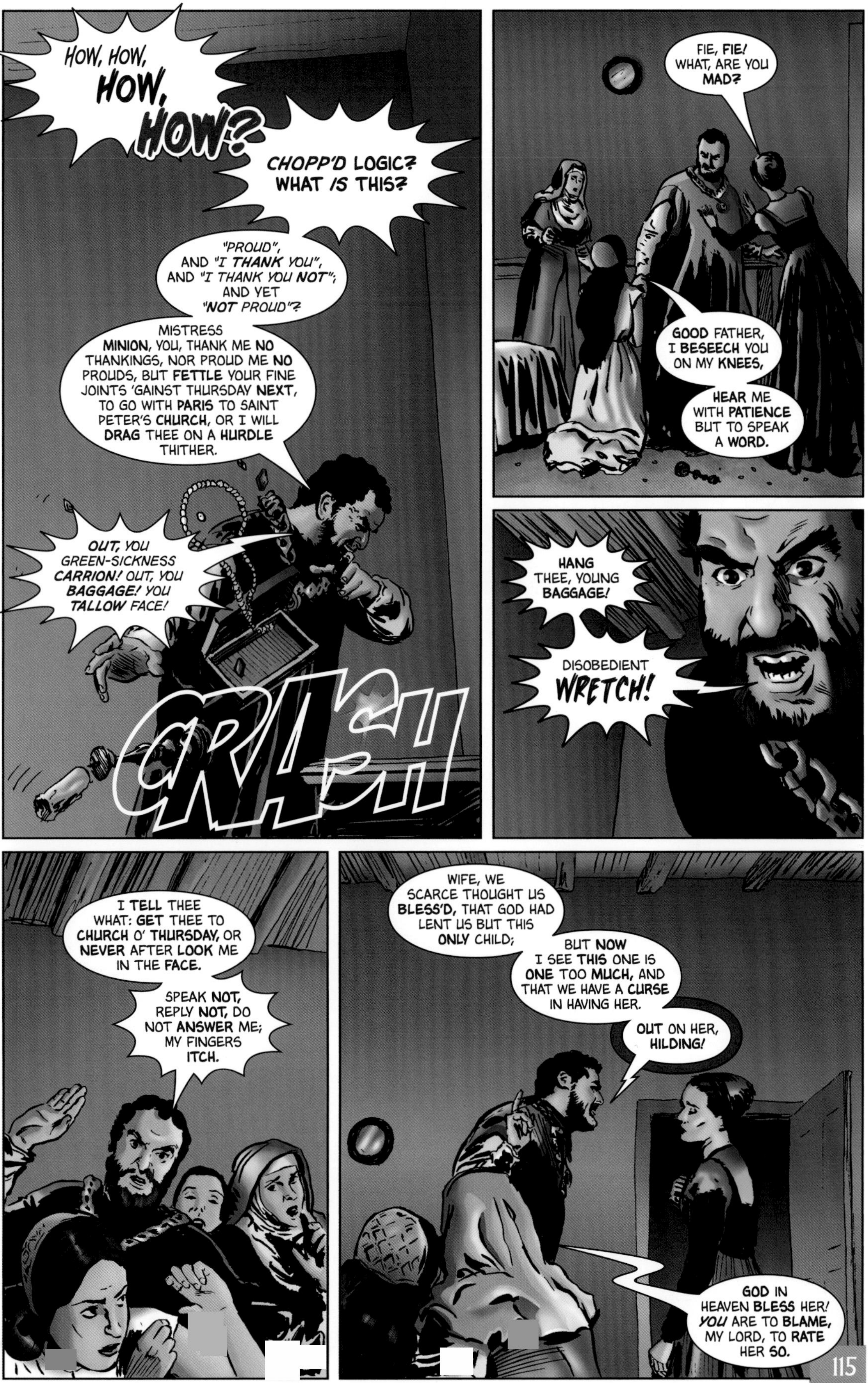
HOW, HOW, HOW, HOW?
CHOPP'D LOGIC? WHAT IS THIS?
"PROUD", AND "I THANK YOU", AND "I THANK YOU NOT"; AND YET "NOT PROUD"?
MISTRESS MINION, YOU, THANK ME NO THANKINGS, NOR PROUD ME NO PROUDS, BUT FETTLE YOUR FINE JOINTS 'GAINST THURSDAY NEXT, TO GO WITH PARIS TO SAINT PETER'S CHURCH, OR I WILL DRAG THEE ON A HURDLE THITHER.
OUT, YOU GREEN-SICKNESS CARRION! OUT, YOU BAGGAGE! YOU TALLOW FACE!
CRASH
FIE, FIE! WHAT, ARE YOU MAD?
GOOD FATHER, I BESEECH YOU ON MY KNEES,
HEAR ME WITH PATIENCE BUT TO SPEAK A WORD.
HANG THEE, YOUNG BAGGAGE!
DISOBEDIENT WRETCH!
I TELL THEE WHAT: GET THEE TO CHURCH O' THURSDAY, OR NEVER AFTER LOOK ME IN THE FACE.
SPEAK NOT, REPLY NOT, DO NOT ANSWER ME; MY FINGERS ITCH.
WIFE, WE SCARCE THOUGHT US BLESS'D, THAT GOD HAD LENT US BUT THIS ONLY CHILD;
BUT NOW I SEE THIS ONE IS ONE TOO MUCH, AND THAT WE HAVE A CURSE IN HAVING HER.
OUT ON HER, HILDING!
GOD IN HEAVEN BLESS HER! YOU ARE TO BLAME, MY LORD, TO RATE HER SO.

AND **WHY**, MY LADY **WISDOM**? HOLD YOUR **TONGUE**, **GOOD** PRUDENCE: **SMATTER** WITH YOUR GOSSIPS; *GO.*

I SPEAK NO **TREASON**.

O! GOD YE GOOD DEN.

MAY NOT ONE **SPEAK**?

PEACE, YOU MUMBLING FOOL!

UTTER YOUR GRAVITY O'ER A **GOSSIP'S** BOWL; FOR **HERE** WE NEED IT **NOT**.

YOU ARE TOO **HOT**.

GOD'S BREAD! IT MAKES ME **MAD**.

DAY, NIGHT, HOUR, TIDE, TIME, **WORK,** PLAY, **ALONE,** IN COMPANY, STILL MY CARE HATH BEEN TO HAVE HER **MATCH'D**:

AND HAVING NOW **PROVIDED** A GENTLEMAN OF **NOBLE** PARENTAGE, OF FAIR DEMESNES, **YOUTHFUL,** AND **NOBLY** LIGN'D, **STUFF'D**, AS THEY SAY, WITH **HONOURABLE** PARTS, PROPORTION'D AS ONE'S **THOUGHT** WOULD **WISH** A MAN;

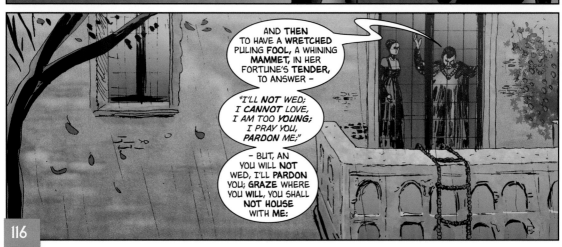

AND **THEN** TO HAVE A **WRETCHED** PULING **FOOL,** A WHINING **MAMMET,** IN HER FORTUNE'S **TENDER,** TO ANSWER –

*"I'LL **NOT** WED; I **CANNOT** LOVE, I AM TOO **YOUNG;** I PRAY YOU, **PARDON ME;"***

– BUT, AN YOU WILL **NOT** WED, I'LL PARDON YOU; **GRAZE** WHERE YOU WILL, YOU SHALL **NOT HOUSE** WITH ME:

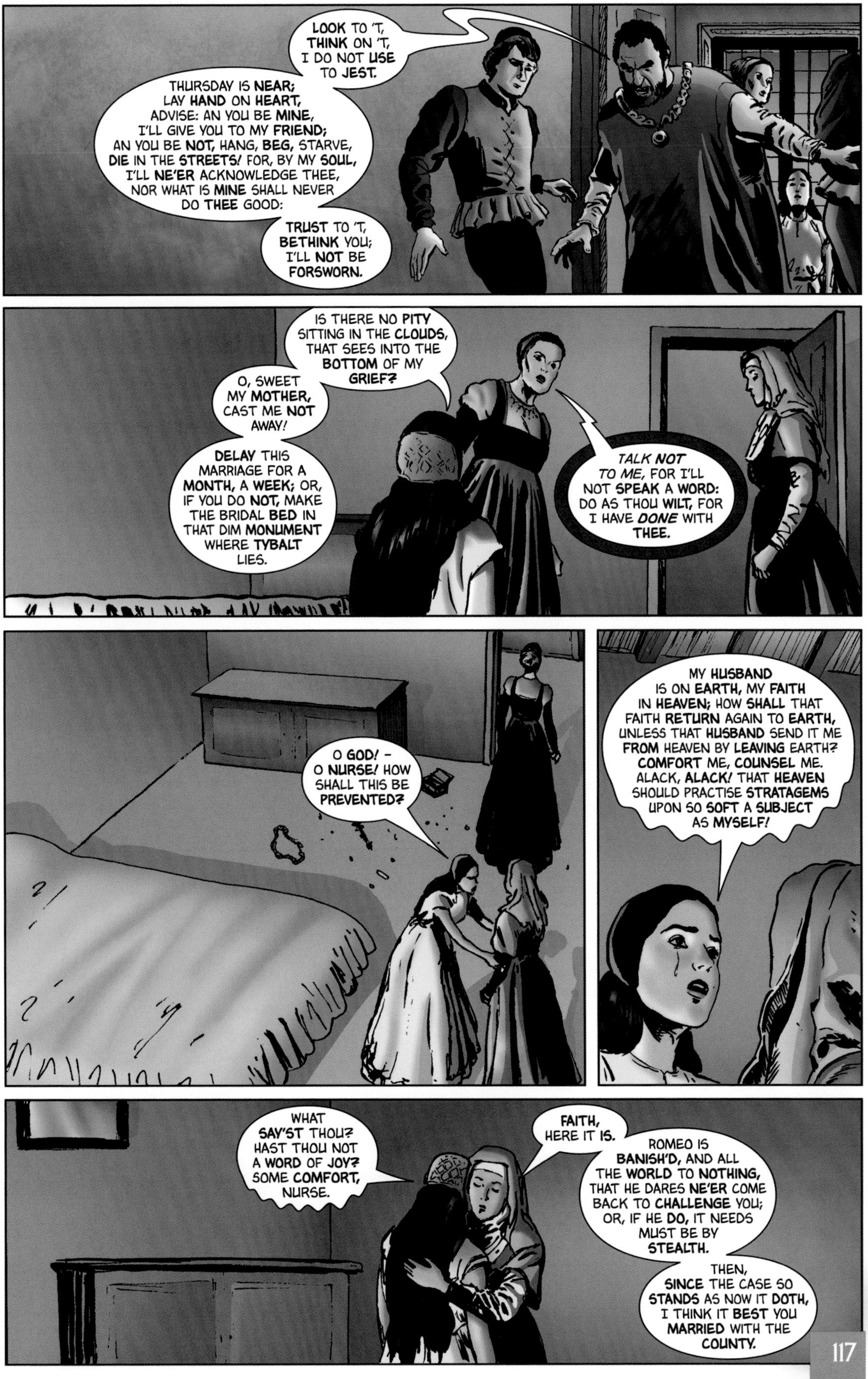

LOOK TO 'T, THINK ON 'T, I DO NOT USE TO JEST.
THURSDAY IS NEAR; LAY HAND ON HEART, ADVISE: AN YOU BE MINE, I'LL GIVE YOU TO MY FRIEND; AN YOU BE NOT, HANG, BEG, STARVE, DIE IN THE STREETS! FOR, BY MY SOUL, I'LL NE'ER ACKNOWLEDGE THEE, NOR WHAT IS MINE SHALL NEVER DO THEE GOOD:
TRUST TO 'T, BETHINK YOU; I'LL NOT BE FORSWORN.
IS THERE NO PITY SITTING IN THE CLOUDS, THAT SEES INTO THE BOTTOM OF MY GRIEF?
O, SWEET MY MOTHER, CAST ME NOT AWAY!
DELAY THIS MARRIAGE FOR A MONTH, A WEEK; OR, IF YOU DO NOT, MAKE THE BRIDAL BED IN THAT DIM MONUMENT WHERE TYBALT LIES.
TALK NOT TO ME, FOR I'LL NOT SPEAK A WORD: DO AS THOU WILT, FOR I HAVE DONE WITH THEE.
O GOD! – O NURSE! HOW SHALL THIS BE PREVENTED?
MY HUSBAND IS ON EARTH, MY FAITH IN HEAVEN; HOW SHALL THAT FAITH RETURN AGAIN TO EARTH, UNLESS THAT HUSBAND SEND IT ME FROM HEAVEN BY LEAVING EARTH? COMFORT ME, COUNSEL ME. ALACK, ALACK! THAT HEAVEN SHOULD PRACTISE STRATAGEMS UPON SO SOFT A SUBJECT AS MYSELF!
WHAT SAY'ST THOU? HAST THOU NOT A WORD OF JOY? SOME COMFORT, NURSE.
FAITH, HERE IT IS.
ROMEO IS BANISH'D, AND ALL THE WORLD TO NOTHING, THAT HE DARES NE'ER COME BACK TO CHALLENGE YOU; OR, IF HE DO, IT NEEDS MUST BE BY STEALTH.
THEN, SINCE THE CASE SO STANDS AS NOW IT DOTH, I THINK IT BEST YOU MARRIED WITH THE COUNTY.

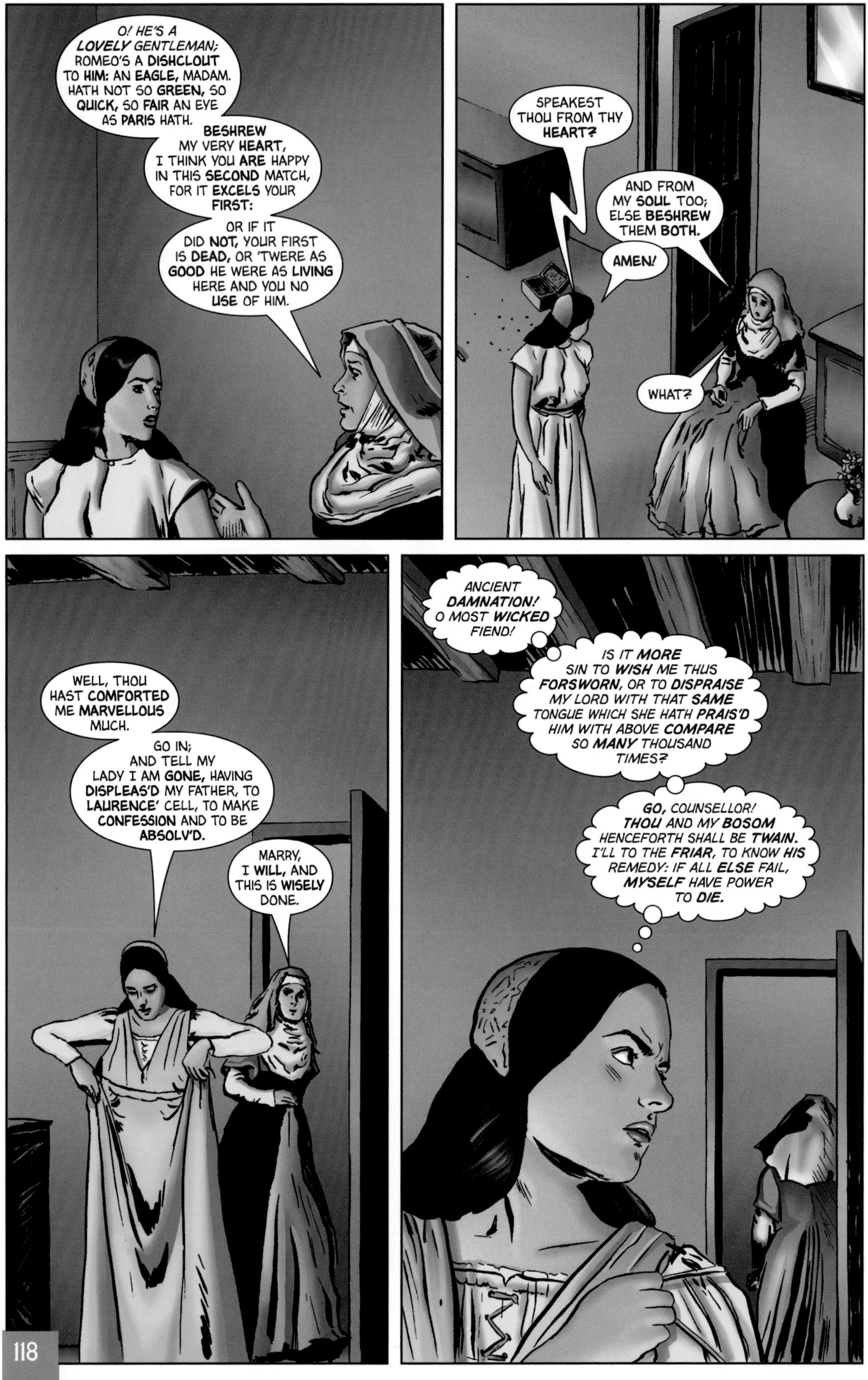
O! HE'S A LOVELY GENTLEMAN; ROMEO'S A DISHCLOUT TO HIM: AN EAGLE, MADAM, HATH NOT SO GREEN, SO QUICK, SO FAIR AN EYE AS PARIS HATH.
BESHREW MY VERY HEART, I THINK YOU ARE HAPPY IN THIS SECOND MATCH, FOR IT EXCELS YOUR FIRST:
OR IF IT DID NOT, YOUR FIRST IS DEAD, OR 'TWERE AS GOOD HE WERE AS LIVING HERE AND YOU NO USE OF HIM.
SPEAKEST THOU FROM THY HEART?
AND FROM MY SOUL TOO; ELSE BESHREW THEM BOTH.
AMEN!
WHAT?
WELL, THOU HAST COMFORTED ME MARVELLOUS MUCH.
GO IN; AND TELL MY LADY I AM GONE, HAVING DISPLEAS'D MY FATHER, TO LAURENCE' CELL, TO MAKE CONFESSION AND TO BE ABSOLV'D.
MARRY, I WILL, AND THIS IS WISELY DONE.
ANCIENT DAMNATION! O MOST WICKED FIEND!
IS IT MORE SIN TO WISH ME THUS FORSWORN, OR TO DISPRAISE MY LORD WITH THAT SAME TONGUE WHICH SHE HATH PRAIS'D HIM WITH ABOVE COMPARE SO MANY THOUSAND TIMES?
GO, COUNSELLOR! THOU AND MY BOSOM HENCEFORTH SHALL BE TWAIN. I'LL TO THE FRIAR, TO KNOW HIS REMEDY: IF ALL ELSE FAIL, MYSELF HAVE POWER TO DIE.

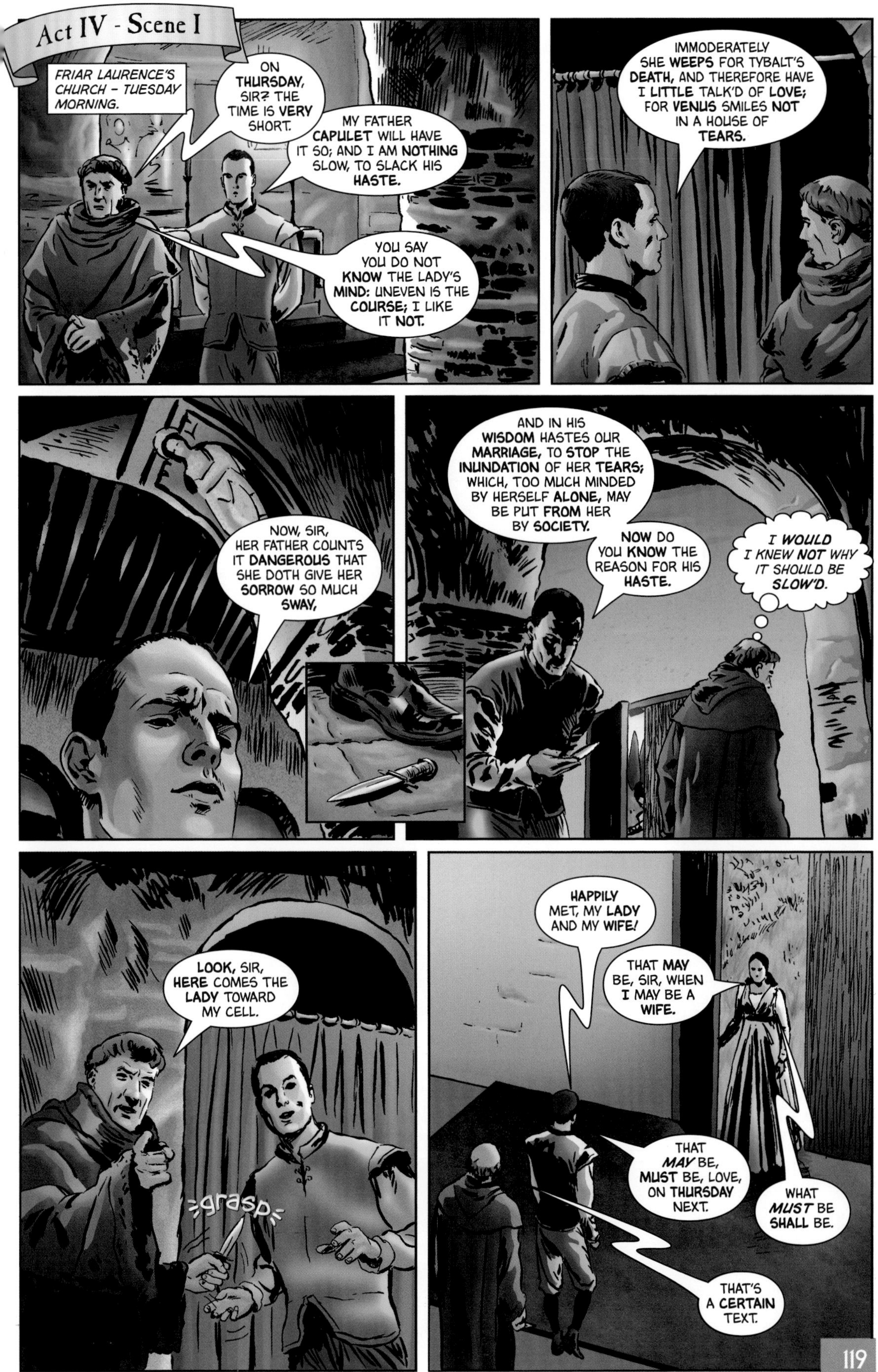
Act IV - Scene I
FRIAR LAURENCE'S CHURCH – TUESDAY MORNING.
ON THURSDAY, SIR? THE TIME IS VERY SHORT.
MY FATHER CAPULET WILL HAVE IT SO; AND I AM NOTHING SLOW, TO SLACK HIS HASTE.
YOU SAY YOU DO NOT KNOW THE LADY'S MIND: UNEVEN IS THE COURSE; I LIKE IT NOT.
IMMODERATELY SHE WEEPS FOR TYBALT'S DEATH, AND THEREFORE HAVE I LITTLE TALK'D OF LOVE; FOR VENUS SMILES NOT IN A HOUSE OF TEARS.
NOW, SIR, HER FATHER COUNTS IT DANGEROUS THAT SHE DOTH GIVE HER SORROW SO MUCH SWAY,
AND IN HIS WISDOM HASTES OUR MARRIAGE, TO STOP THE INUNDATION OF HER TEARS; WHICH, TOO MUCH MINDED BY HERSELF ALONE, MAY BE PUT FROM HER BY SOCIETY.
NOW DO YOU KNOW THE REASON FOR HIS HASTE.
I WOULD I KNEW NOT WHY IT SHOULD BE SLOW'D.
LOOK, SIR, HERE COMES THE LADY TOWARD MY CELL.
grasp
HAPPILY MET, MY LADY AND MY WIFE!
THAT MAY BE, SIR, WHEN I MAY BE A WIFE.
THAT MAY BE, MUST BE, LOVE, ON THURSDAY NEXT.
WHAT MUST BE SHALL BE.
THAT'S A CERTAIN TEXT.

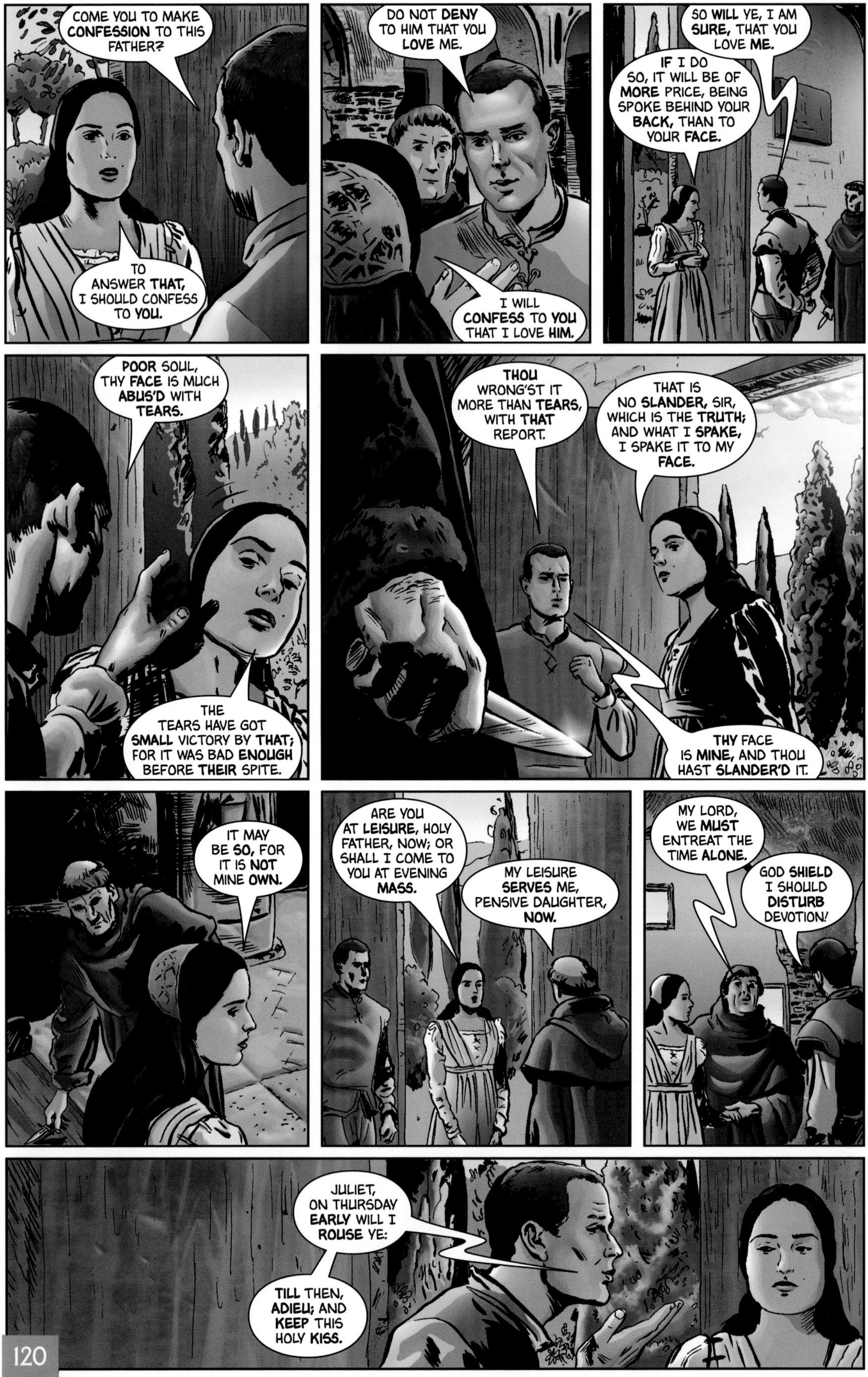
COME YOU TO MAKE CONFESSION TO THIS FATHER?
TO ANSWER THAT, I SHOULD CONFESS TO YOU.
DO NOT DENY TO HIM THAT YOU LOVE ME.
I WILL CONFESS TO YOU THAT I LOVE HIM.
SO WILL YE, I AM SURE, THAT YOU LOVE ME.
IF I DO SO, IT WILL BE OF MORE PRICE, BEING SPOKE BEHIND YOUR BACK, THAN TO YOUR FACE.
POOR SOUL, THY FACE IS MUCH ABUS'D WITH TEARS.
THE TEARS HAVE GOT SMALL VICTORY BY THAT; FOR IT WAS BAD ENOUGH BEFORE THEIR SPITE.
THOU WRONG'ST IT MORE THAN TEARS, WITH THAT REPORT.
THAT IS NO SLANDER, SIR, WHICH IS THE TRUTH; AND WHAT I SPAKE, I SPAKE IT TO MY FACE.
THY FACE IS MINE, AND THOU HAST SLANDER'D IT.
IT MAY BE SO, FOR IT IS NOT MINE OWN.
ARE YOU AT LEISURE, HOLY FATHER, NOW; OR SHALL I COME TO YOU AT EVENING MASS.
MY LEISURE SERVES ME, PENSIVE DAUGHTER, NOW.
MY LORD, WE MUST ENTREAT THE TIME ALONE.
GOD SHIELD I SHOULD DISTURB DEVOTION!
JULIET, ON THURSDAY EARLY WILL I ROUSE YE:
TILL THEN, ADIEU; AND KEEP THIS HOLY KISS.

O! SHUT THE DOOR;

AND WHEN THOU HAST DONE SO, COME, WEEP WITH ME;

PAST HOPE, PAST CURE, PAST HELP!

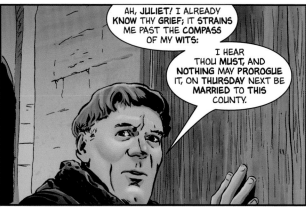

AH, JULIET! I ALREADY KNOW THY GRIEF; IT STRAINS ME PAST THE COMPASS OF MY WITS:

I HEAR THOU MUST, AND NOTHING MAY PROROGUE IT, ON THURSDAY NEXT BE MARRIED TO THIS COUNTY.

TELL ME NOT, FRIAR, THAT THOU HEAR'ST OF THIS, UNLESS THOU TELL ME HOW I MAY PREVENT IT:

IF IN THY WISDOM THOU CANST GIVE NO HELP, DO THOU BUT CALL MY RESOLUTION WISE, AND WITH THIS KNIFE I'LL HELP IT PRESENTLY.

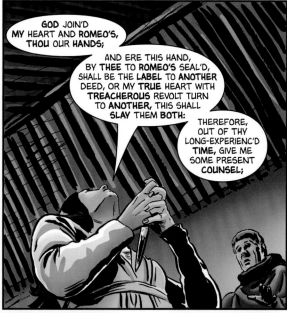

GOD JOIN'D MY HEART AND ROMEO'S, THOU OUR HANDS;

AND ERE THIS HAND, BY THEE TO ROMEO'S SEAL'D, SHALL BE THE LABEL TO ANOTHER DEED, OR MY TRUE HEART WITH TREACHEROUS REVOLT TURN TO ANOTHER, THIS SHALL SLAY THEM BOTH;

THEREFORE, OUT OF THY LONG-EXPERIENC'D TIME, GIVE ME SOME PRESENT COUNSEL;

OR, BEHOLD, 'TWIXT MY EXTREMES AND ME THIS BLOODY KNIFE SHALL PLAY THE UMPIRE, ARBITRATING THAT WHICH THE COMMISSION OF THY YEARS AND ART COULD TO NO ISSUE OF TRUE HONOUR BRING.

BE NOT SO LONG TO SPEAK; I LONG TO DIE, IF WHAT THOU SPEAK'ST SPEAK NOT OF REMEDY.

HOLD, DAUGHTER:

I DO SPY A KIND OF HOPE, WHICH CRAVES AS DESPERATE AN EXECUTION AS THAT IS DESPERATE WHICH WE WOULD PREVENT.

IF, RATHER THAN TO MARRY COUNTY PARIS, THOU HAST THE STRENGTH OF WILL TO SLAY THYSELF, THEN IT IS LIKELY THOU WILT UNDERTAKE A THING LIKE DEATH TO CHIDE AWAY THIS SHAME, THAT COP'ST WITH DEATH HIMSELF TO 'SCAPE FROM IT;

AND, IF THOU DAR'ST, I'LL GIVE THEE REMEDY.

O! BID ME LEAP, RATHER THAN MARRY PARIS, FROM OFF THE BATTLEMENTS OF YONDER TOWER;

OR WALK IN THIEVISH WAYS; OR BID ME LURK WHERE SERPENTS ARE; CHAIN ME WITH ROARING BEARS;

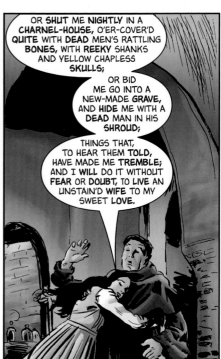

OR SHUT ME NIGHTLY IN A CHARNEL-HOUSE, O'ER-COVER'D QUITE WITH DEAD MEN'S RATTLING BONES, WITH REEKY SHANKS AND YELLOW CHAPLESS SKULLS;

OR BID ME GO INTO A NEW-MADE GRAVE, AND HIDE ME WITH A DEAD MAN IN HIS SHROUD;

THINGS THAT, TO HEAR THEM TOLD, HAVE MADE ME TREMBLE; AND I WILL DO IT WITHOUT FEAR OR DOUBT, TO LIVE AN UNSTAIN'D WIFE TO MY SWEET LOVE.

HOLD, THEN; GO HOME, BE MERRY, GIVE CONSENT TO MARRY PARIS.

WEDNESDAY IS TO-MORROW; TO-MORROW NIGHT LOOK THAT THOU LIE ALONE, LET NOT THY NURSE LIE WITH THEE IN THY CHAMBER:

TAKE THOU THIS VIAL, BEING THEN IN BED, AND THIS DISTILLING LIQUOR DRINK THOU OFF;

WHEN, PRESENTLY, THROUGH ALL THY VEINS SHALL RUN A COLD AND DROWSY HUMOUR; FOR NO PULSE SHALL KEEP HIS NATIVE PROGRESS; BUT SURCEASE:

NO WARMTH, NO BREATH, SHALL TESTIFY THOU LIVEST; THE ROSES IN THY LIPS AND CHEEKS SHALL FADE TO PALY ASHES; THY EYES' WINDOWS FALL, LIKE DEATH, WHEN HE SHUTS UP THE DAY OF LIFE;

EACH PART, DEPRIV'D OF SUPPLE GOVERNMENT, SHALL, STIFF AND STARK AND COLD, APPEAR LIKE DEATH:

AND IN THIS BORROW'D LIKENESS OF SHRUNK DEATH THOU SHALT CONTINUE TWO AND FORTY HOURS, AND THEN AWAKEN AS FROM A PLEASANT SLEEP.

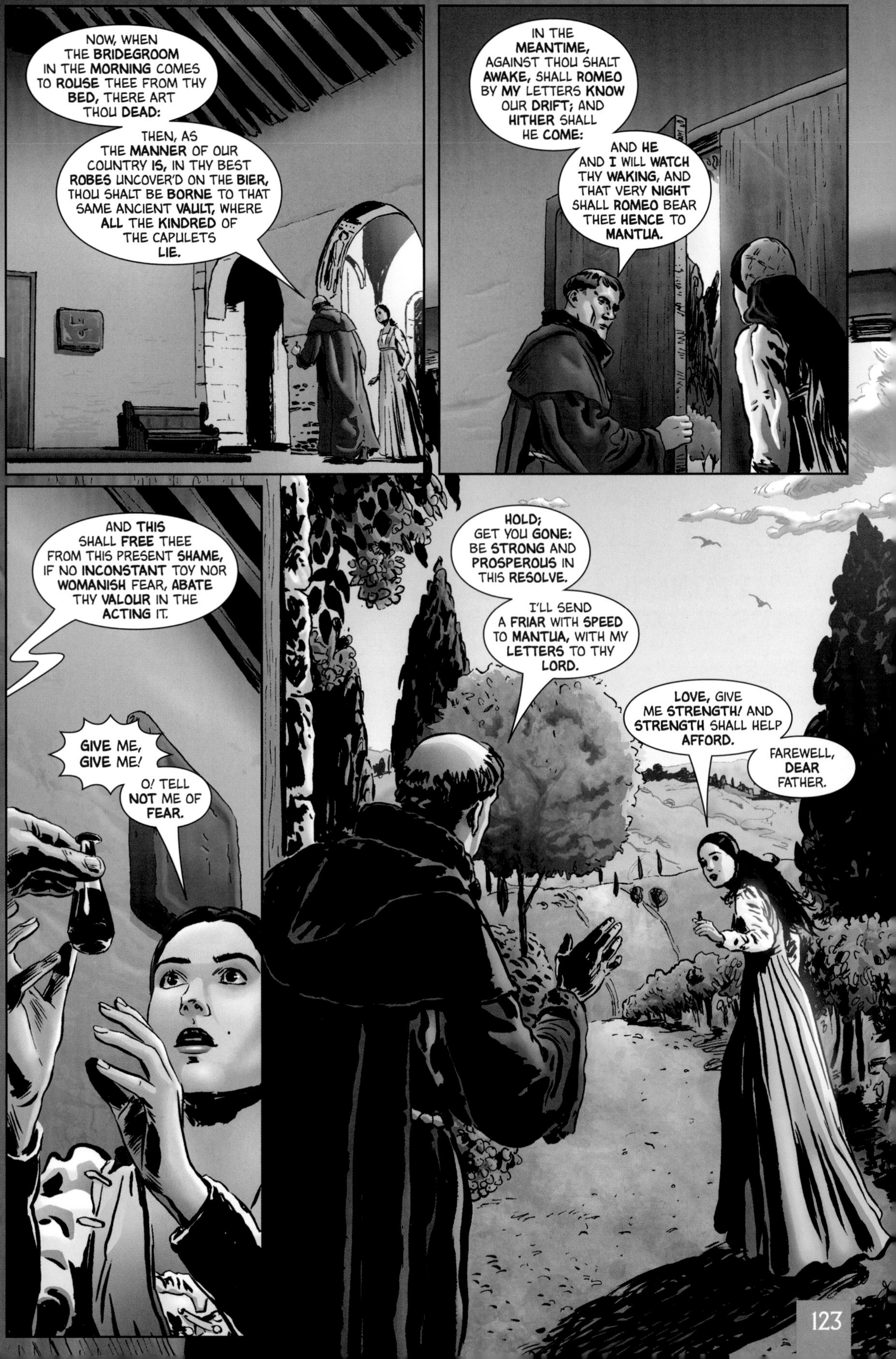
NOW, WHEN THE BRIDEGROOM IN THE MORNING COMES TO ROUSE THEE FROM THY BED, THERE ART THOU DEAD:
THEN, AS THE MANNER OF OUR COUNTRY IS, IN THY BEST ROBES UNCOVER'D ON THE BIER, THOU SHALT BE BORNE TO THAT SAME ANCIENT VAULT, WHERE ALL THE KINDRED OF THE CAPULETS LIE.
IN THE MEANTIME, AGAINST THOU SHALT AWAKE, SHALL ROMEO BY MY LETTERS KNOW OUR DRIFT; AND HITHER SHALL HE COME:
AND HE AND I WILL WATCH THY WAKING, AND THAT VERY NIGHT SHALL ROMEO BEAR THEE HENCE TO MANTUA.
AND THIS SHALL FREE THEE FROM THIS PRESENT SHAME, IF NO INCONSTANT TOY NOR WOMANISH FEAR, ABATE THY VALOUR IN THE ACTING IT.
GIVE ME, GIVE ME!
O! TELL NOT ME OF FEAR.
HOLD; GET YOU GONE: BE STRONG AND PROSPEROUS IN THIS RESOLVE.
I'LL SEND A FRIAR WITH SPEED TO MANTUA, WITH MY LETTERS TO THY LORD.
LOVE, GIVE ME STRENGTH! AND STRENGTH SHALL HELP AFFORD.
FAREWELL, DEAR FATHER.

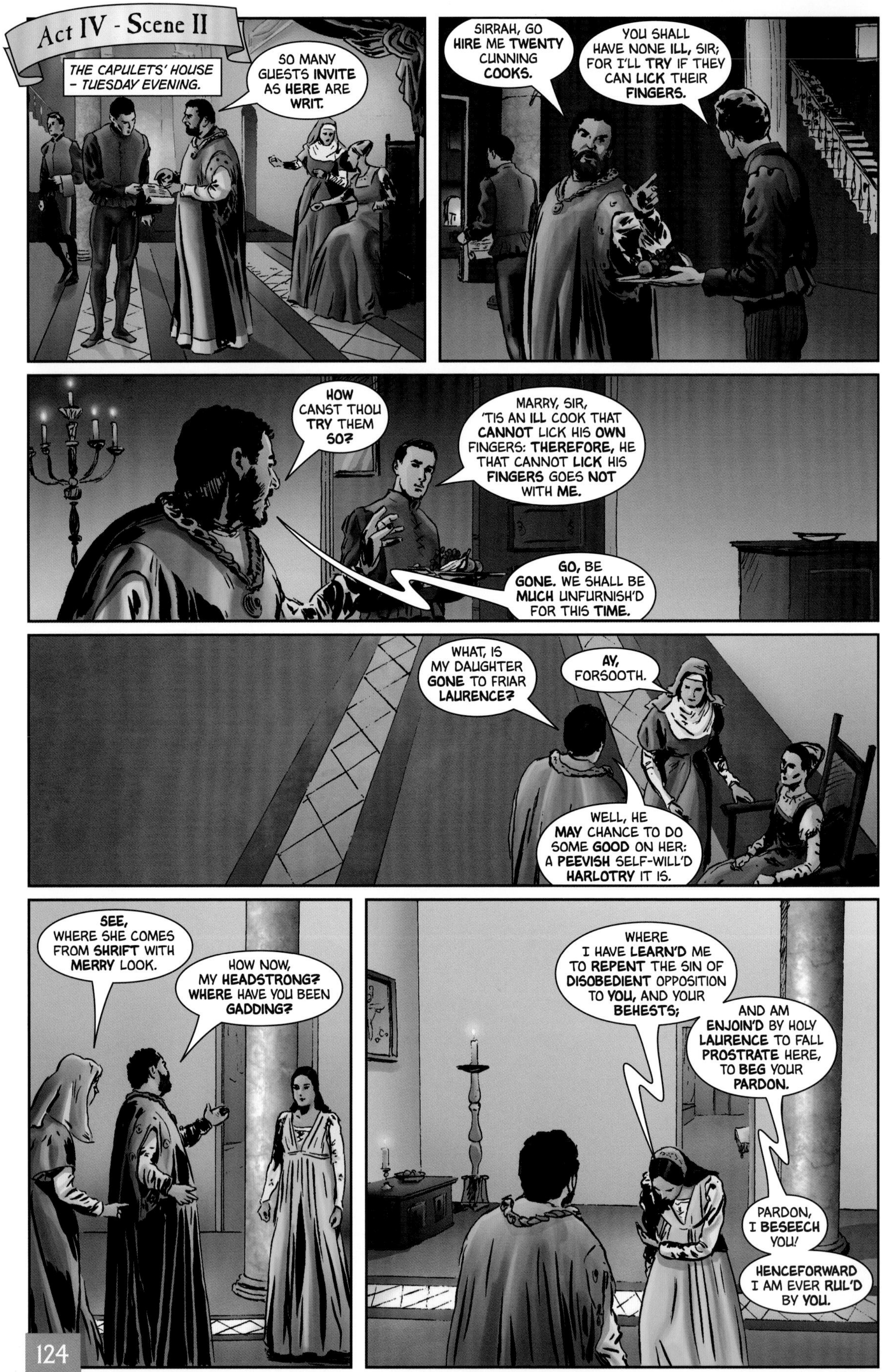
Act IV - Scene II
THE CAPULETS' HOUSE – TUESDAY EVENING.
SO MANY GUESTS INVITE AS HERE ARE WRIT.
SIRRAH, GO HIRE ME TWENTY CUNNING COOKS.
YOU SHALL HAVE NONE ILL, SIR; FOR I'LL TRY IF THEY CAN LICK THEIR FINGERS.
HOW CANST THOU TRY THEM SO?
MARRY, SIR, 'TIS AN ILL COOK THAT CANNOT LICK HIS OWN FINGERS: THEREFORE, HE THAT CANNOT LICK HIS FINGERS GOES NOT WITH ME.
GO, BE GONE. WE SHALL BE MUCH UNFURNISH'D FOR THIS TIME.
WHAT, IS MY DAUGHTER GONE TO FRIAR LAURENCE?
AY, FORSOOTH.
WELL, HE MAY CHANCE TO DO SOME GOOD ON HER: A PEEVISH SELF-WILL'D HARLOTRY IT IS.
SEE, WHERE SHE COMES FROM SHRIFT WITH MERRY LOOK.
HOW NOW, MY HEADSTRONG? WHERE HAVE YOU BEEN GADDING?
WHERE I HAVE LEARN'D ME TO REPENT THE SIN OF DISOBEDIENT OPPOSITION TO YOU, AND YOUR BEHESTS;
AND AM ENJOIN'D BY HOLY LAURENCE TO FALL PROSTRATE HERE, TO BEG YOUR PARDON.
PARDON, I BESEECH YOU!
HENCEFORWARD I AM EVER RUL'D BY YOU.

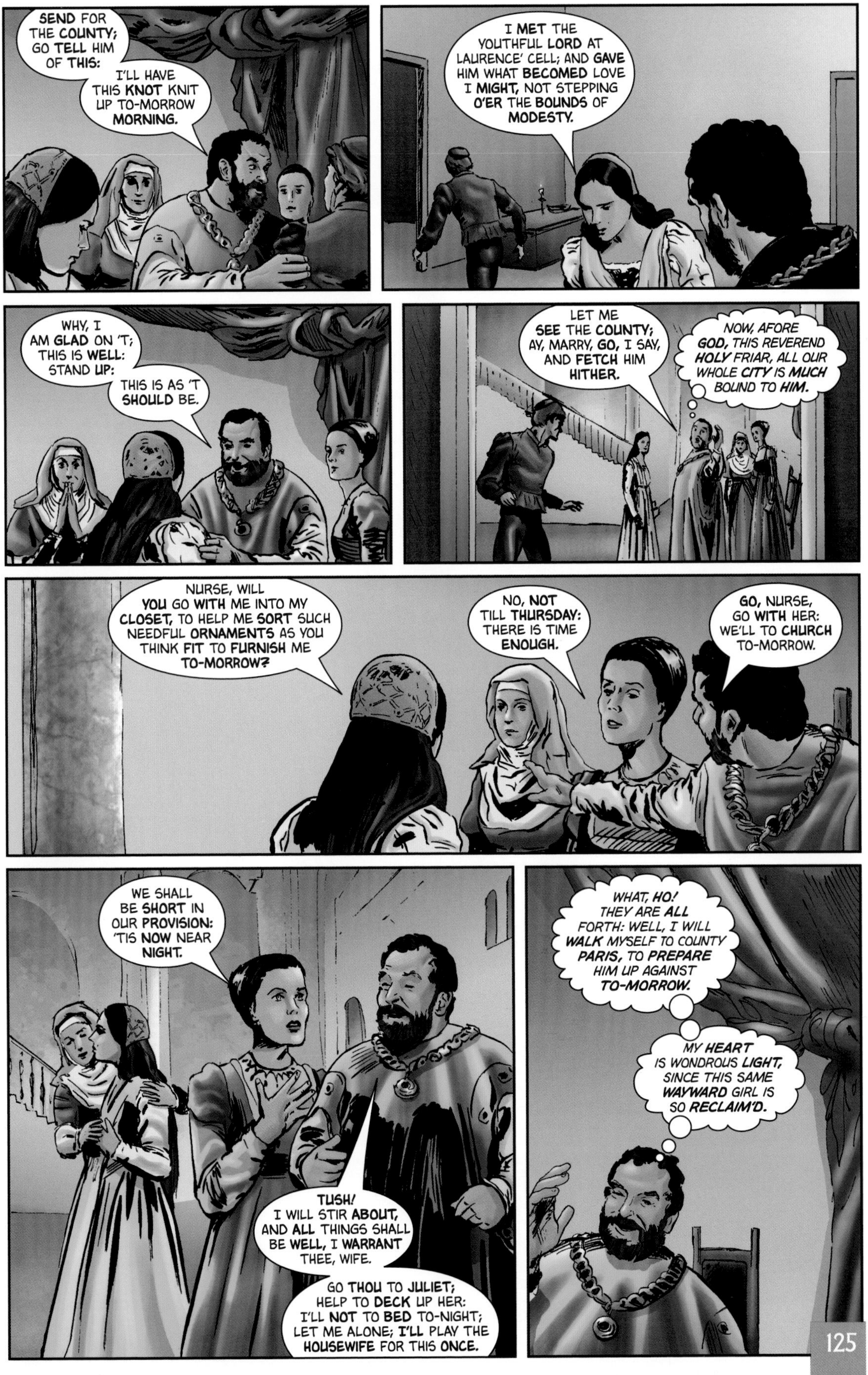
SEND FOR THE COUNTY; GO TELL HIM OF THIS:
I'LL HAVE THIS KNOT KNIT UP TO-MORROW MORNING.
I MET THE YOUTHFUL LORD AT LAURENCE' CELL; AND GAVE HIM WHAT BECOMED LOVE I MIGHT, NOT STEPPING O'ER THE BOUNDS OF MODESTY.
WHY, I AM GLAD ON 'T; THIS IS WELL: STAND UP:
THIS IS AS 'T SHOULD BE.
LET ME SEE THE COUNTY; AY, MARRY, GO, I SAY, AND FETCH HIM HITHER.
NOW, AFORE GOD, THIS REVEREND HOLY FRIAR, ALL OUR WHOLE CITY IS MUCH BOUND TO HIM.
NURSE, WILL YOU GO WITH ME INTO MY CLOSET, TO HELP ME SORT SUCH NEEDFUL ORNAMENTS AS YOU THINK FIT TO FURNISH ME TO-MORROW?
NO, NOT TILL THURSDAY: THERE IS TIME ENOUGH.
GO, NURSE, GO WITH HER: WE'LL TO CHURCH TO-MORROW.
WE SHALL BE SHORT IN OUR PROVISION: 'TIS NOW NEAR NIGHT.
TUSH! I WILL STIR ABOUT, AND ALL THINGS SHALL BE WELL, I WARRANT THEE, WIFE.
GO THOU TO JULIET; HELP TO DECK UP HER: I'LL NOT TO BED TO-NIGHT; LET ME ALONE; I'LL PLAY THE HOUSEWIFE FOR THIS ONCE.
WHAT, HO! THEY ARE ALL FORTH: WELL, I WILL WALK MYSELF TO COUNTY PARIS, TO PREPARE HIM UP AGAINST TO-MORROW.
MY HEART IS WONDROUS LIGHT, SINCE THIS SAME WAYWARD GIRL IS SO RECLAIM'D.

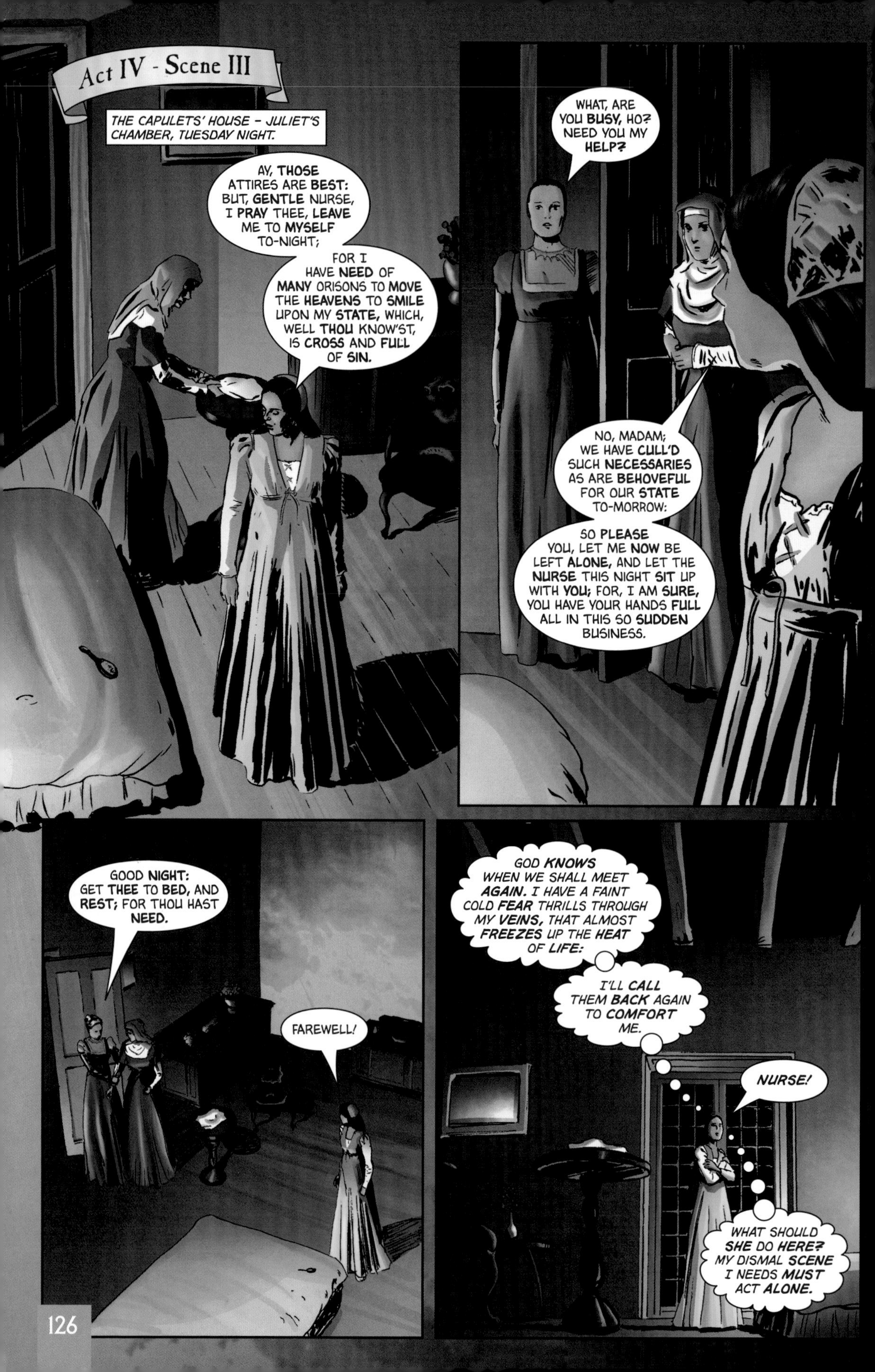
Act IV - Scene III
THE CAPULETS' HOUSE – JULIET'S CHAMBER, TUESDAY NIGHT.
AY, THOSE ATTIRES ARE BEST: BUT, GENTLE NURSE, I PRAY THEE, LEAVE ME TO MYSELF TO-NIGHT;
FOR I HAVE NEED OF MANY ORISONS TO MOVE THE HEAVENS TO SMILE UPON MY STATE, WHICH, WELL THOU KNOW'ST, IS CROSS AND FULL OF SIN.
WHAT, ARE YOU BUSY, HO? NEED YOU MY HELP?
NO, MADAM; WE HAVE CULL'D SUCH NECESSARIES AS ARE BEHOVEFUL FOR OUR STATE TO-MORROW:
SO PLEASE YOU, LET ME NOW BE LEFT ALONE, AND LET THE NURSE THIS NIGHT SIT UP WITH YOU; FOR, I AM SURE, YOU HAVE YOUR HANDS FULL ALL IN THIS SO SUDDEN BUSINESS.
GOOD NIGHT: GET THEE TO BED, AND REST; FOR THOU HAST NEED.
FAREWELL!
GOD KNOWS WHEN WE SHALL MEET AGAIN. I HAVE A FAINT COLD FEAR THRILLS THROUGH MY VEINS, THAT ALMOST FREEZES UP THE HEAT OF LIFE:
I'LL CALL THEM BACK AGAIN TO COMFORT ME.
NURSE!
WHAT SHOULD SHE DO HERE? MY DISMAL SCENE I NEEDS MUST ACT ALONE.

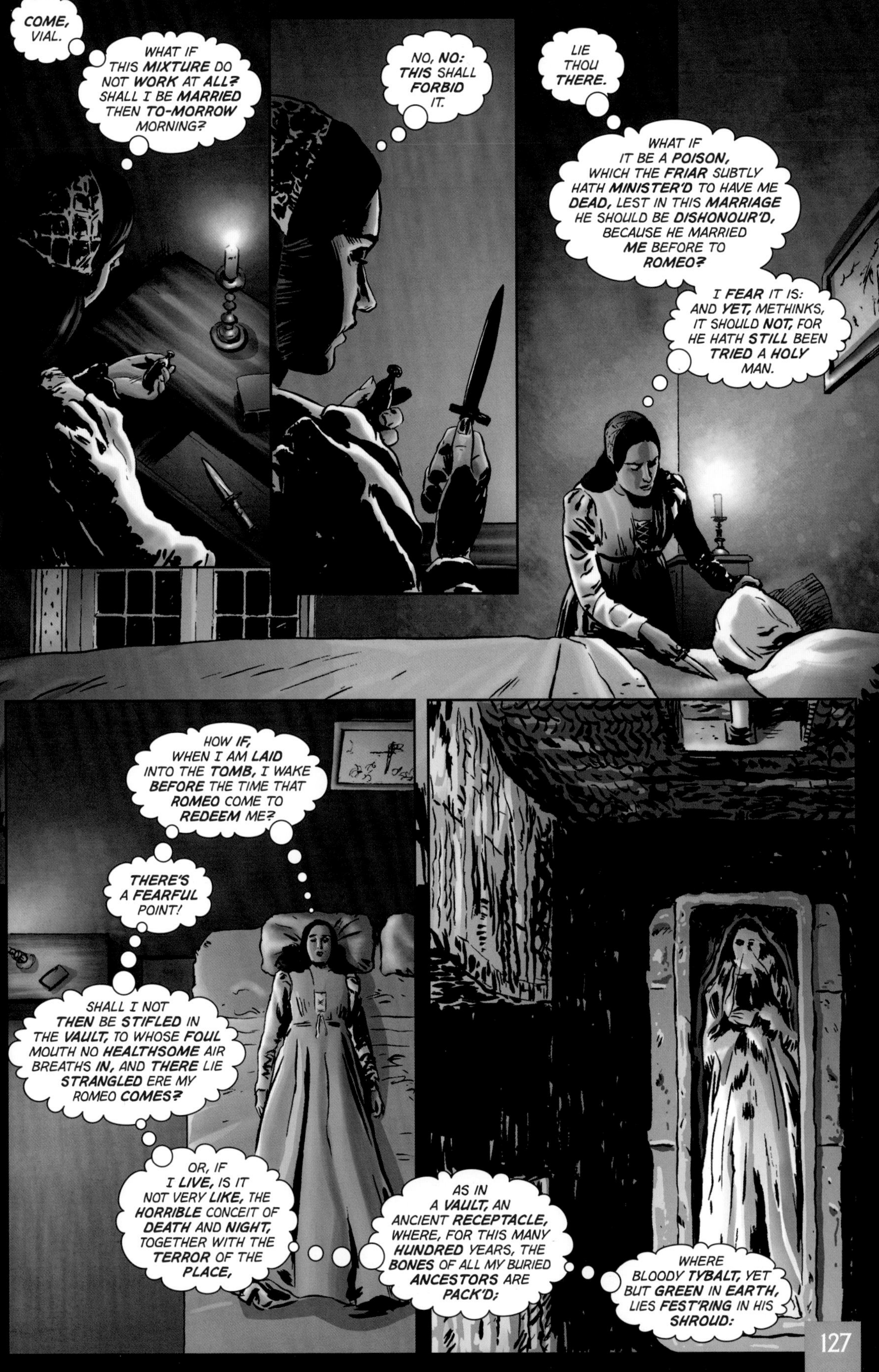
COME, VIAL.
WHAT IF THIS MIXTURE DO NOT WORK AT ALL? SHALL I BE MARRIED THEN TO-MORROW MORNING?
NO, NO: THIS SHALL FORBID IT.
LIE THOU THERE.
WHAT IF IT BE A POISON, WHICH THE FRIAR SUBTLY HATH MINISTER'D TO HAVE ME DEAD, LEST IN THIS MARRIAGE HE SHOULD BE DISHONOUR'D, BECAUSE HE MARRIED ME BEFORE TO ROMEO?
I FEAR IT IS: AND YET, METHINKS, IT SHOULD NOT, FOR HE HATH STILL BEEN TRIED A HOLY MAN.
HOW IF, WHEN I AM LAID INTO THE TOMB, I WAKE BEFORE THE TIME THAT ROMEO COME TO REDEEM ME?
THERE'S A FEARFUL POINT!
SHALL I NOT THEN BE STIFLED IN THE VAULT, TO WHOSE FOUL MOUTH NO HEALTHSOME AIR BREATHS IN, AND THERE LIE STRANGLED ERE MY ROMEO COMES?
OR, IF I LIVE, IS IT NOT VERY LIKE, THE HORRIBLE CONCEIT OF DEATH AND NIGHT, TOGETHER WITH THE TERROR OF THE PLACE,
AS IN A VAULT, AN ANCIENT RECEPTACLE, WHERE, FOR THIS MANY HUNDRED YEARS, THE BONES OF ALL MY BURIED ANCESTORS ARE PACK'D;
WHERE BLOODY TYBALT, YET BUT GREEN IN EARTH, LIES FEST'RING IN HIS SHROUD:

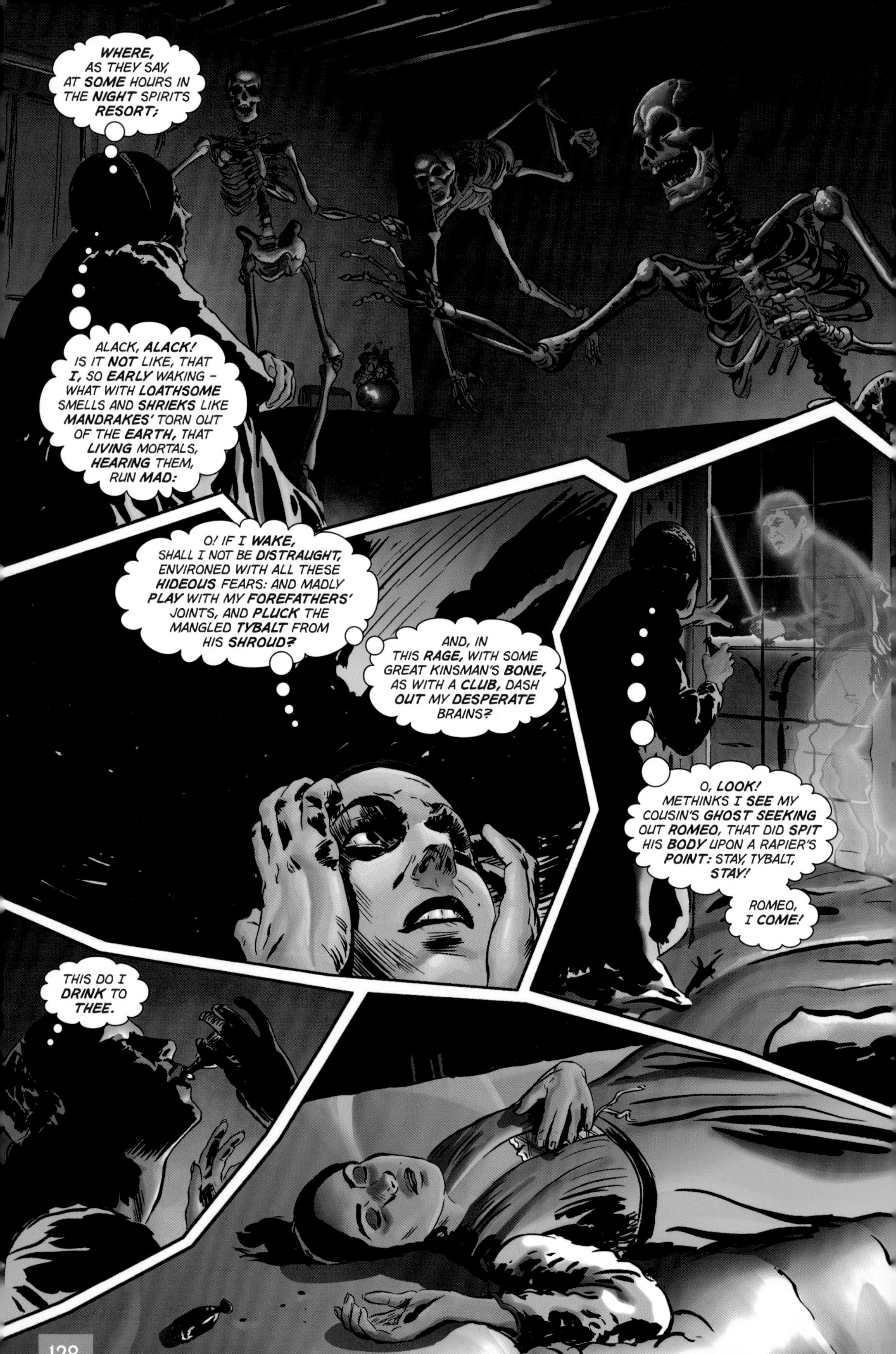
WHERE, AS THEY SAY, AT SOME HOURS IN THE NIGHT SPIRITS RESORT;
ALACK, ALACK! IS IT NOT LIKE, THAT I, SO EARLY WAKING - WHAT WITH LOATHSOME SMELLS AND SHRIEKS LIKE MANDRAKES' TORN OUT OF THE EARTH, THAT LIVING MORTALS, HEARING THEM, RUN MAD:
O! IF I WAKE, SHALL I NOT BE DISTRAUGHT, ENVIRONED WITH ALL THESE HIDEOUS FEARS: AND MADLY PLAY WITH MY FOREFATHERS' JOINTS, AND PLUCK THE MANGLED TYBALT FROM HIS SHROUD?
AND, IN THIS RAGE, WITH SOME GREAT KINSMAN'S BONE, AS WITH A CLUB, DASH OUT MY DESPERATE BRAINS?
O, LOOK! METHINKS I SEE MY COUSIN'S GHOST SEEKING OUT ROMEO, THAT DID SPIT HIS BODY UPON A RAPIER'S POINT: STAY, TYBALT, STAY!
ROMEO, I COME!
THIS DO I DRINK TO THEE.

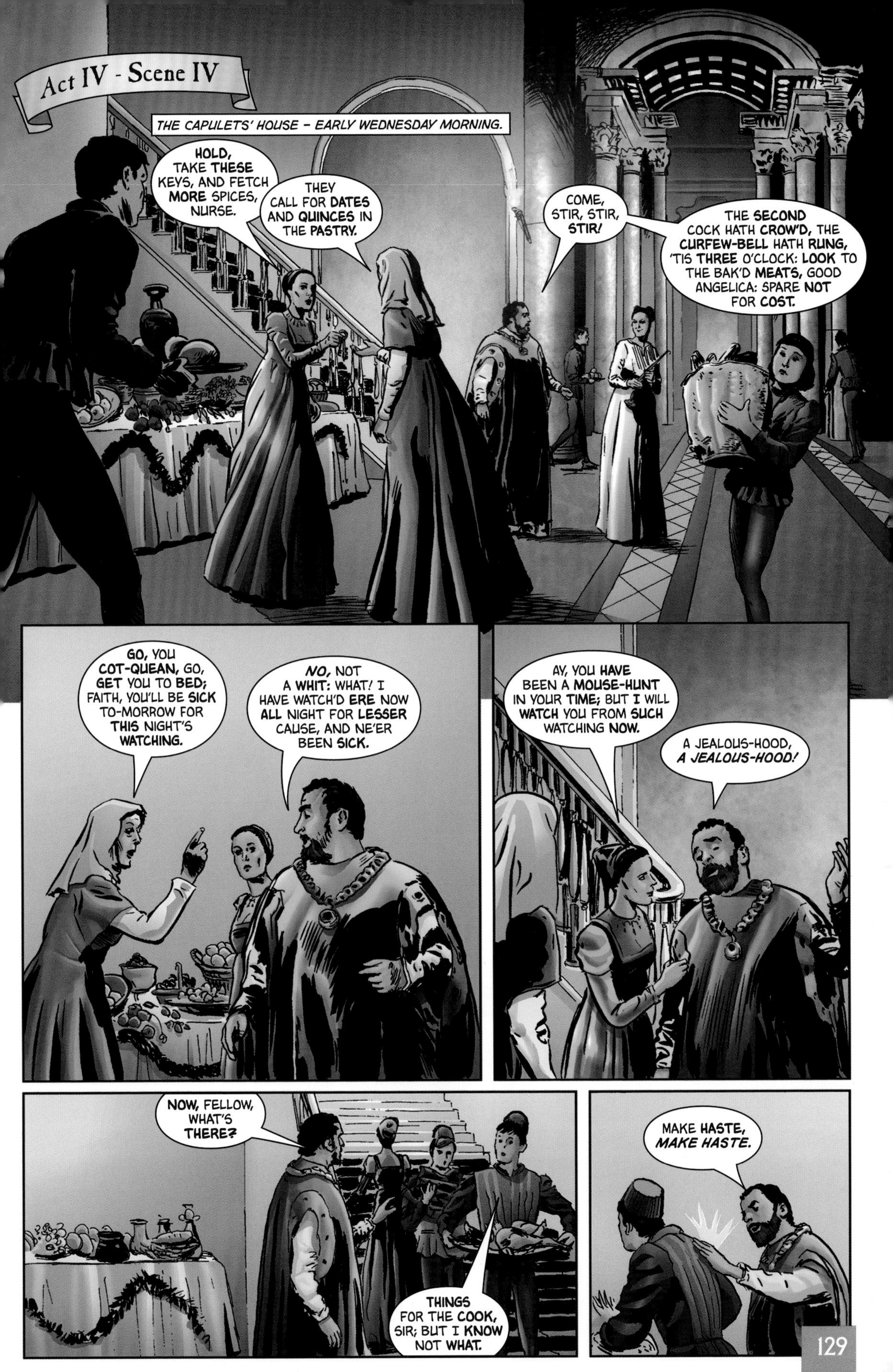
Act IV - Scene IV
THE CAPULETS' HOUSE – EARLY WEDNESDAY MORNING.
HOLD, TAKE THESE KEYS, AND FETCH MORE SPICES, NURSE.
THEY CALL FOR DATES AND QUINCES IN THE PASTRY.
COME, STIR, STIR, STIR!
THE SECOND COCK HATH CROW'D, THE CURFEW-BELL HATH RUNG, 'TIS THREE O'CLOCK: LOOK TO THE BAK'D MEATS, GOOD ANGELICA: SPARE NOT FOR COST.
GO, YOU COT-QUEAN, GO, GET YOU TO BED; FAITH, YOU'LL BE SICK TO-MORROW FOR THIS NIGHT'S WATCHING.
NO, NOT A WHIT: WHAT! I HAVE WATCH'D ERE NOW ALL NIGHT FOR LESSER CAUSE, AND NE'ER BEEN SICK.
AY, YOU HAVE BEEN A MOUSE-HUNT IN YOUR TIME; BUT I WILL WATCH YOU FROM SUCH WATCHING NOW.
A JEALOUS-HOOD, A JEALOUS-HOOD!
NOW, FELLOW, WHAT'S THERE?
THINGS FOR THE COOK, SIR; BUT I KNOW NOT WHAT.
MAKE HASTE, MAKE HASTE.

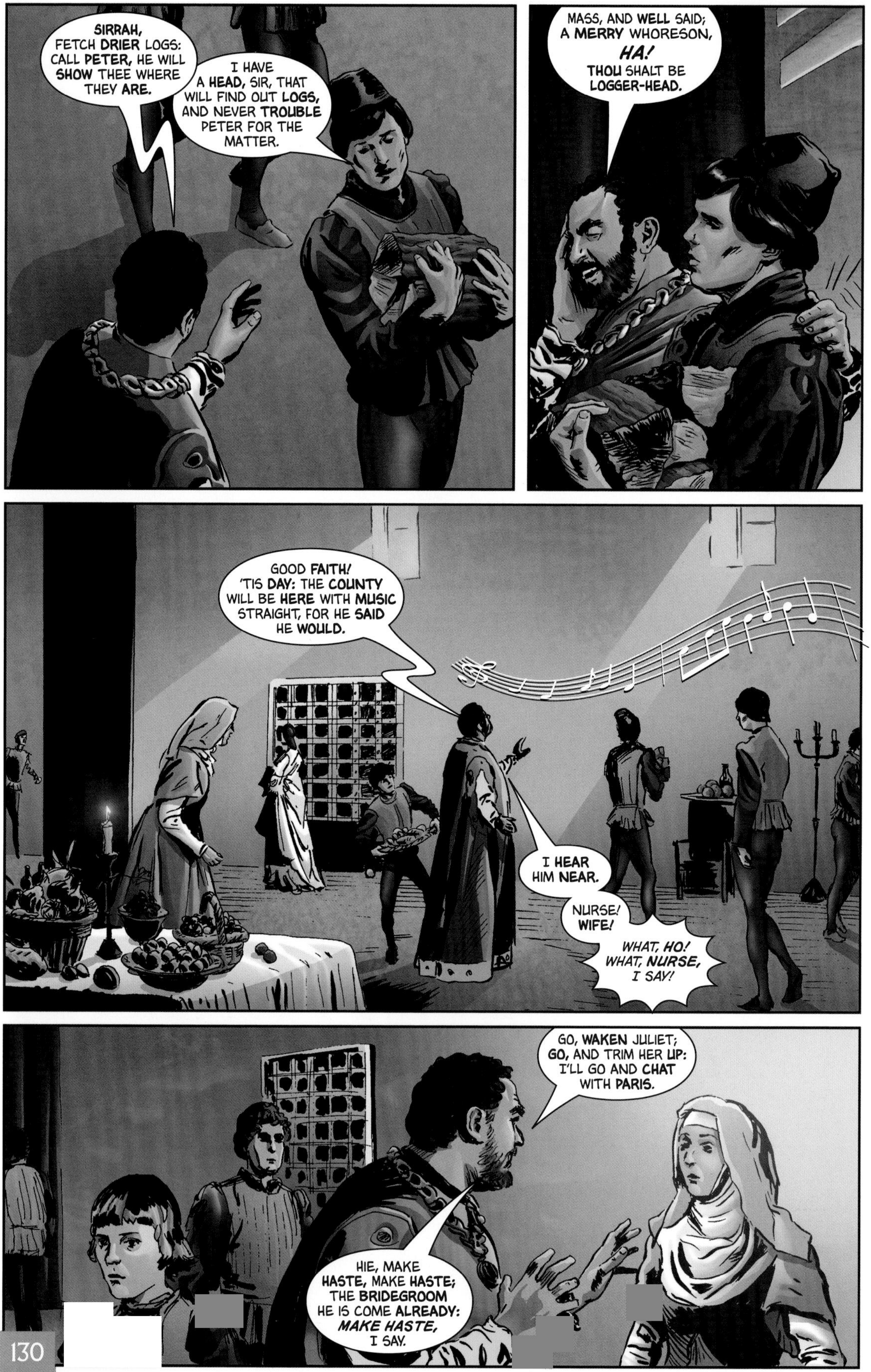
SIRRAH, FETCH DRIER LOGS: CALL PETER, HE WILL SHOW THEE WHERE THEY ARE.
I HAVE A HEAD, SIR, THAT WILL FIND OUT LOGS, AND NEVER TROUBLE PETER FOR THE MATTER.
MASS, AND WELL SAID; A MERRY WHORESON, HA! THOU SHALT BE LOGGER-HEAD.
GOOD FAITH! 'TIS DAY: THE COUNTY WILL BE HERE WITH MUSIC STRAIGHT, FOR HE SAID HE WOULD.
I HEAR HIM NEAR.
NURSE! WIFE!
WHAT, HO! WHAT, NURSE, I SAY!
GO, WAKEN JULIET; GO, AND TRIM HER UP: I'LL GO AND CHAT WITH PARIS.
HIE, MAKE HASTE, MAKE HASTE; THE BRIDEGROOM HE IS COME ALREADY: MAKE HASTE, I SAY.

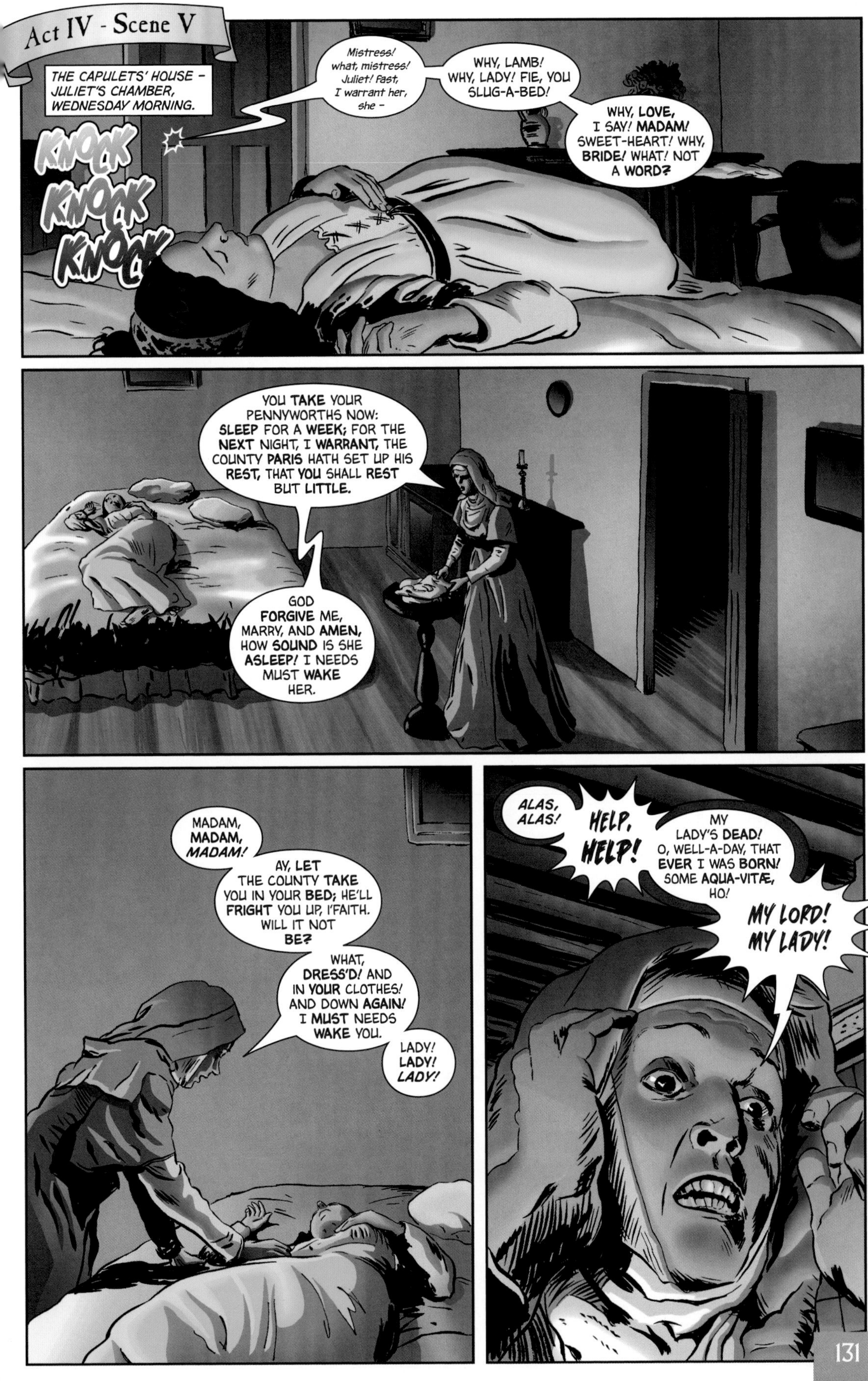
Act IV - Scene V
THE CAPULETS' HOUSE - JULIET'S CHAMBER, WEDNESDAY MORNING.
KNOCK KNOCK KNOCK
Mistress! what, mistress! Juliet! Fast, I warrant her, she -
WHY, LAMB! WHY, LADY! FIE, YOU SLUG-A-BED!
WHY, LOVE, I SAY! MADAM! SWEET-HEART! WHY, BRIDE! WHAT! NOT A WORD?
YOU TAKE YOUR PENNYWORTHS NOW: SLEEP FOR A WEEK; FOR THE NEXT NIGHT, I WARRANT, THE COUNTY PARIS HATH SET UP HIS REST, THAT YOU SHALL REST BUT LITTLE.
GOD FORGIVE ME, MARRY, AND AMEN, HOW SOUND IS SHE ASLEEP! I NEEDS MUST WAKE HER.
MADAM, MADAM, MADAM!
AY, LET THE COUNTY TAKE YOU IN YOUR BED; HE'LL FRIGHT YOU UP, I'FAITH. WILL IT NOT BE?
WHAT, DRESS'D! AND IN YOUR CLOTHES! AND DOWN AGAIN! I MUST NEEDS WAKE YOU.
LADY! LADY! LADY!
ALAS, ALAS!
HELP, HELP!
MY LADY'S DEAD! O, WELL-A-DAY, THAT EVER I WAS BORN! SOME AQUA-VITÆ, HO!
MY LORD! MY LADY!

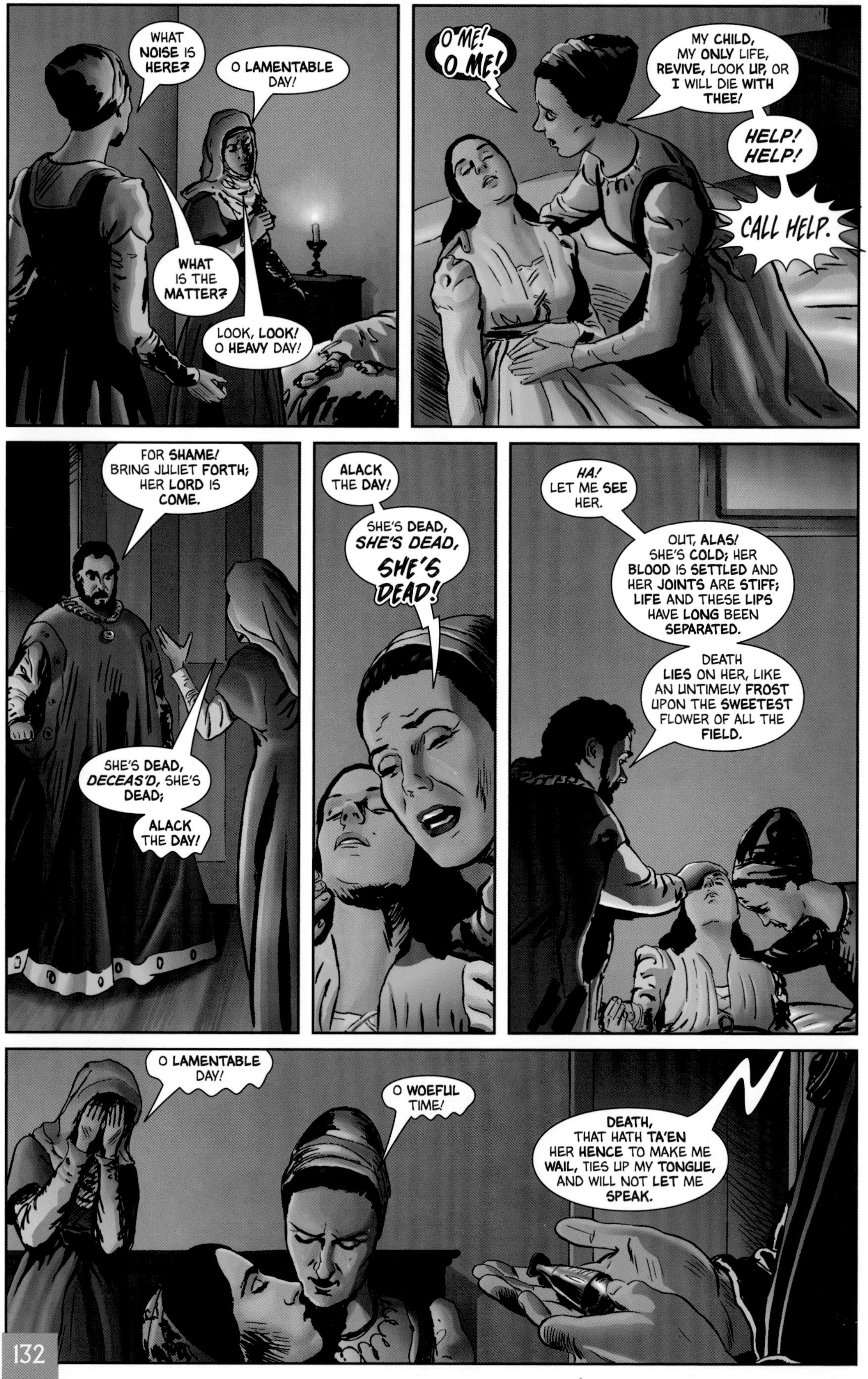
WHAT NOISE IS HERE?
O LAMENTABLE DAY!
WHAT IS THE MATTER?
LOOK, LOOK! O HEAVY DAY!
O ME! O ME!
MY CHILD, MY ONLY LIFE, REVIVE, LOOK UP, OR I WILL DIE WITH THEE!
HELP! HELP!
CALL HELP.
FOR SHAME! BRING JULIET FORTH; HER LORD IS COME.
SHE'S DEAD, DECEAS'D, SHE'S DEAD;
ALACK THE DAY!
ALACK THE DAY!
SHE'S DEAD, SHE'S DEAD, SHE'S DEAD!
HA! LET ME SEE HER.
OUT, ALAS! SHE'S COLD; HER BLOOD IS SETTLED AND HER JOINTS ARE STIFF; LIFE AND THESE LIPS HAVE LONG BEEN SEPARATED.
DEATH LIES ON HER, LIKE AN UNTIMELY FROST UPON THE SWEETEST FLOWER OF ALL THE FIELD.
O LAMENTABLE DAY!
O WOEFUL TIME!
DEATH, THAT HATH TA'EN HER HENCE TO MAKE ME WAIL, TIES UP MY TONGUE, AND WILL NOT LET ME SPEAK.

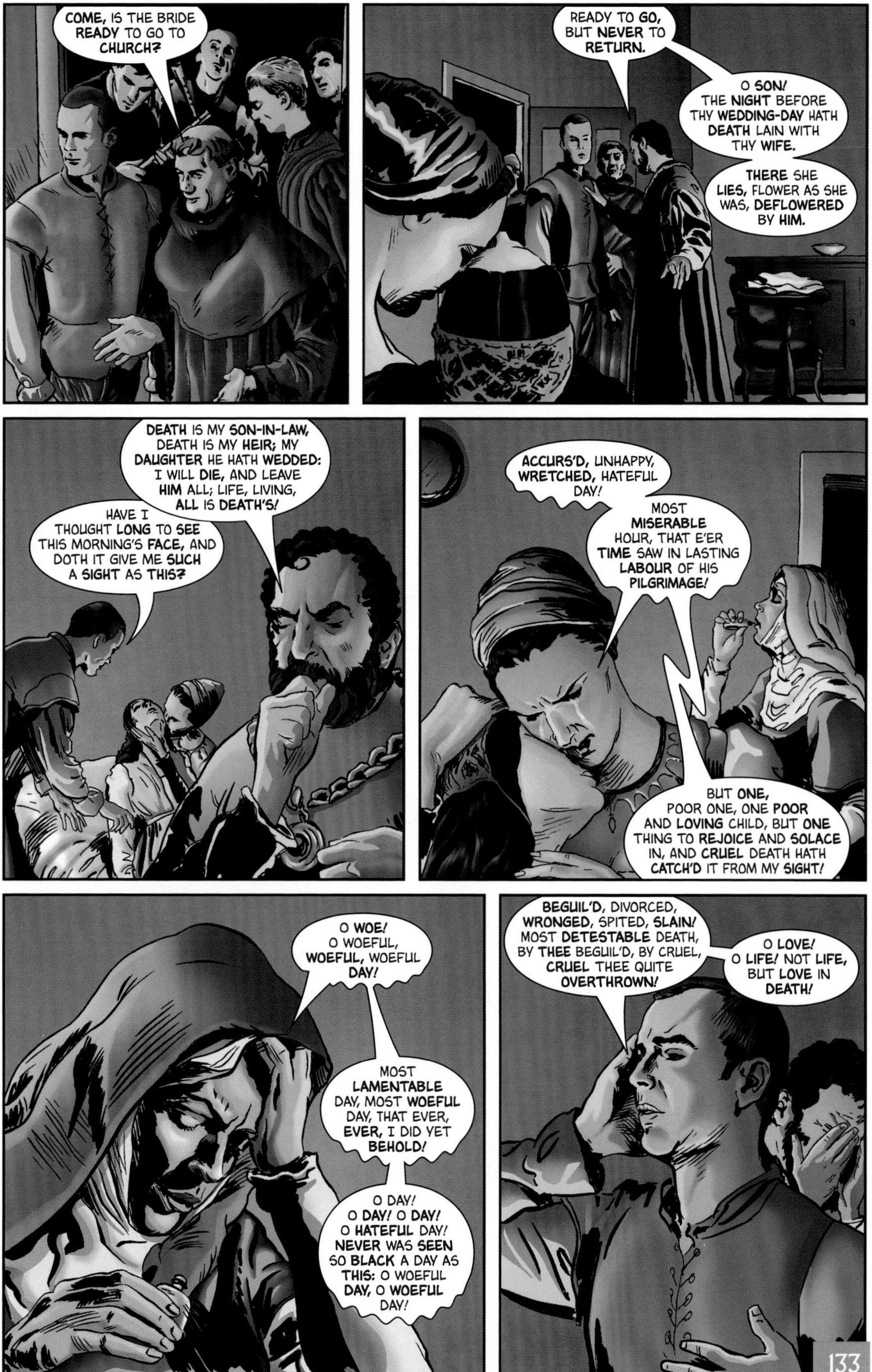
COME, IS THE BRIDE READY TO GO TO CHURCH?
READY TO GO, BUT NEVER TO RETURN.
O SON! THE NIGHT BEFORE THY WEDDING-DAY HATH DEATH LAIN WITH THY WIFE.
THERE SHE LIES, FLOWER AS SHE WAS, DEFLOWERED BY HIM.
DEATH IS MY SON-IN-LAW, DEATH IS MY HEIR; MY DAUGHTER HE HATH WEDDED: I WILL DIE, AND LEAVE HIM ALL; LIFE, LIVING, ALL IS DEATH'S!
HAVE I THOUGHT LONG TO SEE THIS MORNING'S FACE, AND DOTH IT GIVE ME SUCH A SIGHT AS THIS?
ACCURS'D, UNHAPPY, WRETCHED, HATEFUL DAY!
MOST MISERABLE HOUR, THAT E'ER TIME SAW IN LASTING LABOUR OF HIS PILGRIMAGE!
BUT ONE, POOR ONE, ONE POOR AND LOVING CHILD, BUT ONE THING TO REJOICE AND SOLACE IN, AND CRUEL DEATH HATH CATCH'D IT FROM MY SIGHT!
O WOE! O WOEFUL, WOEFUL, WOEFUL DAY!
MOST LAMENTABLE DAY, MOST WOEFUL DAY, THAT EVER, EVER, I DID YET BEHOLD!
O DAY! O DAY! O DAY! O HATEFUL DAY! NEVER WAS SEEN SO BLACK A DAY AS THIS: O WOEFUL DAY, O WOEFUL DAY!
BEGUIL'D, DIVORCED, WRONGED, SPITED, SLAIN! MOST DETESTABLE DEATH, BY THEE BEGUIL'D, BY CRUEL, CRUEL THEE QUITE OVERTHROWN!
O LOVE! O LIFE! NOT LIFE, BUT LOVE IN DEATH!

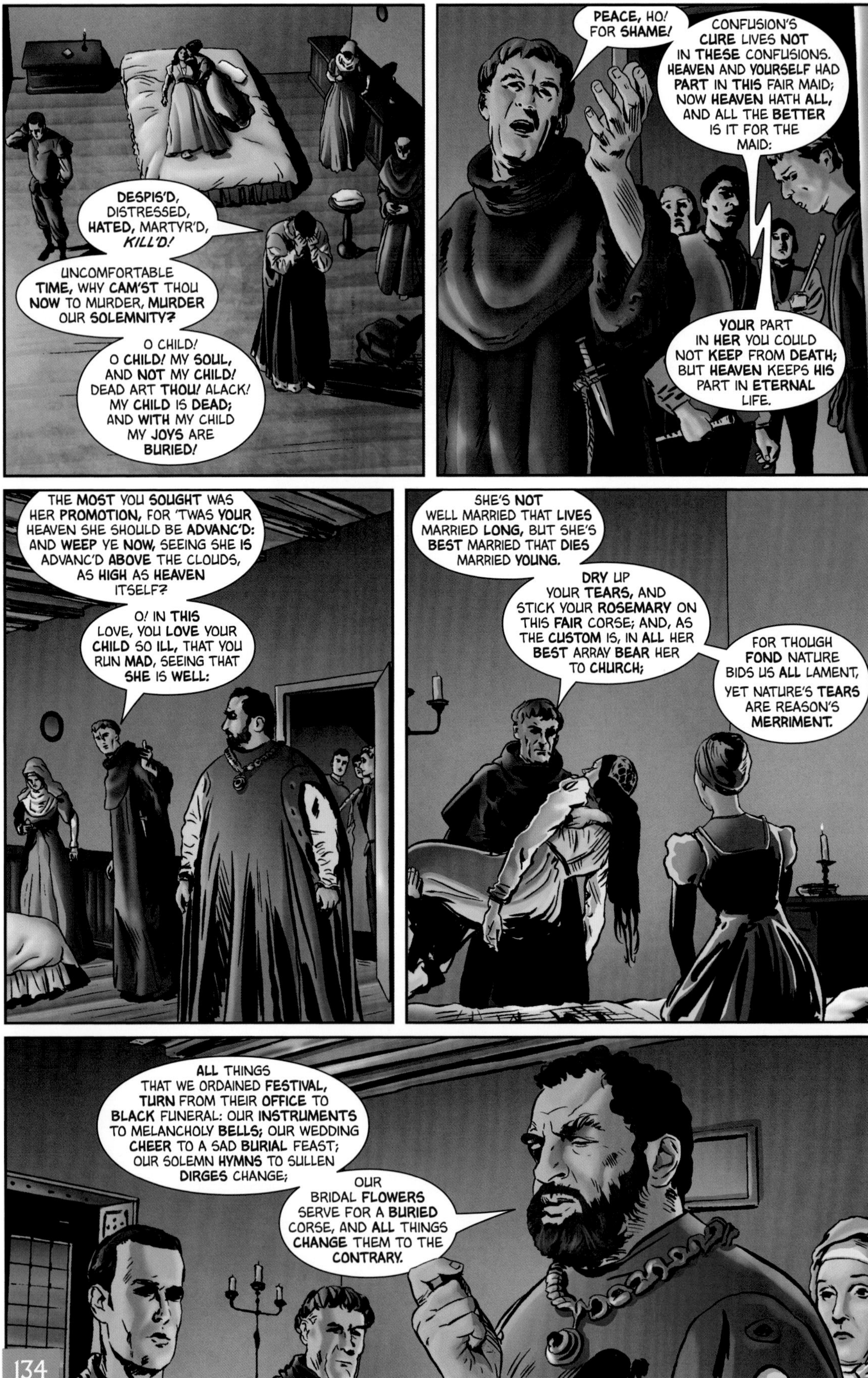
DESPIS'D, DISTRESSED, HATED, MARTYR'D, KILL'D!
UNCOMFORTABLE TIME, WHY CAM'ST THOU NOW TO MURDER, MURDER OUR SOLEMNITY?
O CHILD! O CHILD! MY SOUL, AND NOT MY CHILD! DEAD ART THOU! ALACK! MY CHILD IS DEAD; AND WITH MY CHILD MY JOYS ARE BURIED!
PEACE, HO! FOR SHAME!
CONFUSION'S CURE LIVES NOT IN THESE CONFUSIONS. HEAVEN AND YOURSELF HAD PART IN THIS FAIR MAID; NOW HEAVEN HATH ALL, AND ALL THE BETTER IS IT FOR THE MAID:
YOUR PART IN HER YOU COULD NOT KEEP FROM DEATH; BUT HEAVEN KEEPS HIS PART IN ETERNAL LIFE.
THE MOST YOU SOUGHT WAS HER PROMOTION, FOR 'TWAS YOUR HEAVEN SHE SHOULD BE ADVANC'D: AND WEEP YE NOW, SEEING SHE IS ADVANC'D ABOVE THE CLOUDS, AS HIGH AS HEAVEN ITSELF?
O! IN THIS LOVE, YOU LOVE YOUR CHILD SO ILL, THAT YOU RUN MAD, SEEING THAT SHE IS WELL:
SHE'S NOT WELL MARRIED THAT LIVES MARRIED LONG, BUT SHE'S BEST MARRIED THAT DIES MARRIED YOUNG.
DRY UP YOUR TEARS, AND STICK YOUR ROSEMARY ON THIS FAIR CORSE; AND, AS THE CUSTOM IS, IN ALL HER BEST ARRAY BEAR HER TO CHURCH;
FOR THOUGH FOND NATURE BIDS US ALL LAMENT,
YET NATURE'S TEARS ARE REASON'S MERRIMENT.
ALL THINGS THAT WE ORDAINED FESTIVAL, TURN FROM THEIR OFFICE TO BLACK FUNERAL: OUR INSTRUMENTS TO MELANCHOLY BELLS; OUR WEDDING CHEER TO A SAD BURIAL FEAST; OUR SOLEMN HYMNS TO SULLEN DIRGES CHANGE;
OUR BRIDAL FLOWERS SERVE FOR A BURIED CORSE, AND ALL THINGS CHANGE THEM TO THE CONTRARY.

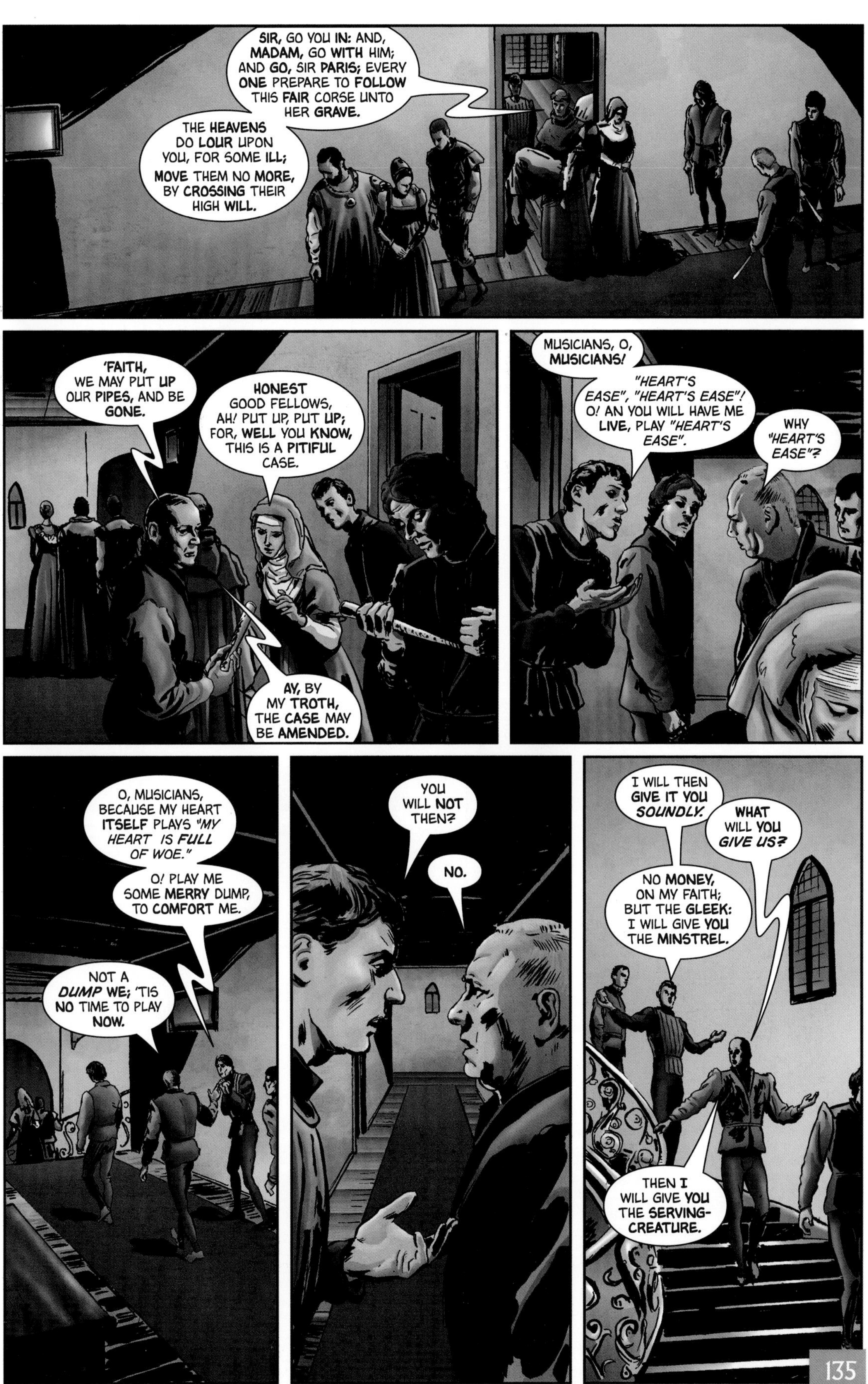

SIR, GO YOU IN: AND, MADAM, GO WITH HIM; AND GO, SIR PARIS; EVERY ONE PREPARE TO FOLLOW THIS FAIR CORSE UNTO HER GRAVE.
THE HEAVENS DO LOUR UPON YOU, FOR SOME ILL; MOVE THEM NO MORE, BY CROSSING THEIR HIGH WILL.
'FAITH, WE MAY PUT UP OUR PIPES, AND BE GONE.
HONEST GOOD FELLOWS, AH! PUT UP, PUT UP; FOR, WELL YOU KNOW, THIS IS A PITIFUL CASE.
AY, BY MY TROTH, THE CASE MAY BE AMENDED.
MUSICIANS, O, MUSICIANS!
"HEART'S EASE", "HEART'S EASE"! O! AN YOU WILL HAVE ME LIVE, PLAY "HEART'S EASE".
WHY "HEART'S EASE"?
O, MUSICIANS, BECAUSE MY HEART ITSELF PLAYS "MY HEART IS FULL OF WOE."
O! PLAY ME SOME MERRY DUMP, TO COMFORT ME.
NOT A DUMP WE; 'TIS NO TIME TO PLAY NOW.
YOU WILL NOT THEN?
NO.
I WILL THEN GIVE IT YOU SOUNDLY.
WHAT WILL YOU GIVE US?
NO MONEY, ON MY FAITH; BUT THE GLEEK: I WILL GIVE YOU THE MINSTREL.
THEN I WILL GIVE YOU THE SERVING-CREATURE.

THEN WILL I LAY THE SERVING-CREATURE'S DAGGER ON YOUR PATE. I WILL CARRY NO CROTCHETS; I'LL RE YOU, I'LL FA YOU; DO YOU NOTE ME?

AN YOU RE US, AND FA US, YOU NOTE US.

PRAY YOU, PUT UP YOUR DAGGER, AND PUT OUT YOUR WIT.

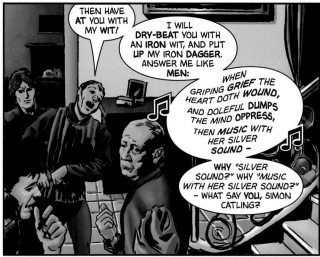

THEN HAVE AT YOU WITH MY WIT!

I WILL DRY-BEAT YOU WITH AN IRON WIT, AND PUT UP MY IRON DAGGER. ANSWER ME LIKE MEN:

WHEN GRIPING GRIEF THE HEART DOTH WOUND, AND DOLEFUL DUMPS THE MIND OPPRESS, THEN MUSIC WITH HER SILVER SOUND —

WHY "SILVER SOUND?" WHY "MUSIC WITH HER SILVER SOUND?" — WHAT SAY YOU, SIMON CATLING?

MARRY, SIR, BECAUSE SILVER HATH A SWEET SOUND.

PRETTY! WHAT SAY YOU, HUGH REBECK?

I SAY, "SILVER SOUND," BECAUSE MUSICIANS SOUND FOR SILVER.

PRETTY TOO! WHAT SAY YOU, JAMES SOUNDPOST?

'FAITH, I KNOW NOT WHAT TO SAY.

O! I CRY YOU MERCY; YOU ARE THE SINGER: I WILL SAY FOR YOU. IT IS "MUSIC WITH HER SILVER SOUND," BECAUSE MUSICIANS HAVE NO GOLD FOR SOUNDING:

THEN MUSIC WITH HER SILVER SOUND WITH SPEEDY HELP DOTH LEND REDRESS.

WHAT A PESTILENT KNAVE IS THIS SAME!

HANG HIM, JACK! COME, WE'LL IN HERE; TARRY FOR THE MOURNERS, AND STAY DINNER.

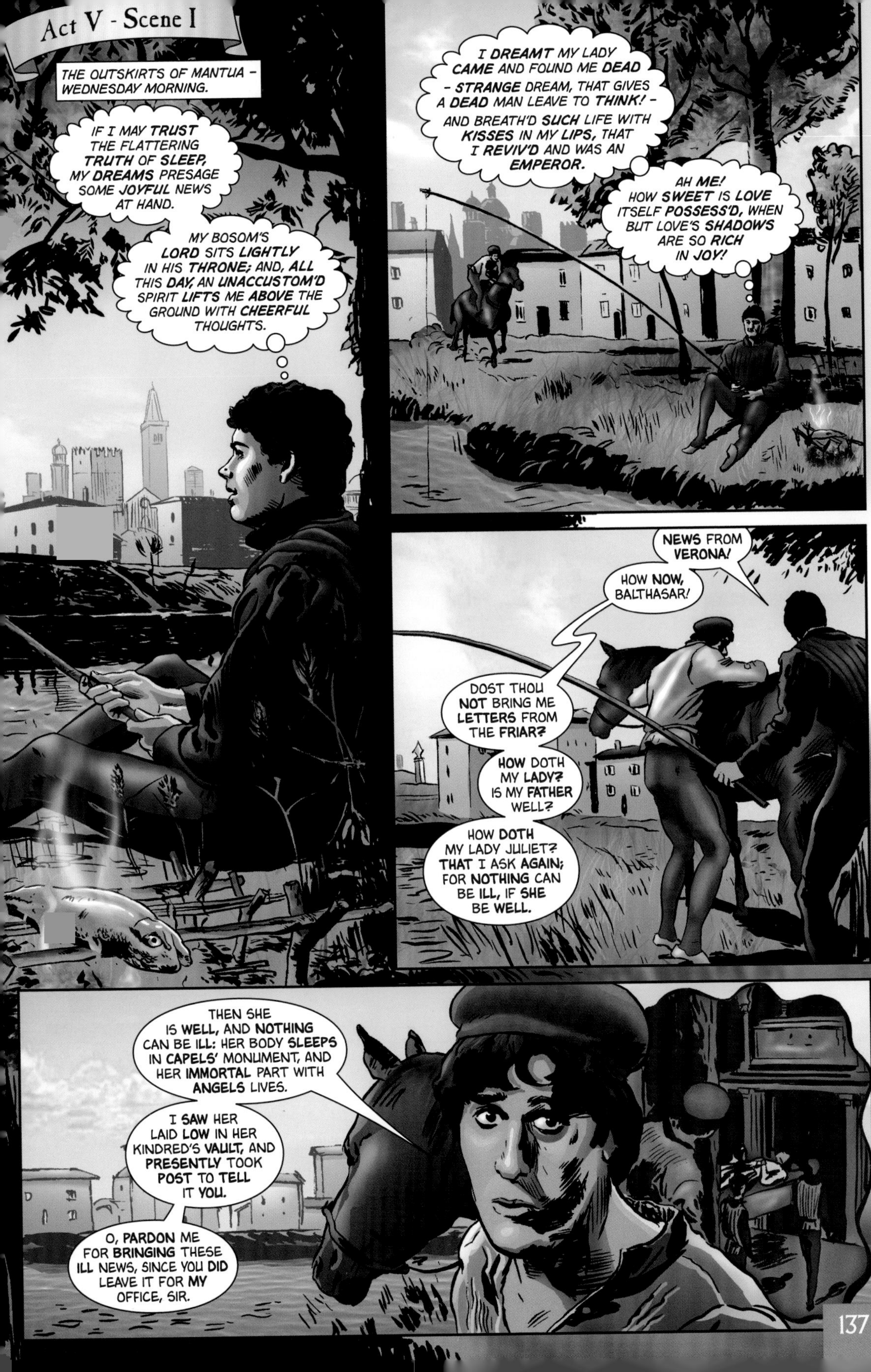
Act V - Scene I
THE OUTSKIRTS OF MANTUA - WEDNESDAY MORNING.
IF I MAY TRUST THE FLATTERING TRUTH OF SLEEP, MY DREAMS PRESAGE SOME JOYFUL NEWS AT HAND.
MY BOSOM'S LORD SITS LIGHTLY IN HIS THRONE; AND, ALL THIS DAY, AN UNACCUSTOM'D SPIRIT LIFTS ME ABOVE THE GROUND WITH CHEERFUL THOUGHTS.
I DREAMT MY LADY CAME AND FOUND ME DEAD - STRANGE DREAM, THAT GIVES A DEAD MAN LEAVE TO THINK! - AND BREATH'D SUCH LIFE WITH KISSES IN MY LIPS, THAT I REVIV'D AND WAS AN EMPEROR.
AH ME! HOW SWEET IS LOVE ITSELF POSSESS'D, WHEN BUT LOVE'S SHADOWS ARE SO RICH IN JOY!
NEWS FROM VERONA!
HOW NOW, BALTHASAR!
DOST THOU NOT BRING ME LETTERS FROM THE FRIAR?
HOW DOTH MY LADY? IS MY FATHER WELL?
HOW DOTH MY LADY JULIET? THAT I ASK AGAIN; FOR NOTHING CAN BE ILL, IF SHE BE WELL.
THEN SHE IS WELL, AND NOTHING CAN BE ILL: HER BODY SLEEPS IN CAPELS' MONUMENT, AND HER IMMORTAL PART WITH ANGELS LIVES.
I SAW HER LAID LOW IN HER KINDRED'S VAULT, AND PRESENTLY TOOK POST TO TELL IT YOU.
O, PARDON ME FOR BRINGING THESE ILL NEWS, SINCE YOU DID LEAVE IT FOR MY OFFICE, SIR.

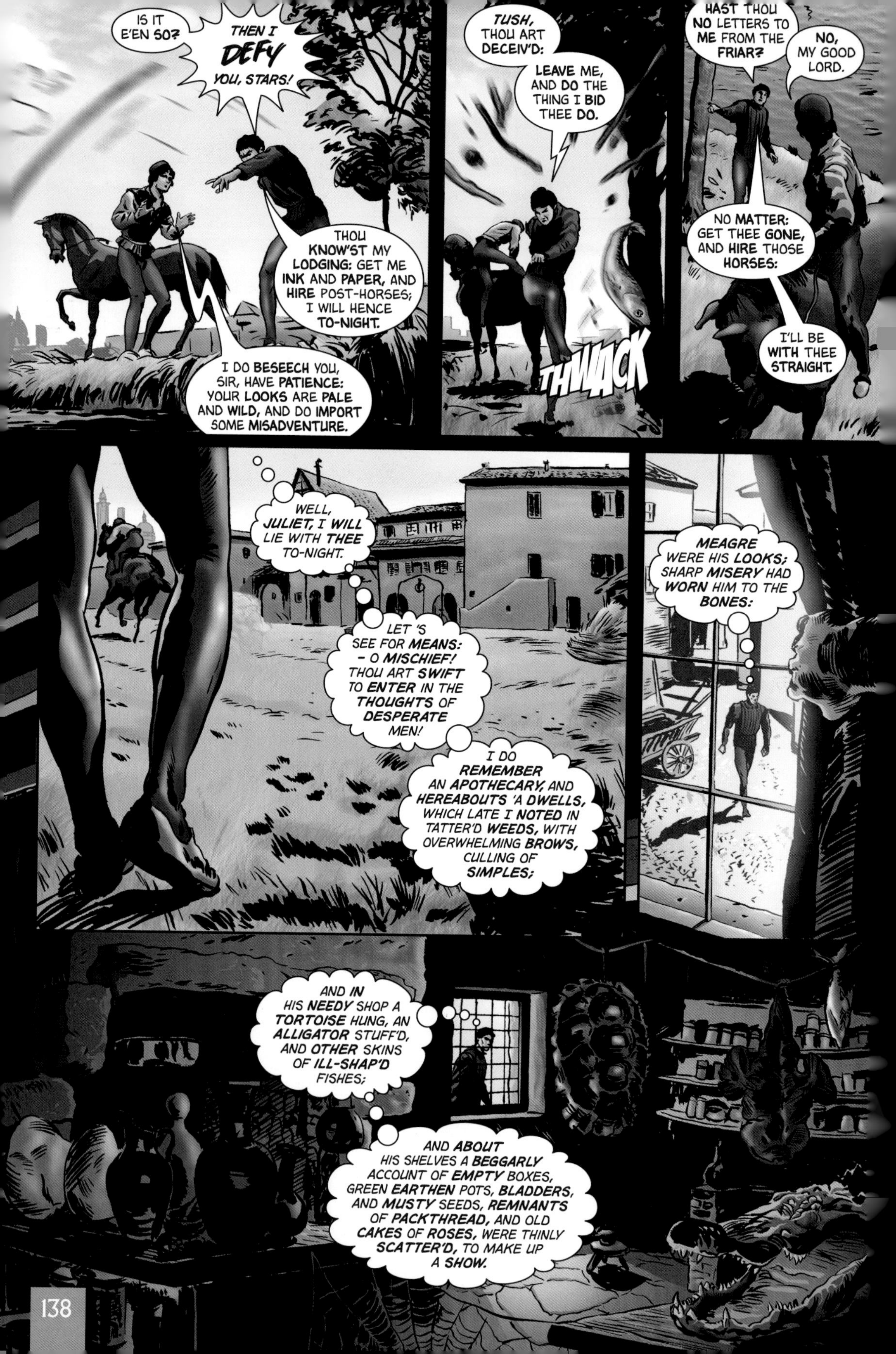
IS IT E'EN SO?
THEN I DEFY YOU, STARS!
THOU KNOW'ST MY LODGING: GET ME INK AND PAPER, AND HIRE POST-HORSES; I WILL HENCE TO-NIGHT.
I DO BESEECH YOU, SIR, HAVE PATIENCE: YOUR LOOKS ARE PALE AND WILD, AND DO IMPORT SOME MISADVENTURE.
TUSH, THOU ART DECEIV'D:
LEAVE ME, AND DO THE THING I BID THEE DO.
THWACK
HAST THOU NO LETTERS TO ME FROM THE FRIAR?
NO, MY GOOD LORD.
NO MATTER: GET THEE GONE, AND HIRE THOSE HORSES:
I'LL BE WITH THEE STRAIGHT.
WELL, JULIET, I WILL LIE WITH THEE TO-NIGHT.
LET 'S SEE FOR MEANS: - O MISCHIEF! THOU ART SWIFT TO ENTER IN THE THOUGHTS OF DESPERATE MEN!
I DO REMEMBER AN APOTHECARY, AND HEREABOUTS 'A DWELLS, WHICH LATE I NOTED IN TATTER'D WEEDS, WITH OVERWHELMING BROWS, CULLING OF SIMPLES;
MEAGRE WERE HIS LOOKS; SHARP MISERY HAD WORN HIM TO THE BONES:
AND IN HIS NEEDY SHOP A TORTOISE HUNG, AN ALLIGATOR STUFF'D, AND OTHER SKINS OF ILL-SHAP'D FISHES;
AND ABOUT HIS SHELVES A BEGGARLY ACCOUNT OF EMPTY BOXES, GREEN EARTHEN POTS, BLADDERS, AND MUSTY SEEDS, REMNANTS OF PACKTHREAD, AND OLD CAKES OF ROSES, WERE THINLY SCATTER'D, TO MAKE UP A SHOW.

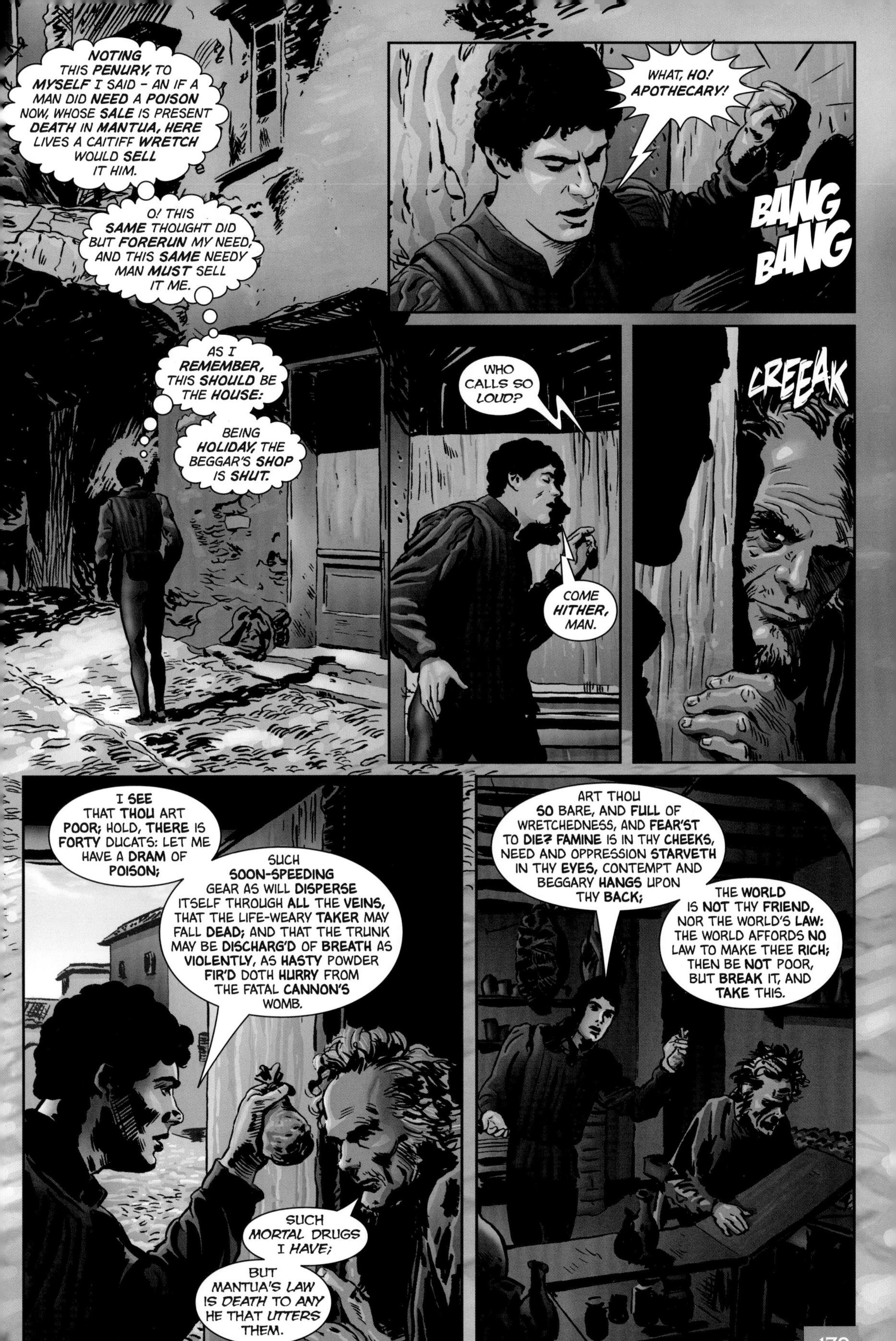
NOTING THIS PENURY, TO MYSELF I SAID - AN IF A MAN DID NEED A POISON NOW, WHOSE SALE IS PRESENT DEATH IN MANTUA, HERE LIVES A CAITIFF WRETCH WOULD SELL IT HIM.
O! THIS SAME THOUGHT DID BUT FORERUN MY NEED, AND THIS SAME NEEDY MAN MUST SELL IT ME.
WHAT, HO! APOTHECARY!
BANG BANG
AS I REMEMBER, THIS SHOULD BE THE HOUSE:
BEING HOLIDAY, THE BEGGAR'S SHOP IS SHUT.
WHO CALLS SO LOUD?
COME HITHER, MAN.
CREEAK
I SEE THAT THOU ART POOR; HOLD, THERE IS FORTY DUCATS: LET ME HAVE A DRAM OF POISON;
SUCH SOON-SPEEDING GEAR AS WILL DISPERSE ITSELF THROUGH ALL THE VEINS, THAT THE LIFE-WEARY TAKER MAY FALL DEAD; AND THAT THE TRUNK MAY BE DISCHARG'D OF BREATH AS VIOLENTLY, AS HASTY POWDER FIR'D DOTH HURRY FROM THE FATAL CANNON'S WOMB.
SUCH MORTAL DRUGS I HAVE;
BUT MANTUA'S LAW IS DEATH TO ANY HE THAT UTTERS THEM.
ART THOU SO BARE, AND FULL OF WRETCHEDNESS, AND FEAR'ST TO DIE? FAMINE IS IN THY CHEEKS, NEED AND OPPRESSION STARVETH IN THY EYES, CONTEMPT AND BEGGARY HANGS UPON THY BACK;
THE WORLD IS NOT THY FRIEND, NOR THE WORLD'S LAW: THE WORLD AFFORDS NO LAW TO MAKE THEE RICH; THEN BE NOT POOR, BUT BREAK IT, AND TAKE THIS.

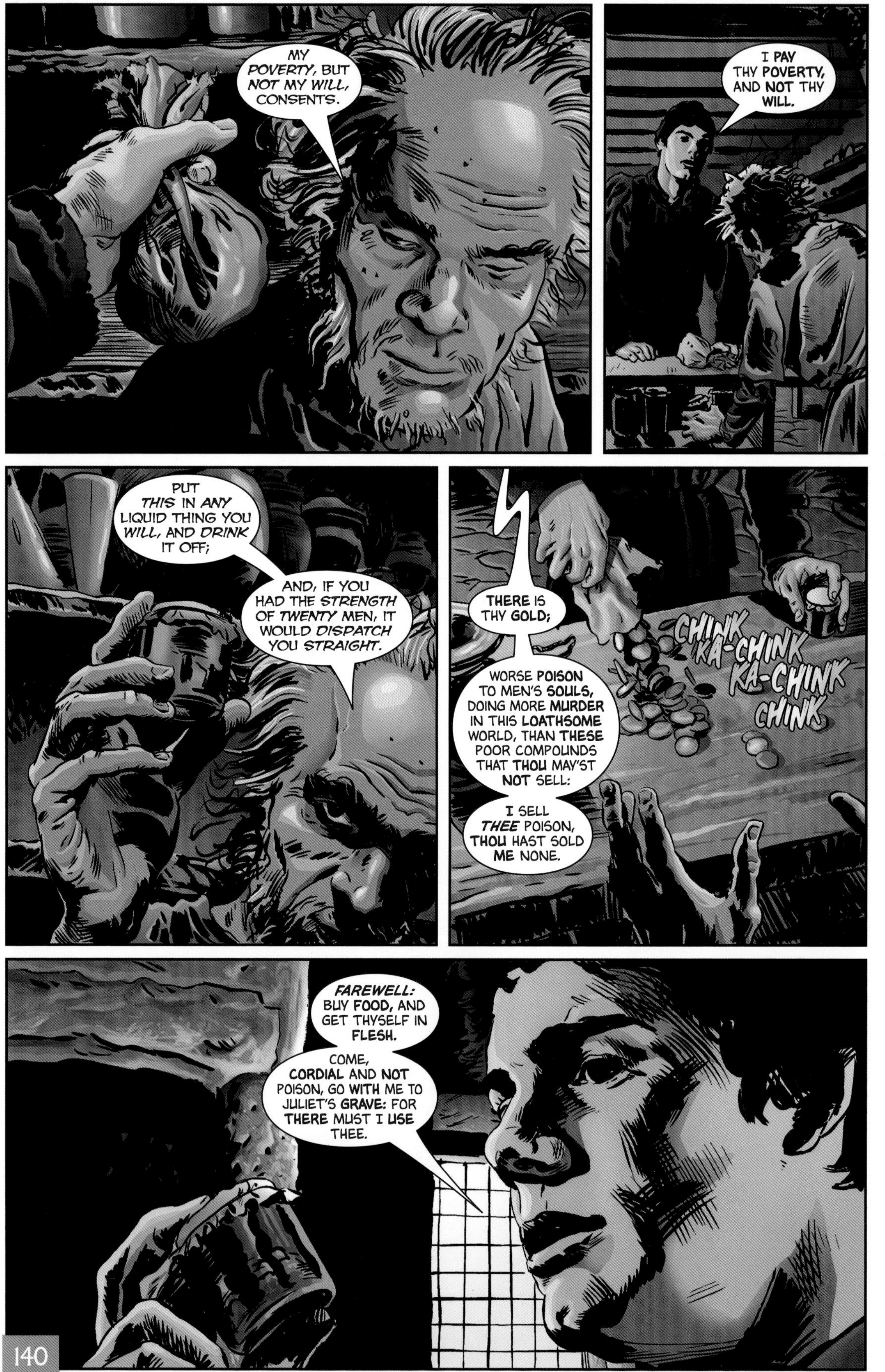
MY POVERTY, BUT NOT MY WILL, CONSENTS.
I PAY THY POVERTY, AND NOT THY WILL.
PUT THIS IN ANY LIQUID THING YOU WILL, AND DRINK IT OFF;
AND, IF YOU HAD THE STRENGTH OF TWENTY MEN, IT WOULD DISPATCH YOU STRAIGHT.
THERE IS THY GOLD;
WORSE POISON TO MEN'S SOULS, DOING MORE MURDER IN THIS LOATHSOME WORLD, THAN THESE POOR COMPOUNDS THAT THOU MAY'ST NOT SELL:
I SELL THEE POISON, THOU HAST SOLD ME NONE.
CHINK KA-CHINK KA-CHINK CHINK
FAREWELL: BUY FOOD, AND GET THYSELF IN FLESH.
COME, CORDIAL AND NOT POISON, GO WITH ME TO JULIET'S GRAVE: FOR THERE MUST I USE THEE.

FRIAR LAURENCE'S CHURCH – WEDNESDAY EVENING.

HOLY FRANCISCAN FRIAR! BROTHER, HO!

KNOCK KNOCK

THIS **SAME** SHOULD BE THE **VOICE** OF FRIAR JOHN.

WELCOME FROM **MANTUA**: WHAT SAYS ROMEO? OR, IF HIS MIND BE **WRIT**, GIVE ME HIS LETTER.

GOING TO **FIND** A BARE-FOOT **BROTHER** OUT, ONE OF OUR **ORDER**, TO ASSOCIATE ME, HERE IN **THIS** CITY VISITING THE **SICK**, AND **FINDING** HIM, THE **SEARCHERS** OF THE **TOWN**, SUSPECTING THAT WE **BOTH** WERE IN A **HOUSE** WHERE THE INFECTIOUS **PESTILENCE** DID REIGN, SEAL'D UP THE **DOORS** AND WOULD **NOT** LET US **FORTH**; SO THAT MY **SPEED** TO MANTUA THERE WAS **STAY'D**.

WHO BARE MY **LETTER** THEN TO **ROMEO**?

I COULD NOT **SEND** IT, – HERE IT IS AGAIN, – NOR GET A MESSENGER TO BRING IT THEE, SO **FEARFUL** WERE THEY OF **INFECTION**.

UNHAPPY FORTUNE!

BY MY **BROTHERHOOD**, THE LETTER WAS NOT **NICE**, BUT FULL OF **CHARGE**, OF **DEAR** IMPORT; AND THE **NEGLECTING** IT MAY DO MUCH **DANGER**. FRIAR JOHN, GO **HENCE**; GET ME AN IRON CROW, AND BRING IT **STRAIGHT** UNTO MY CELL.

BROTHER, I'LL **GO** AND BRING IT THEE.

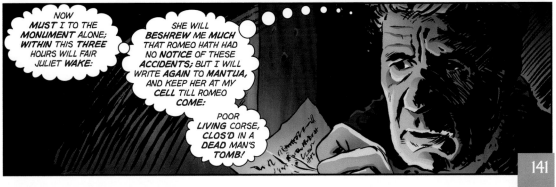

NOW **MUST** I TO THE **MONUMENT** ALONE; **WITHIN** THIS **THREE** HOURS WILL FAIR JULIET **WAKE**:

SHE WILL **BESHREW** ME **MUCH** THAT ROMEO HATH HAD NO **NOTICE** OF THESE **ACCIDENTS**; BUT I WILL WRITE **AGAIN** TO MANTUA, AND KEEP HER AT MY **CELL** TILL ROMEO **COME**:

POOR LIVING CORSE, CLOS'D IN A **DEAD** MAN'S **TOMB**!

141

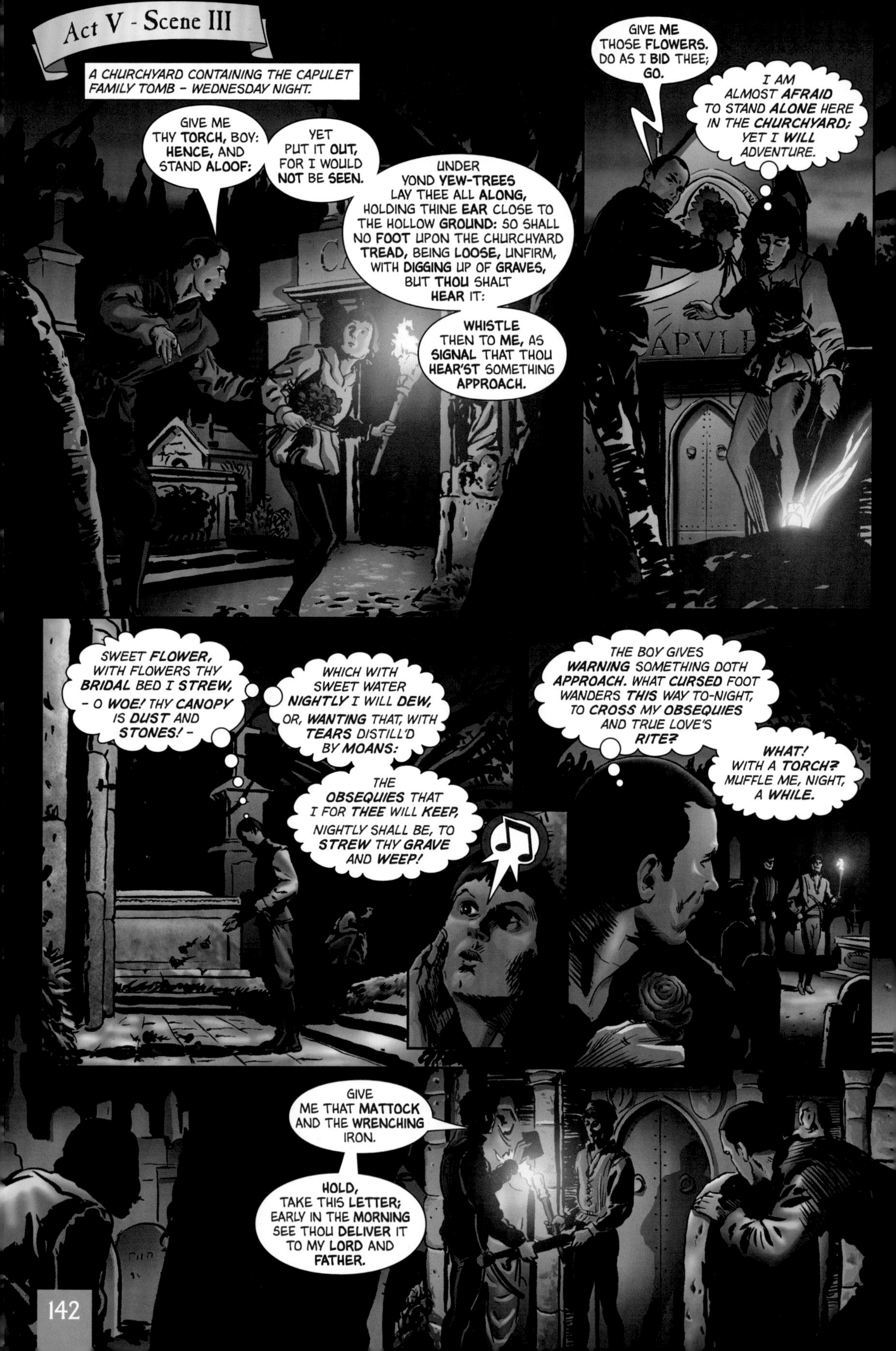
Act V - Scene III
A CHURCHYARD CONTAINING THE CAPULET FAMILY TOMB – WEDNESDAY NIGHT.
GIVE ME THY TORCH, BOY: HENCE, AND STAND ALOOF:
YET PUT IT OUT, FOR I WOULD NOT BE SEEN.
UNDER YOND YEW-TREES LAY THEE ALL ALONG, HOLDING THINE EAR CLOSE TO THE HOLLOW GROUND: SO SHALL NO FOOT UPON THE CHURCHYARD TREAD, BEING LOOSE, UNFIRM, WITH DIGGING UP OF GRAVES, BUT THOU SHALT HEAR IT:
WHISTLE THEN TO ME, AS SIGNAL THAT THOU HEAR'ST SOMETHING APPROACH.
GIVE ME THOSE FLOWERS. DO AS I BID THEE; GO.
I AM ALMOST AFRAID TO STAND ALONE HERE IN THE CHURCHYARD; YET I WILL ADVENTURE.
SWEET FLOWER, WITH FLOWERS THY BRIDAL BED I STREW, – O WOE! THY CANOPY IS DUST AND STONES! –
WHICH WITH SWEET WATER NIGHTLY I WILL DEW, OR, WANTING THAT, WITH TEARS DISTILL'D BY MOANS:
THE OBSEQUIES THAT I FOR THEE WILL KEEP, NIGHTLY SHALL BE, TO STREW THY GRAVE AND WEEP!
THE BOY GIVES WARNING SOMETHING DOTH APPROACH. WHAT CURSED FOOT WANDERS THIS WAY TO-NIGHT, TO CROSS MY OBSEQUIES AND TRUE LOVE'S RITE?
WHAT! WITH A TORCH? MUFFLE ME, NIGHT, A WHILE.
GIVE ME THAT MATTOCK AND THE WRENCHING IRON.
HOLD, TAKE THIS LETTER; EARLY IN THE MORNING SEE THOU DELIVER IT TO MY LORD AND FATHER.

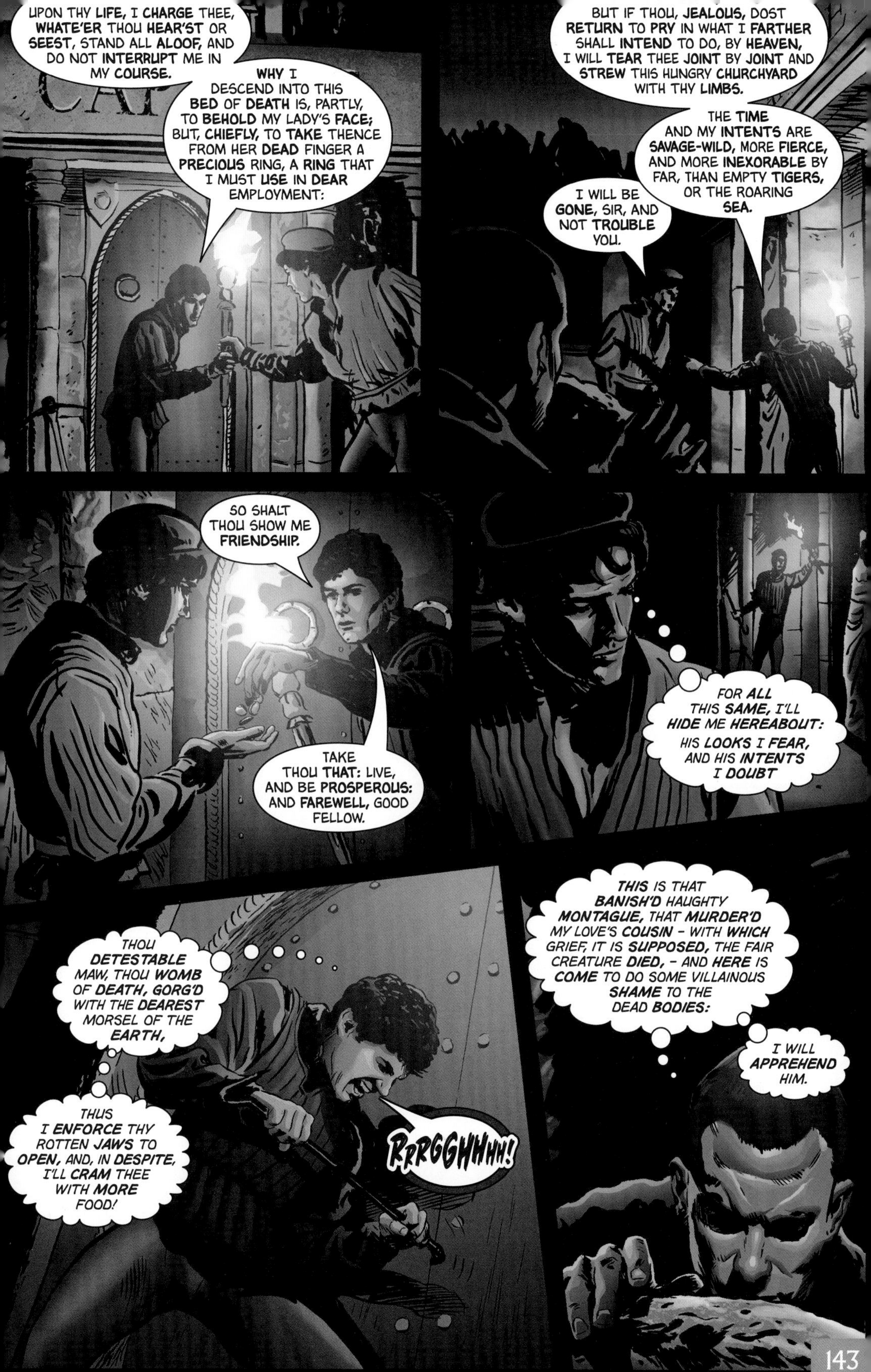
UPON THY LIFE, I CHARGE THEE, WHATE'ER THOU HEAR'ST OR SEEST, STAND ALL ALOOF, AND DO NOT INTERRUPT ME IN MY COURSE.
WHY I DESCEND INTO THIS BED OF DEATH IS, PARTLY, TO BEHOLD MY LADY'S FACE; BUT, CHIEFLY, TO TAKE THENCE FROM HER DEAD FINGER A PRECIOUS RING, A RING THAT I MUST USE IN DEAR EMPLOYMENT:
BUT IF THOU, JEALOUS, DOST RETURN TO PRY IN WHAT I FARTHER SHALL INTEND TO DO, BY HEAVEN, I WILL TEAR THEE JOINT BY JOINT AND STREW THIS HUNGRY CHURCHYARD WITH THY LIMBS.
THE TIME AND MY INTENTS ARE SAVAGE-WILD, MORE FIERCE, AND MORE INEXORABLE BY FAR, THAN EMPTY TIGERS, OR THE ROARING SEA.
I WILL BE GONE, SIR, AND NOT TROUBLE YOU.
SO SHALT THOU SHOW ME FRIENDSHIP.
TAKE THOU THAT: LIVE, AND BE PROSPEROUS: AND FAREWELL, GOOD FELLOW.
FOR ALL THIS SAME, I'LL HIDE ME HEREABOUT: HIS LOOKS I FEAR, AND HIS INTENTS I DOUBT
THOU DETESTABLE MAW, THOU WOMB OF DEATH, GORG'D WITH THE DEAREST MORSEL OF THE EARTH,
THUS I ENFORCE THY ROTTEN JAWS TO OPEN, AND, IN DESPITE, I'LL CRAM THEE WITH MORE FOOD!
RRRGGHHHH!
THIS IS THAT BANISH'D HAUGHTY MONTAGUE, THAT MURDER'D MY LOVE'S COUSIN - WITH WHICH GRIEF, IT IS SUPPOSED, THE FAIR CREATURE DIED, - AND HERE IS COME TO DO SOME VILLAINOUS SHAME TO THE DEAD BODIES:
I WILL APPREHEND HIM.

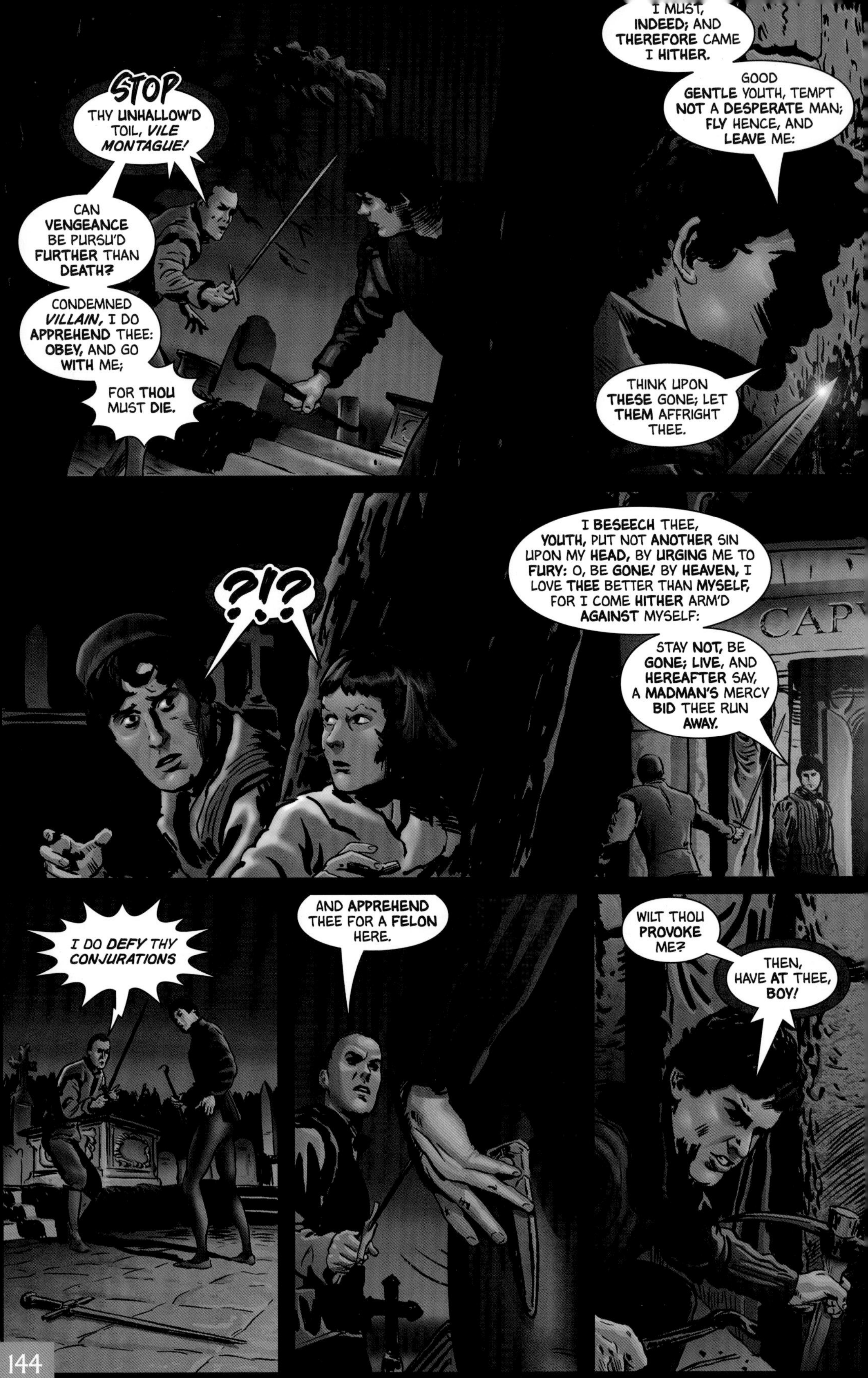
STOP THY UNHALLOW'D TOIL, VILE MONTAGUE!
CAN VENGEANCE BE PURSU'D FURTHER THAN DEATH?
CONDEMNED VILLAIN, I DO APPREHEND THEE: OBEY, AND GO WITH ME;
FOR THOU MUST DIE.
I MUST, INDEED; AND THEREFORE CAME I HITHER.
GOOD GENTLE YOUTH, TEMPT NOT A DESPERATE MAN; FLY HENCE, AND LEAVE ME:
THINK UPON THESE GONE; LET THEM AFFRIGHT THEE.
?!?
I BESEECH THEE, YOUTH, PUT NOT ANOTHER SIN UPON MY HEAD, BY URGING ME TO FURY: O, BE GONE! BY HEAVEN, I LOVE THEE BETTER THAN MYSELF, FOR I COME HITHER ARM'D AGAINST MYSELF:
STAY NOT, BE GONE; LIVE, AND HEREAFTER SAY, A MADMAN'S MERCY BID THEE RUN AWAY.
CAP
I DO DEFY THY CONJURATIONS
AND APPREHEND THEE FOR A FELON HERE.
WILT THOU PROVOKE ME?
THEN, HAVE AT THEE, BOY!

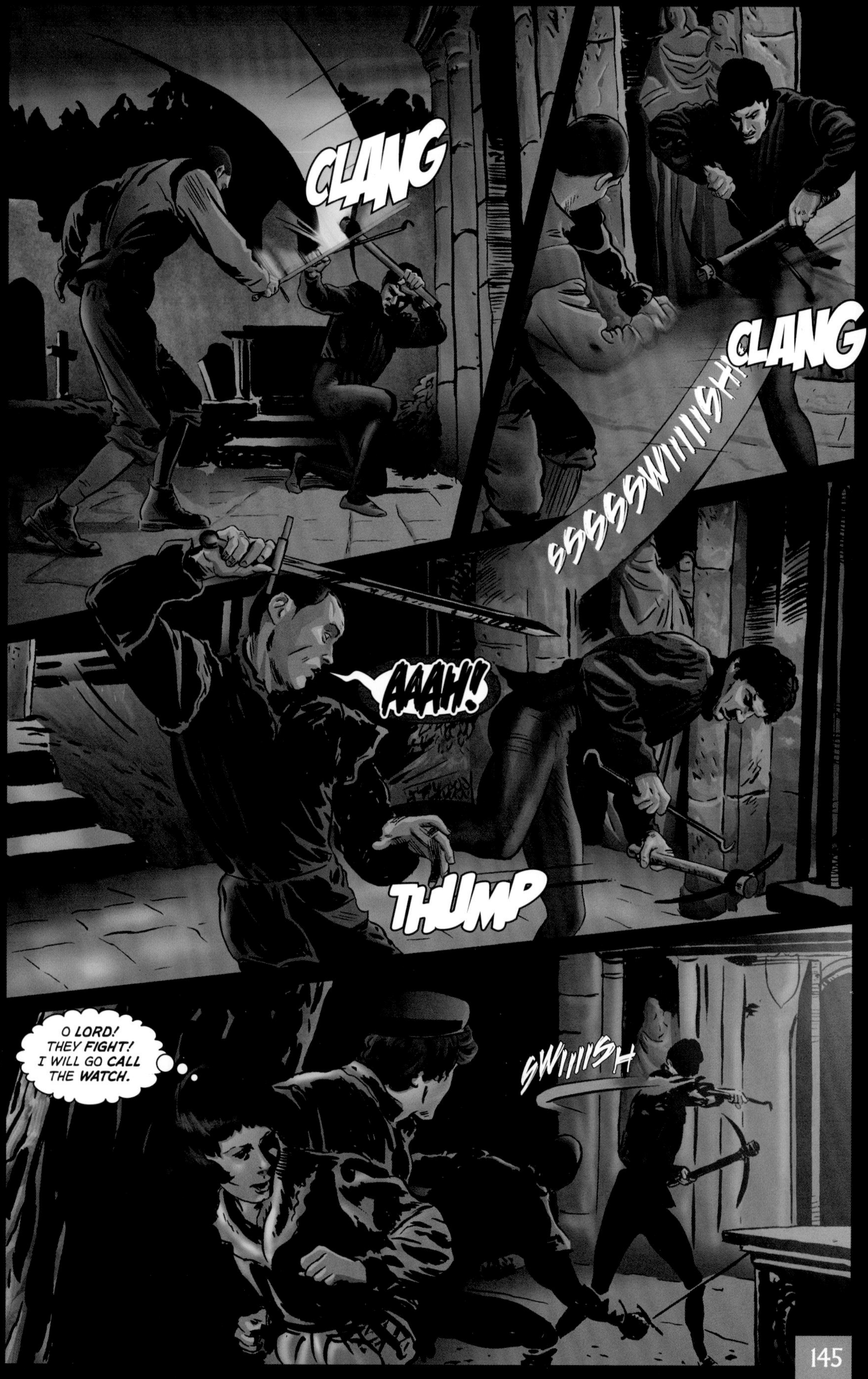
CLANG
CLANG
SSSSSWIIIIISH
AAAH!
THUMP
O LORD! THEY FIGHT! I WILL GO CALL THE WATCH.
SWIIIISH

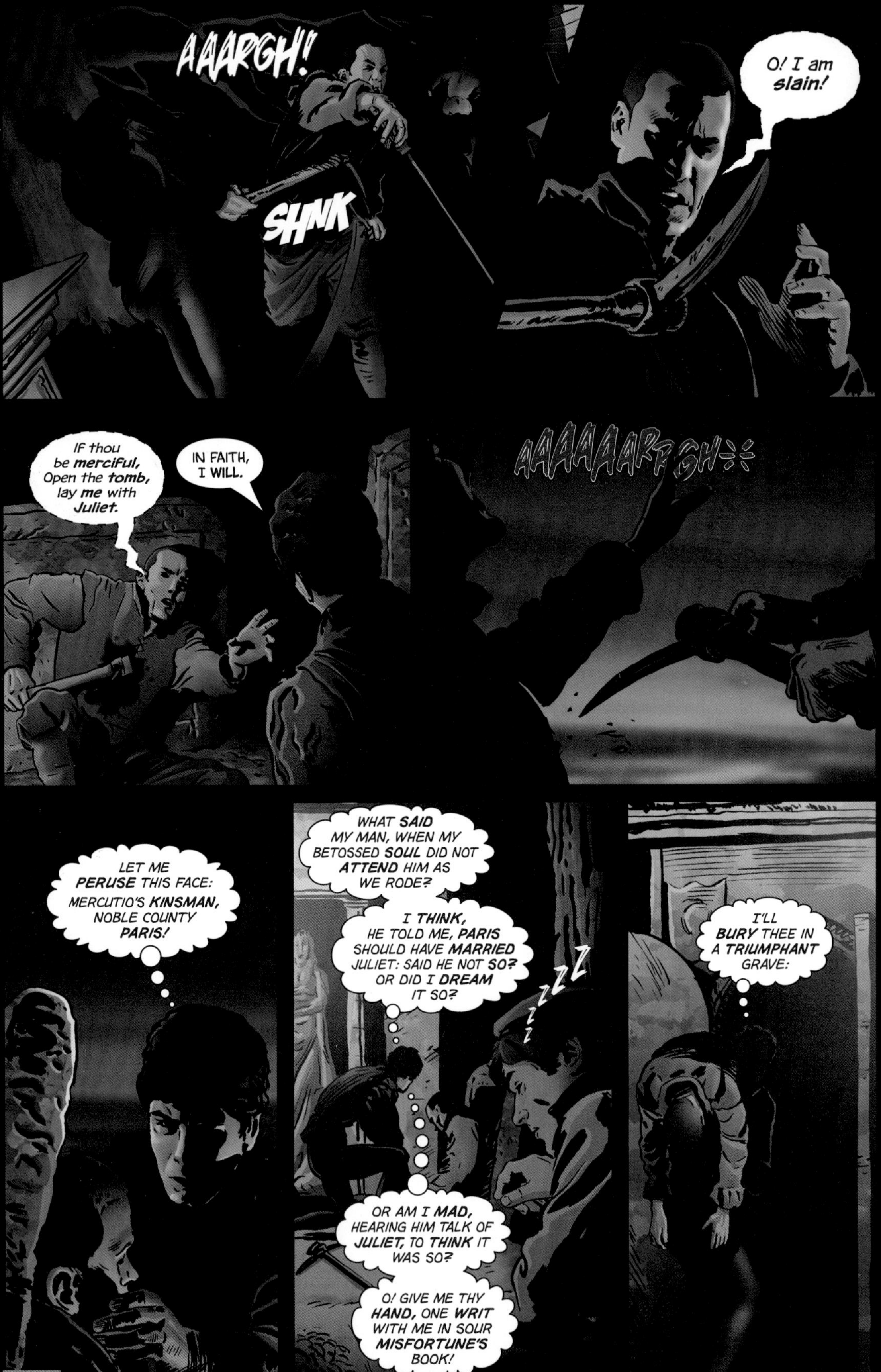
AAARGH!
SHNK
O! I am slain!
If thou be merciful, Open the tomb, lay me with Juliet.
IN FAITH, I WILL.
AAAAAARRGH
LET ME PERUSE THIS FACE: MERCUTIO'S KINSMAN, NOBLE COUNTY PARIS!
WHAT SAID MY MAN, WHEN MY BETOSSED SOUL DID NOT ATTEND HIM AS WE RODE?
I THINK, HE TOLD ME, PARIS SHOULD HAVE MARRIED JULIET: SAID HE NOT SO? OR DID I DREAM IT SO?
ZZZ
OR AM I MAD, HEARING HIM TALK OF JULIET, TO THINK IT WAS SO?
O! GIVE ME THY HAND, ONE WRIT WITH ME IN SOUR MISFORTUNE'S BOOK!
I'LL BURY THEE IN A TRIUMPHANT GRAVE:

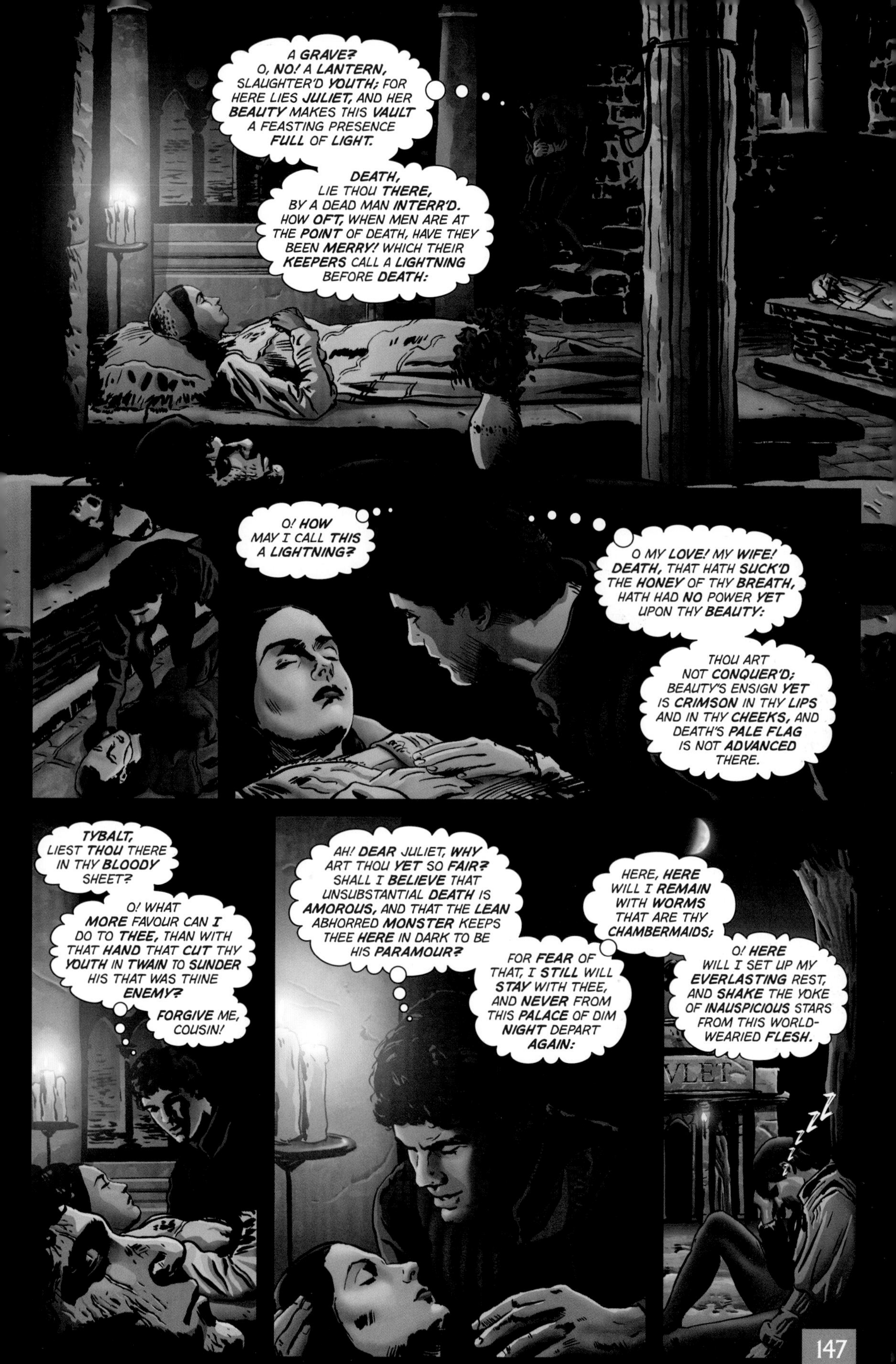
A GRAVE? O, NO! A LANTERN, SLAUGHTER'D YOUTH; FOR HERE LIES JULIET, AND HER BEAUTY MAKES THIS VAULT A FEASTING PRESENCE FULL OF LIGHT.
DEATH, LIE THOU THERE, BY A DEAD MAN INTERR'D. HOW OFT, WHEN MEN ARE AT THE POINT OF DEATH, HAVE THEY BEEN MERRY! WHICH THEIR KEEPERS CALL A LIGHTNING BEFORE DEATH:
O! HOW MAY I CALL THIS A LIGHTNING?
O MY LOVE! MY WIFE! DEATH, THAT HATH SUCK'D THE HONEY OF THY BREATH, HATH HAD NO POWER YET UPON THY BEAUTY:
THOU ART NOT CONQUER'D; BEAUTY'S ENSIGN YET IS CRIMSON IN THY LIPS AND IN THY CHEEKS, AND DEATH'S PALE FLAG IS NOT ADVANCED THERE.
TYBALT, LIEST THOU THERE IN THY BLOODY SHEET?
O! WHAT MORE FAVOUR CAN I DO TO THEE, THAN WITH THAT HAND THAT CUT THY YOUTH IN TWAIN TO SUNDER HIS THAT WAS THINE ENEMY?
FORGIVE ME, COUSIN!
AH! DEAR JULIET, WHY ART THOU YET SO FAIR? SHALL I BELIEVE THAT UNSUBSTANTIAL DEATH IS AMOROUS, AND THAT THE LEAN ABHORRED MONSTER KEEPS THEE HERE IN DARK TO BE HIS PARAMOUR?
FOR FEAR OF THAT, I STILL WILL STAY WITH THEE, AND NEVER FROM THIS PALACE OF DIM NIGHT DEPART AGAIN:
HERE, HERE WILL I REMAIN WITH WORMS THAT ARE THY CHAMBERMAIDS;
O! HERE WILL I SET UP MY EVERLASTING REST, AND SHAKE THE YOKE OF INAUSPICIOUS STARS FROM THIS WORLD-WEARIED FLESH.
ZZZ

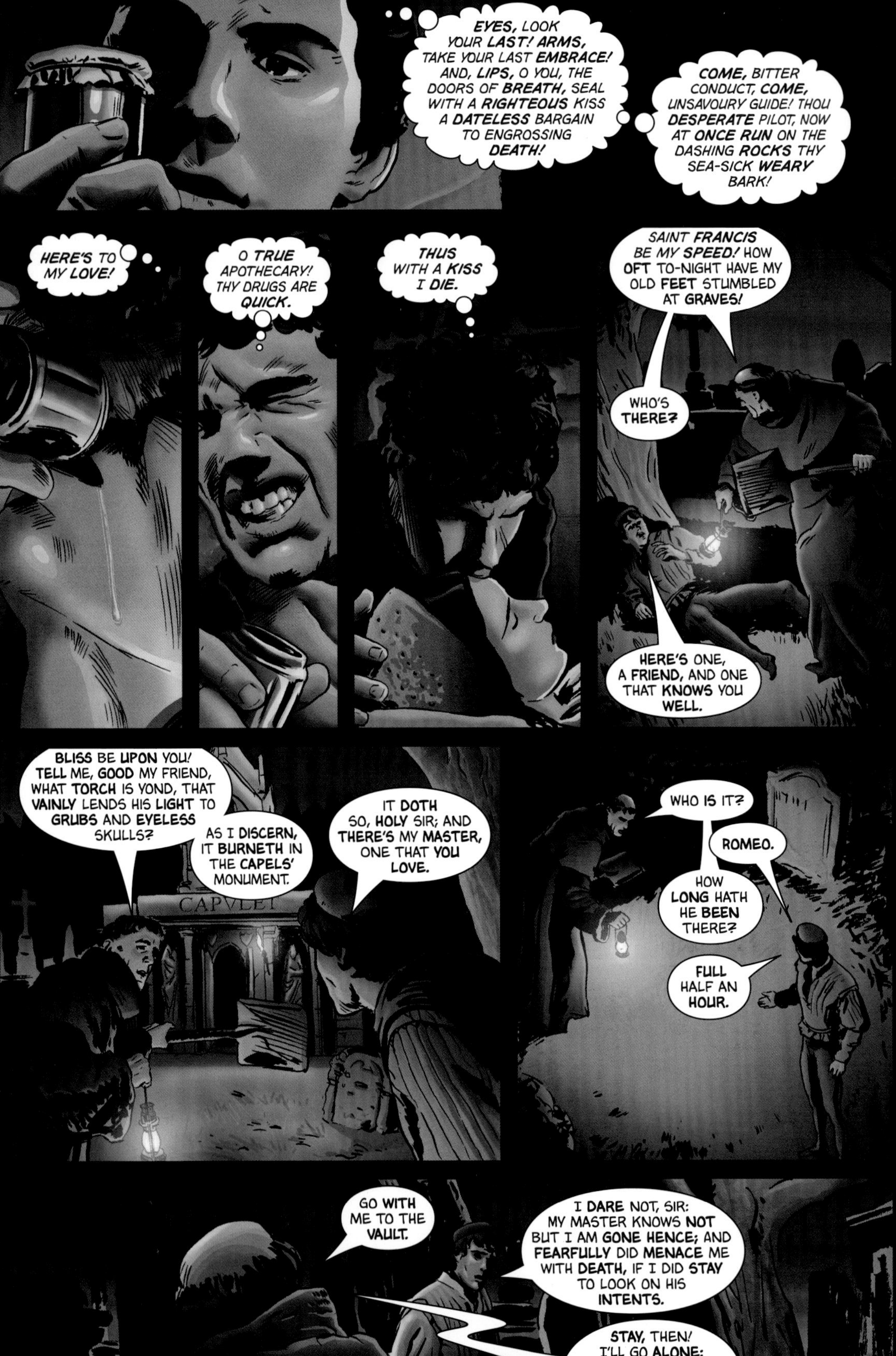
EYES, LOOK YOUR LAST! ARMS, TAKE YOUR LAST EMBRACE! AND, LIPS, O YOU, THE DOORS OF BREATH, SEAL WITH A RIGHTEOUS KISS A DATELESS BARGAIN TO ENGROSSING DEATH!
COME, BITTER CONDUCT, COME, UNSAVOURY GUIDE! THOU DESPERATE PILOT, NOW AT ONCE RUN ON THE DASHING ROCKS THY SEA-SICK WEARY BARK!
HERE'S TO MY LOVE!
O TRUE APOTHECARY! THY DRUGS ARE QUICK.
THUS WITH A KISS I DIE.
SAINT FRANCIS BE MY SPEED! HOW OFT TO-NIGHT HAVE MY OLD FEET STUMBLED AT GRAVES!
WHO'S THERE?
HERE'S ONE, A FRIEND, AND ONE THAT KNOWS YOU WELL.
BLISS BE UPON YOU! TELL ME, GOOD MY FRIEND, WHAT TORCH IS YOND, THAT VAINLY LENDS HIS LIGHT TO GRUBS AND EYELESS SKULLS?
AS I DISCERN, IT BURNETH IN THE CAPELS' MONUMENT.
CAPVLET
IT DOTH SO, HOLY SIR; AND THERE'S MY MASTER, ONE THAT YOU LOVE.
WHO IS IT?
ROMEO.
HOW LONG HATH HE BEEN THERE?
FULL HALF AN HOUR.
GO WITH ME TO THE VAULT.
I DARE NOT, SIR: MY MASTER KNOWS NOT BUT I AM GONE HENCE; AND FEARFULLY DID MENACE ME WITH DEATH, IF I DID STAY TO LOOK ON HIS INTENTS.
STAY, THEN! I'LL GO ALONE: FEAR COMES UPON ME; O! MUCH I FEAR SOME ILL UNLUCKY THING.

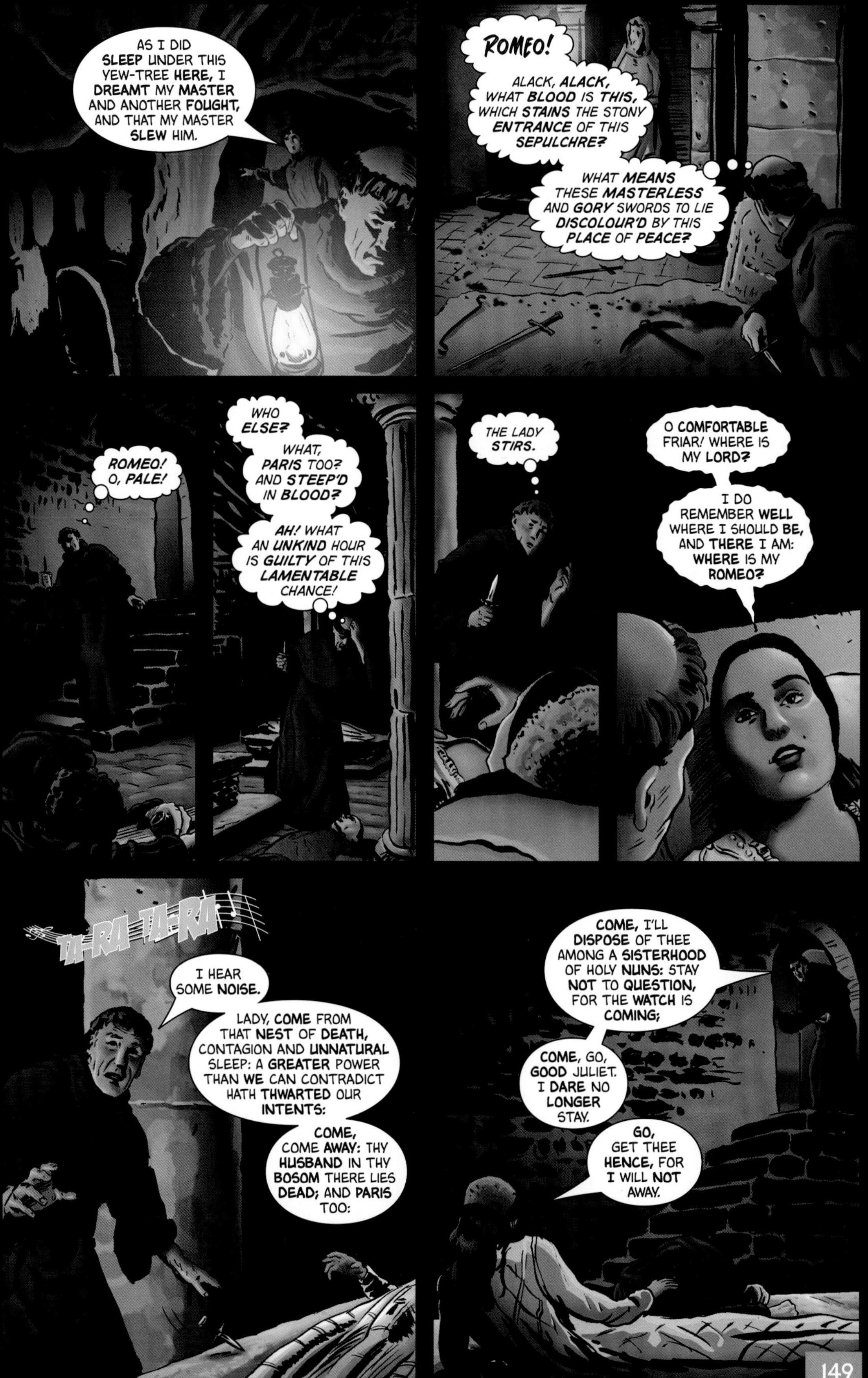
AS I DID SLEEP UNDER THIS YEW-TREE HERE, I DREAMT MY MASTER AND ANOTHER FOUGHT, AND THAT MY MASTER SLEW HIM.
ROMEO!
ALACK, ALACK, WHAT BLOOD IS THIS, WHICH STAINS THE STONY ENTRANCE OF THIS SEPULCHRE?
WHAT MEANS THESE MASTERLESS AND GORY SWORDS TO LIE DISCOLOUR'D BY THIS PLACE OF PEACE?
ROMEO! O, PALE!
WHO ELSE?
WHAT, PARIS TOO? AND STEEP'D IN BLOOD?
AH! WHAT AN UNKIND HOUR IS GUILTY OF THIS LAMENTABLE CHANCE!
THE LADY STIRS.
O COMFORTABLE FRIAR! WHERE IS MY LORD?
I DO REMEMBER WELL WHERE I SHOULD BE, AND THERE I AM: WHERE IS MY ROMEO?
TA-RA TA-RA
I HEAR SOME NOISE.
LADY, COME FROM THAT NEST OF DEATH, CONTAGION AND UNNATURAL SLEEP: A GREATER POWER THAN WE CAN CONTRADICT HATH THWARTED OUR INTENTS:
COME, COME AWAY: THY HUSBAND IN THY BOSOM THERE LIES DEAD; AND PARIS TOO:
COME, I'LL DISPOSE OF THEE AMONG A SISTERHOOD OF HOLY NUNS: STAY NOT TO QUESTION, FOR THE WATCH IS COMING;
COME, GO, GOOD JULIET. I DARE NO LONGER STAY.
GO, GET THEE HENCE, FOR I WILL NOT AWAY.

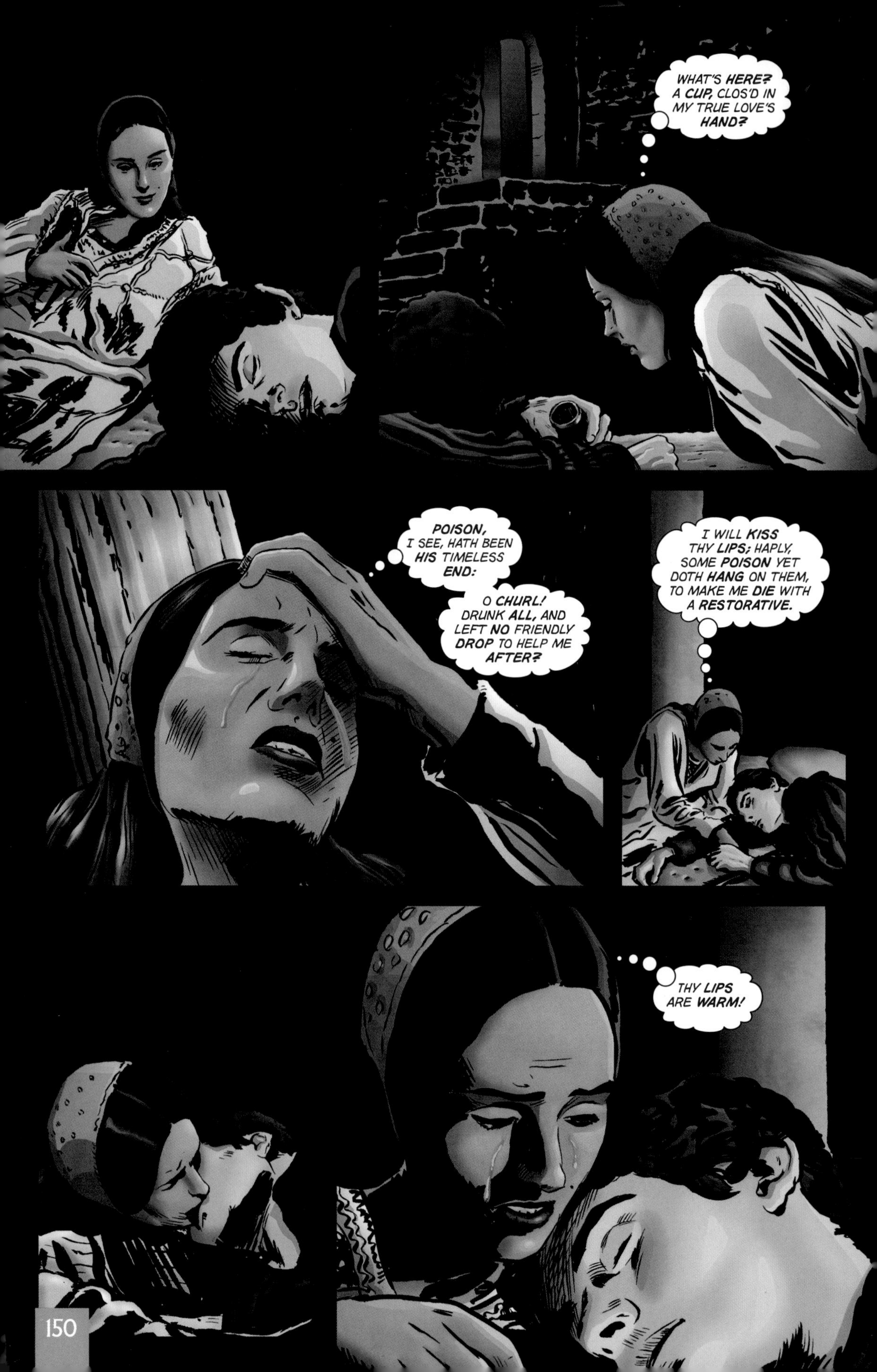
WHAT'S HERE? A CUP, CLOS'D IN MY TRUE LOVE'S HAND?
POISON, I SEE, HATH BEEN HIS TIMELESS END:
O CHURL! DRUNK ALL, AND LEFT NO FRIENDLY DROP TO HELP ME AFTER?
I WILL KISS THY LIPS; HAPLY, SOME POISON YET DOTH HANG ON THEM, TO MAKE ME DIE WITH A RESTORATIVE.
THY LIPS ARE WARM!

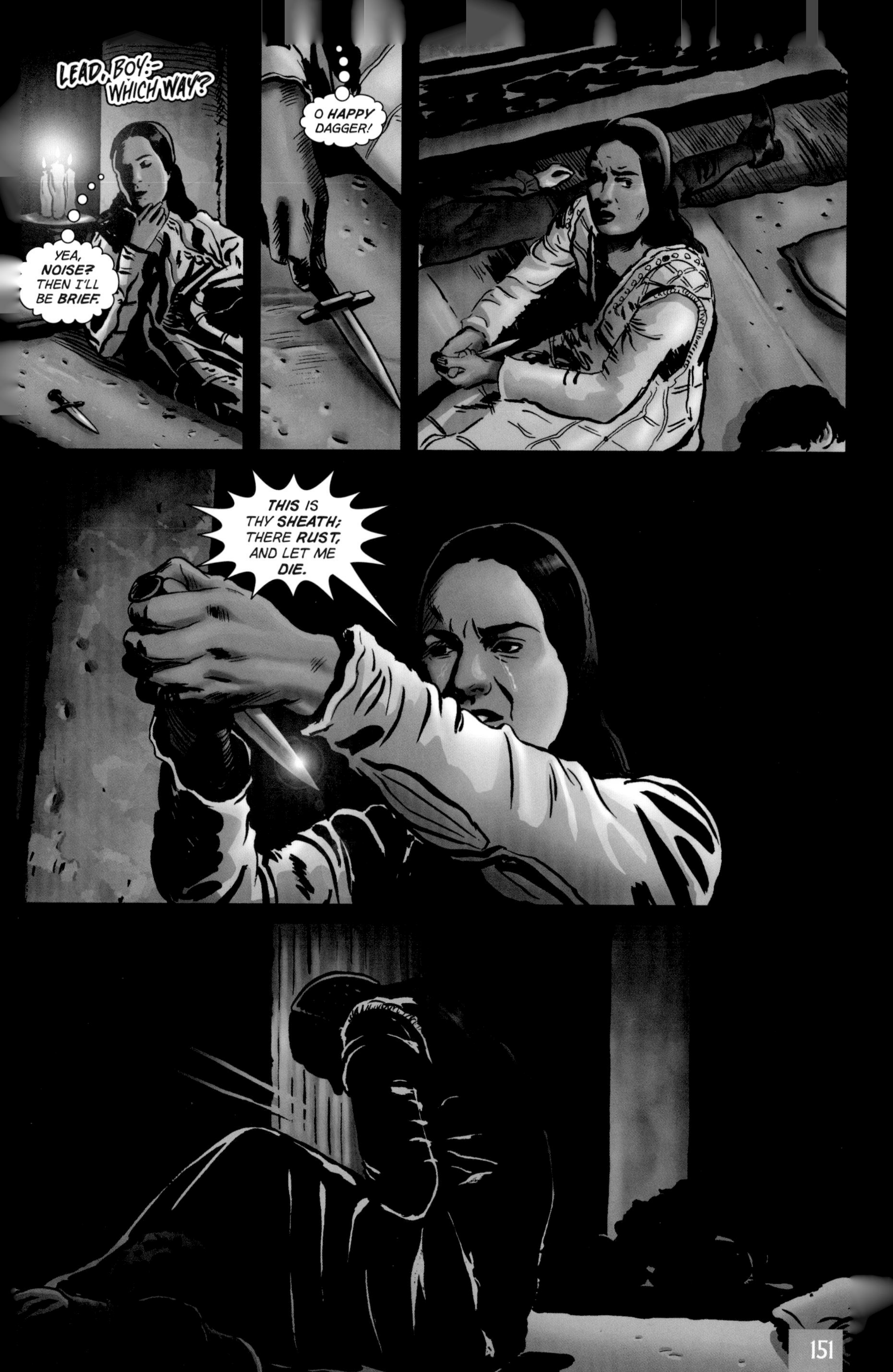
LEAD, BOY:- WHICH WAY?
YEA, NOISE? THEN I'LL BE BRIEF.
O HAPPY DAGGER!
THIS IS THY SHEATH; THERE RUST, AND LET ME DIE.

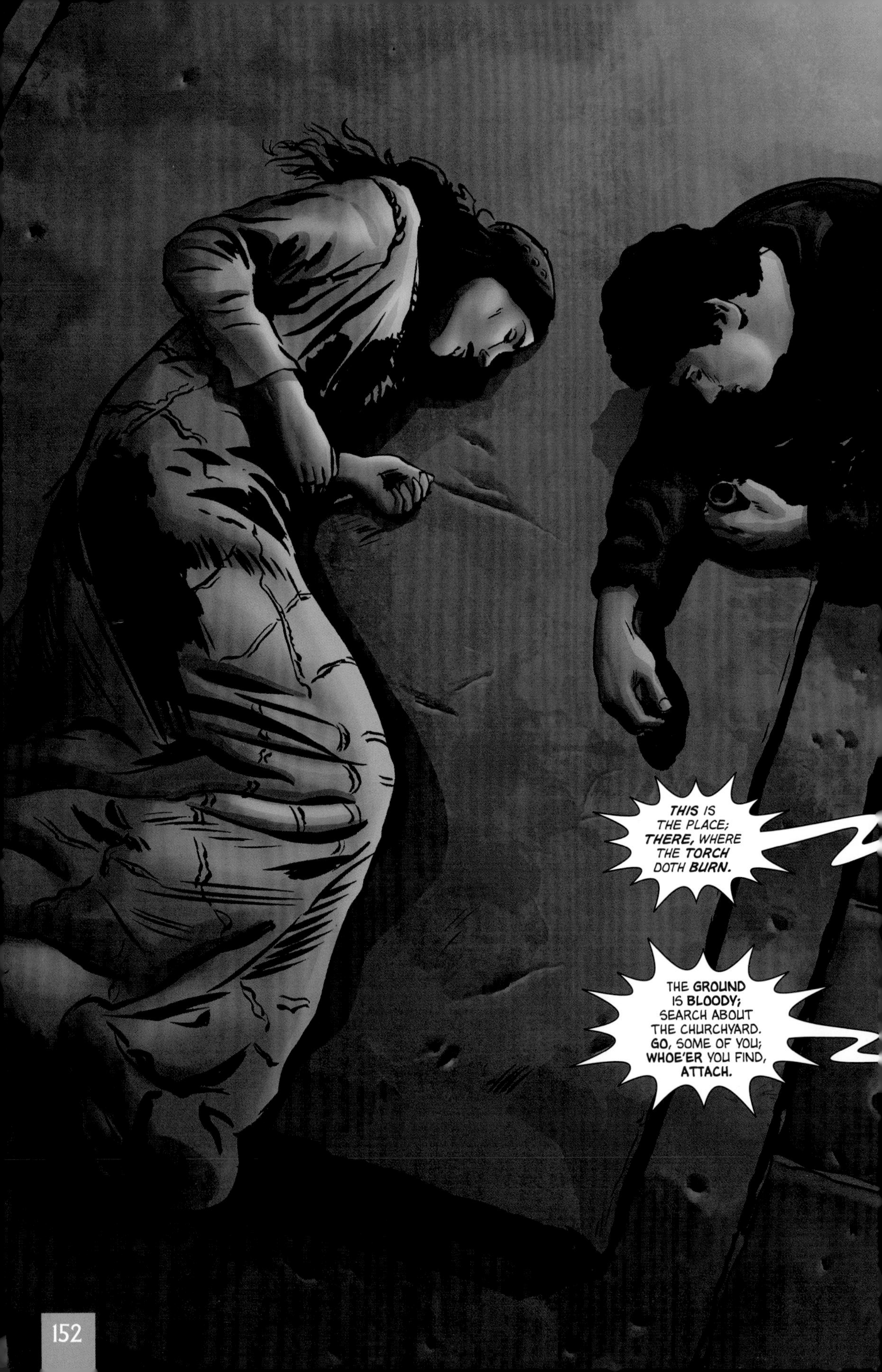
THIS IS THE PLACE; THERE, WHERE THE TORCH DOTH BURN.
THE GROUND IS BLOODY; SEARCH ABOUT THE CHURCHYARD. GO, SOME OF YOU; WHOE'ER YOU FIND, ATTACH.

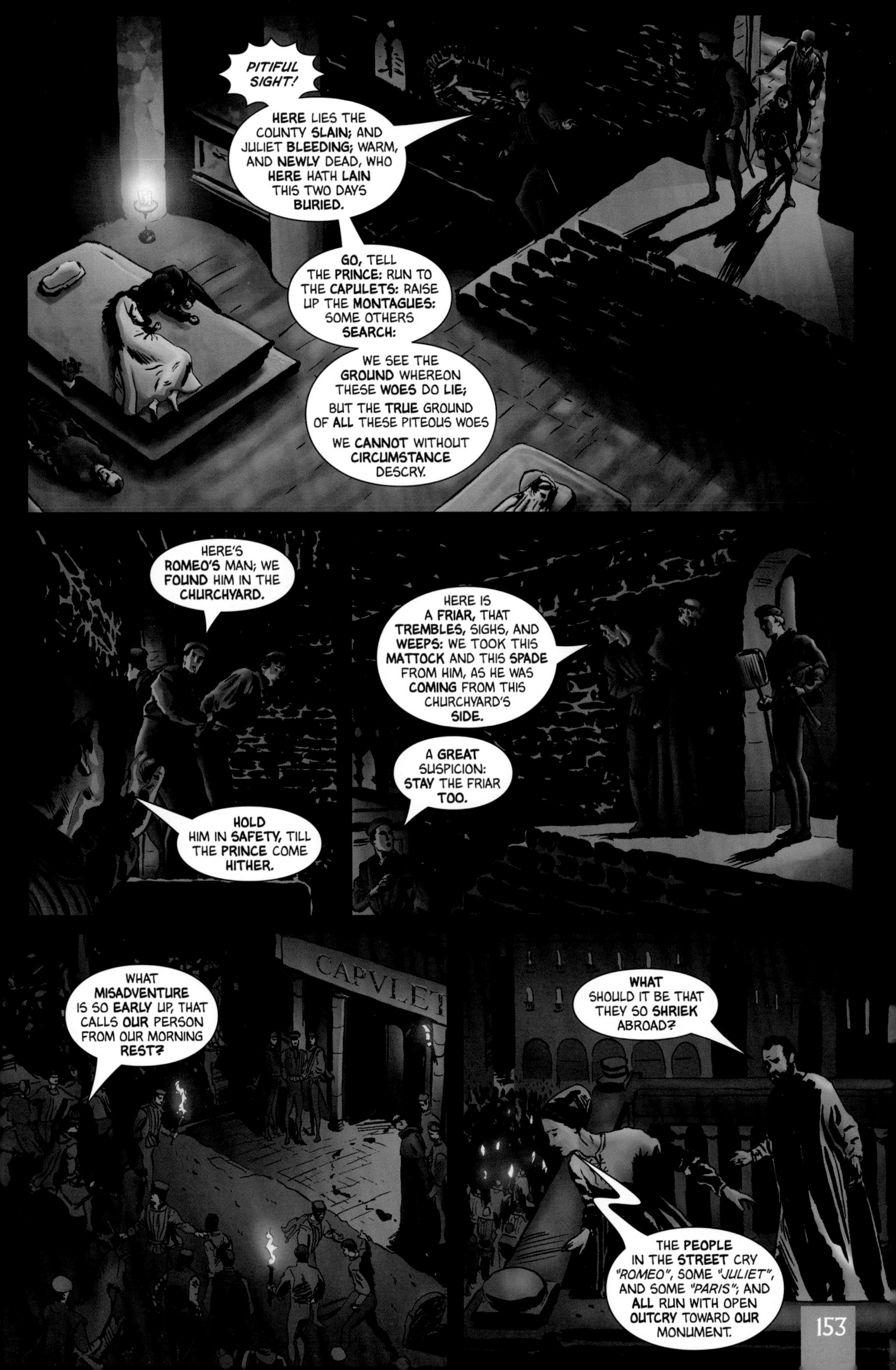
PITIFUL SIGHT!
HERE LIES THE COUNTY SLAIN; AND JULIET BLEEDING; WARM, AND NEWLY DEAD, WHO HERE HATH LAIN THIS TWO DAYS BURIED.
GO, TELL THE PRINCE: RUN TO THE CAPULETS: RAISE UP THE MONTAGUES: SOME OTHERS SEARCH:
WE SEE THE GROUND WHEREON THESE WOES DO LIE;
BUT THE TRUE GROUND OF ALL THESE PITEOUS WOES
WE CANNOT WITHOUT CIRCUMSTANCE DESCRY.
HERE'S ROMEO'S MAN; WE FOUND HIM IN THE CHURCHYARD.
HOLD HIM IN SAFETY, TILL THE PRINCE COME HITHER.
HERE IS A FRIAR, THAT TREMBLES, SIGHS, AND WEEPS: WE TOOK THIS MATTOCK AND THIS SPADE FROM HIM, AS HE WAS COMING FROM THIS CHURCHYARD'S SIDE.
A GREAT SUSPICION: STAY THE FRIAR TOO.
CAPVLET
WHAT MISADVENTURE IS SO EARLY UP, THAT CALLS OUR PERSON FROM OUR MORNING REST?
WHAT SHOULD IT BE THAT THEY SO SHRIEK ABROAD?
THE PEOPLE IN THE STREET CRY "ROMEO", SOME "JULIET", AND SOME "PARIS"; AND ALL RUN WITH OPEN OUTCRY TOWARD OUR MONUMENT.

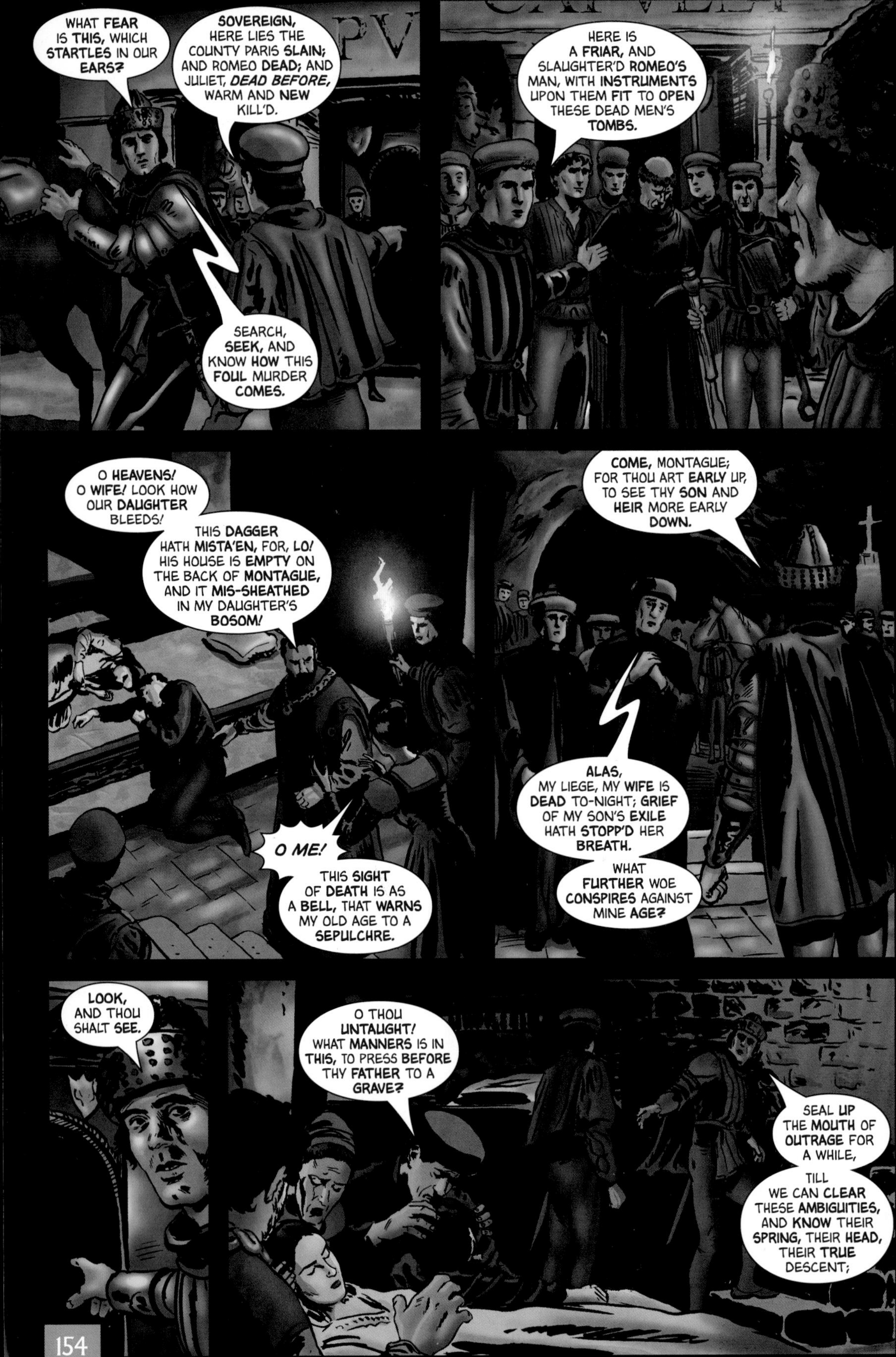
WHAT FEAR IS THIS, WHICH STARTLES IN OUR EARS?
SOVEREIGN, HERE LIES THE COUNTY PARIS SLAIN; AND ROMEO DEAD; AND JULIET, DEAD BEFORE, WARM AND NEW KILL'D.
SEARCH, SEEK, AND KNOW HOW THIS FOUL MURDER COMES.
HERE IS A FRIAR, AND SLAUGHTER'D ROMEO'S MAN, WITH INSTRUMENTS UPON THEM FIT TO OPEN THESE DEAD MEN'S TOMBS.
O HEAVENS! O WIFE! LOOK HOW OUR DAUGHTER BLEEDS!
THIS DAGGER HATH MISTA'EN, FOR, LO! HIS HOUSE IS EMPTY ON THE BACK OF MONTAGUE, AND IT MIS-SHEATHED IN MY DAUGHTER'S BOSOM!
O ME!
THIS SIGHT OF DEATH IS AS A BELL, THAT WARNS MY OLD AGE TO A SEPULCHRE.
COME, MONTAGUE; FOR THOU ART EARLY UP, TO SEE THY SON AND HEIR MORE EARLY DOWN.
ALAS, MY LIEGE, MY WIFE IS DEAD TO-NIGHT; GRIEF OF MY SON'S EXILE HATH STOPP'D HER BREATH.
WHAT FURTHER WOE CONSPIRES AGAINST MINE AGE?
LOOK, AND THOU SHALT SEE.
O THOU UNTAUGHT! WHAT MANNERS IS IN THIS, TO PRESS BEFORE THY FATHER TO A GRAVE?
SEAL UP THE MOUTH OF OUTRAGE FOR A WHILE,
TILL WE CAN CLEAR THESE AMBIGUITIES, AND KNOW THEIR SPRING, THEIR HEAD, THEIR TRUE DESCENT;

AND THEN WILL I BE GENERAL OF YOUR WOES, AND LEAD YOU EVEN TO DEATH:

MEANTIME FORBEAR, AND LET MISCHANCE BE SLAVE TO PATIENCE.

THE PIAZZA, VERONA – EARLY THURSDAY MORNING.

BRING FORTH THE PARTIES OF SUSPICION.

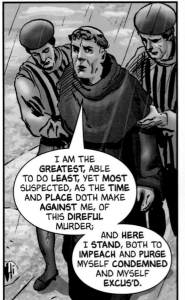

I AM THE GREATEST, ABLE TO DO LEAST, YET MOST SUSPECTED, AS THE TIME AND PLACE DOTH MAKE AGAINST ME, OF THIS DIREFUL MURDER;

AND HERE I STAND, BOTH TO IMPEACH AND PURGE MYSELF CONDEMNED AND MYSELF EXCUS'D.

THEN SAY AT ONCE WHAT THOU DOST KNOW IN THIS.

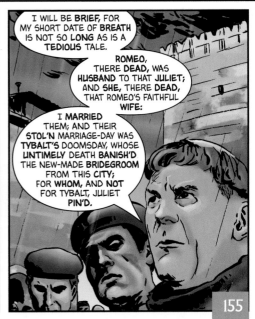

I WILL BE BRIEF, FOR MY SHORT DATE OF BREATH IS NOT SO LONG AS IS A TEDIOUS TALE.

ROMEO, THERE DEAD, WAS HUSBAND TO THAT JULIET; AND SHE, THERE DEAD, THAT ROMEO'S FAITHFUL WIFE:

I MARRIED THEM; AND THEIR STOL'N MARRIAGE-DAY WAS TYBALT'S DOOMSDAY, WHOSE UNTIMELY DEATH BANISH'D THE NEW-MADE BRIDEGROOM FROM THIS CITY; FOR WHOM, AND NOT FOR TYBALT, JULIET PIN'D.

YOU, TO REMOVE THAT SIEGE OF GRIEF FROM HER, BETROTH'D AND WOULD HAVE MARRIED HER PERFORCE, TO COUNTY PARIS:

THEN COMES SHE TO ME, AND, WITH WILD LOOKS, BID ME DEVISE SOME MEANS TO RID HER FROM THIS SECOND MARRIAGE, OR IN MY CELL THERE WOULD SHE KILL HERSELF.

THEN GAVE I HER, – SO TUTOR'D BY MY ART, – A SLEEPING POTION; WHICH SO TOOK EFFECT AS I INTENDED, FOR IT WROUGHT ON HER THE FORM OF DEATH:

MEANTIME I WRIT TO ROMEO, THAT HE SHOULD HITHER COME AS THIS DIRE NIGHT, TO HELP TO TAKE HER FROM HER BORROW'D GRAVE, BEING THE TIME THE POTION'S FORCE SHOULD CEASE.

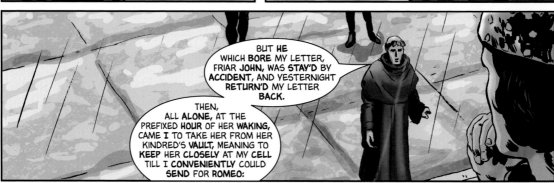

BUT HE WHICH BORE MY LETTER, FRIAR JOHN, WAS STAY'D BY ACCIDENT, AND YESTERNIGHT RETURN'D MY LETTER BACK.

THEN, ALL ALONE, AT THE PREFIXED HOUR OF HER WAKING, CAME I TO TAKE HER FROM HER KINDRED'S VAULT, MEANING TO KEEP HER CLOSELY AT MY CELL TILL I CONVENIENTLY COULD SEND FOR ROMEO:

BUT WHEN I CAME, SOME MINUTE ERE THE TIME OF HER AWAKENING, HERE UNTIMELY LAY THE NOBLE PARIS, AND TRUE ROMEO, DEAD.

SHE WAKES; AND I ENTREATED HER COME FORTH, AND BEAR THIS WORK OF HEAVEN WITH PATIENCE: BUT THEN A NOISE DID SCARE ME FROM THE TOMB, AND SHE, TOO DESPERATE, WOULD NOT GO WITH ME, BUT, AS IT SEEMS, DID VIOLENCE ON HERSELF.

ALL THIS I KNOW; AND TO THE MARRIAGE HER NURSE IS PRIVY:

AND, IF AUGHT IN THIS MISCARRIED BY MY FAULT, LET MY OLD LIFE BE SACRIFIC'D SOME HOUR BEFORE HIS TIME, UNTO THE RIGOUR OF SEVEREST LAW.

WE STILL HAVE **KNOWN** THEE FOR A HOLY MAN.

WHERE'S **ROMEO'S** MAN? WHAT CAN HE SAY TO THIS?

I BROUGHT MY MASTER **NEWS** OF JULIET'S **DEATH**; AND THEN IN **POST** HE CAME FROM **MANTUA**, TO THIS SAME PLACE, TO THIS SAME MONUMENT.

THIS **LETTER** HE EARLY **BID** ME GIVE HIS **FATHER**, AND **THREATEN'D** ME WITH **DEATH**, GOING IN THE VAULT, IF I DEPARTED **NOT**, AND **LEFT** HIM THERE.

GIVE **ME** THE **LETTER**; I WILL **LOOK** ON IT. WHERE IS THE **COUNTY'S PAGE**, THAT **RAIS'D** THE WATCH?

SIRRAH, WHAT **MADE** YOUR MASTER IN THIS **PLACE**?

HE CAME WITH **FLOWERS** TO STREW HIS **LADY'S GRAVE**; AND BID ME STAND **ALOOF**, AND SO I DID:

ANON **COMES** ONE WITH **LIGHT** TO OPE THE **TOMB**; AND, BY-AND-BY, MY MASTER **DREW** ON HIM; AND THEN I RAN **AWAY** TO CALL THE **WATCH**.

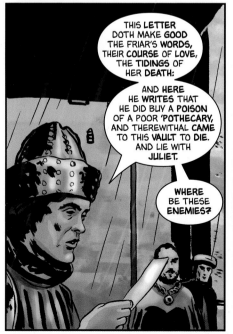

THIS **LETTER** DOTH MAKE GOOD THE FRIAR'S **WORDS**, THEIR **COURSE** OF LOVE, THE **TIDINGS** OF HER DEATH:

AND **HERE** HE WRITES THAT HE DID **BUY** A POISON OF A POOR **'POTHECARY**, AND **THEREWITHAL** CAME TO THIS **VAULT** TO DIE, AND LIE WITH **JULIET**.

WHERE **BE** THESE **ENEMIES**?

CAPULET!
MONTAGUE!

SEE, WHAT A **SCOURGE** IS LAID UPON YOUR **HATE**, THAT **HEAVEN** FINDS MEANS TO KILL YOUR **JOYS** WITH LOVE!

AND **I**, FOR **WINKING** AT YOUR **DISCORDS** TOO, HAVE LOST A **BRACE** OF KINSMEN:

ALL ARE **PUNISH'D**.

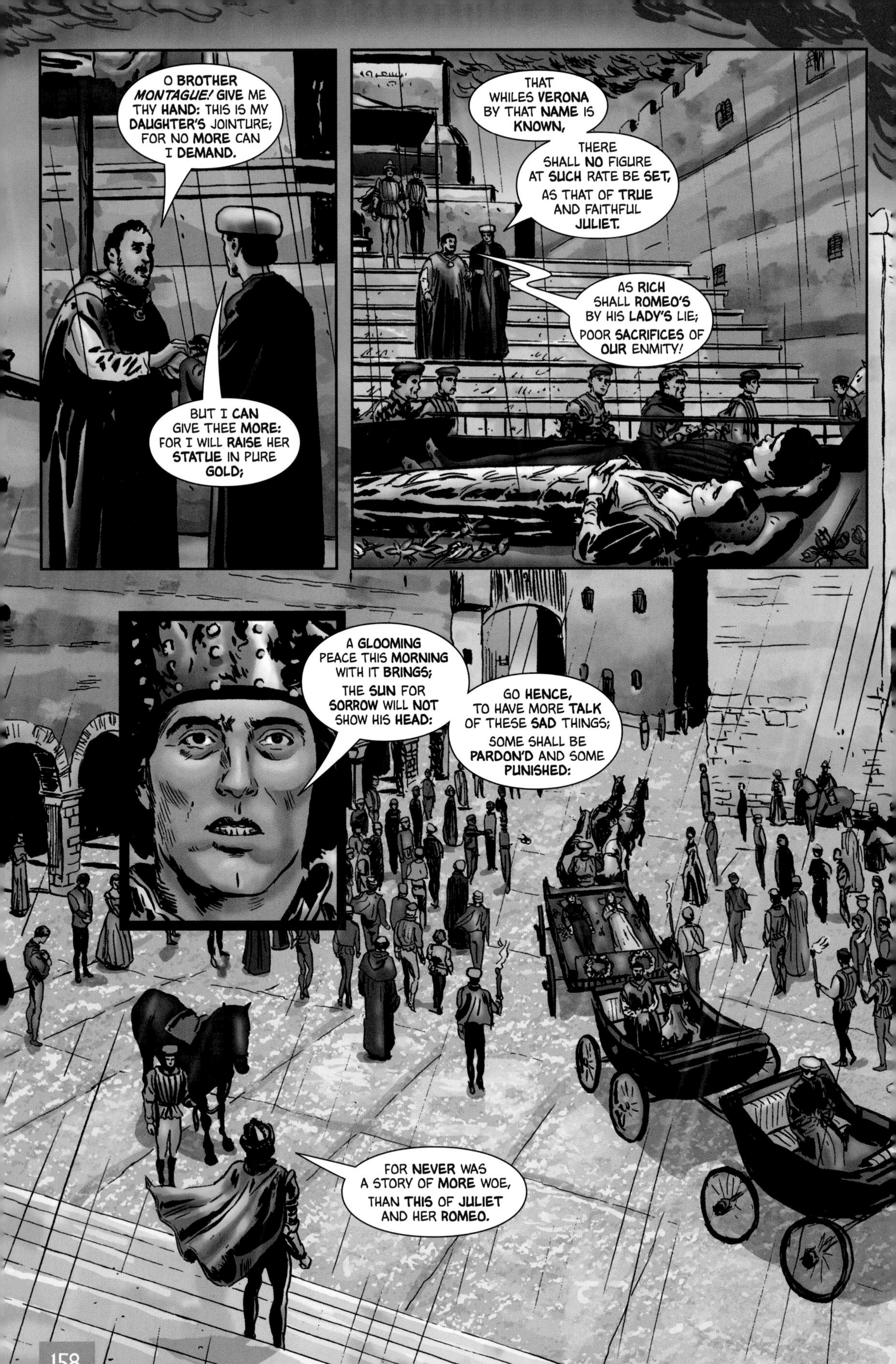
O BROTHER MONTAGUE! GIVE ME THY HAND: THIS IS MY DAUGHTER'S JOINTURE; FOR NO MORE CAN I DEMAND.
BUT I CAN GIVE THEE MORE: FOR I WILL RAISE HER STATUE IN PURE GOLD;
THAT WHILES VERONA BY THAT NAME IS KNOWN,
THERE SHALL NO FIGURE AT SUCH RATE BE SET, AS THAT OF TRUE AND FAITHFUL JULIET.
AS RICH SHALL ROMEO'S BY HIS LADY'S LIE; POOR SACRIFICES OF OUR ENMITY!
A GLOOMING PEACE THIS MORNING WITH IT BRINGS; THE SUN FOR SORROW WILL NOT SHOW HIS HEAD:
GO HENCE, TO HAVE MORE TALK OF THESE SAD THINGS; SOME SHALL BE PARDON'D AND SOME PUNISHED:
FOR NEVER WAS A STORY OF MORE WOE, THAN THIS OF JULIET AND HER ROMEO.

Romeo & Juliet

The End

William Shakespeare

(c.1564 - 1616 AD)

National Portrait Gallery, London

Shakespeare is, without question, the world's most famous playwright. Yet, despite his fame, very few records and artifacts exist for him — we don't even know the exact date of his birth! April 23, 1564 (St George's Day) is taken to be his birthday, as this was three days before his baptism (for which we do have a record). Records also tell us that he died on the same date in 1616, aged fifty-two.

The life of William Shakespeare can be divided into three acts.

Act One – Stratford-upon-Avon

William was the eldest son of tradesman John Shakespeare and Mary Arden, and the third of eight children (he had two older sisters). The Shakespeares were a respectable family. The year after William was born, John (who made gloves and traded leather) became an alderman of Stratford-upon-Avon, and four years later he became High Bailiff (or mayor) of the town.

Little is known of William's childhood. He learned to read and write at the local primary school, and later is believed to have attended the local grammar school, where he studied Latin and English Literature. In 1582, aged eighteen, William married a local farmer's daughter, Anne Hathaway. Anne was eight years his senior and three months pregnant. During their marriage they had three children: Susanna, born on May 26, 1583, and twins, Hamnet and Judith, born on February 2, 1585. Hamnet (William's only son) died in 1596, aged eleven, from Bubonic Plague.

Act Two – London

Five years into his marriage, in 1587, William's wife and children stayed in Stratford, while he moved to London. He appeared as an actor at *The Theatre* (England's first permanent theater) and gave public recitals of his own poems; but it was his playwriting that created the most interest. His fame soon spread far and wide. When Queen Elizabeth I died in 1603, the new King James I (who was already King James VI of Scotland) gave royal consent for Shakespeare's acting company, *The Lord Chamberlain's Men* to be called *The King's Men* in return for entertaining the court. This association was to shape a number of plays, such as *Macbeth*, which was written to please the Scottish King.

William Shakespeare is attributed with writing and collaborating on 38 plays, 154 sonnets and 5 poems, in just twenty-three years between 1590 and 1613. No original manuscript exists for any of his plays, making it hard to accurately date any of them. Printing was still in its infancy, and plays tended to change as they were performed. Shakespeare would write manuscript for the actors and continue to refine them over a number of performances. The plays we know today have survived from written copies taken at various stages of each play and usually written by the actors from memory. This has given rise to variations in texts of what is now known as "quarto" versions of the plays, until we reach the first official printing of each play in the 1623 "folio" *Mr William Shakespeare's Comedies, Histories, & Tragedies*. His last solo-authored work was *The Tempest* in 1611, which was only followed by collaborative work on two plays (*Henry VIII* and *Two Noble Kinsmen*) with John Fletcher. Shakespeare is strongly associated with the famous *Globe Theatre*. Built by his troupe in 1599, it became his "spiritual home", with thousands of people crammed into the small space for each performance. There were 3,000 people in the building in 1613 when a cannon-shot during a performance of *Henry VIII* set fire to the thatched roof and the entire theater was burned to the ground. Although it was rebuilt a year later, it marked an end to Shakespeare's writing and to his time in London.

Act Three - Retirement

Shortly after the 1613 accident at *The Globe*, Shakespeare left the capital and returned to live once more with his family in Stratford-upon-Avon. He died on April 23, 1616 and was buried two days later at the Church of the Holy Trinity (the same church where he had been baptized fifty-two years earlier). The cause of his death remains unknown.

Epilogue

At the time of his death, Shakespeare had substantial properties, which he bestowed on his family and associates from the theater. He had no son to inherit his wealth, and he left the majority of his possessions to his eldest daughter Susanna. Curiously, the only thing that he left to his wife Anne was his second-best bed! (although she continued to live in the family home after his death). William Shakespeare's last direct descendant died in 1670. She was his granddaughter, Elizabeth.

Shakespeare Birthplace Trust

As so few relics survive from Shakespeare's life, it is amazing that the house where he was born and raised remains intact. It is owned and cared for by the Shakespeare Birthplace Trust, which looks after a number of houses in the area:

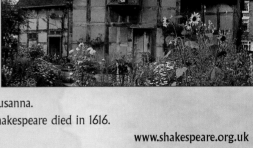
Shakespeare's Birthplace

- Shakespeare's Birthplace.
- Mary Arden's Farm: The childhood home of Shakespeare's mother.
- Anne Hathaway's Cottage: The childhood home of Shakespeare's wife.
- Hall's Croft: The home of Shakespeare's eldest daughter, Susanna.
- New Place: Only the grounds exist of the house where Shakespeare died in 1616.
- Nash's House: The home of Shakespeare's granddaughter.

www.shakespeare.org.uk

Martin Droeshout's engraving of Shakespeare

Formed in 1847, the Trust also works to promote Shakespeare around the world. In early 2009, it announced that it had found a new Shakespeare portrait, believed to have been painted within his lifetime, with a trail of provenance that links it to Shakespeare himself.

It is accepted that Martin Droeshout's engraving (left) that appears on the First Folio of 1623 is an authentic likeness of Shakespeare because the people involved in its publication would have personally known him. This new portrait (once owned by Henry Wriothesley, 3rd Earl of Southampton, one of Shakespeare's most loyal supporters) is so similar in all facial aspects that it is now suspected to have been the source that Droeshout used for his famous engraving.

www.shakespearefound.org.uk

History of the Play

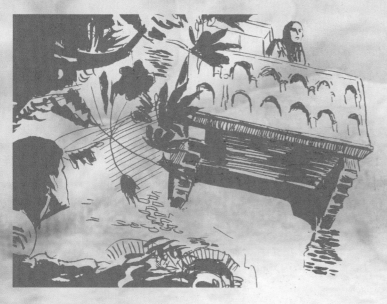

The tale of ill-fated love between Romeo and Juliet is intrinsically linked with Shakespeare, with the famous "balcony scene" providing some of his most enduring phrases:

"But, soft! What light through yonder window breaks?
It is the east, and Juliet is the sun!"
(p55)

"O Romeo, Romeo! Wherefore art thou Romeo?" (p56)

"What's in a name? That which we call a rose
By any other word would smell as sweet;" (p56)

However, as with the vast majority of his works, Shakespeare's play is an adaptation of a story that already existed (*The Tempest* is his only play without a clear source).

Stories of frustrated love are as old as civilization itself and can be found even in ancient myths. The first recognizable form of *Romeo and Juliet* appeared around 1460 by Masuccio Salernitano. In it, Mariotto Mignanelli and Gianozza Saraceni of Siena fall in love and are married in secret by a friar. Shortly afterwards, Mariotto quarrels, fights with and kills a noble citizen. Mariotto is banished from the town, and Gianozza is forced into marriage by her father (who is unaware of her marriage with Mariotto). The friar creates a potion for Gianozza that makes her appear dead, and she is taken to the family tomb. From there, the friar escorts her to husband, who receives word of her death before she can reach him. Mariotto returns to Siena, where he is seized and executed. Gianozza shuts herself away in a convent and soon dies from grief.

Salernitano's story became the inspiration for Luigi da Porto's *Giulietta e Romeo*. Da Porto set the story in Verona, where he was inspired by the two castles just outside the city, each owned by a different family: the Capuleti and the Montecchi, thus introducing the notion of the feuding families. The ending is more tragic than Shakespeare's, with Romeo killing himself by the side of Giulietta, but seeing her revive in his final moments.

In 1554, an Italian writer by the name of Matteo Bandello published his own version of *Giulietta e Romeo*. This story was much more popular than its predecessors. Not only was it translated into English but, importantly for Shakespeare, it became the basis of a 3,020-line poem by Arthur Brooke called *The Tragicall Historye of Romeus and Juliet* (1562). Brooke's poem has all the main characters, albeit with some spelling differences: Romeus Montagew, Juliet Capilet, Prince Escalus, Tybalt, Paris, Friar Lawrence, Juliet's nurse [sic] and even Peter (although he is cited as one of Romeus's men).

Although Shakespeare embellished the story (and of course added his beautiful language) the events can all be found in Brooke's poem — even Friar John being unable to deliver the message to Romeus because of quarantine. It is possible that Shakespeare worked with other sources, too. He may have read the French translation of Bandello's novel, as well as an English version of the story by William Painter called *Palace of Pleasure*. Yet it is Brooke's poem that most closely matches the Bard's great play, as shown in the excerpt, opposite, in which Juliet discovers the name of her new love as the guests leave the masked ball.

The Tragicall Historye of Romeus and Juliet
by Arthur Brooke (1562)

As carefull was the mayde what way were best deuise
To learne his name, that intertaind her in so gentle wise.
Of whome her hart receiued so deepe, so wyde a wounde,
An auncient dame she calde to her, and in her eare gan rounde.
This olde dame in her youth, had nurst her with her mylke,
With slender nedle taught her sow, and how to spin with silke.
What twayne are those (quoth she) which prease vnto the doore,
Whose pages in theyr hand doe beare, two toorches light before.
And then as eche of them had of his houshold name,
So she him namde yet once agayne the yong and wyly dame.
And tell me who is he with vysor in his hand
That yender doth in masking weede besyde the window stand.
His name is Romeus (sayd she) a Montegewe.
Whose fathers pryde first styrd the strife which both your
housholdes rewe.
The woord of Montegew, her ioyes did ouerthrow,
And straight in steade of happy hope, dyspayre began to growe.
What hap haue I quoth she, to loue my fathers foe?
What, am I wery of my wele? what, doe I wishe my woe?
But though her grieuous paynes distraind her tender hart,
Yet with an outward shewe of ioye she cloked inward smart.
And of the courtlyke dames her leaue so courtly tooke,
That none dyd gesse the sodain change by changing of her looke.

Shakespeare contracted the nine months of events within the poem into just five days. While that adds to the tension of the play in performance, it is likely to have been a conscious and practical decision to tailor the story for the stage, as the passing of time is hard to capture in theater.

The play appeared in print for the first time (the *First Quarto*) in 1597. The introduction of that edition tells us that it had already been performed by the time it was published:

An Excellent conceited Tragedie of Romeo and Iuliet, As it hath been often (with great applause) plaid publiquely, by the Honourable the L. of Hunsdon and his Seruants.

It was written before the *Globe Theatre* was built (1599), in the reign of Elizabeth I (which ended in 1603), while Shakespeare was writing for *The Lord Chamberlain's Men.*

The Lord Chamberlain's Men

Until the 1660s, the law prevented women and girls from acting. All parts, even Juliet, were played by males!

Even though Shakespeare's plays were hugely popular, only sparse records exist of actual performances. The earliest official recording of a production of *Romeo and Juliet* doesn't occur until as late as 1662, in a theater in Lincoln's Inn Fields. The famous diarist Samuel Pepys attended the opening night and thought very poorly of it:

"It is a play of itself the worst that I have ever heard in my life, and the worst acted that I ever saw these people do; and am resolved to go no more to see the first time of acting, for they were all of them out more or less."

Despite that early criticism, *Romeo and Juliet* remains one of Shakespeare's best-loved plays, being performed regularly throughout the world, as well as being adapted into other media: classical music (*Berlioz* [1839] and *Tchaikovsky* [1870]), opera (*Gounod* [1867]), ballet (*Prokofiev* [1935]), musical (Leonard Bernstein's *West Side Story* [1957]), movie (many!), and, of course, this graphic novel.

Page Creation

167. **Large** Night. Romeo approaches the balcony and sees Juliet.

	Original Text	Plain Text	Quick Text
ROMEO **(TH)**	But, soft! what light through yonder window breaks? It is the east, and Juliet is the sun! Arise, fair sun, and kill the envious moon, Who is already sick and pale with grief, That thou, her maid, are far more fair than she;	But, soft! what light through yonder window breaks? It is the east, and Juliet is the sun! Arise, fair sun, and kill the envious moon, that is pale and sad because you, Juliet, are more beautiful.	But, soft! what light through yonder window breaks? It is the east, and Juliet is the sun! Arise, fair sun, and kill the moon.

168. Juliet's **POV** from the balcony. She's looking up wistfully at the moon, not down at the ground. She doesn't see Romeo. He stares up at her.

ROMEO **(TH)**	Be not her maid, since she is envious; Her vestal livery is but sick and green, And none but fools do wear it; cast it off.	Don't worry about the moon's jealousy. It is sick and green – the colour of fools and virgins. Get rid of it!	It is jealous of your beauty.

168b

ROMEO **(TH)**	It is my lady; O! it is my love: O, that she knew she were! She speaks, yet she says nothing: what of that? Her eye discourses, I will answer it.	It is my lady; Oh! it is my love: Oh, I wish she knew that I love her. She speaks, but says nothing. It doesn't matter – her eyes do the talking, and I'll answer them!	She is my love!

(+silent panel)

169. Juliet looks down and Romeo ducks for cover.

ROMEO **(TH)**	I am too bold, 'tis not to me she speaks: Two of the fairest stars in all the heaven, Having some business, do entreat her eyes To twinkle in their spheres till they return. What if her eyes were there, they in her head? The brightness of her cheek would shame those stars, As daylight doth a lamp;	I'm being overconfident. She's not talking to me. Two of the brightest stars in the sky have asked her eyes to take their place for a while. Imagine if her eyes were in the sky and the stars were in her head? The beauty of her face would outshine those stars, like the sun outshines a lamp.	She seems to be speaking -- -- but not to me. Her eyes are like stars!

170. Romeo peers out from his hiding place beneath the balcony. Juliet is looking away across the garden, resting her head on her hand.

	Original Text	Plain Text	Quick Text
ROMEO **(TH)**	her eyes in heaven, Would through the airy region stream so bright, That birds would sing and think it were not night. See, how she leans her cheek upon her hand! O! that I were a glove upon that hand, That I might touch that cheek!	If her eyes were up in the sky, they'd shine so bright, the birds would think it was morning and begin singing. See how she's leaning her cheek on her hand. I wish I was a glove on that hand, so that I could touch that cheek!	-- She is so beautiful, leaning her cheek on her hand. I wish I was a glove on that hand, so that I could touch that cheek.

Page 55 from the script of *Romeo & Juliet* showing the three text versions.

1. Script

The first stage in creating a graphic novel adaptation of a Shakespeare play is to split the original script into comic book panels, describing the images to be drawn as well as the dialogue and any captions. To do this, not only does the script writer need to know the play well, but he also needs to visualize each page in his head as he writes the art descriptions for each panel (there are over 600 panels in *Romeo and Juliet*).

Once this is created, the dialogue is adapted into Plain Text and Quick Text to create the three versions of the book, which all use the same artwork.

2. Character Sheets

Because *Romeo and Juliet* is such a well-known play, Will Volley needed very little time to familiarize himself with the characters. However, an artist still needs to "climb into the story" while deciding on the right approach for the artwork. Here you can see Will's designs for Romeo and Juliet, which we instantly agreed upon. The whole process moves steadily towards bringing the play to life and, suddenly, the names "Romeo" and "Juliet" are no longer simply names in a script – they have turned into real people!

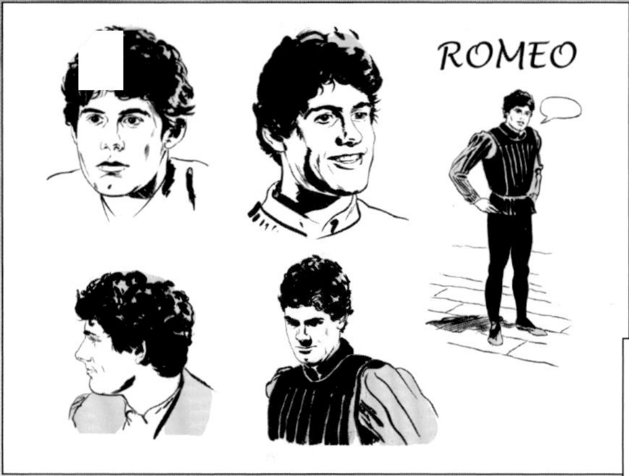
ROMEO

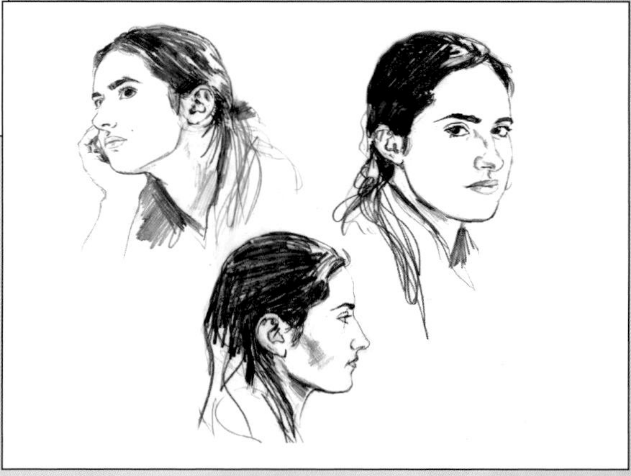

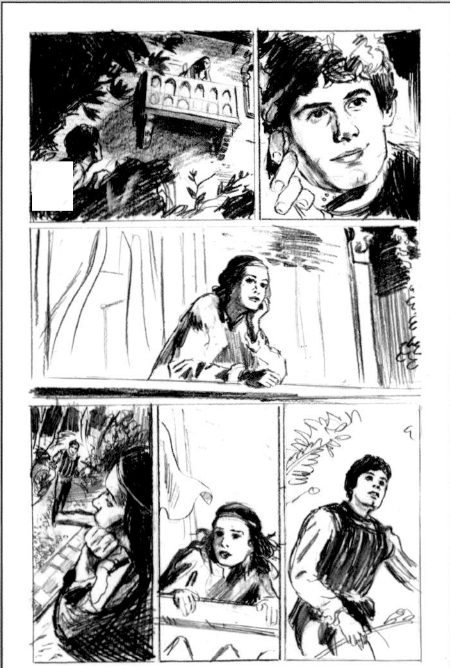

The rough sketch created from the script.

3. Rough Sketch

Armed with the character visualizations, the artist begins work on the 152 pages required for the book. Each page is first sketched out quickly in order to check panel layouts, ensure there is enough space for the lettering, explore continuity elements and to establish the pacing of the action. Will's roughs are very descriptive. As you can see here, he is already considering the lighting of the scenes, how the shadows will fall across surfaces, and so on. These rough layouts are then sent to the editor for approval. If any changes need to be made, it is far easier to make them at this stage from the fast rough layouts than to make changes to finished linework.

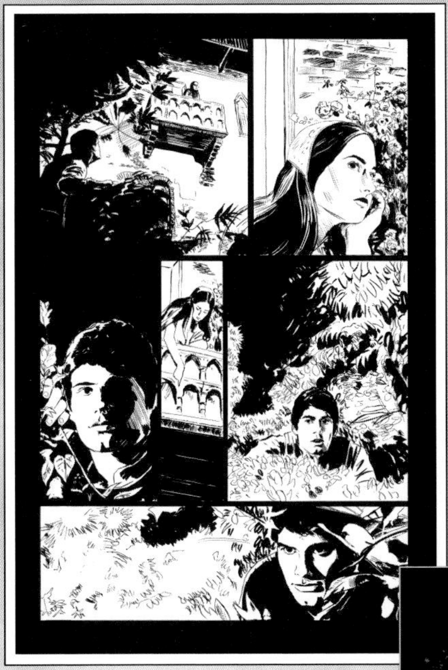

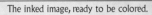

The inked image, ready to be colored.

4. Linework

The process to create the finished artwork begins as soon as the editor agrees to the rough sketch. The artwork is created on A3 art board at approximately 150% of the finished printed size. That magnification allows more freedom when creating the linework and makes for a better final image. As the linework is reduced, it has the effect of "tightening" the art, improving the overall look of the page.

Interestingly, the rough sketch details some artistic elements that won't be tackled until the coloring stage. For example, the sketchy coloring on the sides of faces due to the moonlit scene doesn't appear in the linework because it only deals in stark black and white (and Will doesn't use a technique called "feathering" which is the traditional way to render a curved surface in black and white artwork). Certain textures are added at this stage, such as the folds in the clothing and the rendering of materials, like the stone of the balcony and wall.

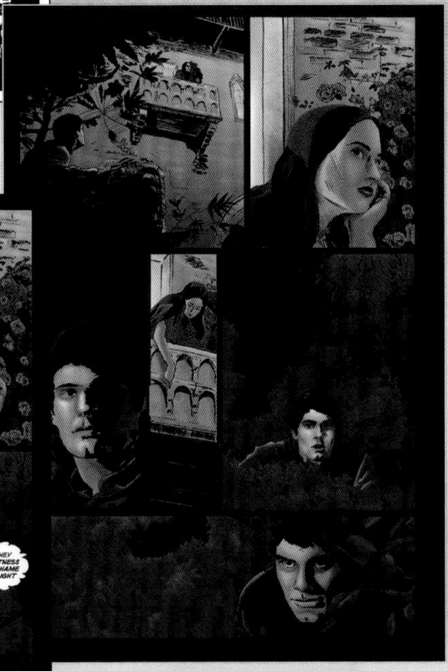

The final colored artwork.

5. Coloring

Adding color really brings the page and its characters to life. There is far more to the coloring stage than simply replacing the white areas with flat color. Some of the linework itself is shaded, while great emphasis is placed upon texture and light sources to get realistic shadows and highlights. Effects are also considered, such as the glow coming from the light in Juliet's bedroom. Finally, the whole page is color-balanced to the other pages of that scene, and to the overall book.

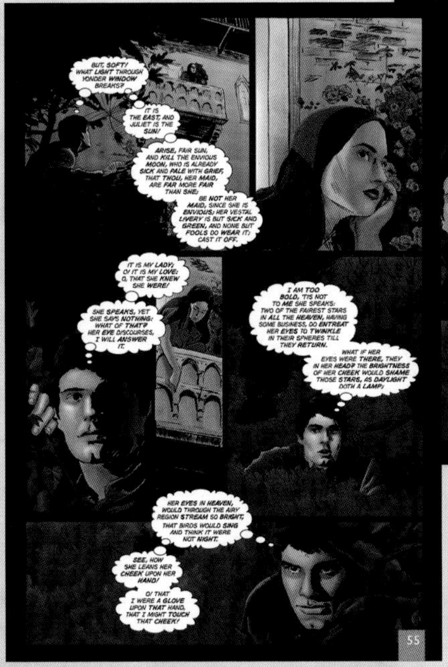
BUT, SOFT! WHAT LIGHT THROUGH YONDER WINDOW BREAKS?
IT IS THE EAST, AND JULIET IS THE SUN!
ARISE, FAIR SUN, AND KILL THE ENVIOUS MOON, WHO IS ALREADY SICK AND PALE WITH GRIEF, THAT THOU, HER MAID, ARE FAR MORE FAIR THAN SHE:
BE NOT HER MAID, SINCE SHE IS ENVIOUS; HER VESTAL LIVERY IS BUT SICK AND GREEN, AND NONE BUT FOOLS DO WEAR IT; CAST IT OFF.
IT IS MY LADY; O! IT IS MY LOVE: O, THAT SHE KNEW SHE WERE!
SHE SPEAKS, YET SHE SAYS NOTHING: WHAT OF THAT? HER EYE DISCOURSES, I WILL ANSWER IT.
I AM TOO BOLD, 'TIS NOT TO ME SHE SPEAKS: TWO OF THE FAIREST STARS IN ALL THE HEAVEN, HAVING SOME BUSINESS, DO ENTREAT HER EYES TO TWINKLE IN THEIR SPHERES TILL THEY RETURN.
WHAT IF HER EYES WERE THERE, THEY IN HER HEAD? THE BRIGHTNESS OF HER CHEEK WOULD SHAME THOSE STARS, AS DAYLIGHT DOTH A LAMP;
HER EYES IN HEAVEN, WOULD THROUGH THE AIRY REGION STREAM SO BRIGHT, THAT BIRDS WOULD SING AND THINK IT WERE NOT NIGHT.
SEE, HOW SHE LEANS HER CHEEK UPON HER HAND!
O! THAT I WERE A GLOVE UPON THAT HAND, THAT I MIGHT TOUCH THAT CHEEK!
55

The finished page 55 with Original Text lettering.

6. Lettering

The final stage is to add the captions, sound effects, and speech bubbles from the script. These are placed on top of the finished, colored pages. Three versions of each page are lettered, one for each of the three versions of the book (Original Text, Plain Text and Quick Text).

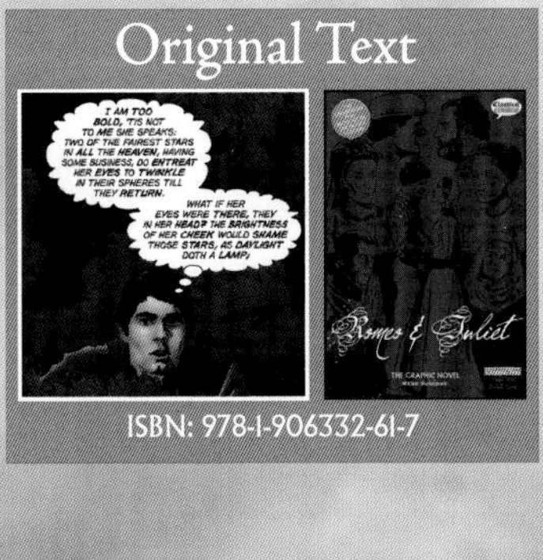
Original Text
I AM TOO BOLD, 'TIS NOT TO ME SHE SPEAKS: TWO OF THE FAIREST STARS IN ALL THE HEAVEN, HAVING SOME BUSINESS, DO ENTREAT HER EYES TO TWINKLE IN THEIR SPHERES TILL THEY RETURN.
WHAT IF HER EYES WERE THERE, THEY IN HER HEAD? THE BRIGHTNESS OF HER CHEEK WOULD SHAME THOSE STARS, AS DAYLIGHT DOTH A LAMP;
Romeo & Juliet
ISBN: 978-1-906332-61-7

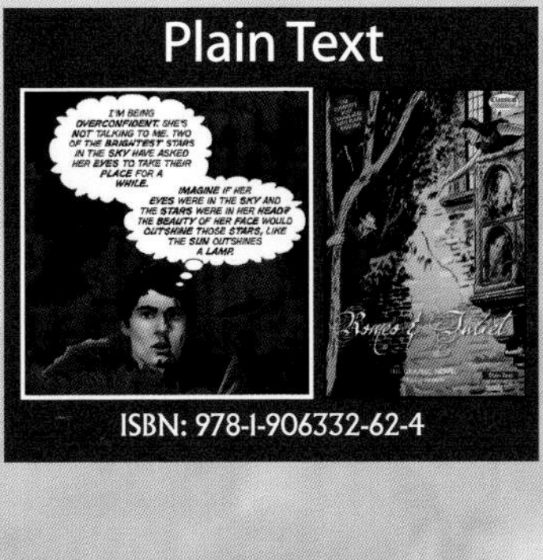
Plain Text
I'M BEING OVERCONFIDENT. SHE'S NOT TALKING TO ME. TWO OF THE BRIGHTEST STARS IN THE SKY HAVE ASKED HER EYES TO TAKE THEIR PLACE FOR A WHILE.
IMAGINE IF HER EYES WERE IN THE SKY AND THE STARS WERE IN HER HEAD? THE BEAUTY OF HER FACE WOULD OUTSHINE THOSE STARS, LIKE THE SUN OUTSHINES A LAMP.
Romeo & Juliet
ISBN: 978-1-906332-62-4

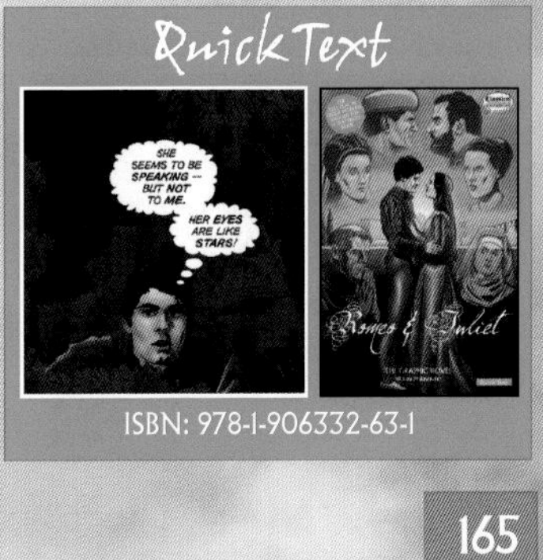
Quick Text
SHE SEEMS TO BE SPEAKING -- BUT NOT TO ME.
HER EYES ARE LIKE STARS!
Romeo & Juliet
ISBN: 978-1-906332-63-1

MORE TITLES AVAILABLE FROM

Shakespeare's plays in a choice of 3 text versions. Simply choose the text version to match your reading level.

Original Text	SHAKESPEARE'S ENTIRE PLAY AS A FULL-COLOR GRAPHIC NOVEL!
Plain Text	THE ENTIRE PLAY TRANSLATED INTO PLAIN ENGLISH!
Quick Text	THE ENTIRE PLAY IN QUICK MODERN ENGLISH FOR A FAST-PACED READ!

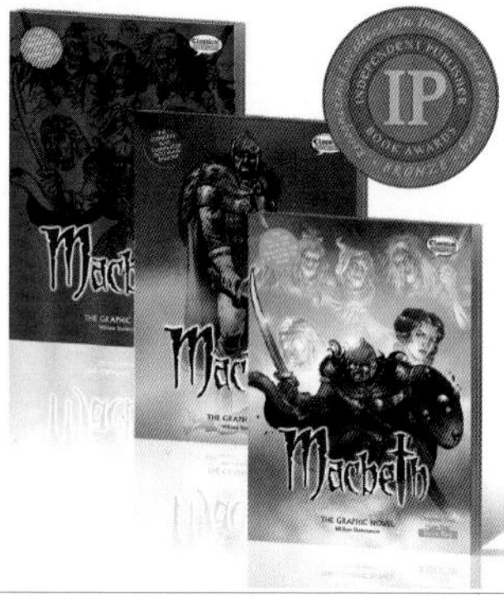
Macbeth
IP

Macbeth: The Graphic Novel (William Shakespeare)

- Script Adaptation: John McDonald • Pencils: & Inks: Jon Haward
- Inking Assistant: Gary Erskine • Colors & Letters: Nigel Dobbyn

144 Pages • $16.95

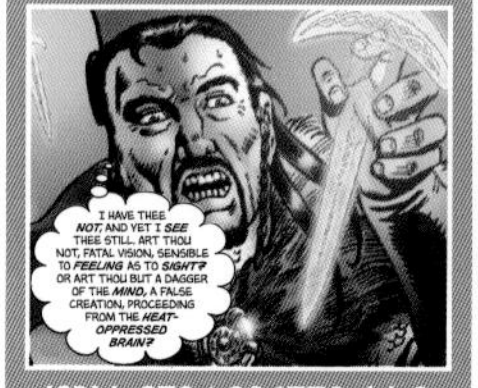
I HAVE THEE NOT, AND YET I SEE THEE STILL. ART THOU NOT, FATAL VISION, SENSIBLE TO FEELING AS TO SIGHT? OR ART THOU BUT A DAGGER OF THE MIND, A FALSE CREATION, PROCEEDING FROM THE HEAT-OPPRESSED BRAIN?

ISBN: 978-1-906332-44-0

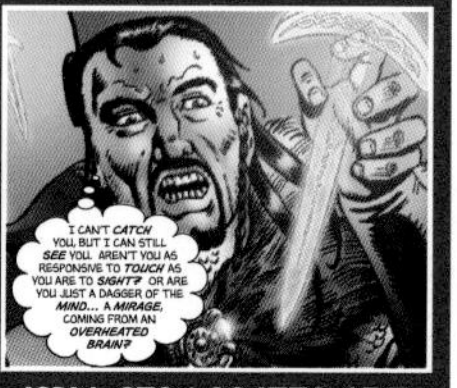
I CAN'T CATCH YOU, BUT I CAN STILL SEE YOU. AREN'T YOU AS RESPONSIVE TO TOUCH AS YOU ARE TO SIGHT? OR ARE YOU JUST A DAGGER OF THE MIND... A MIRAGE, COMING FROM AN OVERHEATED BRAIN?

ISBN: 978-1-906332-45-7

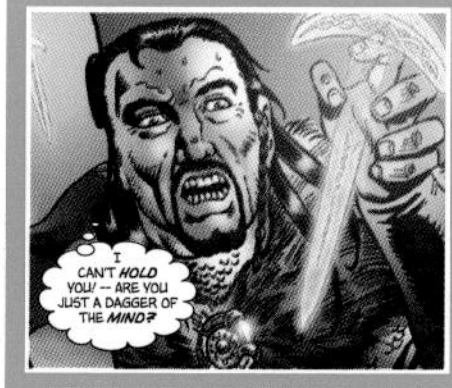
I CAN'T HOLD YOU! -- ARE YOU JUST A DAGGER OF THE MIND?

ISBN: 978-1-906332-46-4

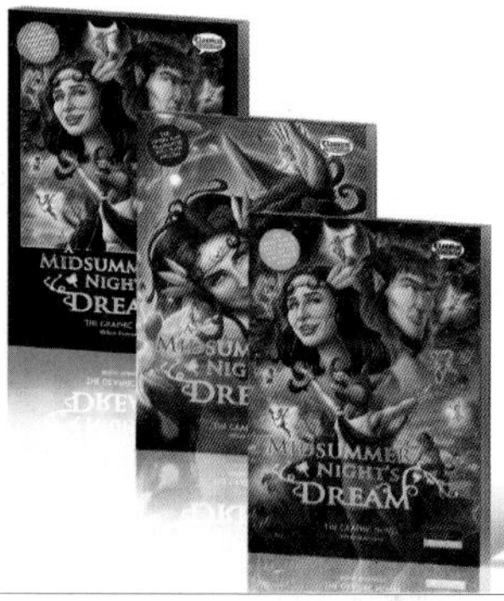
MIDSUMMER NIGHT'S DREAM

A Midsummer Night's Dream: The Graphic Novel (William Shakespeare)

- Script Adaptation: John McDonald • Characters & Artwork: Kat Nicholson & Jason Cardy
- Letters: Jim Campbell

144 Pages • $16.95

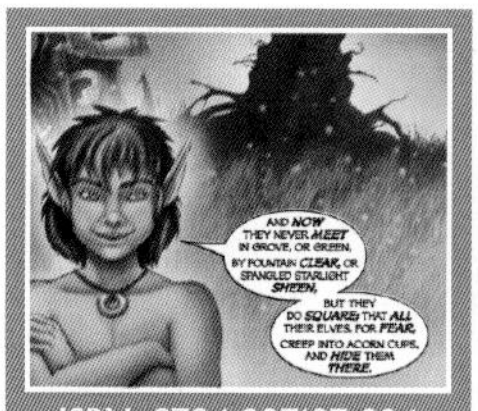
AND NOW THEY NEVER MEET IN GROVE, OR GREEN, BY FOUNTAIN CLEAR, OR SPANGLED STARLIGHT SHEEN,
BUT THEY DO SQUARE; THAT ALL THEIR ELVES, FOR FEAR, CREEP INTO ACORN CUPS, AND HIDE THEM THERE.

ISBN: 978-1-907127-28-1

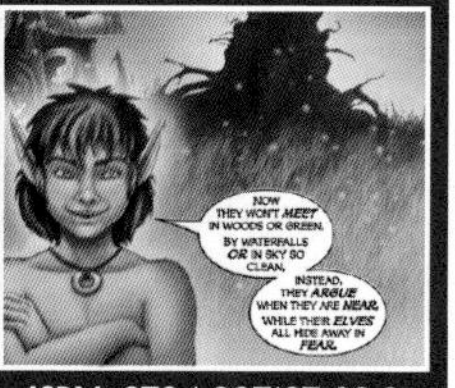
NOW THEY WON'T MEET IN WOODS OR GREEN, BY WATERFALLS OR IN SKY SO CLEAN,
INSTEAD, THEY ARGUE WHEN THEY ARE NEAR, WHILE THEIR ELVES ALL HIDE AWAY IN FEAR.

ISBN: 978-1-907127-29-8

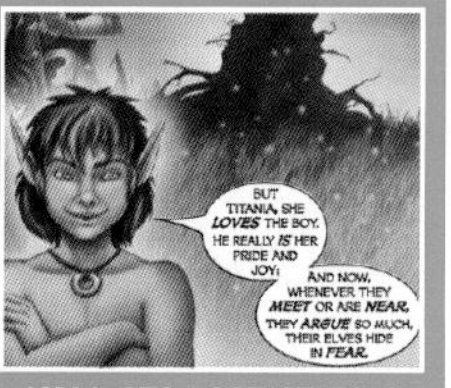
BUT TITANIA, SHE LOVES THE BOY. HE REALLY IS HER PRIDE AND JOY;
AND NOW, WHENEVER THEY MEET OR ARE NEAR, THEY ARGUE SO MUCH, THEIR ELVES HIDE IN FEAR.

ISBN: 978-1-907127-30-4

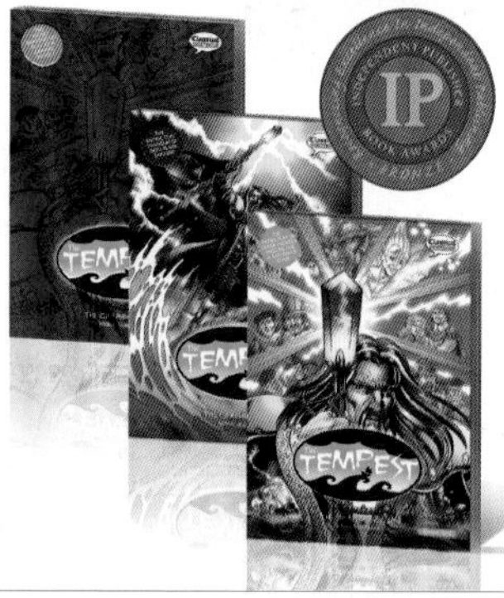
TEMPEST
IP

The Tempest: The Graphic Novel (William Shakespeare)

- Script Adaptation: John McDonald • Pencils: Jon Haward
- Inks: Gary Erskine • Colors: & Letters: Nigel Dobbyn

144 Pages • $16.95

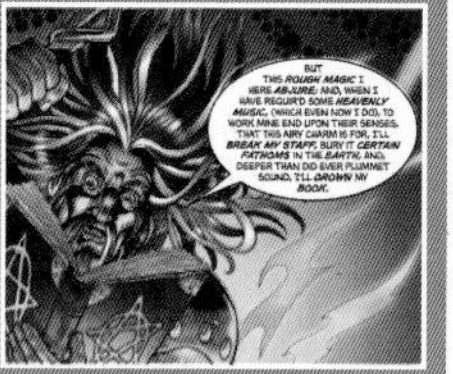
BUT THIS ROUGH MAGIC I HERE ABJURE; AND, WHEN I HAVE REQUIR'D SOME HEAVENLY MUSIC, (WHICH EVEN NOW I DO), TO WORK MINE END UPON THEIR SENSES, THAT THIS AIRY CHARM IS FOR, I'LL BREAK MY STAFF, BURY IT CERTAIN FATHOMS IN THE EARTH, AND, DEEPER THAN DID EVER PLUMMET SOUND, I'LL DROWN MY BOOK.

ISBN: 978-1-906332-69-3

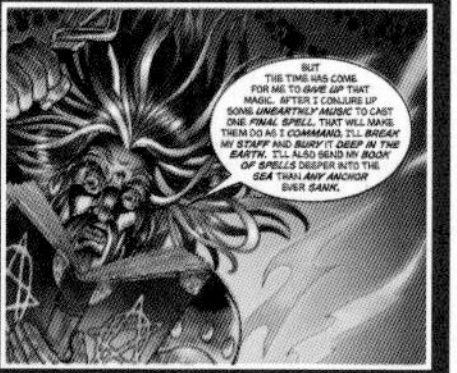
BUT THE TIME HAS COME FOR ME TO GIVE UP THAT MAGIC. AFTER I CONJURE UP SOME UNEARTHLY MUSIC TO CAST ONE FINAL SPELL THAT WILL MAKE THEM DO AS I COMMAND, I'LL BREAK MY STAFF AND BURY IT DEEP IN THE EARTH. I'LL ALSO SEND MY BOOK OF SPELLS DEEPER INTO THE SEA THAN ANY ANCHOR EVER SANK.

ISBN: 978-1-906332-70-9

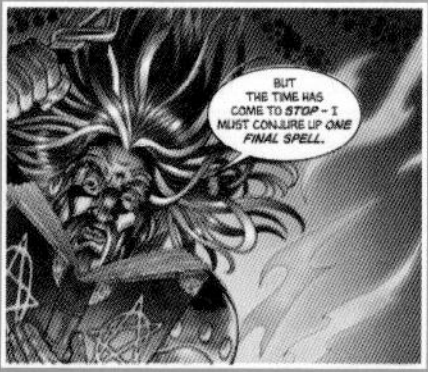
BUT THE TIME HAS COME TO STOP - I MUST CONJURE UP ONE FINAL SPELL.

ISBN: 978-1-906332-71-6

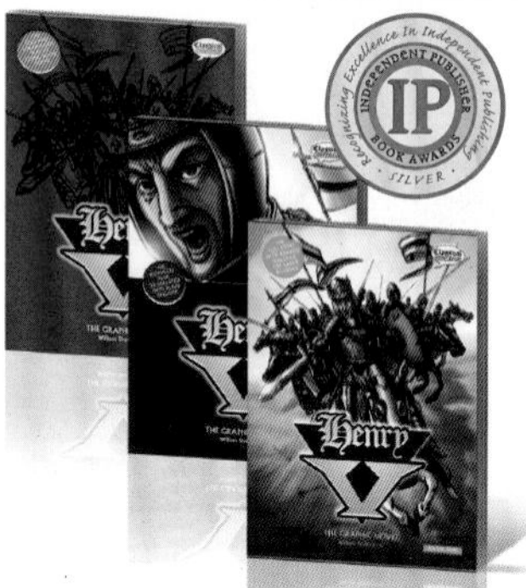
INDEPENDENT PUBLISHER
IP
BOOK AWARDS
SILVER
Henry V

Henry V: The Graphic Novel (William Shakespeare)

- Script Adaptation: John McDonald • Pencils: Neill Cameron • Inks: Bambos
- Colors: Jason Cardy & Kat Nicholson • Letters: Nigel Dobbyn

144 Pages • $16.95

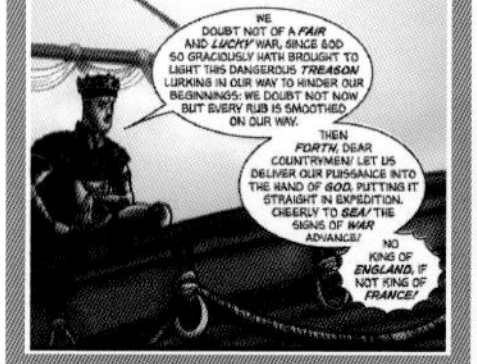
WE DOUBT NOT OF A FAIR AND LUCKY WAR, SINCE GOD SO GRACIOUSLY HATH BROUGHT TO LIGHT THIS DANGEROUS TREASON LURKING IN OUR WAY TO HINDER OUR BEGINNINGS: WE DOUBT NOT NOW BUT EVERY RUB IS SMOOTHED ON OUR WAY.
THEN FORTH, DEAR COUNTRYMEN! LET US DELIVER OUR PUISSANCE INTO THE HAND OF GOD, PUTTING IT STRAIGHT IN EXPEDITION. CHEERLY TO SEA! THE SIGNS OF WAR ADVANCE!
NO KING OF ENGLAND, IF NOT KING OF FRANCE!

ISBN: 978-1-906332-41-9

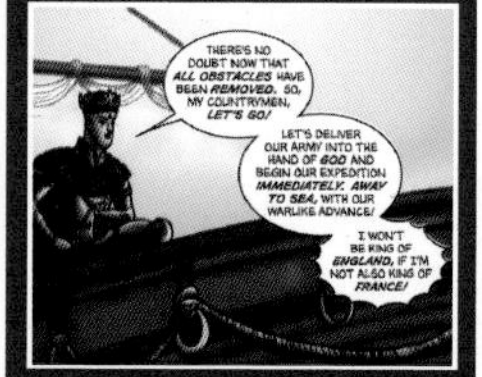
THERE'S NO DOUBT NOW THAT ALL OBSTACLES HAVE BEEN REMOVED. SO, MY COUNTRYMEN, LET'S GO!
LET'S DELIVER OUR ARMY INTO THE HAND OF GOD AND BEGIN OUR EXPEDITION IMMEDIATELY. AWAY TO SEA, WITH OUR WARLIKE ADVANCE!
I WON'T BE KING OF ENGLAND, IF I'M NOT ALSO KING OF FRANCE!

ISBN: 978-1-906332-42-6

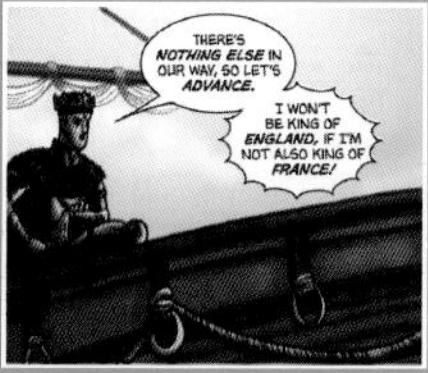
THERE'S NOTHING ELSE IN OUR WAY, SO LET'S ADVANCE.
I WON'T BE KING OF ENGLAND, IF I'M NOT ALSO KING OF FRANCE!

ISBN: 978-1-906332-43-3

OUR AWARD-WINNING RANGE

Classic Literature in a choice of 2 text versions. Simply choose the text version to match your reading level.

Original Text THE CLASSIC NOVEL BROUGHT TO LIFE IN FULL COLOR!

Quick Text THE FULL STORY IN QUICK MODERN ENGLISH FOR A FAST-PACED READ!

Frankenstein: The Graphic Novel (Mary Shelley)

• Script Adaptation: Jason Cobley • Linework: Declan Shalvey • Art Direction: Jon Haward
• Colors: Jason Cardy & Kat Nicholson • Letters: Terry Wiley

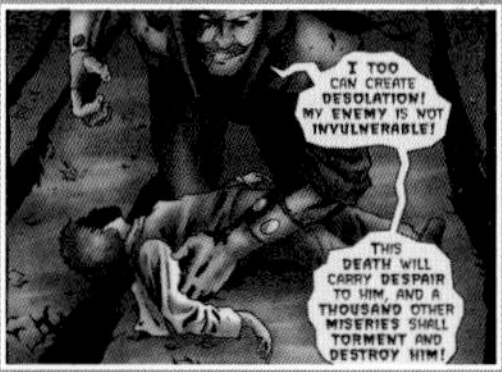
I TOO CAN CREATE DESOLATION! MY ENEMY IS NOT INVULNERABLE!
THIS DEATH WILL CARRY DESPAIR TO HIM, AND A THOUSAND OTHER MISERIES SHALL TORMENT AND DESTROY HIM!

ISBN: 978-1-906332-49-5

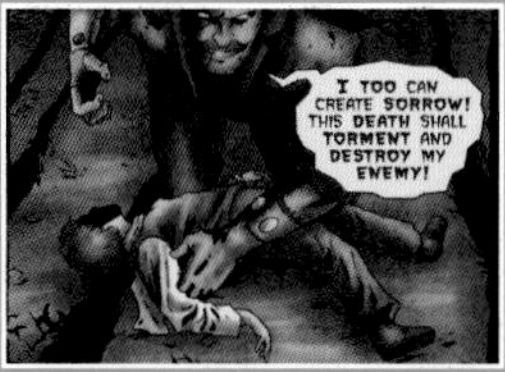
I TOO CAN CREATE SORROW! THIS DEATH SHALL TORMENT AND DESTROY MY ENEMY!

ISBN: 978-1-906332-50-1

"Cursed be the hands that formed you!"

• 144 Pages • $16.95

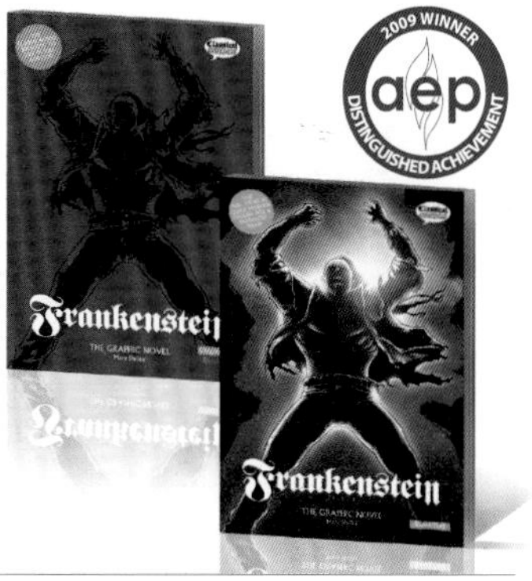
2009 WINNER
aep
DISTINGUISHED ACHIEVEMENT
Frankenstein
Frankenstein

Jane Eyre: The Graphic Novel (Charlotte Brontë)

• Script Adaptation: Amy Corzine • Artwork: John M. Burns
• Letters: Terry Wiley

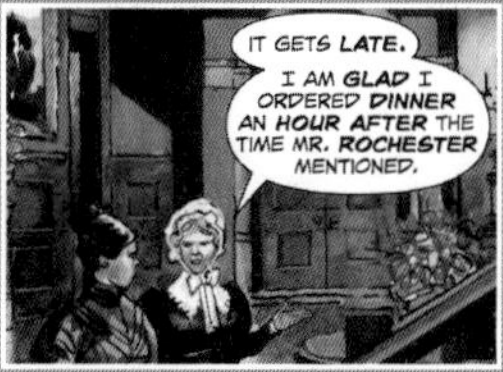
IT GETS LATE.
I AM GLAD I ORDERED DINNER AN HOUR AFTER THE TIME MR. ROCHESTER MENTIONED.

ISBN: 978-1-906332-47-1

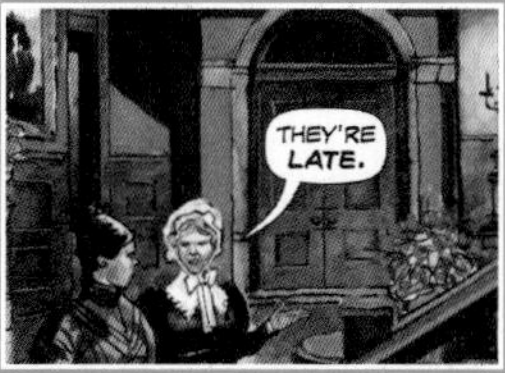
THEY'RE LATE.

ISBN: 978-1-906332-48-8

"I scorn your idea of love and the counterfeit sentiment you offer. And I scorn you when you offer it."

• 144 Pages • $16.95

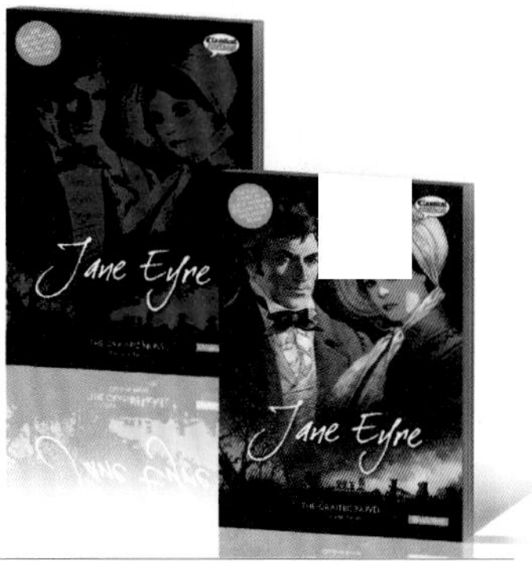
Jane Eyre
Jane Eyre

A Christmas Carol: The Graphic Novel (Charles Dickens)

• Script Adaptation: Seán Michael Wilson • Pencils: Mike Collins
• Inks: David Roach • Colors: James Offredi • Letters: Terry Wiley

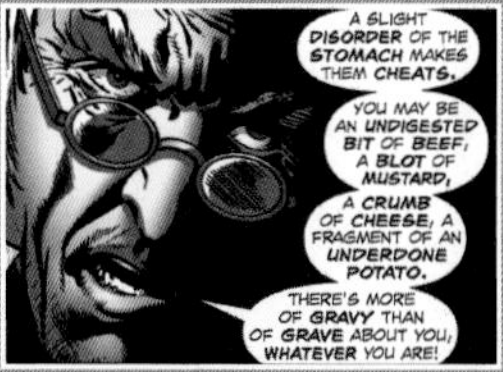
A SLIGHT DISORDER OF THE STOMACH MAKES THEM CHEATS.
YOU MAY BE AN UNDIGESTED BIT OF BEEF, A BLOT OF MUSTARD, A CRUMB OF CHEESE, A FRAGMENT OF AN UNDERDONE POTATO.
THERE'S MORE OF GRAVY THAN OF GRAVE ABOUT YOU, WHATEVER YOU ARE!

ISBN: 978-1-906332-51-8

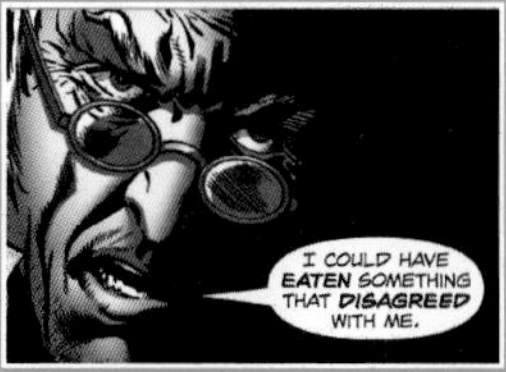
I COULD HAVE EATEN SOMETHING THAT DISAGREED WITH ME.

ISBN: 978-1-906332-52-5

"I will honour Christmas in my heart, and try to keep it all the year. I will live in the Past, the Present, and the Future."

• 160 Pages • $16.95

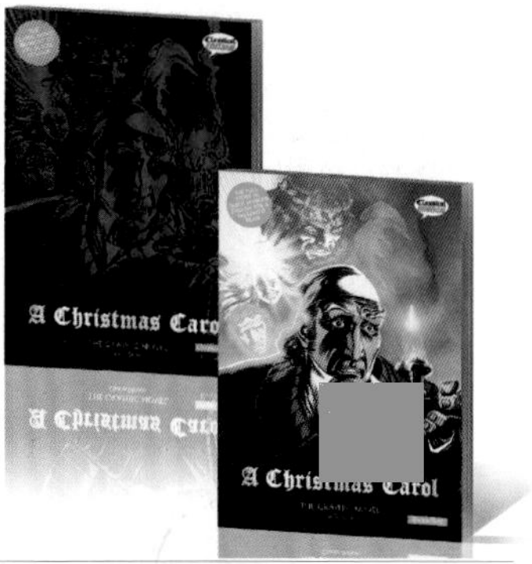

Great Expectations: The Graphic Novel (Charles Dickens)

• Script Adaptation: Jen Green • Linework: John Stokes • Coloring: Digikore Studios Ltd
• Color Finishing: Jason Cardy • Letters: Jim Campbell

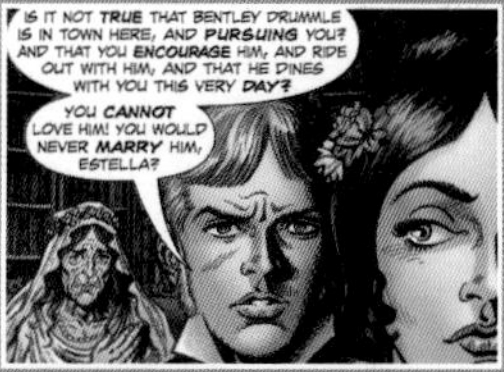
IS IT NOT TRUE THAT BENTLEY DRUMMLE IS IN TOWN HERE, AND PURSUING YOU? AND THAT YOU ENCOURAGE HIM, AND RIDE OUT WITH HIM, AND THAT HE DINES WITH YOU THIS VERY DAY?
YOU CANNOT LOVE HIM! YOU WOULD NEVER MARRY HIM, ESTELLA?

ISBN: 978-1-906332-59-4

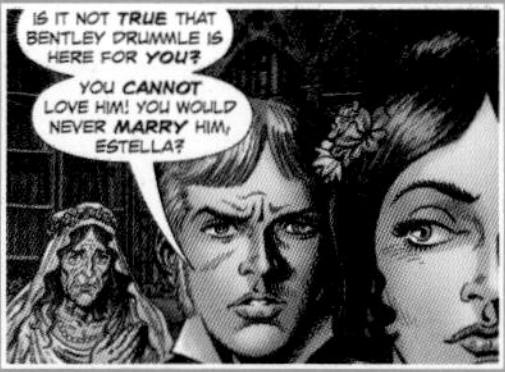
IS IT NOT TRUE THAT BENTLEY DRUMMLE IS HERE FOR YOU?
YOU CANNOT LOVE HIM! YOU WOULD NEVER MARRY HIM, ESTELLA?

ISBN: 978-1-906332-60-0

"I never saw my father or my mother, and never saw any likeness of either of them."

• 160 Pages • $16.95

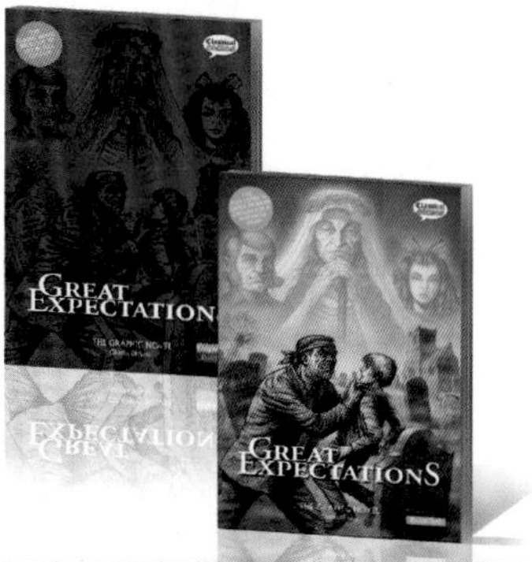
GREAT EXPECTATIONS
GREAT EXPECTATIONS

To see the complete range, and to view samples online, go to www.classicalcomics.com

Romeo & Juliet Teaching Resource Pack

Helping you prepare motivating and stimulating lessons

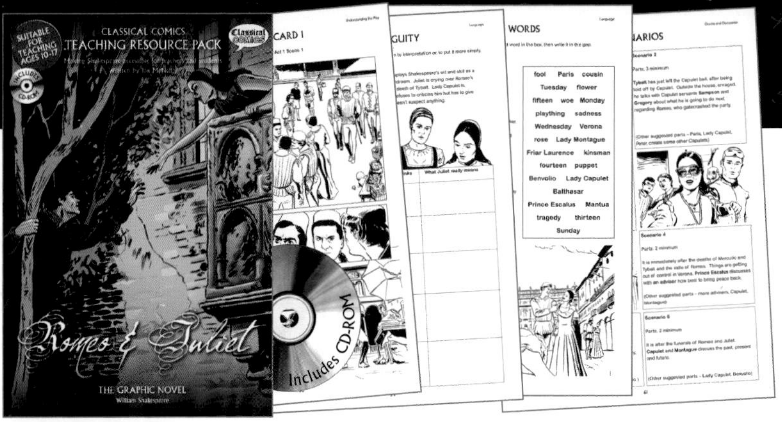
CLASSICAL COMICS
TEACHING RESOURCE PACK
Romeo & Juliet
THE GRAPHIC NOVEL
William Shakespeare
Includes CD-ROM

ISBN: 978-1-906332-74-7

- *Over 100 spiral–bound, photocopiable pages.*
- *Cross–curricular topics and activities.*
- *Ideal for differentiated teaching.*
- *CD includes an electronic version of the teaching book for whiteboards, laptops and digital printing.*
- *Only $22.95*

To accompany each title in our series of graphic novels and to help with their application in the classroom, we also publish teaching resource packs. These widely acclaimed 100+ page books are spiral-bound, making the pages easy to photocopy. They also include a CD-ROM with the pages in PDF format, ideal for whole-class teaching on whiteboards, laptops, etc or for direct digital printing. These books are written by teachers, for teachers, helping students to engage in the play or novel. Suitable for teaching ages 10-17, each book provides exercises that cover structure, listening, understanding, motivation and character as well as key words, themes and literary techniques. Devised to encompass a broad range of skill levels, they provide many opportunities for differentiated teaching and the tailoring of lessons to meet individual needs.

"Thank you! These will be fantastic for all our students. It is a brilliant resource and to have the lesson ideas too are great. Thanks again to all your team who have created these."

"...this is a fantastic way to teach and progress English literature and language!"

"As to the resource, I can't wait to start using it! Well done on a fantastic service."

OUR RANGE OF TEACHING RESOURCE PACKS AVAILABLE

- Only $22.95 each
- 100+ spiral-bound, photocopiable pages.
- Electronic version include[d] for whole-class teaching and digital printing.
- Cross-curricular topics an[d] activities.
- Ideal for differentiated teaching.

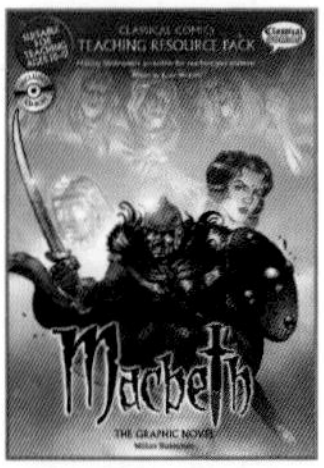
Macbeth

Macbeth
978-1-906332-54-9

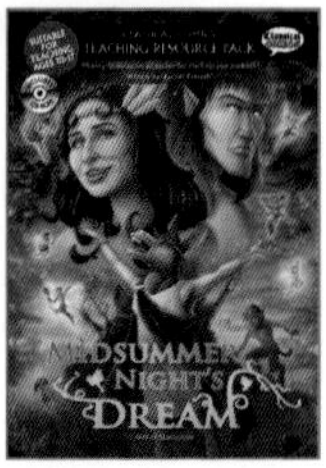
A Midsummer Night's Dream

A Midsummer Night's Dream
978-1-907127-75-5

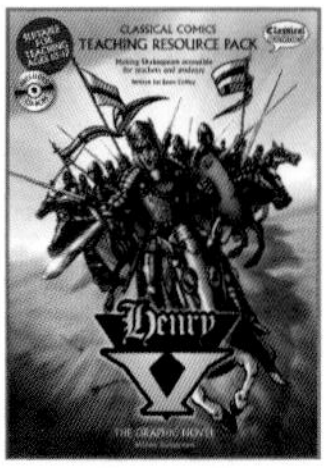
Henry V

Henry V
978-1-906332-53-2

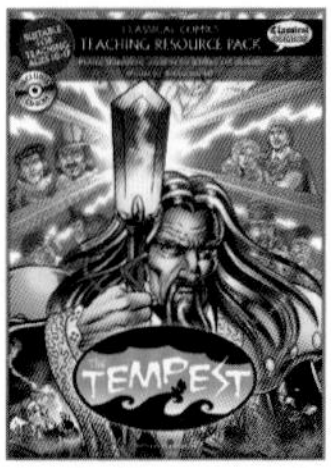
Tempest

The Tempest
978-1-906332-77-8

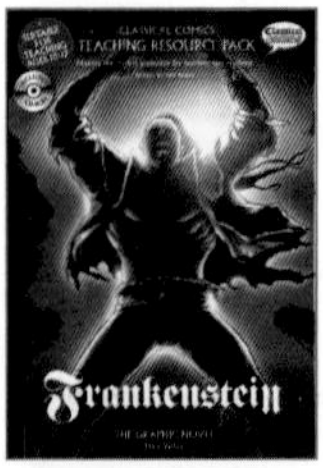
Frankenstein

Frankenstein
978-1-906332-56-3

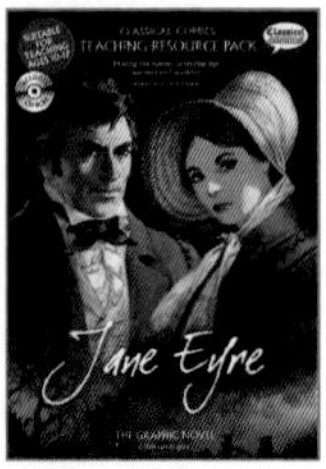
Jane Eyre

Jane Eyre
978-1-906332-55-6

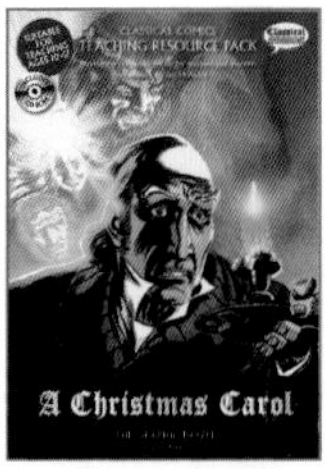
A Christmas Carol

A Christmas Carol
978-1-906332-57-0

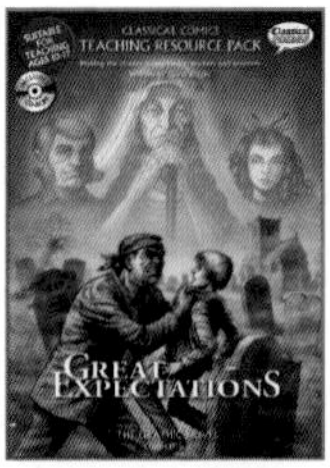
Great Expectations

Great Expectations
978-1-906332-58-7

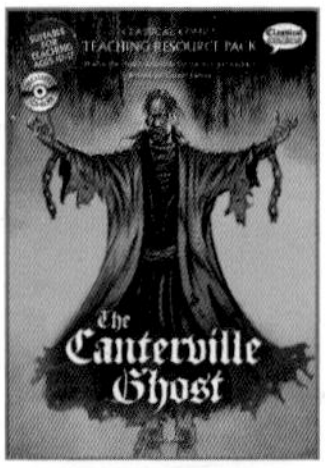
The Canterville Ghost

The Canterville Ghost
978-1-906332-78-5